THE SCOURGE OF
MUIRWOOD

Legends of Muirwood Trilogy

The Wretched of Muirwood
The Blight of Muirwood
The Scourge of Muirwood

THE SCOURGE OF MUIRWOOD

Legends of Muirwood
Book Three

JEFF WHEELER

47NORTH

Text copyright © 2011 Jeff Wheeler
Printed in the United States of America.

Published by 47North
P.O. Box 400818
Las Vegas, NV 89140

Cover illustration by Eamon O'Donoghue

ISBN-13: 9781612187020
ISBN-10: 1612187021
Library of Congress Control Number: 2012943334

To Sharon Kay Penman

I fear everything. This island terrifies me. There are secrets here that I am beginning to discover. My past. My Family. Who I am. These tools are awkward in my hands. It is difficult to describe it. I am used to the laundry, not this vast place full of mirrors. The Leerings here frighten me as well. So ancient. So powerful. The Aldermaston suggested I use this tome to explore my feelings and confront my fears. I must be ready to face the maston test before I can save the kingdoms and before the Blight destroys everyone. So this is what I fear the most. I fear losing the man I love. I fear losing Colvin.

—*Ellowyn Demont of Dochte Abbey*

CHAPTER ONE

Whispers of Death

They rode on horseback, side by side, down a road overgrown with the twisted limbs of monstrous oak trees. The air was full of gnats and gossamer threads of spider silk that gently tickled the face. Martin wiped his cheek hurriedly, staring into the dark woods on either side. The bend ahead was blind—the perfect location for a trap.

"By Cheshu," Martin muttered. "I like not the look of that corner. I do not. This forsaken wood is the only road to Comoros, is it?" He hissed softly and then sniffed at the air, listening with keenness for evidence of the warning that throbbed silently in his heart.

At his side was the man Martin served—the king-maston of Pry-Ree. Martin was the older of the two, but the king had a youthful face. He did not look like a king, for he dressed in a simple shirt and an unassuming leather vest. His hair was an untamed mass of gold and was shorn like a sheep at the nape of his neck. There was a somber expression on his face, which was normal, as he was a man who mused silently much of the day and even more since hatching the plot of a secret marriage to

Demont's daughter. But a smile crept almost unnoticed at times to his mouth, betraying some hidden thought of mirth. He was Alluwyn Lleu-Iselin, though Martin never would have called him by his common name. The king was a man Martin respected and trusted above any other, including the band of men known as the Evnissyen who now clustered around their king, halting as Martin and the king had.

In short, the Evnissyen were the king's protectors, and Martin had trained them all. It was much more than simply that. The Evnissyen were hunters, thieves, schemers, dice-throwers, warriors—the mind in the shadows, whispering advice to their leader. Martin was the man the king turned to after his royal counselors had all argued their positions, blustered for favors and lands, or even plotted his death. The Evnissyen knew all the tangles in the skeins of power, and they ruthlessly plucked at them like harp strings. Martin thought this with satisfaction. It was in his instincts to smell trouble. He smelled it on the road to Comoros.

Lord Alluwyn paused his mount and tugged open the pouch fastened to his wide leather belt. He was a king-maston, showing the glimpse of his chaen just a hint beneath the open collar of his shirt, but he referred to himself as only a *Prince* in his title. Of the Three Blessed Kings of Pry-Ree, he was the wisest, the youngest, and the worthiest to rule them all. That was why the others had already been assassinated, leaving Alluwyn's brother and nephew as co-rulers—neither of whom were mastons or very wise.

After digging into the pouch, the Prince removed a small globe made of refined aurichalcum. It glimmered in the shadows, which made Martin impatient, wondering if anyone skulking in the woods would see it. Staring at the orb, the Prince watched as the spindles set in the upper half began to whirl and spin. Writing appeared in the lower half of the orb. Martin squinted at the tiny markings that only mastons could read. "Well?"

The Prince's face paled. He looked furtively at the road ahead, his face more serious than before. His voice was soft with warning. "A kishion in the shadows ahead. The orb bids me west."

"Into the swamp?"

"The kishion does not want the others in our train, only me. Send them on after we are gone. You ride with me, Martin. Send the rest on to Muirwood."

The Prince did not hesitate after that. Wrapping the reins in one fist, he stamped his stallion's flanks with his spurs and charged into the murky depths of the oak trees. Furious, Martin hissed orders and a warning to the rest of the Evnissyen guard and then rode hard after the Prince. The trees whipped and slashed him as he fought to keep up. The thrill of the chase burned in his stomach. Draw the kishion after them in the moors. Throw him off his original plan—make him react to their movements.

The hunter is patient. The prey is careless.

The kishion was being careless. Not long after charging into the woods, Martin heard the crack of limbs, the thud of hooves from behind. The pay must be considerable for the kishion to risk being so noisy. Martin slowed his beast slightly, listening. The sound of pursuit was gaining on him. Grabbing his bow, he shrugged his boot out of the stirrup and flung himself off the horse, rolling into the mud and muck and then flattening himself against a stunted oak tree. Muddy water dripped down his face, and he brushed it away with his hand, cursing. He had an arrow nocked and darted past several other trees, backtracking. He did not worry about the Prince. He had the orb and could make it to Muirwood without aid from a hunter.

A blur of brown with a milk-stain patch on the nose revealed the pursuer's horse. The kishion was low against the saddle, his mouth twisted into a scowl.

Martin brought back the arrow and loosed it. The kishion saw the motion and swung around the saddle horn the other way, lurching away as the arrow sank into the horse's neck. There was a shriek, a spurt of blood, and then the horse went down. Martin sloshed through the swamp water, drawing another arrow.

The kishion emerged, and Martin sailed the arrow at the killer. Kishion were hired for two purposes: to protect or to kill. So quick, the kishion spun aside, and the arrow sank into the tree behind him. A dagger appeared in the kishion's hand, and it was Martin's turn to throw himself back as it whistled by his ear.

The two glared at each other, circling, drawn closer. There was no taunting—no attempt to persuade or deny. There was only the imminent conflict of sharp-edged blades. Martin drew his gladius and a dagger. He poked the air in front of him, as if testing the distance separating them. He motioned for the other to attack first.

The kishion obliged and lunged at him, a new blade in his hand, going straight for Martin's throat. Their bodies locked for a moment, jabs, cuts, feints, thrusts. Then they parted, circling the other way, eyes locked on each other. Martin's teeth were clenched tight, revealing a sickening half grin. Again the kishion charged him, deftly stabbing at his inner thigh, his fingers clawing toward Martin's eyes. Their arms and limbs smashed against each other. Then they were separated again. There was blood blooming on the kishion's sleeve. Both of them were breathing hard.

"You...you trained...among us," the kishion whispered darkly.

Martin's grin became more pronounced. "You noticed."

Maybe the kishion was losing his strength. Maybe he realized he was already a dead man. He struck at Martin one last time, and then he was subdued, arm twisted in a brutal lock behind him, the blade dropping from the agony of the hold. Martin encircled the kishion's neck with his arm and dropped him like a stone into the murky swamp water until his head was submerged. Martin clenched and squeezed, burying his weight into the man's back, holding him beneath the water as he flailed and struggled for breath. A few more moments while the kishion was starved for air, thrashing violently and desperately, but Martin shrugged harder, squeezing and holding him. Martin felt something break in the kishion's neck.

The struggle ended. He waited longer to be sure, not trusting his instincts. Then he released the dead man and fished through the waters for his fallen gladius. He cleaned it and sheathed it and only then noticed the Prince watching him, his face askew with emotion.

Martin looked at him gruffly. "It was foolish to ride back, my Prince. What if I had lost? A kishion can kill even a maston."

The Prince stared at the corpse, his face in anguish. Martin scowled. He had killed many men in war, and hired killers were no one to feel sympathy for. "Ride on, my Prince. I will search the body for clues as to who hired him."

The Prince stared in silence and shook his head. "I am not squeamish, Martin. It is just what I saw as you drowned him. I saw a girl being drowned by a kishion."

Martin looked around in confusion. "He was certainly a man, my lord. Not even I would drown a woman."

"You might," he said, his voice thick with emotion. "If I asked it of you. If the woman…deserved it. No, what I saw was in the future. A young girl in a dressing gown. The kishion tried to drown her." He trembled for a moment, shaking his head as if dispelling a nightmare. Then he looked down at the orb.

Martin tugged on the kishion's collar to hoist him out of the murky waters. The corpse was limp and soaked.

"Leave him," the Prince said. "We both know who sent him."

"You suspect the treasonous king then? The king you are visiting Comoros to treat with?" Martin said waspishly. "By Cheshu, even with a safe conduct granted, he would try to murder you?"

Prince Alluwyn smirked. "No, the king did not send the kishion. It was his wife."

"The wife? You say it is she? She must be devious and cunning if you suspect her and not her lord."

"There are things I know through the maston ways, Martin. I have long suspected this. There are stories that the kings of Dahomey send only their *daughters* to negotiate treaties. They are notable for their subtlety. There are reasons I cannot explain to you further."

Martin sighed and let the corpse fall with a splash. He made sure the gladius was snug in its scabbard. Then he fished his blade out of the murk and sheathed it in his belt. "We ride to Muirwood then?"

A curious look and a subtle shake of his head came as the reply. "The orb bids me further west. We must ride, while there is still daylight in this accursed swamp."

"Not to Muirwood?"

"Trust me, old friend," he said, his eyes intense. "There is a grove of trees we must visit. Ride with me, Martin. Tell no one what we do."

"The king is expecting us in Comoros in less than a fortnight." He scratched his throat and started toward his own mount. "He is not a patient man. He will take it amiss if we are late."

The Prince was staring westward, his eyes fixed on something only he could see. "I know, Martin. But the way is becoming clearer. The swamp whispers to me. It whispers of death." He sighed. "It whispers of my death."

CHAPTER TWO

Binding Sigil

The fragrance of the Cider Orchard enmeshed with Lia's memories and the churn of feelings she worried would overwhelm her. Throughout her childhood at Muirwood Abbey, she had fled to the Cider Orchard. The tightly clustered rows of trees made it easier to hide and escape kitchen chores. She had plucked hundreds of apples from their stems and nestled in the grass to savor them. She had witnessed the orchard blooming with blossoms or wreathed in smoky mist. The thoughts evoked memories of rushing with Sowe and Colvin to escape the sheriff's men through the orchard—of Getman Smith finding her there and squeezing her arm. One of her most painful memories happened there as well—when Colvin had rejected her and left her alone in the mud and dripping branches. But it was also the place where he had found her again, later, and asked for her help in saving Ellowyn Demont.

Ellowyn Demont.

The name invoked such tangled feelings—hate, envy, pity, respect, jealousy. Especially jealousy. Lia leaned against a tree trunk in the twilight—sighing deeply, stifling a sob—and clenched her fists. Colvin had found Ellowyn at Sempringfall Abbey, sentenced there as a wretched after the kingdom of Pry-Ree was vanquished. She grew up unaware of her name, known as Hillel Lavender because she worked at the laundry. But things were not as they seemed. Hillel was not the real Ellowyn Demont. For some reason, for some cruel reason, Lia had learned too late that she herself was the missing heir of Pry-Ree. She had sacrificed herself for the other girl, believing that Hillel was the true person who had to leave for Dochte Abbey to warn them of the coming of the Blight. But it was not Hillel who needed to go. It was Lia, her leg still throbbing and healing, her hand still aching from the arrow that had transfixed it. The injuries she had sustained were not what pained her the most. It was jealousy—pure jealousy—that the other girl was traveling by sea to Dahomey to warn the inhabitants of Dochte Abbey. She was not traveling alone but with Colvin.

The ache became worse. It robbed her of her ability to think. She had always known herself as Lia Cook. It was every wretched's deepest dream to learn of her parentage. Why had events turned out in such a way? Why was it that Colvin had been led to Sempringfall to find the girl and not to Muirwood? What would have happened if she had been allowed to spend a year with Colvin, as Hillel had, learning languages and scriving, being able to participate in the politics of her uncle, Garen Demont, instead of shying away from them, always too fearful? Did the Aldermaston of Muirwood know the truth? Had he always known?

The jealousy coalesced into anger. The Prince of Pry-Ree, her very own father, had visited Muirwood before her birth. The Aldermaston of Tintern knew who she was. She coughed with a half chuckle. He had even promised to tell her when she returned from Dochte Abbey. She remembered the pity in his eyes. But still, he had not told her the truth. It was the Cruciger orb—a gift left with her when she was abandoned as a baby—that had revealed the truth at last. The Aldermaston knew. He must have known. Yet he had deliberately deceived her. The anger boiled. She had to know why. Colvin was escorting the wrong person to Dahomey. The thought made her feel black inside.

Pushing away from the smooth bark of the apple tree, she strode toward the manor house. It was dusk and torches shone in sconces on the walls. She walked furiously but with a limp. She knew she should not; her leg would throb that night as she tried to fall asleep, but she did not care. The Abbey's walls seemed luminous that night, as if the very stones radiated moonlight before the silver orb appeared in the sky. She loved the Abbey with all her heart. It was part of her. Beneath her hunter's garb, she wore a soft, woven chaen shirt. It reminded her of the maston vows she had made inside. She was a maston, as her father and her mother had been. Being a maston was part of her heritage.

Lia reached the manor house and thrust the door open. Something caught her eye in the corner outside, some movement. She glanced but saw nothing. From the corner of her eye, it had seemed like a person—a man wearing hunter's garb. She paused, staring at the spot, but she could see nothing. She shook her head, realizing that there were many knight-mastons wandering the grounds since the battle. It probably had been one of them.

She approached the Aldermaston's door and opened it without knocking first. She regretted it instantly. The Aldermaston looked haggard at his desk, his eyes red with veins and swollen with lack of sleep. His left hand trembled on the desk, a sign of his age and the strain he had endured. He was talking to Garen Demont, her uncle.

"I am sorry," she offered as their heads turned toward her.

"Is something the matter, Lia?" the Aldermaston said.

"I am sorry for interrupting you," she said, nodding respect-fully at Demont. Her eyes blazed as she stared at the Aldermas-ton. "I must speak with you."

"Come in then, child." His eyes became wary, seeing the flush on her cheeks and the brooding anger in her eyes. "Shut the door. Have you met our hunter, Earl Demont?"

Garen Demont was younger than the Aldermaston, but he was much older than Lia. He was not excessively tall, but he was fit and trim for a man who was nearly fifty. He had survived the battle of Maseve as a young man, escaped the kingdom, and fought for foreign kings in turn. But he had returned at last to challenge the king for his Family's birthright and defeated him at the battle of Winterrowd. Lia had been there and recalled seeing him there, perched on a wagon the evening of the battle, all blood spattered and filthy as he announced their victory in a humble manner. She had not seen him since then until he had arrived at Muirwood to defeat their enemies. His knights had traveled through the Apse Veil, the barrier within each Abbey that allowed someone to pass from one location to another.

His hair was dark and unruly. A maston sword hung from a scuffed leather belt at his hip. He did not have a beard, though the bristles had reformed already and he looked ready for a shave again. He looked at her curiously and bowed his head toward her.

"We have, Aldermaston. Briefly." He gave her a sympathetic look. "I hope you are recovering from your injuries?"

Her heart burned inside of her. He was the only family she had left. He was her uncle, by blood, and he did not know it. She started to tremble.

"What is it you wanted to tell me?" the Aldermaston asked pointedly.

She glanced at him, seeing his eyebrows fold with intensity. He sat back in his chair, wincing with pain as he moved.

"You wish me to speak it now?" she asked, nodding toward Demont.

He gave her a shrewd smile. "Please do."

Her heart throbbed in her chest. What would Demont think of her? How would he react to her news? As she began to speak, her mouth would not open. The force of the Medium slammed into her, cleaving her tongue. She could say nothing. Even breathing was difficult. Her mind whirled.

"Lia?" the Aldermaston asked mildly, but she could see knowledge in his eyes. He knew exactly what was happening to her. Was he doing it to her? Or was the Medium preventing her because it did not want Demont knowing?

She shook her head violently, feeling tears prick her eyes. The thought of something else to say loosed her tongue. "Do you have…any word from Colvin?"

"No," the Earl said, startling her. "Not directly. But we do have word *of* him and of my niece." He looked at the Aldermaston, who nodded curtly. "The king of Dahomey sends us word demanding the release of his sister, Pareigis, into his custody. He has informed us that he will keep my niece and the Earl of Forshee as hostages at Dochte Abbey until we relent." His face hardened with anger. "Our attempts to…contact…the Earl have all been thwarted. If the news you brought from Pry-Ree is true, my dear, that the Blight is coming and it will strike soon, then we must make a decision now on how to save them."

"I agree that we must do something," the Aldermaston said and then paused as a racking cough exploded from his lips. It took several moments for him to regain his composure. He slammed his elbow on the table and leaned forward, expelling his breath roughly. "But releasing the Queen Dowager will do more harm than good. It is a ploy. If what your allies in Hautland have said is true, there is an invasion army assembling. The negotiations are an attempt to distract us from their true aim. We must send word through every village in the kingdom. We must forsake these shores before it is too late."

Demont's brow furrowed with consternation. "Is there nothing, then, that can halt the Blight?"

The reply came as a deep chuckle, wet with phlegm. "Certainly there is. We must abandon all pride. Share our food with the poor. We must act, in a word, with one heart and one mind. But as you well know, that has not happened since the days of King Zedakah. Too many mastons have been killed. Too many abbeys have fallen. How does one stop a rockslide, my lord Earl? We must flee from it before it engulfs us. Lia can guide us to the safe haven in Pry-Ree. There is an abbey there. They know the way."

"Yet you will not tell me where it is," Demont stated simply, his look piercing.

"Not yet, my lord Earl. Continue to send your knights throughout the realm. Those who will listen must come to Muirwood. If our enemies learned where the rallying point was, our escape would be compromised. Bring them to Muirwood."

"What of my niece?" Demont asked, stepping closer, his voice more firm.

Lia's heart throbbed painfully.

"Lord Colvin is an able maston. He is her guardian."

Demont said nothing for a moment. He rubbed his jaw, causing a scratching sound from the bristles on his chin. "Until tomorrow then, Aldermaston. I beg leave of you. It is time to rotate the guard over Pareigis. Even without the kystrel, she is dangerous."

The Aldermaston nodded. "You are wise not to underestimate her. Until tomorrow."

Demont strode from the room and shut the door softly behind him. Lia watched him go, her stomach sick with worry. She turned back to the Aldermaston.

"Send *me* to Dochte Abbey," she said in a low voice.

"You are not fully recovered, Lia. It is a long journey."

She frowned deeply and approached his desk. "I will use the Apse Veil. I can be there tonight and warn him. The orb would show me the way."

The Aldermaston studied her carefully, his expression guarded. "None of Demont's mastons have successfully crossed the Apse Veil to Dochte Abbey. If it were a matter of strength in the Medium, I would suggest you try yourself. But my heart tells me that Dochte has already fallen."

"What?" Lia demanded, planting her palms on the desk. "It is the oldest abbey in Dahomey. If it has fallen, why have we not heard?"

He twisted the tips of his beard. "I have asked myself that question. If the Abbey were burned, we would have heard. But if it were corrupted from within?" He raised his eyebrow at her. "If the Aldermaston succumbed? Dahomey is an ancient kingdom. If Pareigis is a hetaera, then we must assume her Family is as well and that the king of Dahomey has been seduced, as well as the royal Family. Their show of ability with the Medium is done by kystrels. The missives I have received may have been sent deliberately to put my mind at ease—to assure me that they have not fallen when they already have. Perhaps I have been ignoring the signs all along." His words sent a chill through her body, and she shivered. "Perhaps we are the last kingdom to fall."

"The last?" she whispered.

"I fear it may be," he replied softly.

She swallowed, bewildered. Then she looked at him pointedly. "Why did you not tell me?"

"Tell you what, Lia?" he asked, his eyes narrowing.

She was about to say *Ellowyn Demont*, but her jaw froze and her tongue clove in her mouth again. She struggled against the surge of the Medium. But moving her mouth was like trying to lift a boulder with a spoon. She gritted her teeth in frustration, unable to say the words.

The Aldermaston leaned back in his chair, his shoulders slumping with exhaustion. "Now do you understand?" he whispered. "I cannot speak of what we both know to be true. Neither can you."

Lia surrendered against the feeling. "But you are an aldermaston," she said. "Why would the Medium bind us in such a way? It is not...natural."

"Is it any less natural than how Colvin used the Medium to bind Seth's tongue? The curse was removed eventually, but he went without speaking for a year. Imagine what Martin and I endured these many long years. Seth should be grateful that an irrevocare sigil was not used *with* the binding, or he would never have spoken again, in this life or the next." His eyes were serious.

Lia wanted to ask who had performed the binding sigil, but again she was prevented. Angrily, she thought of another question. "How is a binding performed?"

The Aldermaston smirked at her persistence. "A binding sigil, or a binding rune, can be engraved in a tome. A band of aurichalcum is then forged that seals the pages together. The band cannot be opened except by the password. What is written on those pages cannot be spoken. They cannot be uttered by anyone. When someone has the Gift of Seering, they employ the binding runes on their tomes to prevent others from learning the future.

Some with the gift write their visions in language that is difficult to understand or that can be interpreted in more than one way. That protects the knowledge from those who cannot use the Medium. But when the words are plain and easy to understand, they can be sealed with a binding rune to protect them."

Lia studied him carefully. "Do you know how to do this yourself, or were you taught?"

He smiled, as if he were proud of her question. He looked at her deliberately. "I was taught by the Prince of Pry-Ree. Most of what I know of the hidden power of the Medium was taught to me by him. He had a unique way of carving Leerings, for example. He was younger than me but more powerful in the Medium in every way." He paused. "His visit to Muirwood changed my life. Prior to his visit, I was a trifle more concerned with the harvesting of apples and the making of spiced cider."

Lia's heart surged with emotions, and she felt the tears stinging her eyes. More than anything she wanted to ask about her father, but she could not ask it openly. The Medium forbade it. She hung her head, recognizing the truth. The Aldermaston had never intended to hide from her what he knew. For some reason, her father had felt the secrecy was so important that he had prevented the knowledge from being shared.

"Why?" she said, struggling to find her voice through the tears. "Why must it be secret? Martin knew?" Her heart ached to tell Colvin, but she realized with despair that even if he stood before her, she would not be able to tell him.

The Aldermaston's look was full of sympathy. He nodded curtly. "Martin struggled with it. He always did. He looked for ways to circumvent the binding rune. He is defiant by nature. When you..."— he paused, choosing his words carefully—"...were abandoned at the Abbey, as a wretched, I was expecting there to be a tome with you.

Instead there was the orb. No one ever learned what happened to the Prince's tome. It is still missing. I can use the orb, but I cannot leave the grounds. My office requires me to be here, at Muirwood. I think...the Prince...protected this information in such a way to prevent it from being told to the wrong person. Or people. You see, even if I wanted to tell the truth, I could not." His eyes gave her a meaningful look that said much she did not understand. He knew, she realized, even more than he had said, more secrets he was powerless to reveal.

Lia sighed, feeling exhausted suddenly. "Then what must I do? What does the Medium expect from me?"

His look was full of sorrow. "You already know, Lia." His voice was soft and firm. "Ellowyn Demont must go to Dochte Abbey to warn them. Get some sleep, child. You must rest and heal. The Abbey will continue to heal you. You have made good progress each day. But still, there is little time left to us."

She nodded and went to the door. Pausing at the threshold, she studied his face, and he studied hers. There was no anger or resentment within her any longer, only determination to find a way to tell Colvin who she really was. She sighed, realizing how thickheaded he could be. But she would try. She had to try.

After shutting the door gently, she walked down the hall and joined the cool night air. Her leg throbbed from the punishing pace she had allowed herself that day. Her temples clanged like kettles. She was so distracted that she did not see the shadow of the man until it mixed with hers. Whirling, she caught sight of a man detaching himself from the darkness to approach her. His hand rested on a gladius blade.

"You are the Pry-rian lass?" he asked softly in the language of her deceased father, her heritage, her homeland.

She had seen him before and recognized the face from Tintern Abbey.

I failed at the Leerings again today. There is one that frightens me more than the others. Let me describe it. The image is of two serpents woven together, their heads facing each other. It forms a circle. Most of the Leerings I see are shaped like faces, but this one is different. It is small. I see this symbol everywhere in Dochte. The Aldermaston says it is an ancient rune, that the serpent is one of the manifestations of Idumea. There are seven manifestations of Idumea. Dahomey embraces the manifestation of the serpent. I believe him, but it makes me afraid. There are serpents engraved everywhere. People keep serpents as pets here. There are no rats or voles. I will try again tomorrow to speak to the Leerings. There is one that will stop the Blight. Colvin said I must hurry. There are things he will not tell me. If Lia were here, he would tell her.

—Ellowyn Demont of Dochte Abbey

CHAPTER THREE

Kieran Ven

Lia understood the language of the Pry-rians. It startled her to hear it on the Abbey grounds, and it startled her even more that she recognized the man. The last time she had seen him, he was picking fruit from a small, enclosed garden behind Tintern Abbey where Colvin hid. Her hand dropped to her gladius hilt.

He smirked. "You were brave enough to pass the mountains of the Fear Liath," he said. "No doubt you are equally brave enough to face me with a blade. But given your limp, I would suggest against it."

Lia tried to calm her heart, to let him sense her confidence instead of shock. "How did you get here?" she demanded of him. "The waters have not subsided. The land is flooded for leagues around the Abbey." He was not wet.

"I do not wish to be seen," he replied, not answering her question. "Follow me."

With that, he stepped back into the shadows and started toward the rear of the kitchen. It was dangerous, she realized. What was he doing there? Why had he come? She stood rooted in place, fingering her weapon, wondering whether to return and warn the Aldermaston or find Seth to accompany her.

His voice drifted from the dark. "It is a beautiful moonlit night and mild enough that others will be wandering the grounds, so if I am to remain unseen, as is my desire, I must withdraw to where fire cannot reveal me."

Lia was intrigued by his choice of words. They were almost musical the way they came out of his mouth. There was a different manner of speaking in Pry-Ree, a different way of expressing ideas. Rather than being alarmed, it calmed her. Cautiously, she ventured into the shadows and followed him to the copse of oak trees at the fringe where she had observed Colvin at his swordplay more than once. She was tensed, ready to cry out if surprised by anyone else.

"Explain yourself," Lia said, listening keenly for the sounds of others. She remembered how Colvin and Ellowyn had been lulled into a trap by Martin. She glanced around and searched the darkness for any sign of others.

"I am alone," he said.

"Who are you?"

"My name is Kieran Evnissyen, though I am called Kieran Ven, which means 'night' in the tongue of this land. I do most of my work after sundown. I am part of the Evnissyen—as are you."

Lia walked in a half-circle around him, forcing him to turn to keep her in view. "What is that name? Is it a Family name?"

"It was, long ago. But those abandoned by their parents use it now. We are the protectors of the royal Family. Advisors to the nobles of Pry-Ree."

"Their abductors as well, it would seem," Lia said. "This is not your first journey to this land."

"I confess it. I know that our aldermaston sent Ellowyn to Dochte Abbey. It was clearly the Medium's will. We did not oppose it. Now it bids us rescue her from that den of snakes…and hetaera."

Lia gasped as he said the word.

"I know you are a maston," he said with a nod of approval, "as am I. It is unusual for Evnissyen but not unheard of. Which brings me to the answer you were seeking at the first. I arrived at nightfall, crossing the Apse Veil from Tintern. The way to Dochte was sealed. I could not pass. So I was sent here. My mission is to join Martin in Dahomey. I was told you would come with me willingly." He cocked his head. "Or should I fetch a rope?"

"Martin?" Lia gasped. She stopped circling the enigmatic man and rushed him, gripping his sleeve. He reacted defensively but let her seize him.

Another smirk. "He felled the Fear Liath, girl. We were trying to join you—to aid you in your mission. We lost two to that beast, but Martin finished the kill and rid the mountain of that demon. He booked passage on a ship from Bridgestow and left before you even made it back to this forsaken country. You have the Prince's orb. You will lead me to Martin. We leave at dawn."

Lia stared at him in surprise and chafed at his presumption. "I serve the Aldermaston of Muirwood, not Tintern. I must seek—"

"Permission? You are such a child. I have been an Evnissyen since my birth. How old are you? Seventeen? I have twice as many years behind me. I have been to Dahomey many times. I know the road to the island Abbey. I know the woods full of stones and flooded with boulders. I know the port of call, Vezins. But Martin insisted that I bring you with me, so I must insist that you come along whether the old man wills it or no. I am not normally this polite."

This is polite? she thought darkly. "Why do you come now?" Lia said, challenging him.

His eyes were dark, brooding. "Because we cannot wait any longer. Whitsunday is past. The apples are harvesting and will be mashed into cider. The cider will be drunk at the winter celebration. The winter celebration is when the Blight will come. It will strike at Twelfth Night, the beginning of winter. We must be on the ships before the winter storms arrive and prevent us from sailing. The plague stirs from Dochte Abbey on Twelfth Night."

As he spoke, an image bloomed in Lia's mind: a Leering stone carved into a circle made of entwining serpents. As she looked at it, it began to glow with fire.

Lia blinked, and the vision was gone. She stared at Kieran Ven coldly. "Before I go anywhere, I must speak with the Aldermaston."

"For your sake, I hope he says yes."

***

"Let me help you comb the tangles out of your hair," Sowe offered. The kitchen smelled lovely for an egg crackled on a skillet and pottage boiled on the cauldron. Lia's rucksack was full of food and a change of garments. A full quiver of arrows rested by it, and the bow sleeve stood straight against the fringe of the doorway.

"Thank you," Lia said and sat patiently while Sowe began working on the wild tangles in her always-unmanageable mass of hair.

Pasqua ladled syrupy treacle into the dish and then pressed it into her hands with a spoon. "You are scarcely fit to walk, Lia. Another day or two would do you some good. Why not delay?" She reached out and touched Lia's cheek tenderly.

"Traveling to Dahomey will take time. The Aldermaston would like me to leave before dawn when others will not see me go."

"I am almost finished," Sowe said, hurrying with the task. She pinched a clump of golden twisty hair and then ran her hand over Lia's head. "I will miss you again. I have never left Muirwood once. You have been so far."

Lia was not sure if she detected envy in Sowe's voice or not. She looked up at her friend. "Do you wish you were going?"

Sowe smiled and shook her head. "Edmon is going to take the maston test. I should like…to be here when he does." She blushed and looked down.

Lia took her hand and squeezed it. They had different temperaments. Sowe was shy and reserved, the greatest beauty in the Abbey since Reome had left after Whitsunday. She did not act conceited or haughty. She almost seemed unaware of the effect she had on the boys—especially one Edmon, Earl of Norris-York, who doted on her shamefully when he was allowed inside the kitchen.

"I will miss you," Lia said, squeezing her hand again.

Sowe leaned down and kissed Lia's cheek. "I worry for you without Colvin to protect you, even though I know you can care for yourself better than the knight-mastons can. Pasqua is grateful Martin is still alive. She cried when you told her the news. Do you think the Aldermaston will forgive him?"

"I do not know. He forgave Seth, though, even after his betrayal. Well, the voyage on the ships will be a long one, I imagine. We will all need to learn forgiveness before we reach the destination." Lia took a spoonful of the porridge and savored the mix of spices and treacle with the oats.

Pasqua rubbed her hands together, looking forlorn. "I am not sure I want to leave," she said with a sigh, glancing up at the tall beams supporting the huge roof. The fires in each corner of the kitchen were glowing, cooking the bread and sending the heat upward and then swirling back down to warm them. "Maybe I will stay with the Aldermaston. I do not relish the thought of a long sea journey. My knees have been aching, and I do not like walking." She glanced around at the kitchen again, her eyes brimming with tears. "But then I have the thought that if I do not go, I will never meet your little ones."

"Pasqua," Lia said archly, "there are no promises made to either one of us. Please do not speak of children before any man has even plighted his troth."

Pasqua gave her a smile with a glint of teasing in it. "Many of the noble born marry at your age, child. Some even younger are married as children. Since two young nobles are interested in you both, do not dismiss my words too hastily. I should have shooed them both away with a broom instead of encouraging them with gooseberry fool. I love Muirwood. There is no other place that is home to me…save where you two are. You are my daughters, after all, in every way except birth. But considering the pain and trouble you have both put me through so often, would a true mother have suffered more than I?" She grinned at them, tears dropping from her lashes. She hugged them both, so fiercely it stole Lia's breath for a moment.

"Have a care," Pasqua whispered and then kissed Lia soundly. "Did you remember the orb?"

Lia had forgotten it. "Thank you," she said gratefully and took another bite while she fetched the orb from behind the secret stone where she hid it. Then, fetching and donning her cloak, she took one last Muirwood apple from the basket and wrapped it in oilcloth to protect it. She intended it as a gift for Colvin. She finished the meal and then bid Pasqua and Sowe farewell and took her leave of the kitchen.

Kieran Ven waited in the shadows outside. The grounds were thick with morning mist, which would help hide their departure.

"You dawdle," he said stiffly, walking briskly toward the Abbey. "Most ships begin to leave at dawn. There is an abbey on the eastern side of Comoros that is near the docks. Hurry, lass, or we lose another day."

"The hunter is patient," Lia reminded him.

"I have patiently limited my scolding to your punctuality. We will discuss your other failings later."

Lia chuckled to herself and thought he was a rather petulant man. "Please, do not spare my feelings. I am quite used to my faults being pointed out by complete strangers."

"I am not trying to insult you."

"Nor are you complimenting me." Lia stopped and stared at him. "My leg is throbbing already. I understand the urgency, Kieran. But I cannot walk as quickly as you right now."

"My apologies," he said, bowing his head deftly. "At your pace then."

Lia continued walking and approached the Abbey, which rose before them like a mountain of stone. The flowers from the grounds were a gentle reminder that she had packed a bunch of purple mint in her rucksack as well. She craved seeing Colvin again and wondered how long it would take to reach Dochte Abbey.

"Where is the Queen Dowager being kept?" Kieran asked softly. His gaze wandered the grounds around them quickly, zigzagging from bench to tree to flowerbed as if every shrub held a threat.

"There is a guest house on the opposite end of the Abbey. She is under guard night and day."

Kieran pursed his lips. "She should be executed and her head delivered to her brother in a basket."

Lia stared at him in shock. "That is cruel."

He shook his head. "The world she manipulates is cruel. The destruction of the Blight is a result of her actions and the actions of those like her. An Evnissyen advises. Sometimes we do what must be done. If a king must die to save his people, then so be it. With her death, it removes the Dahomeyjan king's pretext for war. It forces him to react rather than us. Demont is bold, but he is too merciful. Here we are."

They had reached the door of the Abbey. "Have you crossed the Apse Veil before on your own?" he asked her.

She shook her head.

"Then I will go first and then bring you across. That is the way it is done."

"I understand."

As they started up toward the archway and the door, it opened from the inside and a knight-maston emerged, his face red from running. His eyes were wild with intensity.

"What news?" Lia asked, for they were blocking the way out.

He was panting and sagged back against the archway. "You are the Aldermaston's hunter. I recognize you. I seek Demont, but you can tell your master." He wiped his mouth on his arm. "The Earl of Dieyre escaped Pent Tower last night. The bells are ringing throughout Comoros. They say he is bound for Dahomey, that a ship was waiting for him. He swore he would return with an army and execute every maston for treason."

Lia felt a spasm of fear strike through her. The Earl of Dieyre was Colvin's sworn enemy. Since his capture after the battle, he had refused to reveal where he had hidden Colvin's sister, Marciana. Lia had promised Colvin before he left that she would use the orb to find her.

They let the knight-maston pass, and he ran through the fog toward the manor house.

"If you are a maston, can you read Pry-rian?" Lia asked Kieran. She could not read because it was not allowed at Muirwood.

He nodded.

She withdrew the Cruciger orb from the pouch at her belt. His eyes narrowed as he stared at it. *Find Marciana Price*, she thought. The pointers on the orb began to spin and whirl. It pointed southeast, towards the king's city. A single word appeared on the lower half of the orb, written in the slanted scrawl of the Pry-rian language.

Kieran looked at it and then stared at her. "Who were you searching for?" he asked her. "Dieyre?"

"What does it say?"

"Comoros."

CHAPTER FOUR

Comoros

Lia felt the Medium engulf her like a flood as she gripped Kieran's hand and he pulled her through the Apse Veil. It was a dizzying rush, a swirl of color and sound, and then a violent shudder as if her insides were wrenched apart and then thrust back together. As she stumbled through on the other side, she staggered and nearly fell, overwhelmed with the sensation. The Medium was a power she respected, though she still did not fully understand it. For most of her life, she had felt it strongly without even realizing its subtle influence. But it was not until she passed through the Apse Veil into Comoros that she realized how strongly it was felt in Muirwood. In Comoros, the whisper of it was nearly gone.

Lia choked. The air was thick with smoke and sour with the stench of filth. Even deep within an abbey, the smell was blinding in its intensity. There was but a little spark of the Medium, a dull throb that was painfully unnoticeable.

"Where are we?" Lia said, wrinkling her nose and feeling the first throbs of worry.

"Claredon Abbey," Kieran said. "Near the docks of Pent Tower, as luck would have it. There are ships there ready to sail to Dahomey." He parted the Apse Veil for her to let her pass first.

She crossed the curtain, which did not glow as it did in Muirwood. Looking back, she saw seven Leerings carved into stone pillars. It was the same seven themes she had seen before, but the workmanship was different. A bearded man. One of a lion, another of a sheep. Another of a snake, which made her pause as she thought of the Leering she had seen in her mind during the vision. She also noticed one with a blazing sun and another of a twisting vine with flowers and leaves. The last was a bull with horns. The workmanship was different but still beautiful. They showed the seven aspects of Idumea, another world that existed far away—a world where the city gardens of the Idumeans beckoned all mastons.

They left the Abbey, and Lia stopped short at the whirl and commotion of Comoros. The Abbey was small, unlike Muirwood, and it was on the eastern outskirts of the infamous city. The gates were barred, but the porter opened for them without question, since only mastons could travel the Apse Veils. The porter was an older man with silver hair, crooked teeth, and a pleasant smile.

"Any travelers from Dahomey recently?" Lia asked him on a whim, pausing to touch his arm.

His smile wrinkled into a pursed grimace. "Not in a long while, girl. The Dochte Mandar do not allow it."

"Who?" Kieran asked.

"The Dochte Mandar. Be wary of them, mastons." Lia did not understand the word but nodded and was about to move on, but the porter grabbed her sleeve. "The person you seek is at Lambeth Manor."

Lia startled and stared at him in confusion.

He bunched up his mouth into a frown and nodded. "I have lived here a good many years. I was abandoned as a wretched and chose to stay to fulfill my vow. I was shown great kindness by a noble prince once—a noble prince who came down that road yonder, paused on his horse, and paid me a gold sovereign. He said a girl would come through Claredon with hair like yours. That was a long time ago. I had forgotten it until just now. Something made me remember. The Medium, no doubt. There you have it. My message is delivered. Now I can spend the gold crown."

Lia felt the tiniest throb. She took the old porter's hand and squeezed it. He opened the gate and let them pass into the wild throngs filling the street beyond.

"What was that?" Kieran said, his brows knitting together. "Whom do you seek?"

"We must go to Lambeth first," Lia said.

"Whatever for?"

Someone bumped into Lia from behind, nearly knocking her over. The street was teeming with travelers and carts. The gutters were choked with manure and mud. Kieran grabbed her arm and pulled her with him, walking southward. "You must walk quickly in this city. Do not gawk so. Who is at the Lambeth?"

"A person I came here to find," Lia answered.

He gave her a sharp look of incredulity. "Do you have any idea how many people live here? There are three dozen abbeys alone, I think, just serving Comoros. You think you can find a single person?"

"Yes, I can," Lia said. "I have the orb."

"Think, girl. If you pull it out, you will have every thief in Comoros with knowledge of it before the midday bells toll. Keep your hand around it. There are cutpurses everywhere."

"You said you have been here," she said, growing annoyed at his tone.

"I have," he answered. "I hate it. Do you see that fortress? We are not even inside the city gates right now. Pent Tower is the castle keep and the royal manor that protects the king's Family and guards the king's enemies. Are you seeking Dieyre? He is an enemy to us."

Lia shook her head violently. "He is the last man I want to see."

"All the better, for his reputation is known in Pry-Ree. Whom do you seek?"

"Someone he abducted. I made a promise, Kieran. The orb said I would find her here. And the porter said where."

He grabbed her arm and steered her against the wall before a cart crashed into them. The jolt of it stunned her. A swarm of flies buzzed about her face, and she shuddered. She was used to the moors and wilderness, not this hive of movement. She felt the Myriad Ones thronging them but taking no notice.

He was tall and looked down at her with fury. "We must catch a boat to Dahomey today," he said, his teeth gritting with frustration.

"I am not stopping you," she replied evenly, looking into his eyes with determination.

"Martin said you must come."

"I do not obey orders from Martin," she said. "Or from you. I obey the Aldermaston of Muirwood."

He shook his head, obviously biting his tongue. "Muirwood is a bit far. You used me to cross here. You said nothing of this other person when we left."

"And you have told me all of your secrets?" Lia replied. "Are we going to stand here bickering in the street for much longer? The day is wasting."

"I hate this city," he replied, his teeth clenching. His look was full of loathing.

"It will not take long before I share your sentiment. Go on without me then. But I will likely find Martin before you will. *After* my errand is done."

He snorted, hands planted on his hips in frustration. He glanced at her, as if judging whether he should simply truss her up and carry her to the docks. "You are still limping. I cannot abandon you in a place like this."

"I can take care of myself," Lia said evenly.

Kieran whirled and grabbed a man toting a cart. The man spluttered with surprise, his face twisting with anger. "My pardon, good sir. Where is Lambeth? What part of the city?"

"Oy, you are a rude sort!"

"Oy, where is Lambeth?" Kieran repeated, his face a mask of anger. He seemed to take the other man's temperament and adapt it to himself immediately, like changing his shirt.

The carter nodded toward the road ahead. "Across the bridge. In the Stews." He looked at Lia, and his face twisted into a sickening smile—a leer. "She will fetch a decent price. Even with that awful tangle of hair. The Stews—have at it and leave me be!"

***

There was no way to describe the king's city Comoros—no words fitting or suitable to a girl raised in the shelter of Muirwood. It was, Lia decided, the worst place in the world. The streets were narrow and sliced this way and that, the buildings crammed and topped and then crammed and topped more until the roofs seemed to sway in the wind. Laundry clothes were hung from poles in the windows to dry. The streets were caked with filth, and the air was rancid. It was busy and violent. Once she thought she saw a knight-maston weaving through the crowd, but he covered his sword with his hand to hide the insignia. Just when Lia thought it could get no worse, they reached the bridge that straddled the mighty river and crossed it into the Stews, and Lia realized that life on the other side was even worse.

In the Stews, everything was for sale and everything sought for a price. Someone offered Lia gold crowns for her hair. Another wanted to pay for a kiss. No one would direct them to Lambeth for free, forcing them to venture into an alley and use the Cruciger orb for direction. The oppressiveness of the Stews hung so heavy that even the orb was sluggish in its response. The Medium was stifled. There was no feeling it, as there were no abbeys south of the river.

"This is where some venture who do not want to be found," Kieran said, his face tight with revulsion. "The Blight is already here. You can feel it. Come on, then. It is daylight yet, and this sort of town gets worse after dark. You may trust my word on that, girl. I have been acquainted with the night for many years."

"You have been here?" Lia asked, stuffing the orb back in its pouch.

He shook his head. "Few mastons would dare it." She saw his eyes narrow back at the mouth of the alley. "We were followed."

Seizing her arm, he pulled her back the way they had originally come, toward the mouth of the alley instead of deeper. There were four men approaching, their eyes dark with hunger and mischief.

Lia's hand throbbed. Her body became sick with the thought of fighting. Her leg was throbbing from the hard walking that day. "The other way is open. Why are we approaching them?"

"Are you really that simple? Their job is to frighten us deeper into the alley where even more are waiting. Better odds with four than twenty."

"Oh," Lia said, ashamed that she was not thinking like a hunter. The men approached, and she could see the apprehension on their faces. One of them gave her a look that made her stomach sour.

"Are you lost?" one of them said, holding out his hand disarmingly. Lia noticed the dagger in his other hand, a small dirk.

Kieran walked straight toward them, pulling her close to him. "My sister is ill," he said, his voice suddenly trembling with fear. "Let us pass. We have no money save for the healer."

"She does look ill," the man replied, his grin widening. "I know a place where she might lay down." The others chuckled.

"No...no...it will be well. We are looking for the guildhall. Do you know where it is?"

"The guildhall? You are on the wrong side of the river, sir. If you would like it, I could—"

Kieran stepped in and smashed the heel of his hand into the man's nose. Lia saw the spurt of blood, the shocking stream of crimson, and then the second man was down on the cobbles as well. She saw the gladius in Kieran's hand. He whirled around and cracked a man's skull with the hilt, dropping him.

Lia felt her body lurch as the final man grabbed at the pouch holding the orb and tried to slit the tether with his knife. All around her, things whirled, and before she could think, she reacted. She caught the wrist holding the knife and pulled him toward her, jamming the edge of her hand into his throat. His eyes bulged as he spluttered and choked. Twisting his wrist, she pulled harder and swung him around and into the side of a building, head-first. He collapsed in a heap.

Kieran sheathed his gladius, nodded to her approvingly, and motioned her to follow. They entered the street as the four men twitched and moaned.

"You told them the guildhall because you wanted their friends to chase us somewhere else," she said.

He gave her a wry smile. "And just moments ago, I was beginning to think you were totally useless. You have the makings of an Evnissyen in you. Tell me more about this girl we are hunting down, other than that she is Lord Price's sister. Is she a maston? Can she cross the Apse Veil?"

"No, but she studies to be one."

"Is she the kind of girl who will help us save her or hinder us?"

"What do you mean?"

"Can she handle a blade?"

"I have never seen her."

"A scholar then. How boring. Have you given any thought as to how we will rescue her? Or were you leaving that detail to me to consider?"

Lia grit her teeth. "No one is making you do this, Kieran."

He sighed. "You are not defenseless, I will give you that. But you are young and inexperienced. I was trained for the city. You were trained for the woods. They are both wild and savage but in different ways. What I am asking, Lia, is what we will do when we find the Lambeth? Were you planning to knock on the porter door and ask for her?"

"The Medium will tell me," Lia answered. "It always does."

"Really? You can actually feel it in the Stews? I have not felt its spark since we left the Claredon this morning. This is a sick and diseased place. It will succumb to the Blight in a moment, if it already has not. You think the Medium will direct us to her?"

Lia craned her neck and felt a throb in her heart. For the last several moments, her eyes had rested on a girl ahead of them, carrying a basket against her hip, wearing a shawl to cover her hair, though some of the locks escaped, and she recognized the color.

"It already has," Lia said and started to walk faster. The girl walked and dodged through the street ahead of them. Lia recognized the stride, the muscles on her arms. But as they approached, the girl turned sharply to an alley, hunched over, and retched into the gutter. She was sick. No one took notice of her except Lia.

"What is it?" Kieran asked, seeing her stare. "The girl? That is Forshee's sister?"

Lia shook her head, watching as the girl wiped some spittle on the shawl. She hefted the basket of laundry again. Lia had a glimpse of her face.

"No," Lia whispered. "Her name is Reome Lavender. I know her from Muirwood." The insight struck her as it always did: just a little whisper of knowledge. Just as it had pointed her out in the crowd. Without seeing her face, Lia knew. "She is with child. Dieyre's child," she whispered.

CHAPTER FIVE

Lia's Leering

The swamp filling the lowlands of Muirwood was known as the Bearden Muir, but neither Prince Alluwyn nor Martin Evnissyen knew it by its local name. For them, it was a wet and sick land, so different from the lush valleys of Pry-Ree, which were thick with fat sheep and jackrabbit and thrush. No, the swamps reminded them more of the mountains, the ancient mountains called the Myniths where ancient beasts roamed and tortured travelers with their worst fears. The Bearden Muir was full of sinkholes and bogs, clouds of gnats, and crooked oaks crowning the bumps of land protruding from the swamp.

The two men on horseback rode into a clearing on the slope of a hillside that wound down to a little hamlet fixed near the sea. The wind whipped at their cloaks, and large blots of rain spattered the ground. The Prince looked down at the orb, which had stopped spinning.

"By Cheshu, a village," Martin muttered. "At long last. Is that Muirwood? I do not see the Abbey. Is it hidden in the woods?"

"It is not," the Prince replied, his shoulders sagging with exhaustion. Lightning streaked across the sky, and the ripples of thunder made the horses nervous.

"A village is a village. We can find a bed and a meal at least." Martin rubbed his hands together with enthusiasm. "I would like as not to eat a jackdaw raw right now, feathers and all. If we hurry, we may find a place to rest before the night falls."

The Prince shook his head, staring down at the valley floor. "We will not rest here. We ride southeast all night for Muirwood."

"Muirwood is to the south? Why did we wander so far west?"

The Prince lifted his finger and pointed to the valley. The rain came in heavy sheets around them. The storm whipped at their faces. "That is where our enemy will fall. This field before us. Do you see that hill yonder? There he will die." He chuckled through the howling wind. "I can see him, Martin. I can see him quivering with fear, shrinking from the battlefield. He is clutching my flag, Martin. It is a misty morning. He holds *my* standard when he dies."

The Evnissyen nudged his horse closer, staring into the black rain, and clenched his teeth with the discomfort of being soaked and saddle sore and robbed of a night's lodging. "Why does he hold your standard, my lord? How did he get it?"

"He will get it after I am dead. As he has done with others before me, he will hoist my banner as a threat to his enemies. But hoisting it will kill him. That is where he will fall. From an arrow loosed from that slope. Do you see it? Where the ground pitches beneath that giant oak?"

"That *is* a large oak, my lord. Not questioning your lordship's eyesight."

"It should not be there."

"What?"

"That oak should not be there. There needs to be a little cave for her to sleep. A shelter from those who pursue her." He paused, staring at the giant oak. He wiped the rain from his face. Martin knew he could speak enigmatically at times, but this was different. He was talking about the future as if he were living there instead of the present. He shook his head, a stern expression on his mouth. "That oak should not be there."

Martin leaned forward in the saddle, feeling impatient. "Shall I tell it to move then, my lord? If it offends you, I can go down to the village and fetch an axe." *And a meal*, he thought blackly.

"Close your eyes. You must not witness the maston sign."

This also had happened before. Martin despised the maston secrets. Not even the Evnissyen dared penetrate an abbey to learn them. The Prince forbade it. Martin clutched the saddle horn, shivering from the hair as it dribbled down his leather hood. He closed his eyes, grimacing.

Suddenly everything went white, and a blast of thunder nearly shook him off his horse. The animals screamed with fear and bucked frantically. The noise was so loud that Martin could barely hear the shrieking stallions. He twisted around on the saddle after calming his beast, and the oak was afire, blazing despite the surge of rain.

"I said I would fetch an axe!" Martin roared, staring at the Prince, who stroked his stallion's mane and whispered to it soothingly. The animal was preternaturally calm.

"An axe would not do," the Prince replied. "The rains will wear away the earth at the roots, leaving a little cave. It will be ready when she needs it."

"Who?"

"The girl in my vision."

"Do you know who she is? Is this the girl who was drowned by the kishion?"

"It is the same, though he did not kill her. She managed to kill him."

Martin looked at the Prince, who had a strange expression on his face. An expression of pride. "Who is this girl, my lord? Who is this ghost you hunt?"

"She is not one of the Unborn, Martin. It is the future that I see. There is one more place we must stop before Muirwood. The Medium bids me east again. But before you join me, ride over to the burning tree. You will find branches that have been preserved thick with acorns. Collect the acorns and bring them to me—all of them. Gather as many as you can."

"I am collecting acorns now?" Martin said, exasperated. "Acorns!"

"You will see, Martin. Gather them and then join me in the valley beyond. There is something else I must do first, and you cannot see it."

***

Of all the tasks Martin had been given to perform during his duties as the Prince's advisor and protector, gathering acorns near a forsaken swamp marked one of the most humiliating. The tree was thick with them, as he had been told. There were hundreds to gather, and Martin wondered at the reason. During one of his sea voyages, he recalled some wisdom he had learned from a sea captain that enabled him to lead other men. The wisdom was that when men were employed in labor, they were contented. On the days when they worked, they were good-natured and cheerful, and having done a good day's work, they spent the evenings with mirth. But on idle days they were mutinous and quarrelsome—finding fault with their pork, the bread, the cider—and in continual ill-humor. That sea captain, Martin recalled, had a rule to keep his men constantly at work. When his second once told him that they had done everything and there was nothing further to employ them about, the sea captain ordered them to scour the anchor. Martin himself was known to employ that device with the Evnissyen, choosing to keep their minds and bodies active with too many orders rather than not enough.

When he finished filling his saddle bag with acorns, he mounted and followed the Prince's trail back over the ridge of the hill and into the muck-ridden sludge of the moors. The storm raged in the sky, the constant vivid lightning making it easy to spot the trail in the dark. The wind howled around him, as if warning him away from what lay ahead. He gritted his teeth, plodding into the eye of the storm. The stallion faltered with the strain of mud at its hooves. A burned smell drifted in the air.

Picking the fallen acorns was like scouring the anchor. He was certain of it. Could a man really see into the future? How was it possible since it had not happened yet? Or was the future like a river, bound by rocky banks and flowing from the high ground to the low ground? Knowing the pitch of the land, knowing the bounds, one might guess where a boat would end up at any time along the course. Was that it?

Another white blast of lightning scarred the sky, forcing Martin to shield his eyes. But in the light, in that moment of total glory and vividness, he had seen something. Martin shook his head, trying to steer his stallion toward what he had seen. It was the Prince, standing in the middle of the moors, his horse nearby and neighing. That was not what Martin remembered. It was the boulder hovering in the sky.

Another surge of lightning, another throaty roar of thunder. The Prince stood in the middle of the valley, his hand raised high. Before him, a huge slab of boulder hovered in the air.

"By Cheshu!" Martin swore, unable to believe what he saw. He wiped the rain from his eyes and stared again, trying to see through the blackness once more. Lightning lit up the sky overhead, the image revealing the boulder slowly coming down, as if it were hoisted in the arms of some invisible harness. The Prince's skin glowed white. In the flash that followed next, the boulder was firm on the ground. Martin started. The Prince had collapsed.

Martin kicked the horse's flanks and rode hard down the hillside to the valley. The hooves churned and splashed up mud. As he reached his master's side, Martin shook himself out of his stirrups and came down. The Prince's face was ashen.

"My lord!" He felt for the throb of his heartbeat, and it was there, just a tremulous little thing. "My lord Prince! Are you awake? Can you speak?"

The Prince's eyes fluttered open. He was exhausted. "A little rest, Martin. Then I will be well." His voice was barely a whisper.

"I brought the acorns. My saddlebag is full." He wiped rain from the Prince's face. The sky drenched them.

"Scatter them," the Prince whispered. "All around the stone."

"You want me to scatter them? But why?"

The Prince grimaced with pain. Air hissed through his teeth. "Do it," he repeated. "They will remind her of home when they are grown. Remind her...of Muirwood."

"My lord? Who is this girl you keep seeing? Who is she? Is it your bride? Is it Demont's daughter? Is she in danger?"

A smile twitched on the Prince's mouth. "Danger," he whispered. "When is she not in danger? You must help...protect her, Martin. Train her. Evnissyen—she must be trained as one. You must teach her to survive. To live. She will save...our people... from the Blight."

"Your wife? Your young wife in Dahomey? Demont's daughter?"

"No," the Prince gasped, shaking his head against Martin's arm. "No. My daughter."

His arm trembled as he lifted it, finger pointing to the boulder that moments ago had hovered in the air. When the lightning flashed again, Martin saw the Leering carved into its face.

It was the face of a young girl with rivulets of unruly hair.

I learned today that my grandmother first studied at Dochte Abbey when she was my age. I had always believed she came as a learner at twelve. My mother, however, did not study here because she was not the daughter of a king. But my grandmother was the daughter of a king, and the sister of one, and so by rights could study here. The Aldermaston showed me her tome. When people pass the maston test here, they promise to grant their tome to the Abbey to protect the knowledge they contain. My grandmother was married when she was nine years old to an earl. How awful I felt for her. Her first husband died when she was my age. They had no children together, though he spawned a brood from his first wife. My grandmother swore an oath that she would never marry again unless he was a maston. I think her first marriage was very tragic. She studied at Dochte Abbey and passed the maston test within her first year. The Aldermaston said that women learn quickly in Dochte Abbey. He also told me that my grandmother fell in love with another earl— Sevrin Demont. The Aldermaston said that at the time, the people believed that Sevrin had seduced my grandmother because she was the sister of the king and that he wanted power through her. But I have read her tome. It is clear to me that she wanted him and that she influenced the king to get what she wanted. I did not realize a woman could have so much power.

—Ellowyn Demont of Dochte Abbey

CHAPTER SIX

Lambeth Manor

Lia and Kieran followed Reome to Lambeth Manor, a stone fortress built in the heart of a rundown neighborhood in the center of the Stews. The grounds were blocked by ivy-fed stone, tipped with spikes, but there were tree branches visible within, revealing some open inner area beyond the walls. The manor had a large main keep that rose up in the north apex of the grounds, but it was not as imposing as the citadel of Pent Tower. Still, it was impossible to see inside the grounds of Lambeth, and as Reome approached one of the porter doors at the rear, Lia motioned for Kieran to hold back.

"What are you going to do?" Kieran asked.

"Talk to her and learn what I can. Then I will take her shawl and basket and go inside."

The look he gave her was beyond astonished. "That is your entire plan?"

"I am not asking you to go with me."

"You are asking to be caught or killed," he said, seething. "We have found Lambeth. Let us study it for several days to learn their routines, their faces, their weaknesses…"

Save Marciana.

The jolt from the Medium was so strong and insisting it made her eyes blur with tears. She saw Reome reaching for the knocker and knew she had to act.

Glaring at Kieran, she whispered, "If you do not wait for me, I will understand. But the Medium bids me to do this."

Lia summoned her courage and advanced, closing the distance before Reome knocked. "So this is where you live now?"

Startled, Reome jerked around and stared at Lia in surprise. It was clear she had recognized Lia's voice. "What are you doing in Comoros?" Her eyes betrayed loathing as well as fear. "Is he paying you as well?"

Lia noticed Reome hug the basket protectively and had a suspicion. She reached for the wicker rim and lifted the blanket covering the wet contents. Within the basket were several green gowns, too fancy and expensive to belong to Reome. The workmanship showed a master seamstress, and the color was the kind that Marciana preferred.

"She is here, Reome," Lia said. "This is where Dieyre is keeping Marciana."

Reome bit her lip. "Who sent you? The Aldermaston?"

Lia nodded.

"I hate that old man. I…I like it much better here than Muirwood." Her eyes were filling with tears.

"In the Stews? Reome…this is not your home. Dieyre escaped the tower last night. Did he come back? Is he here now?"

Reome still clutched the basket to her stomach, but she wiped tears on her arm. "No. He is in Dahomey. That is where…why are you here? How did you find me?"

"I am a hunter, Reome. You always teased me about that. I have hunted Colvin's sister."

"I must go inside," Reome said, trying to pull away, but Lia gripped the edge of the basket tightly.

"What did Dieyre promise you?" Lia asked.

Reome showed her teeth. "I do not have to answer to you. This is where I work. If I do not return, they will look for me."

Lia stepped closer, pitching her voice lower. "Did he promise he would claim the baby, Reome? Or will you abandon it as a wretched as *you* were abandoned?"

The look in Reome's eyes was haunted. It spoke of misery, of sleepless nights, of tortured hopes. She struggled with her emotions, her face contorting with pain.

"How did you know that?" Reome whispered faintly. She trembled, her skin going pale. "I have told no one save him."

Lia touched Reome's arm. "Go back to Muirwood."

Reome's lip trembled. Tears dribbled down her cheeks. "He will not…take me back…not after all I have done."

Lia was not sure if she meant the local blacksmith or the Aldermaston. "If you stay in Comoros, you will die. So will the babe. It is true, Reome. You must believe me. A great sickness is coming. It will sweep over every land, every kingdom. There is only safety in Muirwood. The Aldermaston will take you back. I promise you he will. Did Dieyre promise to bring you to Dahomey?"

Reome sniffled and nodded. "He has a manor there. Better than this one. He promised I would never work. That I could live there and raise the child. I was told he sent for me, that I would leave on a ship. Tonight."

Lia angered at the lie. She knew the truth as soon as Reome had spoken. She saw it flash in her mind like a blaze of lightning. "No. He will keep you here. You are the decoy. It is Marciana who is leaving tonight in your place. You are her disguise.

Do you see my friend over there? The tall one in the shadows? He will show you a safe place to go. Where are they hiding her? In the keep?"

Reome shook her head.

"You must tell me."

Reome flinched. "It will be my death if I do."

"I will protect you. Believe that. I will take your place and go inside. Let me free her, and you can both go back to Muirwood. Please, Reome. You must tell me where she is." Lia pushed the thought at her—along with her will, her intentions, her desire to protect Reome and her child. The Medium throbbed in the air and softened the look on Reome's face.

"The east tower. That one," she said, pointing. "But Lia, you cannot get to her. She is guarded day and night by a man. He… he frightens me. He said he would kill me if I told anyone she was here. They say…he kills mastons."

A kishion.

Lia sighed deeply. She clenched her jaw and nodded firmly. The Medium would protect her. She pulled on the basket. "Give me your shawl."

"Lia, I know you are a hunter…"

"You cannot go back there, Reome. Muirwood is the only place you can save your child. Do you have any money?"

"I have a little."

"Then go home, Reome."

She bit her lip. "How do you know…that Dieyre is lying? He is a noble. He would not abandon me."

Lia stared her in the face. "I know Dieyre better than you do, Reome. I know about his false promises. You see, he tried to kill me. Quickly, give me your shawl." The urgency to rescue Marciana burned inside her, compelling her to act quickly.

***

In the courtyard at the center of the Lambeth grounds was a giant oak tree, leafless and dying. Maybe the choking air had finally destroyed its growth. Perhaps some wasting sickness had struck its branches, which were huge and pointed every direction like a sharpened hedgehog burrowing in the mud. Moss grew on one side, and clumps of mistletoe buds were thick in the boughs. It was a dead thing—a shell of a tree. For a moment, it reminded Lia of the oak forest surrounding Muirwood, and a chill went through her heart. The scarf covered her hair, and she had traded cloaks with Reome to hide her hunter leathers. She had no time to conceal her bow stave, so she had given it to Reome to hold and sent her away with the arrow quiver. Lia carried her dirk with the hand supporting the basket beneath and had her unsheathed gladius hilt in the other hand, the blade resting atop the damp garments but underneath the wrap to conceal it. She wanted two weapons ready when she faced the kishion.

Martin had trained her well. She knew all the locations where to stab a man and kill in one thrust. She realized she might only have one chance to kill him. It was kill or be the victim herself. The Medium had led her to Comoros. Strangely, her life felt as if she were a small boat bobbing on a river rushing wildly through a maze of rocks and rapids. It pulled her quickly, no matter how she longed to slow it.

Her heart beat frantically as the porter opened the door and let her in. She did not acknowledge his curt greeting and merely tromped inside, clutching the basket to her bosom as she quickly surveyed the courtyard and saw the oak. The inner yard was a giant circle, grown with sod and ringed with cobblestones. She counted three doors giving access to the manor house from the interior and one directly at the base of the tower Reome had pointed to. She took the pathway to the right and followed it toward the tower, her heart pounding in her ears. She wished she could have checked the Cruciger orb. Glancing at the upper windows, she noticed the heavy curtains blocking them. She had no idea what was happening inside.

A raven caw startled her, and she noticed the black bird perched atop a flag spike. The building was larger than the Aldermaston's manor house; it was two stories compared with one, and the towers rose to a third height, the main keep rising the highest of them all. The tower she sought was on the edge of the grounds, connecting to an outer wall with spikes fastened into the stone like a ridge of teeth. She crossed the path to the door and shoved at it with her basket. A porter opened the door and looked at her curiously. Lia glanced behind him and saw a stone stairwell ascending up the gullet. There were no other guards.

"Set the basket down by the brazier," the porter told her. "I will carry it up later. They wish no interruptions."

Lia nodded, carried the basket into the chamber, and set it down by the brazier. She released the gladius blade resting in the basket but turned the dirk over in her hand to conceal it from him.

"Move along, girl." He waved for her to leave the way she had come.

Lia walked toward the door and saw him glance outside and look at something that interested him. His distraction was all she needed. Her hunter training flowed back to her, filling her with knowledge. There was a spot on the back of the skull. With the dirk handle, she clubbed him there. His eyes rolled back in his head, and she caught him as he fell and laid him out on the floor. Then she shut the door softly and glanced up the stairwell winding its way up within the tower. She could hear the murmur of voices but could not discern any of the words.

Hefting the basket of laundry, Lia gripped the gladius hilt again beneath the wrap and started up the stone steps. Her leg throbbed with the effort. Doubts struck at her thoughts, but she batted them away. Having faced a kishion before, she knew that their training exceeded hers. The last time, she had been surprised and unprepared for the encounter. It had ended with her face down, drowning in a bathing tub. She gritted her teeth, preparing herself for another fight. Part of her wished Kieran was there. Two against one would make it easier, but the porter door would not have opened if he had seen them both. She did not want to think about Kieran and what he was thinking about her at that moment. His expression was one of disgust when she had revealed her lackluster plan. Follow the Medium. That was all she could do.

As Lia made the loops up the stairwell, the voices grew louder. Torches hung in racks along the wall, lighting the way. At the top of the stairs, a wooden door barred the way. Lia's hand trembled as she reached for the handle to pull it open. There was no crossbar on it, and it opened to her touch. The voices became clear, and so did the presence of the Medium. It fluttered in her heart powerfully, bringing tears to her eyes once again. She recognized the powerful feelings, but it felt forced and not tamed.

"You must persuade your brother to join us," said a man's voice. "When the kingdom falls, do you think he will be allowed to keep his earldoms if he is on the losing side? Do you think he will keep his head? Lord Dieyre has promised him amnesty in return for your willing consent to be his wife. With his authority, I offer you his plighted troth and will accept yours in return. You must promise to marry him when you reach Dahomey. His affection for you is sincere. Do not doubt that."

"I love him, but I cannot accept him," Marciana replied. Her voice was throbbing with emotion.

"Why not?" The voice was a sneer.

"He is not a maston."

"You have sworn to yourself that you will only marry a maston. But what a foolish oath to make to yourself, child. What will you do when there are no mastons left? Marry your brother?" The voice dripped with sarcasm. Lia heard an accent in the speech, and she recognized it as Dahomeyjan. "You are the price Dieyre demands. You are the only person who can save your brother's life. Even now, he is under guard at Dochte Abbey in Dahomey. He is being treated fairly and courteously. But should you refuse this arrangement, he will be sent into the dungeons. There are serpents in the dungeons, my lady. If he were to fall asleep, he will be bitten and poisoned. Do not trifle with me, child. You must promise to marry Lord Dieyre. You must say it for it to be binding. You must agree."

The Medium throbbed even stronger, and as Lia opened the door, she heard Marciana sniffling and crying. The only light in the chamber was the light of fire. The air was thick and hot and smelled strongly of incense.

"I am thirsty," Marciana moaned.

"Then drink some more cider," the man replied.

"I will not drink it," she said. "Water—just a little water."

"Then tell me you will swear your betrothal to Lord Dieyre. I will bring you water. I will summon it fresh from a *gargouelle*.

Cold, clean water to soothe your thirst. But you must first swear it. Or drink the cider."

As the door opened slowly, Lia saw Marciana in a rich crimson gown with black and gold trim. There were ornaments of gold in her hair, which was loose and thick about her shoulders. The bodice of the gown was cut low in the Dahomeyjan style, similar to what Lia had seen the Queen Dowager wear. Marciana looked tortured—her eyes brimmed with tears. She shook her head, pacing the far side of the chamber where thick curtains blocked the sun. She crushed her fists against her forehead and sobbed, pacing, wracked with her feelings. Lia's heart burned with anger.

The man in the room wore a black cassock. His hair was short and cropped, and he had a disdainful look on his face. His eyes glowed silver as he turned and looked at Lia.

"I gave *orders* to leave the basket below," he said in a sulky tone. The Medium swirled around Lia, enveloping her in ribbons made of iron. Fear exuded from the man. It made her think of Almaguer. She shuddered with terror at the feelings swarming her body. The Myriad Ones sniffed about her, so thick it felt the room was bursting with them. They swarmed around Marciana, sending their thoughts into her, willing her to bend to their will. Lia's heart panged with compassion for Marciana. She knew what it felt like.

"I beg your pardon," Lia mumbled, bowing her head. She skirted to the side to drop the basket near a brazier. "Would you like me to hang them to dry?" she asked with a quaver in her voice.

"Yes," the man said impatiently. "If you must. Then leave us."

There was a changing screen near the brazier, and Lia walked to it and discovered several other garments—some thin chemises and another gown. She carefully withdrew the first damp gown and fitted it to the pegs on the changing screen so it could dry by the fire. Sweat ran down her cheeks.

"Will you answer me, Lady Marciana?" he said, turning his attention back. "Will you please explain to me again why you will not marry the lord Earl? Do you not care for him?"

"I do," Marciana said, sobbing.

"You think him not clever enough for you? He is too old and doddering for you? There are many girls from your station who are forced to marry as children. The king orders them to be wed, despite their feelings. Can you imagine that? Being forced to marry a man at fifty as the Queen Dowager was forced to marry your dead king? You are being given a choice! A chance for wealth. A chance for power. A chance to have children who will love you and adore you. To be a mother, as you did not have one. Do you not long for that? To be a mother? To comfort and nurture a sweet baby? Can you imagine holding that son or daughter in your arms? Can you comprehend the joy of hearing its first cry?" The voice was mesmerizing, and it filled Lia with hungers she had never experienced before. She slammed the thoughts away because they distracted and ensnared. They wove through the most delicate part of her feelings. But the threads were not pure in their intent.

"He can give that to you," the man continued, his voice barely a whisper. "Even joys and pleasures you do not comprehend. Is it wrong to crave children, my lady? Can you imagine holding the child, suckling him, loving him? Does not your heart crave these things? Your baby. Your own. Will you not accept Lord Dieyre's offer of marriage? I am not asking you to yield to the binding, just a promise that you will when you reach Dahomey. Let him declare his feelings for you himself. As I told you, he is no longer a prisoner of the Crown. He is not in rebellion against the throne but a champion of the young king and an enemy of the usurper, Garen Demont. You know this to be true. He is the only one who can save you and thus save your brother. Can you be so selfish?"

Lia looked at Marciana's eyes. She was tortured, exhausted, and weak. How long had she been captive, living in the Stews, unable to know what happened to those she loved? The air was perfumed and cloying. Lia was sure the cider had been treated with other herbs or had been allowed to spoil and strengthen its flavor. The man in the black cassock, the kishion, manipulated her feelings with deftness and cruelty.

"I am so thirsty," Marciana said with a tremulous sigh. She was begging.

"Then drink the cider," came the reply, and he poured some from a bottle into a golden cup and offered it to her. His back was to Lia as she started toward him stealthily.

"Water," she pleaded.

"Just a sip, to quench your thirst," he promised, holding up the chalice.

Lia pushed the dirk blade into his back. She knew right where to stab, right where his air would spill out. The fabric slit. Blood bloomed on her hand, warm and hot. He gasped, thrashing. His neck jerked around, his silver eyes burning into hers, sending her into a daze of panicked emotions as he died. In that instant, she could see into his frenzied thoughts, full of terror because the Myriad Ones would leave his body now.

He slumped to the floor, and Lia let him fall. She lowered the shawl.

Marciana looked at her, puzzled, confused. Then her eyes widened with shock and horror. "The kishion," she hissed. "Behind you!"

Lia heard the body swing down from the rafters and fall like a sure-footed cat. The kishion blocked the doorway leading out. She realized, too late, that the man in the black cassock was not the kishion after all. She realized also that her gladius was still in the basket.

CHAPTER SEVEN

Broken

Oh Lia, he will kill us both!" Marciana whispered. "He has not left me since Muirwood."

The hunter was patient. The prey was careless. Lia swallowed, trying to contain her fear. She wished again, pointlessly, that Kieran was with her. Her mind raced as she glanced about the room, looking for a way to shift the balance.

"Stay behind me," Lia said. The kishion started toward them with twin daggers in his hands. He had the same dead eyes she had seen before, a man utterly devoid of feelings. A scar ran down his left cheek. His eyes were blue, his hair cropped short. There was something in the look of his mouth, some rugged quality of his chin that told her he had survived many fights and killed many—even women.

Lia glanced at the nearest brazier, remembering that it was fire that had destroyed her previous enemy. There were no Leerings in the tower, no stone sculptures, but there was fire, and she had the Gift of Firetaming. It would not burn her.

She shifted to the right, keeping as much of the room between them as she could. The windows were all blocked by heavy curtains.

The idea bloomed in her mind. *Force the enemy to react to your plans, instead of reacting to his.* She was not fully healed and feared the kishion's skill at knife-fighting eclipsed hers. If she focused on her strengths, it would give her a better chance.

The kishion studied her, weaving closer, watching her feet as she moved, seeing which leg she favored. She tried to keep from wincing at her throbbing leg. He was judging her abilities.

"I offer terms," Lia said. "Will you negotiate?" She moved closer to the brazier.

"The challenge lures me," the kishion replied. "Not the gold. Drop the dirk, and I will kill you quickly. You murdered a Dochte Mandar. They will want you dead for that, and it will not be a pleasant death."

Lia darted as he spoke. She had hoped he would respond to her, to distract his mind from her true intent. The brazier glowed with burning coals, and the black iron was white with ash. Flames filled its bowels and offered light from between the thick slats. It had four tiny legs keeping it up, and Lia gripped the bars and shoved it over, spilling the flaming coals onto the nearest curtain. The metal was warm against her hand, but it did not burn her. The curtain erupted into a sheath of flames.

She tried to use the Medium to control the fire, but there was not even the spark of it in the tower any longer. It could never be forced by a maston, only pleaded with or persuaded. She was on her own yet still. Black smoke began to fill the room. The curtain blazed, sending fire up to the wooden rafters.

The kishion lunged at her.

He was faster than she thought he would be, but there was something new in his eyes—a little hint of fear at the crackling flames. She had changed the balance of the duel. He had experience with fire. He knew how fast it would devastate the room.

Lia watched his feints, refusing to react to them, to be distracted. He suddenly dropped low and tried to sweep her bad leg with his boot, but she moved aside and sliced toward his ear. He deflected it with a dagger, and she whirled around behind him, trying to draw him after her. It worked. He had seen how lethal she could be with a dirk and slashed at her with his other hand. Lia jumped away from the cut and saw Marciana backing away from the kishion, toward another curtain.

"Get to the door!" Lia told her, stabbing carefully at the kishion, trying to push him back into the blaze of the curtains. If she could get close enough, she could shove him into the burning mass, but he recognized her plan and went after Marciana.

Lia intervened, slashing at his arm. Smoke swirled in the room, obscuring everything, her movements and his. Suddenly the kishion's blade lashed out at her, the dagger at her ribs. He stabbed just above the leather girdle she wore, beneath her breast. She felt the point of the blade rip against her shirt, tear it, and then glance away.

There should have been pain. There should have been a cut. She realized to her surprise that the dagger had not penetrated. The shirt was torn, but the blade had stopped against the chaen beneath.

There was another look in the kishion's eyes. It was a blow that should have impaled her, and instead, it had not even harmed her.

"Maston," he murmured.

Lia clawed at his eyes with her fingers. She felt his skin tear as her fingernails bit into his flesh. With her other hand, she stabbed and managed to land the blade into his arm as he deflected it from his throat. He snarled once and backed away, his eyes burning from the smoke. Red tears tracked down the side of his face with the scar. Blood.

The door opened, and Marciana fled the room.

"No!" the kishion bellowed. He hoisted his dagger and threw it after the fleeing girl. Lia watched helplessly as it whistled and spun, end over end. In her mind, she remembered Astrid being cut down by such a stroke, the blade burying itself in his lower back. She willed the blade to stop; she willed it to miss. In Marciana's place, the dagger was caught mid-air by Kieran.

There he was, filling the doorway with his size as he strode into the room.

"Take him together," Kieran said.

The kishion looked back and forth at them, seeing the change in the battle and blaze and the naked gladius in Kieran's other hand.

Lia stomped on the kishion's foot and slammed her dirk against his head, but he responded quickly and deflected the second blow, though her foot had managed to meet his.

Kieran moved like a serpent strike, the blade flashing with the light from the blazing room. The gladius and the dagger met, clanging and hissing as the two engaged. Lia looked for an opening, but the two were a mass of arms and legs. Instead, she rushed to the basket of wet garments and retrieved her gladius. The air was so full of smoke that she could barely see either man, but both were coughing. So was Marciana, kneeling on the floor at the base of the doorway, watching as the kishion and the Evnissyen fought.

There was a grunt, a hiss of pain. Kieran's face was masked with soot. The two smashed into each other again, stabbing, feinting, thrusting. Then the kishion was swung around and struck a bedpost, his head whacking it so hard that spittle sprayed from his mouth. Kieran had lost the dagger somehow, but his fist buried in the kishion's ribs, and she heard the bones snap. Then a knee went up, and the kishion doubled over. He popped up quickly again, striking Kieran in the face with his palm.

Kieran staggered back, grimacing, and Lia noticed blood on his sleeve as a wound stained his shirt. With a scowl of hatred, Kieran struck so fast his gladius sunk into the kishion's gut. He pulled it out just as quickly as the dead man slumped to the ground.

"You are wounded," Lia said, seeing the rivulet of blood coming from his arm.

"So glad you noticed," he replied curtly and then coughed violently. He surveyed the blazing room, the fire thrashing the rafters. He moved quickly, stepping up on a chest, and yanked down another set of curtains from the windows by the iron bar.

"To the stairwell before we choke to death!" he ordered. "Did you light the room afire? You did, I know it. Foolish, foolish girl!"

Lia rushed to Marciana and helped her stand and then pulled her down the stairwell.

Marciana's eyes were swollen but thankful. "I begged the Medium that you would find me in time," she whimpered. "I am so grateful, Lia. Where is Colvin? Is he truly in Dochte Abbey? He is in great danger."

"What precisely do you consider our present situation to be?" Kieran shouted from behind. "A maypole dance? Lia, break that window. Dieyre's men will have gathered at the door below by now. I lowered the crossbar, but it will not hold for long."

She noticed the banging coming from below. The windows were narrow and veiled, the glass dark with soot. She tried to unfasten them, and Kieran just grunted in amazement.

"I said smash them, girl! We do not have much time!"

Lia used her gladius hilt and struck the window, smashing it. He joined her on the stairs, dropped the mass of curtains, and helped her crush the window panes. Then, heaving the mass of curtain over the edge, he let it tumble down the side. Then he fixed the curtain rod against the wall on each side of the window to act as a brace.

He looked down below and winced, shaking his head furiously. He glanced up at the room and saw the fire blazing down the stairwell. "The curtain only reaches partway down. We will have to jump the rest. Lia, you first. Climb to the end of the curtain, hang there, and then fall. Quickly, girl!"

"Will the curtain hold my weight?" she asked.

"Only one way to know. Go!" He coughed against his arm, gripped her waist, and hoisted her up the window ledge.

Lia sheathed her gladius in her belt and grabbed the curtain. She started outside and heard some fabric rip, and her stomach lurched when she saw how far it was to the ground below. Above, the roof of the tower was blazing. Smoke came from the window above, calling attention to Lambeth for all to see. There was nothing but cobblestone below her, which would not cushion a fall. Several bystanders in the street were pointing and shouting in worry. She lowered herself hand over hand down the length of the curtain until she was at the lowest part. She dangled from the curtain, trying not to be dizzy, and glanced down at the street. It looked so far away.

Jump.

The whisper in her thoughts compelled her.

She fought down her fears and let go of the curtain. Plummeting like a stone, she struck the cobbles below with jolt of pain. It was not so far as it seemed after all, and she sighed with relief.

"Lia!" came a voice. Reome rushed through the bystanders on the street to her.

Lia realized through her daze that they were outside the manor walls. The tower window was on the exterior wall of the grounds. Lia was grateful and hugged Reome quickly. When she turned back, she saw Marciana coming down the length of curtain. Ash sprinkled down from the blaze of the tower beams above. Cinders rained as well, stinging her eyes as she looked up. Marciana struggled against the fabric, but she lowered herself down as well. She reached the end of the curtain.

"Jump!" Lia said. "It is not far!"

There was a smashing sound as the door to the tower was finally forced open. Shouts and the thunder of boots on the stairwell sounded.

Marciana dropped, and Lia and Reome both tried to catch her to break her fall. The force of her impact knocked them all down, but she was safely on the ground and spluttered with the smoke. Then, sobbing, she clung to Lia's neck and wept.

Marciana turned and looked up at him, shaking her head. "We were too heavy," she cried. "He was holding the curtain with his hands."

Kieran was out the window next, starting down the curtain length. They all stood as he hurriedly descended. But there was a ripping noise as the curtain came loose. Marciana shrieked. Lia stood in shock as he fell. She tried to rush in and cushion him but could not move fast enough. She watched the look and blaze of pain contort his face as he landed on his back. His head whipped back on the stone cobbles with a sickening crunch. His body lay still. Bystanders gasped with shock and scattered back, some screaming. The alleyway emptied, save for the girls.

Lia stared at Kieran's body in shock. A stream of blood ran in the grooves of the cobblestones. Soot and ash rained down on them. She looked up at the mass of fire and then down at the fallen man. The Medium surged inside of her, building stronger and stronger. It was a flood, the pressure mounting, squeezing her, blinding her.

Marciana stared at Kieran, stricken, her eyes brimming with tears. Reome looked pale seeing a dead man at their feet.

"Close your eyes, both of you!" Lia screamed. They obeyed and she lifted her hand in the maston sign.

Lia made the maston sign by raising her hand in the air and touching the dead man's forehead with her other. She recognized the pattern now, as she had seen it before. There was something sacred about death, especially a death offered as a willing sacrifice for others to live. She had participated in that sort of end herself, which allowed the Abbey's defenses to flood the lowlands surrounding Muirwood and destroy the Queen Dowager's army. The Medium's will had been fulfilled, and its power now could be fully invoked. Not for her benefit—never for her own benefit. But for the greater good of all.

"Kieran Ven, I Gift you with life. You will live, and you will heal." Her voice thickened with emotion as the power of the Medium continued to rush through her. "By Idumea's hand, you will live, Kieran Ven. You will live, and you will heal."

The power of the Medium continued to surge through her. There were screams in her mind throughout Comoros. She could hear them all, a cacophony of despair and accusation. She could sense the blood of dead mastons calling out to her, clinging to her soul and shaking her with fury and revulsion. *We are the dead mastons of this kingdom, murdered by our king because we would not forsake our oaths—the oaths which you have sworn yourself to pass the Apse Veil! Avenge us!*

The Medium was a roar in her ears. The ash and cinders thickened like hail. It was still growing inside of her. It raged like the fire within the crumbling tower. Lia straightened, her hand still held high in the maston sign. Her blood thundered and boiled. She could only see the blaze of the fire above her. Her hand was pointed toward it—not to quell it, but to feed it. She sensed the fire's greedy urge to consume.

Unbidden words filled her mouth. They came in a foreign tongue, the ancient language of the Idumeans, given to her through her Gift of Xenoglossia. "*Pyricanthas. Sericanthas. Thas.*" It was the sacred language to control fire. In her mind, it was nightfall, and she saw the Stews burning.

The Aldermaston of Dochte Abbey helps me a great deal. He explains the tomes in such a clear way that I am beginning to understand them. It used to be so frustrating when Colvin explained things because I could not understand what he was saying, even though I wanted to, and he grew angry. The key is to see the inner meanings. The Aldermaston showed me several passages today, for example, that spoke of the First Parents in the Garden of Leerings. It was of a serpent who whispered the truth of what they needed to do to gain the knowledge they required. The serpent is one of the aspects of Idumea. It is clear to me now. A way was provided to whisper the truth. That is a symbol of the Medium. The symbol of the serpent is the greatest manifestation of the Medium's power. When I explained this knowledge to Colvin, he looked at me differently. It was a look of respect. I have never seen him look at me that way before. It happened often when Lia was nearby, and it always made me jealous. Today it made me dizzy.

—Ellowyn Demont of Dochte Abbey

CHAPTER EIGHT

Flames of Comoros

H e is finally waking," Reome announced, drawing Lia away from the doorway to the bedside.

Kieran's eyes fluttered open, and he stared up at Lia in confusion. Then his face grimaced with pain—uncontrollable pain. His teeth clenched, and he groaned.

"I fell," he gasped. His neck muscles strained as he lifted his head.

"You are alive," Lia said soothingly.

His face was tortured with pain. He clenched his jaw, willing himself to maintain control, to keep from blurting out with his suffering. His fingers clenched within the blanket. "My back is broken," he said darkly.

Reome stifled a moan of horror.

"You will heal," Lia said, touching his shoulder.

Kieran's face contorted with pain, but he breathed through his nose and mastered it. "I smell smoke. Are we near Lambeth still?"

"No, it is eventide. The smoke is on the wind. Comoros is burning."

He looked at her, his face confused. "The whole city? Ablaze? How?"

Lia looked down at her hand. "The fires came from Lambeth. Everything was built so close together. It went from rooftop to rooftop. Then it burned the bridge. It rages still."

Sweat dripped down Kieran's temples. He reached with his hand and gingerly touched the back of his head. He looked confused. He spoke to her in Pry-rian, masking his language so Reome would not understand. "I thought…I remembered…hitting my head. Then blackness. Then the Apse Veil." He wiped his face slowly. "I died."

"It was not your time to die, Kieran Ven."

The look he gave her was full of pain and fury. "It was my time to go to Dahomey. I had a duty to perform, and you thwarted it."

She shook her head. "It was the Medium's will that we journeyed to Lambeth."

"You say it as if you could command it. As if you did command it to summon me to that burning tower." He frowned with fury. "I have never done anything so foolish in my life. I deserve to be dead. I was careless. But there was a need drawing me after you. I could do nothing but worry and pace after you left. Almost at once I regretted it. So I left the laundry maid in the shadows, climbed the wall like a thief, and ran after you. Someone saw me, of course, and summoned the servants and the guards. I had to knock down four men just to get to the tower door, and then the flames!" He winced with a spasm. "You nearly got us all killed."

The door opened, and Marciana entered, her face smudged with soot, her gown ruined by the smoke. "I heard voices. He has come around?"

Lia had never seen Marciana look so disheveled, but some of her strength had returned. The weeping child from the tower was gone now. The only gown she had was the one Dieyre had left her, and she clutched at the bodice with one hand to guard her modesty. There was fire in her eyes, especially after she learned from Lia that Reome was carrying Dieyre's child.

"Ah, the reason for our delay," Kieran said gruffly, still muttering in Pry-rian. "And my downfall."

"Be civil," Lia advised back. "She is the sister of an earl who is Demont's ally."

Marciana held up her hand. "Please...do not speak in a language I cannot understand. Lia, please, I insist. I owe you my gratitude, Kieran Ven. I wish to express it myself. You saved my life today."

Kieran looked at her coldly. "Your gratitude is of no recompense to me, my lady. You were not my mission. Permit me a little disappointment that I cannot stand to greet you properly. I do not want or require your sympathies."

"I said be civil," Lia said thickly.

Marciana looked at him, surprised at his tone. "You were injured on my behalf, like it or no. I owe you every courtesy, despite how you treat me." She looked at Lia next. "It is all arranged. We have secured room aboard a small fishing vessel, which will take us upriver in the morning. There, we will hire out a carter and return to Muirwood."

Kieran interrupted. "I do not want to *go* to Muirwood. Send me to Pry-Ree."

Marciana shook her head. "Impossible. It is too far, and you need a healer. You will convalesce at Muirwood."

Lia set her hand on Kieran's shoulder as she saw him ready to argue. "We all understand your desire to return to your homeland. Muirwood is the gathering point. They will be better able to care for you there."

"I do not wish to be cared for, nursed, or in general, pitied. Who are you to control my destiny in such a way? I would rather be tossed in the cargo of a ship headed to Bridgestow and take my chances amidst the vermin."

Marciana looked at Lia and then back at Kieran. "Men are insufferable when they are hungry. Have you eaten since this morning? You have not. Reome, my dear, can you see to some food? Thank you so very much. I will not forget your role in freeing me. I will safeguard you. Thank you." After Reome left, Marciana folded her arms and squinted at Kieran. "Did my brother treat you any worse than this after you saved his life, Lia?"

Lia also folded her arms and glared down at Kieran. "He has not retched on you yet, Ciana, but give his stomach a moment after he has eaten, and I will hazard he just may."

"I am doomed to never walk again and you mock me," Kieran said, closing his eyes and shaking his head. His face contorted with pain, and he writhed on the bed.

Marciana approached and grabbed his hand and squeezed it fiercely. "Then I shall be your crutch, your stay, your helper. If you cannot walk because of me, then I will walk for you. If you were not in that tower today, then I would have taken a knife in *my* back. When I saw you coming up the stairs, when I looked into your eyes, I knew the Medium had summoned you to save me."

She turned and smiled at Lia. "How many times have I heard your story, Lia—that if you trust in the Medium, if you think and believe and hope, you will be saved?" Tears brimmed in her eyes, and she shook her head firmly to master them. "I will not cry. I have shed too many tears this last fortnight. If I start again, I fear I may never stop and I will die of drowning."

She swallowed and breathed deeply. "I must never see Dieyre again. Please, Lia. You must keep him from me. I was being broken by that evil man, that Dochte Mandar. I nearly surrendered to his will. I was so thirsty, and all they would offer is this sweet cider that dulls your mind. He used a kystrel. I could feel it for what it was. I knew it for what it was, but I was powerless to resist it. It changed my feelings, Lia. I hated Dieyre for kidnapping me. I hated him for taking me away from those I care for." She shook her head again. "Now I am in love with him against my will, and these conflicting feelings are torturing me. I know they are not real. I know they were planted in my soul by a foul and evil man. But they are part of me now. I only hope that when I pass the maston test, I will be able to banish them forever."

Marciana looked at Lia pointedly. "As you passed it. When did you, Lia? I did not know you were a maston too until you made the sign." There was a look of awe in her face.

"After you left Muirwood in the night." Lia felt abashed, seeing not only awe but also a hint of envy in her eyes. She rubbed the spot on her shirt where the kishion's knife had ripped the fabric but could not pierce her chaen. Being a maston had saved her life.

"Does Colvin know?"

She nodded, and the grin on Marciana's face was blinding in its intensity. "You must save him, Lia. You told me that he and Ellowyn are hostages at Dochte Abbey. That is where the Dochte Mandar come from. I do not know if they move in secret, but they are powerful with the Medium. There are rumors that they are coming to take over the abbeys in our kingdom, to change our customs. In Dahomey, I heard from some of the knights that were escorting me here that they opened the abbeys for all to enter— that the secret rites of the mastons are being changed and proclaimed openly. They insist all must receive these rites. They say that we are keeping knowledge from the people to hoard power.

There are riots by those demanding to be let inside the abbeys. It is beginning to happen in our kingdom as well."

"But what about the Leerings protecting them?" Lia said, angered.

Marciana looked sad. "They are failing. Many learners have returned home and said the Leerings are not working anymore. Lia, the Blight is coming quickly. I can feel it. We do not have much time to stop it."

Lia saw the nervous look in her eyes, the wild fear. She hugged her tight, grateful that she could face Colvin with the knowledge that his sister was safe. It was a burden she no longer had to carry.

It was Kieran who spoke next. "You cannot stop it. The Blight comes by Twelfth Night. I was alive when the Blight came to Pry-Ree. I do not wish to be here when it comes again. We leave in ships for another shore. It is less than a fortnight from now."

Marciana straightened and looked him firmly in the eye. "If that is where the mastons go, then so will I." She squeezed Lia's arms. "Fetch my brother, Lia. Bring Colvin and Ellowyn back to Muirwood."

Lia wished she could tell Marciana the truth about herself. She opened her mouth to try, but the Medium forced her not to speak the words. Truly, she had not really expected it would let her. "I will use the orb to find a ship to Dahomey. I will leave in the morning."

"I do not know how many ships will be sailing in the morning," Marciana said. "There is so much damage by the fire. But consider this: there is another port eastward. Doviur is the major port on our eastern shore. The straits there are the nearest point to Dahomey. I could send a mounted escort. If you rode hard, you could be there in the morning."

"Does Doviur have any abbeys?"

"There is one abbey in that Hundred. It is called Augustin Abbey."

A feeling of peace came through her. "Then that is my road to Doviur. I will leave tonight."

"Let me send an escort with you," Marciana pleaded.

"They are needed here, Ciana. Those who will flee must go. They must warn others before the Blight comes. This is our last chance to warn them."

She looked over at Kieran and took his hand in hers, gripping it firmly. "There is something about the Leerings in Muirwood. They will heal you faster than you think. And you will walk, Kieran Ven." She squeezed his hand. "I know it."

"You are not what you seem," he answered softly, his face enigmatic.

She looked him in the eye, wishing she could tell him. Something passed between them, a spark of recognition. "Do I remind you of someone?" she asked simply.

He studied her face, her eyes. He looked as if he would speak, but his jaw clenched shut. Then he opened his mouth and said, "Yes."

She patted his hand, thanking him with her eyes. *You did me service this day, Kieran Ven. I will not forget it.* She was about to withdraw her hand, but he clenched it tightly, making her wince.

"I was trained in the city. You were trained in the woods. Let me teach you what I know. Maybe some of it will help you." He shifted slowly, wincing. "Dahomey is a land of great wealth. It sits in the center of many kingdoms. Just as Muirwood is the oldest in your realm, Dochte is the oldest abbey in Dahomey. It is the richest abbey in Dahomey. It is situated on an island, off the northwestern shore. When the tide leaves, it opens a land bridge to the island. It is dangerous to time it, for if the tide comes in during the journey, you will drown in quicksand. The orb will help you. When the tide comes in, sometimes there are fishing boats that will row you to the Abbey. Where there is great wealth, you will find corruption. The Abbey is built on top of the island. It is surrounded by the village of Dochte. There are huge walls separating the village from the Abbey proper on the dome of the hill. The walls are enormous. It is actually a giant castle, five or six stories high, that surrounds the sanctuary.

"The Abbey itself rises like a spike in the center of the island. It must have required two hundred years to build it, stone by stone. It is impressive. The village houses are lower down and are not as imposing. The only way in or out of the Abbey is through the main gate in the wall. I was able to enter because I was a maston, but I recall the disdain with which I was treated because of my clothing. Even though I was an ambassador from Pry-Ree, I was treated with contempt because I did not look like one. This is important, Lia. You may be allowed in because you know the maston signs, but you will stand out because of the way you dress. The women of Dahomey are very particular in their appearance."

Lia understood and looked down at the soot stains on her shirt. "Are you afraid I will barge into Dochte the way I did at Lambeth?"

"It had crossed my mind," Kieran said pointedly.

"I would give you this gown I am wearing," Marciana offered. "Except I have no other gowns. They were all burned in the fire."

"I cannot wear it," Lia said, shaking her head. "I appreciate the warning, but the orb will show me another way. I think… perhaps…it is the reason I have had it all these years."

Another pulse of warmth in her heart confirmed it.

Lia patted Kieran's hand again. "I will see you again in Muirwood. Thank you. I am…proud of you, Kieran Ven."

There was a voice, a whisper in her mind so faint she barely heard it. *I wish I could serve you in Dahomey, my lady—daughter of my Prince.*

You will serve me again, she answered in her mind, pushing the thought at him. *In a far country where there is no Blight.*

A small smile crept on his mouth, and he nodded at her.

It was the first spark of hope Lia had since learning of the binding sigil. If she could not tell Colvin the truth with her words, perhaps she could tell him with her thoughts.

CHAPTER NINE

Augustin Abbey

It was the first time Lia had tried to cross the Apse Veil on her own. Summoning her courage, she focused her thoughts on Augustin Abbey, repeating it over and over in her mind. The Medium swirled around her, sending a pricking feeling of dread deep inside her heart. There was something terrifying about the possibility of going so far with one footstep. It was even more terrifying to think that if she focused hard enough, she could step over to Idumea itself, where the power of the Medium would probably devour her. Reining in those thoughts, she took several deep breaths and then walked forward through the shimmering curtain. The wrench of time and distance made her dizzy and nauseous. For a moment, she tottered, nearly falling. Her balance returned gradually, so she leaned against the side of the pillar and struggled to calm her heart.

As she opened her eyes, Lia noticed the surroundings had changed. The construction was beautiful but different. This Abbey was bigger than Muirwood, more impressive in its design and craftsmanship. Glancing around as she walked, she noticed the lush furnishings, the ribboned ironwork, the white tassels, and gauzy curtains. Walking deliberately, she approached the Rood Screen separating the chambers and promptly met several cassocked mastons, who were wearing white with golden trim.

"Where do you hail from?" one of them asked her, his face curious. "How old are you, child? You cannot be eighteen years, if that."

"I am Lia from Muirwood," she replied. "This is Augustin?"

"Muirwood." There was something in the way he said it, the sudden wrinkle in his forehead that alarmed her. "The Aldermaston will wish to speak with you."

"Have there been others?" she asked, watching their three faces for signs of a reaction. They all looked uneasy, wary, and a little disgusted by her sudden appearance.

"Knight-mastons," another answered gravely. "Come, child. The Aldermaston will speak with you."

"I am on urgent business," Lia answered, approaching them cautiously.

"We will not delay you long," replied the third.

Lia felt a shiver of apprehension. She followed the three mastons to the exterior door where there were several porters on duty holding lanterns. There was a strange smell in the air, the odor of incense. The floor tiles had been scrubbed and waxed until they shone like glass.

"Bring her to the Aldermaston straightaway," one of the mastons said. "She is from Muirwood."

The porter nodded and started down the path away from the huge Abbey. Lia followed, suspicious, but the porter did not deviate from his path and brought her immediately to a large and spacious manor, festooned with flags surrounded by gardens sculpted into the maston symbol of two offset squares. Every shrub had been painstakingly cut and molded, creating intricate shapes and hedgerows. The air carried the strong scent of a fishpond, though she could not see it through the blackness. Even at night there were gardeners at work, pruning and tending and cleaning the grounds. Some glanced up at her as she passed, but most focused on their duties. The porter escorted her to the doors of the manor house, which were guarded by servants holding long, polished black staves. The doors were opened for them as they ascended the steps, and Lia entered the voluminous main corridor.

Her boots thudded against the polished tiles, and she was struck with the splendor of the place, especially in contrast to the manor house in Muirwood. There were vases full of fresh flowers, mirrors and bowls, and sculptures of polished stone. There were rows of small pillars with spherical orbs the size of pumpkins polished to a shine as decoration, for she could discern no other purpose for them. Tall velvet curtains flanked the walls and hung from silver rods. She inhaled through her nose and discovered the faint scent of incense again, permeating the air, though she did not see any braziers.

"This way, lass," said the porter as she nearly stumbled into him when he stopped.

"The grounds are impressive," Lia said.

"Augustin is the only abbey in this Hundred," he replied. "Ahead, if you please." He knocked on the door firmly.

The door opened, and a venerable maston appeared, wearing a silvery cassock with black threading.

"Tell the Aldermaston he has *another* maston visiting from Muirwood," the porter said.

Lia noticed the inflection in his voice and was surprised when the aged maston nodded and motioned for Lia to enter.

"Your name, child?"

"I am Lia."

"So young to be a maston," he observed. His brow furrowed as he examined her unkempt appearance. She felt awkward being in such a pristine place.

"Who is it now?" complained a voice thick with a northern accent. He rose from a stuffed couch, a goblet in his hand which he set down on a marble pillar. He was very young for an alder-maston, probably not even fifty. His hair was shorn very close to his scalp, and it was dark, with occasional slivers of gray. He was healthy, athletic, and approached with a swagger, his mouth twisting into a scowl at the look of her.

"Look at you, as filthy as a beggar. You are a maston, are you? You hail from Muirwood?"

"I do," Lia replied, nodding respectfully but bristling at the Aldermaston's tone.

"How old are you?" he demanded.

"I am nearly sixteen."

"Sixteen? And you passed the maston test, did you? What is your Family name? Would I know it?" He raised the goblet and took another sip of the drink, which smelled strongly of apples. It was probably cider.

"I do not think so," Lia replied, hedging. "I am on a journey to Doviur."

"I know most of the Families in your Hundred, even the minor ones, like the Fesits. I would have heard if any passed the maston test so young. Who is your Family?"

Lia clenched her fists, trying to calm her anger. "I must be leaving. I am sorry to have disturbed you."

"You will not tell me? I command you to speak. This is my domain, my hospitality." He paused, looking at her again, more closely. "You have no Family, do you? I can see it in your bearing, your countenance. You must be a wretched." He looked genuinely startled. "He elevated a wretched?" he murmured to himself. "Is that the new fad in Muirwood these days? Anyone who can kindle a *gargouelle* spark can take the test? I should have known. Cunning old fool."

If Lia's temper was not already smoldering, it suddenly blazed white hot. She said nothing, for any words out of her mouth would have been insulting.

The Aldermaston took another drink, regarding her closely. "So why are you bound for Doviur, my dear? Did Gideon Penman suspect that I would fail to warn the port cities about his imagined dangers? That I would not see through his ploy to legitimate Demont as usurper and king? Flee to Muirwood—there is danger! Leave your homes or you will all be destroyed! Bah! Does he truly think I am that naïve?"

A cold feeling ran down Lia's back. "You have not warned them?" she asked, aghast.

"Warn them of what? You are a wretched, so what can you possibly know about the ways of the world?" He turned away from her, cradling his goblet, and then turned on her fiercely, his dark eyes smoldering with anger. "Let me educate you, child. Your aldermaston conspired to murder the king. An anointed king! Why? Because the king had threatened to revoke his tax immunity. The king's tax can only be collected in the jurisdiction of the king's sheriffs. Poor Almaguer was murdered too. Child, do you not understand that Muirwood is the richest abbey in the realm? Did you not know that this cider, this *Muirwood* cider that everyone craves, has tripled in price over the last three years? I am sure his coffers are fit to burst with the wealth he has earned from the cider trade. Enough wealth to lure Demont back from overseas and pay for his army of pretended mastons." He reached out and handled the smoke-stained fabric of her cloak. "One would *think* he could afford to attire his wretcheds more appropriately."

Lia gritted her teeth, furious at the accusations. "I can assure you that the Aldermaston of Muirwood is not as wealthy as you presume. The Blight is real. Manifestations of it are ravaging the woods in our Hundred. Have you not heard of Sempringfall Abbey? It was burned."

The man snorted. "It is a lie. It is a story you have been told because you trust an old man who cannot stand to lose his power and influence. Word of the king's murder has reached our ears. I have it on good authority that the High Seer of Avinion has sent instructions for him to be arrested and brought to trial here, at Augustin. The wild tale of a great Blight coming is just a distraction. Every time the earth shudders, or a storm ravages a crop, or a new pestilence kills the grain, there is a quick opinion that we are being wicked and that it is the Blight. The Medium would not destroy the inhabitants of seven kingdoms. It is blasphemy even to suggest it."

Lia shook her head. "You *must* warn the people. Even if you do not believe it is real, it is your duty to warn them. You are an aldermaston—"

"I know very well who I am, child." He gave her a look of condescending smugness. "Gideon will not be the Aldermaston of Muirwood for much longer. When the High Seer's missive arrives, I will be taking it personally to deliver. I have it on good authority, you understand, that the post will be given to me." There was something in his eyes, a look of glee that was nearly incoherent. He raised the goblet to his mouth and frowned to learn it was empty. He thrust it angrily into the older maston's hand with a nod to go fill it again.

He looked at her, and his voice was a little slurred as he spoke. "You are sixteen, you say? What position do you serve? I see a weapon—a girl with a weapon. Is that a bow on your shoulder? It is. You are a hunter then?"

Lia nodded, clenching her teeth.

"I should like to see how well you hunt. In the morning, you will bring me a pheasant for my afternoon meal. Or a pig. You are no doubt used to hunting the pigs that root amidst the oaks of Muirwood. I hear they are especially delicious. Pig and cider."

"I have duties to perform in Doviur. I beg you excuse me."

The Aldermaston leveled his eyes at her. "Even were I to let you go and you managed to return to warn Gideon in time, do you think it would really matter? Muirwood will be mine at last. The most ancient abbey in the realm will finally become the grandest. When I become its aldermaston, there will be no more profits spent on Demont and his pitiful army. Then perhaps he will finally be persuaded to end this fruitless contest for power." He put his hand on her shoulder, his thick, heavy hand. "A pheasant. Or a pig. You may hunt on my grounds, but you cannot leave them. I forbid it. You serve *me* now, child."

Lia stared in his eyes, saw the intensity there—the deliberateness. How many other knight-mastons had he waylaid?

She reached up and put her thumb on the back of his hand and her fingers around the edge of his palm. With a quick twist and jerk, she yanked his arm around and brought him to his knees with a howl of pain. She bent the wrist backward, driving him into the tile. She flexed the wrist harder, making him yelp.

"I serve the Aldermaston of Muirwood," she said tightly. "If any of your people try and stop me, I pity them."

"I am an aldermaston!" he quailed, his voice throbbing with pain. "I will invoke the Medium to destroy you!"

There was nothing in the air, not even the faint murmur of the wind.

"By all means try," she replied, waiting a moment for anything to happen. When nothing did, she shoved him away from her. The older maston was returning with a fresh cup of cider, his eyes popping in shock to see his master handled thus. But he did not approach her.

Lia turned and walked back out the door, flinging it open as she walked. The Aldermaston let out a rush of commands.

"Give me that! You fool! Summon my guards! Do not let her escape. The Earl of Dieyre said he would pay handsomely for her. Get her! Get her!"

Lia ran down the huge corridor, her heart pounding, her stomach thrilling. She reached the doors and yanked them open as the sound of clattering steps echoed throughout the vast maze. The door servants were there, holding the black, polished staves. They turned and crossed them, barring her way.

She stomped on one's foot, wrenched the staff out of his hands, and dropped him with a single blow. The other man looked stunned as she whirled the staff around. He deflected it, but she switched ends and jabbed the rounded end into his throat. He clutched his neck, dropping his staff with a loud clattering noise, and Lia braced herself on the steps. She saw the wretcheds gathering around, the gardeners with spades and pruners with shears, others with brooms and rakes and young girls with polishing rags and tubs of wax. She understood it now—that the Aldermaston of Augustin did not want to see his wretcheds working, so he made them work at night. They labored and toiled so that during the daylight, he would not be bothered with looking at them. Reaching into the pouch at her waist, she withdrew the Cruciger orb and summoned its blinding light. It enveloped her like a blazing sun.

"The Blight is truly coming!" she shouted. "It strikes by Twelfth Night! Flee to Muirwood for safety. Flee this place before it comes!"

In her mind, she willed the orb to work, to guide her to a safe road where she could escape into the woods. That was her domain, her place of strength where her skills would outmatch any of theirs. The light of it was dazzling, so bright it made her wince. The spindles spun and then pointed a clear path toward a giant hedge maze.

CHAPTER TEN

Doviur Caves

The smells and sounds of the woods were comforting, familiar, and haunting with memories. The scent of pine was strong in the air, and Lia's rushed pace prevented her from being cold. She walked with her hood down, listening for any sound that would betray an enemy. She had walked for a league at least and her feet were tired and sore, but she had endured worse before and knew her strength would last. She had to reach the port of Doviur by morning, and she decided to walk until she could smell the salty air before stopping and resting. The orb guided her, pointing the way through the tangle of trees, stumps, and fallen trunks.

A memory from the Bearden Muir flitted through her mind as she traversed the woods. She remembered the feeling of her filthy dress clinging to her skin, the grit buried underneath each fingernail, her hair a tangled mess. Those were details, but the bud of the memory was Colvin first teaching her how the Medium worked. It was the revelation that all actions in the world originated from the seeds of thought, deliberately sown and nurtured, and then the Medium maneuvered events to bring them to pass. His desire to join Garen Demont's forces at Winterrowd had brought him Muirwood Abbey and laid him as a wounded stranger in the care of Lia. She recognized, a bit ironically, that his desire to find Ellowyn Demont had unwittingly been fulfilled as well.

It was her turn now to focus her thoughts on reaching him. The desire to find a ship to Dahomey consumed her. She had to hurry, for something was going to happen if she did not. The Blight would start at Dochte Abbey, and more than anything else, she wanted to protect him from it. She worried about him, so far away. What was he doing at that moment? Asleep and dreaming? What were his dreams? Was he awake at that moment, staring out some window at a night sky, sharing the scene of the moon high above that painted everything silver? Or was he in a dungeon, as Marciana suggested, cold and miserable and terrified of the dark, confined space?

Meeting the Aldermaston of Augustin had shoved her inside a new cauldron of worries. She could still see the naked ambition in his eyes, his craving to inherit Muirwood. So much of what he had said was utter nonsense. She had worked closely with the Aldermaston and had never seen even the remotest shadow of opulence that she had witnessed in Augustin. Instinctively, she realized the Queen Dowager's hand. Augustin was subverted by the hetaera. Some of his words had brought thoughts to her mind, memories of the past. She recalled the sheriff, Almaguer, and his threats to destroy the Aldermaston. It was as if he had known that a change in leadership would happen and was looking forward to it. She shuddered to think of what life at Muirwood would have become under the direction of someone like the Aldermaston of Augustin. Had he not said that the price of cider had tripled in three years? Another memory nagged at her—it was the Queen

Dowager's age. She had been fifteen when she married the old king and come from Dahomey. Three years ago. The webs of spider thread were nearly invisible, but Lia could make them out—subtle, calculating, coldblooded. She had not succeeded at first in toppling the most ancient abbey in the realm. But Lia could tell it was clearly her aim.

A fresh breeze brought the telltale musk of seawater. Lia looked up, inhaling the smell. She withdrew the orb again and summoned its power, asking it to find her shelter where she might sleep safely until dawn. She needed a cave, a warren, fallen tree—something that would hide her from sight and allow her a chance to rest before searching for a ship at Doviur. The orb responded to her need, the spindles pointing clearly toward the seashore.

Lia followed the trail it offered, weaving through the last vestiges of forest until it opened into a sweeping range of lush hills. In the distance, she could hear the foam and churning of the surf as the ocean collided with it. The sky was ablaze with myriads of stars and a moon as bright as a torch. The air was cooler, and she tugged her cloak around her throat to fend off the chill. She descended the hill, seeing the flat slate of sea in the distance, the moonlight rippling off the crests. The land pitched down lower, and she slowed her walk, glancing at the orb to guide her to a safe path. The hill ended abruptly, revealing a jagged cliff down to the thrashing surf below. The orb guided her to a small, steep path down the edge of the rocks. There was enough light to see, but her heart spasmed with worry and she moved stealthily down the edge.

The cliffs were made of chalk and flint and crushed easily against her hand and boots. Noises from the ocean echoed off the slabs of stone, filling her with the apprehension of falling. Partway down the hillside, she noticed the giant maw of a cave—black against the silvery cliff. She stumbled slightly in the wet grass and went down but skidded to a halt, her heart thudding in her throat. Carefully she scooted down the hillside toward the exposed cave. The Cruciger orb affirmed it was her destination. The ocean reached the mouth of it on one side, rushing in, swirling, slinking back. A large, moss-covered boulder was mired in the thick, grassy growth higher up. It was singular seeing the massive boulder there, apart from the cave, apart from the rock. As she approached, she felt the Medium emanating from it and realized, with fascination, that there was a Leering carved into the rock, hidden by the moss.

The ground leveled out in front of her, and she approached the hidden glen quickly. The boulder was taller than her, rounded on one side and flat on the other. Cautiously, she lifted her hand and touched it. To her relief, it was pure—untainted by the Blight. In her mind, through her Gift of Seering, she could see other mastons who had used the cave for shelter. The Leering had been there for hundreds of years, protecting the entrance to the cave, which water had hollowed out. Using her thoughts and will, she activated the Leering's protection and set it to guard the entrance by frightening away anyone who wandered nearby. In her blood, she felt the Medium churn awake, and the cave emptied of seawater. The Leering repelled the salty water as it did intruders, and she noticed the entrance dry out. The waves crashed farther away, against the cliff's side instead of at the breach. She was grateful to the Leering and thanked it in her mind before stepping off the grassy hill and into the sand and pebbles of the wash.

Using the orb for light, she entered the cave and found a spot of dry sand where she stretched out after removing her rucksack and bow and settled down with her cloak as a blanket. She set the orb in the sand and summoned fire into it, using its glowing surface to warm her hands and body. Weariness engulfed her, and she laid her head down, banishing the light from the orb with a thought, and felt the darkness shroud her. She could not see, not even her hands before her face, but she could hear the murmur of the sea foam. In the darkness, she thought of Colvin.

Her memories flitted this way and that, like little butter-flies scattering over a well-known patch of sunny grass. The first journey was through the mist to the cave where Maderos lived, a spot where the boulders floated in the air, suspended by the Medium's power, where she had helped him find shel-ter from the sheriff of Mendenhall. She remembered next crouching over his body as Almaguer's men had kicked him and abused him. In her mind, she saw Colvin as she walked away from the fire consuming a stand of oak trees after sum-moning it to destroy the evil men. He had caught her and car-ried her to a safe place, where she slept. She remembered the promise of meeting again at Whitsunday, a whispered promise that he had not fulfilled because of his duty to find and protect Ellowyn Demont. She sighed deeply, jealous of the year the two had spent together and jealous now of the time they were together in Dahomey.

Colvin had returned at last, surprising her one night in the kitchen. She squirmed at the memory of shouting at him, itching and healing from a poisonous sap that had stained her. Another memory—despite the dirt, the tattered hunter's garb, the spots of mud and grime, he had let her hold his hands to warm and com-fort him in a cave beneath the Muirwood grounds. She savored the memory, the intimacy of the moment. But not as much as she savored another cave, made of ash and charred wood—high in the mountains of Pry-Ree. She would never forget that dark, frigid night as they huddled together in the husk of a fallen tree so huge its roots had forged a cave. It was a moment she would always remember—the night he had finally confessed his love.

Closing her eyes, she reached out to him with her thoughts. *Colvin?*

He was so far away, in another country, in an abbey that could no longer be reached by the Apse Veil. If the Medium could connect worlds, could it not bridge such a distance?

There was nothing in reply, no flicker of thought or awareness other than her own. Her heart twisted with pain at being away from him. She would have given all she possessed to find a way to be with him at that moment. It was a desperate yearning, a craving so strong it stung her eyes with tears. In the quiet of the cave, it felt as if she were all alone in the world.

Lia shifted in the sand, sitting up and feeling her emotions swell inside her. The weight of it came crashing down on her. What if they failed? What if *she* failed? What was she supposed to do at Dochte Abbey? Warn them that the Blight was coming? But would they listen to her, a wretched, and not Ellowyn, who had the appearance of a lady of rank? In her mind, she had clung to a secret wish that after rescuing Colvin and Ellowyn, they would return to Muirwood and ask the Aldermaston to marry them and bind that marriage with an irrevocare sigil before the end came. The binding would last forever, and Colvin would be hers. That is what she wanted, even more than learning to read and engrave.

The doubts began to play with her then. The sneaking doubts that poked at her, jabbed her with icy fingers.

What if Colvin changed his mind? What if Pareigis won and managed to turn over Muirwood to the Aldermaston of Augustin before she returned? What if there were no abbeys left by the time she and Colvin met?

Her heart raced. Her blood pounded in her ears. She had not known who she truly was when he had left her. He had been in love with her for most of his life—at least in love with the *idea* of her. She would be sixteen. He was twenty. In her mind, she had imagined there being time to marry—if not at Muirwood, then Tintern surely. The aldermaston in Pry-Ree knew her true identity. Would he perform the binding ceremony? But what if the Queen Dowager learned of Tintern's existence? What if there were no abbeys left in the world?

Lia squeezed her hands together, pushing another thought into the aether. *Colvin, can you hear me? Colvin, my love, can you hear my thoughts? I am Ellowyn Demont. Please hear me—I am she. I am coming, my love. I am coming for you.*

She paused, holding her breath—listening to her thoughts, her insights, her connection and strength with the Medium.

She heard nothing save the crashing of the waves.

***

Lia abandoned the shelter at dawn. She used the Leering at the mouth of the cave to summon water to drink and bathe in. Her hair was an impossible mess, but she held it up and let the water splash on her neck and then soak her hair. Long ago, Colvin had held up her hair while she bathed. The memory made it difficult to think. She wiped the soot from her face, cleansed the ash from her hair, and brought fire to summoning, enough to make the water steam. A seagull looped in the sky above her, as if curious about the human invading its cliffs.

Lia squeezed the water from her hair, arranged her cloak and rucksack. She found some bread that Pasqua had packed and ate it hungrily, along with strips of cool beef, and broke off some cheese from the small slab. In her rucksack, she saw the bundle she had packed and opened it quickly, staring at the apple she was saving for Colvin. She stared at it, studying the splotches on the skin, and then held it to her nose and smelled it. There was the scent, the reminder of Muirwood. Her thoughts turned to the Cider Orchard, at the trees that had produced the fruit she held in her hand. Somehow the Queen Dowager was claiming Muirwood through its fruit. The price of cider had tripled. Perhaps she was arranging that—buying up all the casks after it left the grounds. She had come to Muirwood for Whitsunday and had offered free cider to those who had been allowed to dance around the maypole. The Aldermaston of Augustin had been drinking the cider. It was the drink that Marciana was offered in the tower in Lambeth.

In her mind, the pieces clove together, making a whole. The Queen Dowager was corrupting the kingdom through Muirwood's cider. Was there a poison she was adding to it that enabled her to control the minds of others? Such a harmless thing, a cup of cider, an innocent thing. But what if she was twisting it to serve her purposes?

The Medium whispered to her as she stared at the Leering. Yes, there were poisons. Dahomey was the land of poisons and serpents and subtlety. In her mind, she saw a symbol—two intertwining serpents forming a circle. She had seen it before, in her mind, when Kieran Ven had shared with her when the Blight would strike. In the deepest reaches of her thoughts, she realized that the symbol was connected to the coming of the Blight.

Just as clearly, she realized that she was going to where that symbol would be found.

CHAPTER ELEVEN

The Cider Orchard

The middle of an orchard of apple trees was a peculiar place to hold a meeting, but Martin did as he was told and patrolled the edges of it, alert for signs of intruders, while the Prince and the Aldermaston inspected the fruit and conferred quietly together. A few awkward learners had ventured toward the rows of trees to spy, but Martin waved them on with a growl in his voice and a curt nod to move on. After making the rounds twice, he ventured back into the trees and easily found them.

The look on the Aldermaston's face alarmed Martin. He had a chalky pallor, his eyes intense on the Prince's face. As Martin approached, the Aldermaston gave him a look full of daggers, his teeth baring into a hiss. "We are not finished speaking," he said tightly, unable to control his anger at the interruption.

"It is all right," the Prince said. "I wish him to know."

"But *I* do not wish it," the Aldermaston replied stiffly. His face was warped with angles and wrinkles, with an expression of emotions flashing hot and cool across his brow. "I have never encountered someone so Gifted in the Medium. If what you say is true…"

The Prince gave him an arch look and then a twisted smile. "If? You doubt already? That does not bode well for me, Aldermaston."

He clenched his jaw and his fists. "I am reeling from what you have told me. The preciseness of your visions. The way you describe events that have not occurred as though they were in the past. I am unfamiliar with the Gift of Seeing. I do not mean that I doubt your word."

The Prince approached a thin tree and rubbed his hand along the bark. He stared from the base and up the trunk to the first crown of limbs. "My grandfather had this Gift. My own father did not or else he would not have plummeted to his death from Pent Tower. I cannot imagine choosing that fate."

"But to know of your own death…beforehand. How have you endured it?"

The Prince stared at the bark closely, his fingers slowly stroking it. "The same way you will learn to," he answered softly. "It is a burden to know the future. And a blessing. Look at this tree, Aldermaston. The fruit is nearly ripe. Soon you will harvest it. You have that knowledge because you have seen it before. The ripening and the harvest is a familiar experience. So it is with the future." His voice grew husky. "This grove will be a place dear to her heart." He winced saying the words, and Martin caught the glint of an unshed tear in his eye, invisible to the Aldermaston.

The Aldermaston bristled, his emotions flaring to anger again. "Your…your daughter, as you said."

The Prince turned and looked at him, a penetrating look. "In time, you will care for her as if you had been permitted to rear your own. She will heal the chasm in your heart that was breached when your lady died last year, though I cannot expect it of you now."

The Aldermaston was like a huge gray stone. His face was impassive, his eyes speaking quite loudly, *How can you ask this of me?*

The Prince plucked a bud of ripening fruit from the stem and held it close to his nose, smelling it. He turned it over in his hand several times. "What else would you know from me before we leave for Comoros?"

"Tell me of my enemy. Tell me of the woman who will bring about my death."

"She is hardly a woman yet. The queen of Dahomey is with child, I believe."

"Yes, I did hear that she was."

"The child she carries is your enemy." The Prince looked amused at the Aldermaston's shock. "When I said your enemy was the queen of your realm, what I meant was that she will be. The king's current lady wishes me dead. But she will be poisoned herself by a kishion from Dahomey, giving the king the excuse to marry again. The Dahomeyjan king will offer his young daughter. She is your enemy, Aldermaston. An unborn babe. But does it not make sense? Are not the Myriad Ones called the Unborn? This child will be very powerful. There is something in the lineage of that Family, especially the daughters. They do not require a kystrel to manipulate the Medium after their training. When they use one, it does not leave a mark on their flesh. She will have enormous power at controlling emotions. Men will do her bidding, even those you think impervious. Be warned, Aldermaston. You will be betrayed in the end by someone you trust."

Martin noticed the narrowing of the Aldermaston's eyes. His lips were hard and white, his expression growing chalkier. "Will you tell me who?"

The Prince shook his head. "It is not important that you know it. Remember that those from Dahomey are expert at cunning. They are quite devious. But remember also that the wisdom of the Medium is greater than all the cunning of the Myriad Ones."

The Aldermaston turned away, shaking his head slowly. He seemed in agony. With a violent gesture, he rounded on the Prince. Martin stepped forward, wondering if he would need to restrain the old man.

"You ask too much of me!" he roared. "I have never met you before, Prince Alluwyn. Yet you come here to my abbey and tell me it will succumb to the Blight. That there is nothing I may do to prevent it. You presage my death in a most cruel manner, and yet I must invite the very serpent who will bite me into my trust and care? I must shield her in Muirwood for the purpose of my own destruction and to protect *your* daughter, who must be abandoned here as a babe?" His face was livid. "How can you ask this of me?"

The Prince was calm, his voice soft-spoken. "I do not ask you to suffer needlessly, Aldermaston. It is not I who requires it of you, but it is the Medium's will. I am but the messenger. When I leave, it will be up to you to try and thwart the future. If you even can. I am only trying to prepare you for what is to come. It will take great courage to face this queen, your enemy. I have written this all in my tome, and I will put a binding rune on it. You will not be able to speak of it to anyone."

The Aldermaston clenched his fists and stepped closer, his size towering over the Prince. "You mean to say that I cannot even tell your daughter who she *really* is? I must raise her as a wretched when she is truly the heir of the kingdom of Pry-Ree? Why? Again I must ask…why?"

"My wife is the daughter of Sevrin Demont, who was very strong in the Medium. The strongest in this kingdom was only an earl. I am the strongest of my Family, even stronger than my grandfather, who was renowned for his Gifts. The houses of Lleu-Iselin and Demont will produce a child who will be exceptionally strong with the Medium, Aldermaston. Her Gifts will emerge at an age that will startle you. By the time she is fourteen or fifteen years, she will be ready to pass the maston test, even if she has never glimpsed or understood the meaning of a tome. Believe me, our enemies will be watching for her.

"Think of how powerful she would become with a kystrel. Think if she became proud or vain or filled with her own self-importance. If she is to fulfill her destiny—the destiny I shared with you—then she must never know who she is until the Medium teaches it to her. That is the only future I see where she can suc-cessfully accomplish her task. She is a voice of warning before that most terrible Blight comes and devastates the seven kingdoms. She must go to Dochte Abbey, to the very nest of vipers, and pro-claim it there. Only with the Medium compelling her, guiding her footsteps and her words, will she be able to do what she is meant to do. Any distraction of feeling or selfish inclination will destroy her." He took a step forward and grabbed the Aldermaston's arms. "I have seen that future, Aldermaston. I have seen the death of this land. I have also seen its rebirth. Just as these tree limbs will hang barren of fruit and leaves during the winter, the season will come on its heels and new life and growth will take its place. It is not for her alone that I do this, but her entire progeny and for all those who will survive and prosper because they heeded her warning. By this final sacrifice, I can save my people and yours. *You* must be her father while I cannot be."

The Aldermaston's mood shifted. He was a keen man, and he had picked up on something the Prince had said. Martin saw his eyes narrow. "You said your…*wife*. You are not married currently. Is that also a glimpse into the future?"

The Prince smiled cryptically. "We are married already, Aldermaston. She was bound to me by irrevocare sigil, though we have never met. I dare even suggest that our unusual marriage was one of the reasons Comoros invaded Pry-Ree. It is also the reason I am finally suing for peace. She was coming to me by sea and was captured at sea and is now being held for ransom at Pent Tower, where my father died. The king is not a maston, though. He will insist we marry again, and we will to please him. But she is my wife and will forever be, though it feels as if every Myriad One in existence thwarts our attempts to unite."

The Aldermaston shook his head, amazed at the revelation. Martin wanted to sneer at him. He had been in Dahomey when the ceremony happened—not inside the Abbey, of course, for he was not a maston. But he had met the girl and brought tidings of her back to the Prince.

The Aldermaston cleared his throat. "There are rumors, muttered gossip really, that Sevrin Demont's wife wore a kystrel. They say she was the cause of his downfall at Maseve—that it was how she persuaded the marriage to Demont to occur."

The Prince looked unmoved. "I have heard worse rumors."

"Is it true? You say Demont's blood is strong with the Medium, but did that strength come legitimately? Do you marry the daughter of such a one? I know your wife was never allowed to study at Dochte, for she was not the daughter of a king, but her mother may have taught her."

"That is my concern and none of yours. Thank you, Aldermaston, for your hospitality. My men are rested, and we ride in the morning for Comoros. Martin, will you show me that giant oak in the woods you discovered? I would not want to leave Muirwood without seeing its mighty branches."

The Aldermaston looked as if he had aged another dozen years during their interview. "You are welcome to roam the grounds as you see fit. There is an excellent view of the Tor from the slopes of the cemetery."

The Prince smiled and nodded. "Yes, the cemetery. I imagine the view will be splendid. Until it floods. Thank you again, Aldermaston. Come, Martin."

The Prince walked through the lush apple orchard. The buzz of flies wafted in the wind. Martin glanced back at the Aldermaston, who paced the orchard, collecting his thoughts and emotions.

Martin coughed in his hand. "You did not tell him about the cider, my lord."

The Prince shook his head. "He has enough to worry about. He would not care for us to visit the Tor if he knew what else I have seen."

"Will he obey you?" Martin asked. "Will he raise the child as you instructed?"

The Prince cocked his head slightly, giving Martin an unnerving look. "That is why I must leave you here, Martin. You must guarantee she reaches Dochte Abbey when it is time. You will not be going with us to Comoros."

Martin stared at him in shock, his insides writhing with pain. "By Cheshu!" he hissed.

The king arrived with the Earl of Caspur, not the king of Dahomey— our king. There was great enmity between Colvin and Caspur, but the king forbade them to quarrel. He said he wants to bring peace to the realm and heal the rift between Demont and the Queen Dowager. He intends to pass the maston test at Dochte Abbey, and the Aldermaston has agreed to let him try. The king has joined my private lessons. He is nearly my age and very clever. He knows about reading, but he has not had the patience to learn engraving. He whispered to me that he will have his scrivener do that for him. He attempted to read over my shoulder and see what I write in my tome, but I did not permit him. It is for my secrets and not to be shared. He is very kind, and his humor reminds me somewhat of Edmon. I miss those evenings in the kitchens of Muirwood. How simple and peaceful they were. Here there is studying all day long and dances and fetes until late into the night. The cider is delicious, but I only sip a little. Colvin will not drink it. During the dances he broods. I wish he would ask me to dance. Sometimes I stare at the dancers with great interest, but he ignores me. I do not think he cares to dance.

—Ellowyn Demont of Dochte Abbey

CHAPTER TWELVE

The Holk in Doviur

S hips of every mast and size thronged the port of Doviur. Hundreds of gulls squawked and swooped, mirroring the commotion existing on the piers below. The horizon was a tangled skein of ropes, poles, masts, and large hooks and cranes. Lia kept the Cruciger orb hidden within the fold of her cloak and stared at the spindle as it pointed the way she needed to go. Her request was simple—*find me a ship that will bring me to Dochte Abbey.* The orb obeyed, allowing her to weave in and out of the crowds, through plumes of charcoal smoke and the sick aroma of decaying fish.

The vessels were of different sizes, but they were similar in design. They had tall masts rigged with triangular sails, some folded, some flapping. Burly men worked to load and unload the ships, some cursing and others struggling against their burdens. As she had experienced in Comoros, she could feel no trace of the Medium in Doviur, and she had not felt it since leaving the cave that morning. The Myriad Ones skulked and sniffed, enjoying the feelings of anger and impatience that permeated the air.

Lia walked purposefully, feeling stronger and yet wondering how she was going to beg passage aboard the vessel she found. She had some money given her by the Aldermaston, but she was not certain what it would cost.

As the orb led her closer to the ship she sought, her mind wondered at what she would say. Though she desired passage to the Abbey, she realized that it might not be possible to land there directly and there might be some foot travel required. Desperately, she wanted to reach Dahomey, to find Colvin and warn him of the dangers they faced. The Medium continued to guide her, but there was a worried twist in her stomach, a feeling that every delay should be avoided.

The orb spindles changed direction, leading down a dock aisle. Berthed at the end of it was a ship that dwarfed those around it. Instead of triangular sails, it was rigged with several square sails, with a hive of masts and rigging. Sailors thronged the deck, some scurrying up and down ropes. The sides were dark and caked with slime and pitch. It was enormous, a huge mass of wood and cloth and rope. A small row of barrels were pushed up the gangplank, probably provisions for the journey. Several discarded ropes were being collected and wrapped. It seemed as if the loading was nearing an end.

The spindles pointed toward the ship unmistakably. Summoning her courage, she concealed the Cruciger orb and advanced. As she drew near, the whistles began, and several members of the crew took immediate interest. They were a rowdy sort. She frowned as she approached.

"What seek ye, lass?" one of the sailors crooned. "A kiss ere we disembark?"

"Do not waste your charms," said another. "She is my girl and came to bid me farewell."

"In the frigid depths of Sheol," said the former, shoving the man. The retaliation was swift.

They spoke her language but with an accent strange to her ears. It reminded her a little of Dieyre's manner of speech. Both he and Colvin had come from farther north.

"I must speak with the captain," Lia said firmly, pushing her thoughts at them with her will.

"But does he wish to speak with you?" replied the man she addressed, his expression regarding her with interest. "What is your business?"

She nearly told him, but the Medium whispered to be silent. Instead, she gave him a serious look, shoving the thought at him again.

"Who are you, lass?" said another sailor, one coiling a rope.

"I must speak with the captain." A thought struck her mind, and she said it before she could stop herself. "He is expecting me."

There was a surprise in their faces. "Expecting you?" one challenged disrespectfully.

The one coiling the rope jammed him with an elbow. He was older than the two young sailors, his face grizzled and pocked, but he was notable for very sharp, gray eyes. He observed Lia and nodded. "I will take you, lass."

"You will take her, Malcolm? What right do you have—"

"As much right as any man here. Shut your mouth before I do. Follow me, lass." He did not look back at her and started up the gangplank. Lia shuddered involuntarily and followed, for the commotion on the dock had attracted the eyes of the crew. Many whistled and jeered at her, and she swallowed the deep feeling of nervousness that clung to each breath. She saw that several had noticed her gladius, which raised eyebrows and infused them with curiosity. She kept her hood up, hiding her tangle of hair, but she could see them peering at her face as she approached. The sailor with the rope, Malcolm, if she had heard correctly, reached the main deck and turned back, offering her his hand to assist her. When she took his grip, she felt the Medium spark between them. He stared into her eyes and she returned the look, but neither said anything.

She walked across the crowded deck, feeling the leers and grins surround her. He shoved past several rude sailors who hung so close there was hardly room to pass. Lia followed, uncomfortable by the press of bodies. A few whispers reached her ears that she had been purchased by the captain to sport with on the journey. Greedy eyes stared at her hungrily, and a spasm of panic nearly threatened her composure. She trusted the Medium implicitly, but she felt she was in real danger. Guarding her fears, she kept her face solemn and resolved as she walked, remembering her courage when she had faced Almaguer's men in the Bearden Muir.

Another man stepped in the way, one with hair as black as midnight and a wary look. "Who is this, Malcolm?"

"The captain is expecting her," replied her escort.

"Do your work. I will take her from here." He gazed at Lia with confusion and distrust.

"Sorry, sir. I must bring her to the captain."

He spoke the words softly, almost too soft to hear, but Lia felt the spark of the Medium. The black-haired man started, looking confused, and then railed on the crew to get back to work. His gray-eyed gaze met hers, and then he led her under the bulkhead into the narrow passage back to the captain's quarters. He did not knock, only twisted the handle and pushed the door open.

"The Aldermaston will see you now," he said, nodding to her.

Lia startled at the word, and then gave him a thankful bow and proceeded. Upon opening the door, she saw the lushly furnished quarters and smelled the strong scents of breakfast lingering in the air. The captain was older, probably in his fifties, with streaks of gray in his reddish hair and beard.

Lower your hood.

Lia obeyed and entered the quarters, shutting the door behind her.

The noise drew his attention and his eyes lifted to her face. The effect of seeing her was unmistakable on his countenance. He paled instantly, his eyes widening with startled shock. His mouth parted silently, gaping. Sweeping the hat from his head, he crushed it against his leather tunic. She had never seen him before in her life, but he stared at her as if he had known her all the while.

Say nothing.

Lia stared at him, guardedly, feeling her hair fall about her shoulders as she shook it loose from the cowl.

"No," he said with a moan, shaking his head. He rubbed his eyes, blinking furiously. There were tears glistening there. He wiped his mouth and beard, staring at her, struck by so many conflicting emotions that she pitied the haunted expressions. Never had she had such an encounter—been the source of so much distress at meeting a man for the first time.

Lia stared at him, waiting for him to speak.

His chest heaved with emotion, his face tortured with regrets. When he spoke, his voice was half-strangled. "How you do look… like…her."

"Do you know who I am?" Lia asked.

He nodded slowly. His teeth were bared like a wolf's. "How can I forget the face that has been my demon these many years?" His lips quivered, tense as leather stretched over drums. "By Sheol, look at you!" He swallowed and started to cough.

"I seek passage to Dahomey," Lia said firmly. "You will bring me to Dochte Abbey."

"The serpent's lair," he whispered. "What…seek you…amidst the Dochte Mandar?"

"My own errand," she answered. "How do you know me?"

"I cannot say."

She cocked her head, challenging him with her eyes.

His mouth twisted into a snarl. "For many years I have not been able to speak of it. My crew has changed, save one—he who brought you to me. Malcolm was the only one left." The captain walked around the edge of his table and approached her. His breath stank of decay, but she willed herself not to flinch. She had gutted enough wild boar in the woods surrounding Muirwood not to lose her stomach so easily. His hand lifted to her cloud of wavy hair, and he touched it gingerly, his eyes closing with a memory that obviously pained him. "My mouth must be silent on certain matters, lass. I cannot speak of them, for I am cursed by Sheol for what I did. Do you know who I am?"

Lia shook her head slowly, feeling the menace of his presence so near to her.

"My name is Tomas Aldermaston." He sneered at her. "A jib, my lady. A mock. I was born in the northern Hundreds, a wretched of Dun Pharlain Abbey. After serving my time, I went amidst the shipbuilders of Dun Pharlain town on the mouth of Firth River. There I learned to be a crew member. They called me Aldermaston instead of Tomas Crew because I was a wretched. But I learned the trade well. I served under several captains and had a gift for turning a profit. But the greatest profit I ever earned was arresting the king's cousin on a voyage to Bridgestow. She was marrying a prince, you see, against the king's wishes. We caught her cog easily enough, and my men did their work well. We only killed the Evnissyen left to protect her. The rest…we spared." His eyes bore into hers. "I shall never forget that lass. I shall never forget her, though I live to be a hundred and forty." He turned away from her and walked back to the table, staggering as he did. His voice was muffled, but she could still hear him speaking.

"I was paid two hundred crowns. Two hundred. A ransom greater than any I had earned. I would give every farthing of it back. I would give tenfold back and drown in Sheol if I could bring back the tide and do it again." He looked back at her, his eyes full of suffering. "She was held in Pent Tower for three years. She was kept from her husband for the first three years of their marriage." His teeth chattered. "And she died in the birthing chamber. Snuffed out, like a golden wax taper." With a sweep of his arm, he scattered everything off the table. Lia started as the sacks of coins, the tuns of spice, the flagons all crashed and spilled on the wooden floor. He slammed his fist down on the table, so hard she wondered if he had broken his hand. Whirling at her, he approached again, his finger fixed in the air.

"I can say no more of what I know. My tongue cleaves to my mouth when I try to speak more of it. These many years have the memories tormented me. I would recognize your face anywhere. I know who you are. You bid me take you to Dahomey? We were departing to Dahomey this very morn. You bid me take you to Dochte? Then you shall go there and torture those fools and haunt them instead of me. I have a shipment of cider due thereabouts." He scratched his cheek roughly, staring at her with anguish. "I am yours to command. If you bid me sail you into the Great Deep, I will do it. Most captains fear to sail beyond the outer island, but I fear it not. There is a stirring in me that says I will sink into Sheol, or else brave the seas beyond those islands ere I die. This ship was built to ride the high seas. There is no distance too great. It lures me. It whispers to me. If you bid me sail you there, I will, lass. I fear it not."

"I do not doubt it, Tomas Aldermaston," Lia said, her heart wrestling with the implications of what he had revealed. If her heart was telling her true, she was standing before a man who had known her mother. "Is your ship very fast?"

A crooked grin met her in reply. "She is big and fast, my lady. Nothing outraces the *Holk of Doviur*."

CHAPTER THIRTEEN

Crossing the Storm

To spare Lia any further indignities from the crew, Tomas Aldermaston offered her his quarters while he went up on deck and made ready to sail. Lia opened the bolted shutters and watched the port of Doviur recede from sight as the giant ship lumbered away. The wind was gusty, and the ship had an odd sway that made her nervous and queasy. The sound of shouting, the creak of floorboards, and the whine of ropes all flooded her with sounds and sensations. The captain's chamber was decorated with fine workmanship, the furniture fashioned with wooden pins to lock the pieces to the ground and keep them from shifting with the vessel's swaying.

Lia grew weary of waiting and so went to the door and slowly opened it. A mass of bodies moved about the deck, but there was a man stationed at the door. It was the one she had met earlier coiling the rope. He looked at her and shook his head slowly. "Stay hidden, lass. Best if the crew do not see you."

She realized that he had taken to guarding the door to prevent other members of the crew from harassing her while the captain was distracted with other duties. He nodded to her to go back in, and she obeyed.

With nothing to do, Lia cleaned up the mess spilled about the floor and then sat by the edge of the bed. The lurch and roll of the ship made her drowsy.

She awoke when thunder boomed overhead, and sat up straight. The chamber was dark, though it was still daylight, she reasoned. Rain came slanting down through the open windows, which she hurriedly fastened shut. Enormous storm clouds filled the skies, and the ocean was a cauldron of boiling water. Lia lost her balance as the ship suddenly pitched forward, and she had to grab the table to keep from falling. She was grateful she had not eaten in a while. Her stomach was horribly upset.

The floor contained puddles of seawater that had sloshed in from under the door. Another violent pitch the other way made Lia desperate for a handhold to brace herself. Each rise and fall made her stomach giddy and then sick. Thunder boomed overhead, and lightning flashed like silver daggers. Shouts from outside the cabin were full of rage and even the keen of fear. Lia managed to get to the door again and opened it. Her protector was no longer there. Water sluiced through the passageway and soaked her boots. Foamy waves breached the high walls, crashing onto the wet crewmen, who struggled to tame flapping ropes and sails.

Railings were nailed into each wall, so she gripped them carefully and forced herself out of the dim corridor to the main deck. There was only a handful of crew about. She reckoned the rest were below deck to spare them from the storm's wrath. Lia's eyes bulged as she watched the sea drop perilously in front of her, and the nose of the great boat went down at a steep angle. She gripped the rods hard, using her feet to brace herself between the two walls as the ship sliced down the trough and up the other side. Seawater submerged the prow when it struck the valley of the wave. Hand over hand, she pulled herself forward. The wind was thick with salty water, and soon her hair hung in clumps.

A body appeared in the corridor. It was the black-haired sailor, the one who had scowled at her when she first boarded. The look he gave her was lethal. "Go back to the room, foolish girl! Sheol is punishing us because you are on board. Go back at once!"

Lia cowered at the fear in the man's eyes. His words were angry, but his countenance was terrified. The ship plunged again, and Lia started to slip, so she used both hands to grip one rod.

"Go back!" he roared at her.

Lia obeyed, fighting against the slick flooring to make it back to the captain's quarters. After shutting the door, she staggered to the captain's bed and thrust herself on it. Each pitch of the waves terrified her. The storm blew with fury and rage. Something inside nagged her that it was because of her somehow. The shutters rattled, and thunder continued to explode overhead. Lia squeezed her eyes shut and trembled.

***

The storm raged for days. Lia was sick, exhausted, and frightened by its ferocity. In all the gales that struck Muirwood, she had a sturdy roof overhead, and though there were leaks, they were not the kind that threatened her life. The crew worked furiously to bail water, mend cracks, and fix spars, their actions continually compromised by the dashing waves and violent pitching of the *Holk*. Tomas Aldermaston was rarely in his quarters, retiring there only when exhaustion overwhelmed him, sleeping a few short hours, and then rushing back to the helm to battle the storm's fury.

He entered the cabin again, his face wretched with fatigue and despair. "She cannot endure much more of this pounding," he said, conflicted. Then he stared at her. "The crew says the storm is because of you."

Lia looked incredulous. "They think that I brought the storm?"

"Aye, and many seek to throw you overboard to prove it will cease. It is unlucky to sail with womenfolk. Others say you are cursed. It's a crewman's fear, yet they are angry. I have never suffered a storm as great as this one—not in all my years at sea."

Lia moved slightly, adjusting her legs around the edge. Her stomach was taut with hunger, but she dared not eat with the general queasiness she felt. "I did not bring this storm, Tomas. Surely you believe that?"

He leaned back against the door, as if holding it closed to protect her. "Are you aware of sailors' myths? Do you know of the kingdom of Ilkarra in Sheol?"

Lia shook her head, though a shiver ran through her at the word. She understood the language through her Gift of Xenoglossia. Ilkarra was the representation of the underworld, the land of the dead.

The ship pitched again, nearly throwing Lia off the bed. She clutched at the rails and held on. Tomas wedged his boots against a post and held on. He grimaced with anger. "We will break apart. I have lost three men to Sheol already. Maybe we will all perish." His eyes narrowed when he looked at her. "Your journey must be important if you bring a storm upon us."

Lia frowned. "I brought no storm with me."

"Not you yourself—but your thoughts. What seek ye in Dochte Abbey?"

"I am only a messenger," she said. "As I told you last night, I warn them about the Blight."

"Then Sheol mayhap does not wish to be warned," he replied.

"Who is Sheol?" Lia asked. "You have mentioned that name. The sailors curse by it."

"Aye, they do. Sheol is the Queen of the Sea. Queen of the Unborn. The sea is the gateway to her domain, to Ilkarra. When men die, their bodies are returned to the earth, but their souls sink down into Ilkarra. Sheol is what *we* call her: the Queen of Storms; the Queen of the Unborn; the Whore of all the earth. The mastons call her Ereshkigal. Did you know that, lass?"

The name sent a shiver up Lia's spine. She stared at him in shock and surprise. "How do you know that name?"

"Sometimes a maston is careless with his whispers. Sometimes they speak in their sleep or when they are tempted. Sometimes they do not mind the abbey doors as they ought and a young wretched sneaks in and overhears the maston rites. Ereshkigal is the mother of hetaera. Is that what you seek in Dochte Abbey?" His eyes squinted at her, his face jutting forward intensely. "Do you seek to join them?"

"I am no hetaera," Lia answered distastefully. "They are my enemy."

He nodded. "Some believed that my prisoner, all those years ago, was one. That she had power over storms. That she was Ereshkigal made flesh. But she was a maston. I promise you that. She was a maston, and she could calm a storm." He swallowed heavily. "I cannot speak what I cannot say. Can you...save us, child? Can you banish these winds? You may be the only thing that can save us now."

Lia stared at him. "Me?"

"I have done all that I can. My ship will break up. She is already beginning to. In my pride, I thought I could ride her out. I thought I could bring you safely there. But I see now that I cannot. The crew thinks you are causing the storm. Except Malcolm. He says you will save us from it."

A furious pounding sounded on the door. Tomas whirled and opened it, and the black-haired crewman stumbled in, sea-drenched and gasping.

"She's foundering! Captain, she's foundering!" His face was livid with emotions, mostly fear. The sky keened with the wind.

Tomas turned back to Lia with a look of supplication.

Lia advanced, swaying with the ship, and stepped out into the storm. The lashing washes had swamped the main deck, and crewmen clung to ropes to keep from going overboard. She was blinded by the stinging saltwater, but she squinted as she pushed on, ignoring the howls from the crew when they saw her. She used her arm to shield her face, her vision blurring, and then she saw the gray-eyed crewman, Malcolm—the one who had brought her to the captain to begin with. He was drenched but his expression calm. He nodded to her slowly.

Lia summoned her courage.

Then a cry from one of the crew reached her ears. "Save us!"

It was picked up by another. Then another. "Save us! Save us! Save us from Sheol!"

"Shut your eyes!" she cried out. "Do not watch what I do."

The Medium began to churn within her, before she even raised her arm to the maston sign. She gripped the wooden bar to keep her balance. Water splashed across her face. Foam hissed like ten thousand serpents.

She remembered the night of the great storm in Muirwood. It came back to her in a rush. Jon Hunter, sopping wet, holding rings in his hand. Pasqua refusing to bake the required loaves of bread. Sowe asleep beneath her blanket. Lia saw the Aldermaston's eyes, heard the tone of his voice. *The rains have plagued us quite enough. They will cease. Now.*

"Be calm," Lia said softly, gently, coaxingly. "Be still."

The Medium roared inside of her, flooding her senses with light and force. She stared at the ocean, stared at the roiling waves as the wind died around them. The groans from the *Holk* settled as the waves slipped back down harmlessly. She lowered her hand and stared next at the crew and found them squatting, gripping their ropes or poles and shielding their faces from her as if she were too bright too look at.

The sea was calm. Gentle waves lapped against the hull as the water drained from the ports and doors. There was a hiss and curse in her mind—a presence retreating, fading into the distance. It was familiar to her. It terrified her. The Gift of Seering opened up her mind, and she saw the darkness receding from the ship, tossed away like a heavy blanket. In her mind's eye, she saw Pareigis hunched over a firewell within Muirwood Abbey, scowling furiously. The presence she had sensed was the Queen Dowager's. It was familiar to her because she had felt it not just in Muirwood, but she recalled feeling it earlier than that. The night before the battle of Winterrowd, she had been plucked by an invisible hand, a hand so powerful she had assumed it to be the king's will, his mind. But she realized it was another hand; it was the Queen Dowager who had been the puppet master.

The Queen Dowager is the form Ereshkigal uses to walk the earth—one of her many forms. It is her sanctuary you approach.

Lia's feelings shriveled inside her when she finally realized that another hand controlled the Queen Dowager. She could sense that presence still, vast as a starlit sky. The Queen of the Unborn was on the earth. She could assume human form by forging a link through a kystrel. Lia realized it fully that the Queen Dowager's Family members were her chosen minions, her disguise to live in the world. From generation to generation she had been born and born again. Pareigis was young. But the being dwelling inside her was as ancient as Idumea.

I am confused and miserable. How can I know the truth of what I am told? The Aldermaston of Dochte says that if the Blight is coming, it may be my destiny to stop it and not just warn of it. I must pass the maston test soon, or it will be too late. The king has told me that it is my destiny to marry him, that our alliance will put an end to the civil war and make our kingdom mighty again. He is a kind person, so very thoughtful, but something in his manner makes me distrust him. Or maybe it is because in my heart, in the deepest part of my heart, I cannot bear the thought of marrying anyone but Colvin. I could be the queen of the realm—yes, me! But I do not desire it.

There is never time to sleep in this place. It is study and celebration, study and celebration, every night going later and later. I am so weary. How can I pass the test when my mind is so tired? The Aldermaston thinks I am nearly ready. I can hear the whispers of the Medium now. They are all around me. This place is so full of the Medium. In Muirwood, I could scarcely hear anything. But after several days in Dochte, the whispers are clear. I especially hear them at night. What is my destiny? What am I supposed to do? Colvin says I must surrender to the Medium's will. I do not think he understands what that means, for every time I look at him, when his eyes seek my own and he smiles in encouragement, the Medium whispers that he will be mine. How I hope it is true. I would give up a kingdom to be his.

—*Ellowyn Demont of Dochte Abbey*

CHAPTER FOURTEEN

The Spike of Dahomey

The *Holk of Doviur* was listing badly, forcing the crew to bail water and work at shoring up the cracks in the seams before she foundered and sank. The beating from the storm had mangled the rigging, terrified the crew, and jeopardized the massive hull. There was no doubt, though, in any of the crew's mind, that Lia had saved them from destruction. As she walked above deck, they looked at her with respect and awe. Some had even asked her for her blessing.

Tomas Aldermaston shouted orders, striding vigorously on the deck and pointing this way and that, identifying new dangers that threatened them. He stared at the deep shelf of the sea, tame once more, and beckoned for Lia to join him. She did.

He kept his voice pitched low, and it was thick with anger. "We are lost," he whispered. "That storm blew us hither and yon, and I cannot get my bearings until the night. We should have seen Dahomey shores by now, but I cannot say whether we will see their shores or ours first. We faced the wrath of Sheol, we did. But now we are lost, and I fear we will take in more water before we can make it to a harbor to mend the *Holk*."

Lia nodded and walked behind him, staring over the bulwark to the flat line of the sea. The waves rippled in little foamy caps, and she breathed in the salty air. "The sun is over there, so we sail southward?"

"Aye," Tomas replied. "That is about the best course I can choose. The gap between our two countries is narrowest between the cities of Doviur and Ushuaia. Dochte Abbey is farther west, but if we have gone past the Spike of Dahomey, we could sail south forever and not reach it until the sea starts to boil."

"What is the Spike?"

He scowled and frowned, chewing on his thoughts savagely. "The coastline is not flat, lass. There is a bulge of land that comes out like a dagger spike. I know not how far west we were flung, you see—not until nightfall when I see the stars. But we lose precious time and increase the danger."

Lia stared into the sea, thinking. Her father had thought of everything. Untying the knot at the pouch, she withdrew the Cruciger orb.

"Well that is a pretty sight," Tomas Aldermaston said, his eyes growing hungry from the glimmer of pure gold. "Look at how the top bobs and spins. A curious workmanship, lass. Where did you get it?"

Lia ignored him and stared down at the spindles. *Show me the way to Dochte Abbey,* she thought, summoning its powers. The spindles spun around once and pointed due south, the direction they were headed. *Show me Martin.* The spindle did not change. *Show me Colvin.* No change. *Show me Hillel Lavender.* Again, the spindle remained true.

Putting her hand on Tomas's shoulder, she squeezed and nodded. "We will be there before nightfall. The orb never lies."

Indeed, it did not. Before much time had passed, the lad in the crow's nest hollered he could see land. The rest of the crew rushed to the view and watched the kingdom of Dahomey appear across the horizon. A collective cheer rose up, and sailors pumped their fists in the air, shocked with relief that they had cheated death during the crossing. Additional crew members touched the edge of her cloak, nodding respectfully to her. The crew clapped each other on the back and went back to their chores with vigor, and the listing ship hobbled closer to the edge of Dahomey.

"That is the Spike," Tomas told her, motioning toward the jut of land. "If we follow the coastline south, we will meet with Dochte Abbey at the edge of it. There is no harbor at the Abbey, but there is one about two leagues to the west—the town of Vezins. The tide defends the Abbey twice a day, you see. When it comes in, it is an island. When it goes out, the road opens. No army has ever been able to lay siege to it. No fleet could attack it because of the tides and the lack of deep water. It took a hundred years to raise it. We will anchor in Vezins, and from there you must walk to the Abbey. You can cross in the morning, when the tide goes out. I would say hire a village lad, but you have that golden ball to guide you."

Lia felt the throb of the Medium in her heart. She gripped Tomas's forearm tightly and blinked tears from her eyes. "You must wait for me or wait for word from me. I warned you the Blight is coming by Twelfth Night. We do not have long now. If I must flee Dochte Abbey, if they will not listen, I will need a way to escape. Can you fix your ship quickly? More importantly, will you wait for me?"

Tomas's eyes widened with surprise. "You would have me sail you away from this land?"

She gazed deeply into his eyes. "I may need you to sail me to the edge of the world, Tomas Aldermaston. There is a gathering place. There are ships that will carry us to a distant shore where the Blight cannot touch us. I would have you with us when we go."

The Medium churned inside her heart. Tomas's arm trembled where she gripped it. She knew that he could feel it as well. He glanced down at her hand, as if it burned him. A single tear went down his cheek.

"I will wait for you," he whispered hoarsely. "Ever since I was a lad, I dreamed of sailing to the edge of the world. I built the *Holk* to survive such a voyage. She will be ready, lass. She will be ready when you need her. And I will be your captain."

***

The *Holk* docked at the port of Vezins. There was much shouting with those on shore, for they were the first ship to arrive since the storm had battered the harbor, and all were curious to hear that they had sailed through it. As Lia was about to begin the walk down the gangplank, Malcolm seized her cloak. She turned and stared at him, noticing the peculiar look in his gray eyes.

"This is Vezins, lass. Do you speak the port speech?"

"I can manage it," she replied, smiling wryly. She turned to go, but his grip tightened.

"We thanks thee, lass," he said, switching languages to Dahomeyjan but with a different accent and manner. "Thou sav'dst us from the gale."

Lia nodded to him, puzzled by the look in his eyes and his more formal manner of speech. She had noticed his eyes when they had first met. There was something odd about him, something she could not make out.

"Thou art welcome," she answered, her Gift matching his tone and accent, and she paused to see if he would explain himself.

Malcolm did not. He simply released his grip on her cloak and motioned for her to proceed down the ramp. She did, glancing back at him once, and she saw he was still watching her. When she looked back at the path ahead, she was struck with a paralyzing fear. The dock swarmed with sailors who were painted with dazzling tattoos. All the people she saw had ink stained on their skin. There were cobweb-like patterns on their arms, necks, and even across some bald heads. She raised the cowl of her cloak to shield her face and walked through the throngs, noticing every man and woman thus disfigured with tattoos. There was a humid haze of languidness in the air. Men walked and shuffled with staggered steps. Indolent men were resting on the ground, cradling a mug of drink. The smell of cider was thick in the air, a yeasty smell that made what little hunger she had vanish. Eyes followed her. People brushed past her, and she felt hands reaching for her pouches, her bag. Clutching the pouch with the orb tightly, she used her forearms to thrust people away from her who came too close. It seemed that everyone was drunken. Their speech was lively and relaxed and followed the more formal manner of speech that Malcolm had demonstrated. Though their faces had varying forms of tattoos, none she met had glowing eyes.

Lia retreated into a side alley where it was dark and where she did not see anyone loitering except one man sleeping. She opened the pouch and summoned the orb's power, asking it to guide her to an inn where she could find a guide to Dochte Abbey who could help her with knowledge of the tides. The spindles were sluggish, as if the very air of Vezins made it difficult for them to move. They pointed the way, and she noticed it immediately, a short, squat house smashed between two larger ones, and she walked across the crowded street toward it. Night was falling quickly, and she wondered if it would be safer to sleep outside the port town.

Lia pushed open the door, and the strong smell of incense flavored the air. Huge wagon wheels with torches were hung from chains in the rafters. The inn was a giant main floor with ladders leading up to wooden lofts constructed around the perimeter. It reminded her vaguely of the Aldermaston's kitchen, for it was about the same size. The lofts seemed to be where the visitors slept. Strings were hung with curtains to offer a little privacy.

The innkeeper was a woman, probably forty or fifty years old, with brown hair streaked with gray. She did not have any tattoos, but she scowled at Lia when she entered.

"Thou wilt not find any cider here," she said harshly in Dahomeyjan, waving at Lia in annoyance. "But if thou seekest a meal and lodging, that I have."

Lia was relieved. Most of the patrons were sailors, hunched over bowls and slurping the soup. They had tattoos, but the innkeeper woman approaching her warily did not, though she was trying quite unashamedly to look past Lia's hood.

Lia thought a moment and then decided to use court Dahomeyjan instead of port speech. She did not want to pretend to know her way. "I do not want any cider," Lia replied, feeling the words come out of her mouth effortlessly.

The woman cocked her head. "You sound foreign."

"I just arrived today," Lia answered. "I am hungry. May I have some of your soup?" An idea struck her, a way she might begin to earn the woman's trust and gain some information from her.

"Dost thou need a pallet? Or is it the soup only thou cravest?"

"Let me first taste the soup. Then I will decide."

The innkeeper scowled at her and then walked back toward the large oven in the corner where a huge cauldron was bubbling and seething. It smelled overcooked and ill-made. The woman scooped up a spoonful of scalding soup, and Lia tasted it gingerly. It was hot but had no flavor except for a little marrow.

"Dost thou want soup and a room or just the soup?" the innkeeper repeated, folding her arms and staring at Lia archly. She pitched her voice lower. "When the men-folk see thee, they will bother thee. They will offer thee gold to touch thee. If thou camest here to sell thyself, go elsewhere."

Lia sipped from the spoon again. "If anyone touches me, I will break their hands."

That earned her a smile. "What seekest thou?"

"A guide to Dochte Abbey. When must I leave to make it with the tide?"

The innkeeper nodded shrewdly. "Thou knowest what thou art asking. A fine kettle of fish. Who told thee to come hither?"

Lia smiled and handed her the spoon.

"Jouvent!" the innkeeper said gustily. A boy of about ten approached from the room, holding a cap in his hands. He was tall and husky for ten, with dark hair that was combed straight down his forehead, the tips like quills, and he had pale blue eyes. He was young, but he had the wary look of a cat, ready to jump or pounce. His eyes belied his age. They looked haunted by things he must have witnessed.

"Aye, mother?" He glanced from the innkeeper to Lia, speaking in a soft tone. He nodded to Lia respectfully.

"The lad can take thee to Dochte Abbey. But thou must depart whilst it is yet dark. We are quiet and good for sleep and rest, such as we are, because we serve no cider." She brushed her hand through Jouvent's hair. "Soup, pallet, and a guide. What wilt thou pay me?"

There was something in her eyes that Lia trusted. She was an honest woman living her best in a hive of filth and treachery. The way she caressed the boy's hair revealed something of her personality that reminded Lia of Pasqua.

"Knowledge worth a hundred crowns," Lia answered and watched the woman gape in shock.

"What art thou jesting at?" she challenged, laughing with surprise. "A hundred crowns? Thou dost not look as if thy had ten. By my troth, thou dost not."

Lia looked at the cutting table next to the cauldron. She gave the wise innkeeper a fresh look. "I will teach you how to make a soup that will fill your inn every night. Soups and breads and desserts. I know many recipes. If you let me stay here, I will teach you some of what I know." Lia looked at the boy. "Would you like to taste a real soup, Jouvent?"

His eyes widened hungrily. "Aye, my lady."

"Then you must pay attention and watch me. I will teach you."

"Where didst thou learn to cook?" the innkeeper said, curious now. Something unspoken passed between them as Lia took an onion from the table. She peeled back the crackling skin and smelled it. It was fresh.

"When I was Jouvent's age, I learned to cook for an aldermaston. These are good onions. Let me show you how to cut them. There is a way to cut them very fine. You need spices. I can show Jouvent how to gather plants on our walk to the Abbey. Here, let me show you."

Lia began to cook. It all came rushing back to her. There were beans to soften, strips of salt pork to add, and spices. From her rucksack, she withdrew spices they had never seen before but that smelled wonderful. Both watched her with fascination as she worked, quickly and deftly, adding new aromas to the bubbling cauldron. The smell in the inn began to shift, and so did the mood. Others entered, but it was not a rowdy crowd, and many left as soon as they learned there was no cider.

With a sharp knife, Lia smashed a clove of garlic and mixed it with the onions and then added them to the soup, scraping the wooden board clean and then adding some salt and crushed peppers. She smelled the soup, tasted it often, and then sprinkled some sprigs of thyme leaves.

Jouvent stared at the pot, his eyes wide with hunger and anticipation.

"Taste it," Lia whispered. He obeyed, producing a spoon from his pocket and gently ladled some soup into his mouth. The expression on his face pleased her.

"Aye, my lady. It is good soup," he mumbled.

Lia nodded and tousled his hair. "You watch people, Jouvent. You learn by watching. I will dare say that you know many tales and stories."

He nodded shyly.

"What news from Dochte Abbey?" she asked.

He took another spoonful of soup and devoured it. He fished around for a chunk of meat and then chewed it, nearly burning his tongue. When he finished, he looked at her again. His eyes were wise beyond his years, as she had noticed earlier. "Talk of marriage and war. The king of Comoros, he has come thither to study at the Abbey. If thou wilt listen, thou wilt hear he shall marry a lass. She be the heir of Demont. They shall marry and stop all the warring in that accursed land." He slurped more of the soup. "If they do not marry, there will be a war. There be too many from Comoros here and they crave the warring to happen.

Dost thou know who stays at the Lily here in Vezins? Another earl from Comoros, he be. A fine swordsman. Thou may call him Dieyre. An' he is paying ten crowns for the boy or man who brings him word of a boat a comin' from Comoros. I know've a boat just arrived from Doviur, but the *Holk* was not the vessel he seeks." He seemed ashamed all of a sudden, as if he realized he was talking too much.

But Lia could not control her expression of dismay. She could do nothing but stare in shock at the little boy who, between mouthfuls of soup, had just revealed the worst news she could imagine. If the wretched who believed she was Ellowyn Demont consented to marry the king, what impact would it have on Lia if the truth became known? She had no desire to marry the young king whose father she had slain with a Pry-rian arrow. Even though he had been under the guardianship of Garen Demont, she knew he must have been corrupted by Pareigis. The thought of being forced to marry him sickened her.

It was equally alarming to learn that Dieyre was in Vezins. When she thought of Reome carrying his child, she wanted to run him through with her gladius. How much suffering he had caused and continued to cause. He was undoubtedly waiting for a ship to bring Marciana to him. What would he do when he learned it was not coming? She could see the additional pieces of the Queen Dowager's plan locking together. At Muirwood's cloisters, Lia had witnessed Dieyre promoting marriage between Ellowyn Demont and the young king. He had tried to persuade her to aim for it.

She realized with a very real throb of terror that she had very little time to thwart it.

CHAPTER FIFTEEN

Jouvent

L ia stayed up late baking bread, pizzelles, and even a sam-
bocade. The soup cauldron was scraped empty before the
guests had settled for the night, sharing ladders to climb
up to the loft curtains. In the time she had spent with them, she
had learned the innkeeper's name—Huette—and also learned the
Jouvent was not her natural son. She had lost three children to
fevers and sickness and then lost her husband to the sea. Instead of
despairing, she had started the inn to support herself. On a stormy
night that had battered the dock-bound ships, a young woman
from the Abbey had come. She was very ill and very rich and very
much with child, and Jouvent had been born by the hearth that
night. The young woman was determined to abandon the child at
the Abbey, but Huette had persuaded her to leave the child with
her since bringing it out into the storm would have killed it for certain. The young woman did not care what happened to the child,
so long as she was rid of it. She never left her name, and she never
came again. Lia stared at the boy as the innkeeper shared the story.
Though a sickly thing at birth, he had managed to survive the winter and had grown strong and sturdy ever since.

The guests were all settled before midnight, and Huette tamped down the fires, locked the door and windows, and started sweeping up the spills and crumbs from the rush matting. Jouvent stared into the chimney, at the soot-choked Leering carved into the wall at the back of it. He stared at it long and hard, but nothing happened.

"Why do you stare at the gargouelle?" Lia asked him softly.

He did not look at her. He shook his head.

"Tell me," she whispered.

"Mother warned me never to tell of it. Too many Dochte Mandar about. They know when things happen."

Lia stared at the Leering's eyes and summoned its power with a thought, just enough to make the eyes glow red.

Jouvent looked at her knowingly. "Thou art a maston," he whispered. He did not ask her to confirm it. He already knew.

"When did you realize it?" she answered softly, watching Huette as she cleaned the tables and decided to join her and help.

"I saw a peek at thy chaen," he answered, his eyes meeting hers. "Earlier. I meant no disrespect, but I saw it and then I knew what it was."

"How did you know?"

"The mastons find us," he whispered. "Somehow they know they are safe here. Thou art safe here. In the morn, I will take thee to the Abbey. But I must warn thee. The Dochte Mandar have promised fifteen crown for any maston turned in. It is a lot of coin, my lady, and my mother and I are poor. But we always have enough to eat. Somehow, there is always enough. I judge it that by not turning thee in, there are blessings on our house."

Lia smiled at him and stifled a yawn.

"Thou shouldst sleep," he said. "Lay on my pallet, near the fire. I shall help Mother."

Lia could not argue, for she was exhausted. She stretched out on the pallet near the oven and stared at the winking embers as they died, one by one. Little bits of ash sizzled, and she breathed in the scents and flavors that reminded her hauntingly of Pasqua's kitchen. In her mind, she could hear the old woman bustling about, thumping ladles and fussing over stubborn dough. The guests at the inn had enjoyed her treats that night. She had earned some lavish compliments, and the extra coin had made it the most prosperous evening throughout Huette's time as an innkeeper.

Nestling beneath her cloak on the pallet, her thoughts drifted back to Muirwood again, and she relished the memories. Long evening talks with Sowe after Pasqua had gone to bed. The thrum of the rain on the roof shingles during the wet season. How curious that her skills in the kitchen had served her so well. As she lay there, turning it over in her mind, an idea began to bloom. Maybe her skills at cooking would help her get inside Dochte Abbey. Was she just going to arrive and try to declare herself? No, that did not make sense. She wanted to find Colvin first, and if not Colvin, then maybe Martin. There was so much going on that she needed to warn them about.

Her stomach wrenched with a crushing feeling of longing when she realized that Colvin was so near. Would she see him on the morrow? Would it be possible to get close enough to see him? The thought sent another spasm through her, twisting her heart cruelly. She was so thankful to have the Cruciger orb and how it would help her find them. Would the next evening be spent with him? Would she be able to tell him who she really was? She realized that thinking of him would make sleep impossible. Squeezing her eyes shut, she forced away thoughts of the new day. Sleep—she desperately needed to sleep.

The pallet was comfortable, the smells so soothing, that she drifted off to sleep, remembering vividly the Aldermaston's kitchen at Muirwood. She dreamed of the night of the great storm, the night when Colvin had been brought there by Seth, bleeding and unconscious. A knock at the door had announced the arrival. A fitful knocking. A persistent knocking.

"Get thee gone, we are closed!" Huette hissed through the door. "There is no cider here. Get thee gone!"

The voice answering was gruff and heavily accented—the accent of her native country. "Open thy door. We serve the Earl of Dieyre."

Lia's blood went cold, and she sat up instantly.

"Go thy way!" one of the patrons roared from the loft. "We care not!" Mutters of assent came from others.

The knocking turned louder. Lia was about to warn her when Huette lifted the crossbar and opened the door a small way. "I do not care who thy master is!" she railed. "Thou art foreigners and I shall hail the—"

She was flung backwards as the knight shoved past her to enter—four men, wearing Dieyre's colors. Recognizing their tunics made her stomach clench with dread. She did not know any of them, but their arrogance and pride would have announced them as Dieyre's men without any livery.

"Hold thy tongue, woman," one of them said. "Rail not against us." Their eyes searched across the room, looking at the empty tables and the curtains up in the loft. Each gripped a sword hilt menacingly. Four men, alert and angry.

Another man stepped forward, looking at Jouvent. "Lad, here is a coin. Is there a young lass here with golden hair? She arrived in the *Holk* before twilight. She has hair like flax or gold, and it is wavy with frets. The Earl will pay handsomely if she is found. Dost thou know where she is, lad? Dost thou?"

"It be rude to accost us thus," Huette said with fury. "Thou art not welcome here. Take thy crow coins and fly with them. Buy cider to quench your thirst. Be gone!"

Jouvent slowly backed away from them, toward the front door. He did not look at Lia once. "Aye," he said slowly, "I have seen the lass."

"Have you now?" said the knight, walking toward him firmly.

Jouvent backed away even faster. "I shall tell thee what I know. Give me thy coin first, to help me mother." He looked ready to run. Lia saw the fifth knight enter from outside. Jouvent saw him too late, and the man's hand clamped down hard on his shoulder.

The boy struggled suddenly, wriggling like he was made of nothing but slippery eels, but the knight clenched hard and steadied him.

"If thou hurts him," Huette warned angrily, seizing the knight by the collar, but he shoved her back.

"Lia," the new arrival said in her native language. His voice carried through the inn. "We know you are here. You were foolish to stay in one place so long. There are five of us, girl, and Dieyre has already warned us what you are capable of. He does not wish you any harm. He only seeks to speak with you. Come with us and then you will be at liberty. I give you my word, Lia." He squeezed Jouvent's arm so hard the boy yelped with pain.

Lia stood fully in the corner where she was concealed. Already Huette and Jouvent had sacrificed for her. "I am reassured by your promises," Lia said tartly. "I know full well the Earl of Dieyre is a man of his word. When it suits him."

The five turned and faced her. They each wore chain hauberks, covered by the tunics of their master, as well as black velvet capes. The one holding Jouvent leered at her. "Well, it is true. But he informs us that you were wounded severely not long ago, that your hand might still be mending, and your leg. You seem hale to me, though. As I said, he only wishes to speak with you."

"I come willingly," Lia answered, sighing, and approached them. They seemed to watch her warily. She looked at each of their faces, at their smug presumption that any one of them could outmatch her. They were servants of the best swordsman in seven kingdoms, so they had a reputation at least to uphold.

Jouvent shook his head warningly at her, his eyes quailing with fear and pain.

Lia's stomach wrenched with knots as she approached the knights. She knew she had to be unpredictable—throw them off their guard. She glanced toward the nearest window and wondered if she would have the strength to break it as well as fling herself out of it in time. The scattered tables and chairs would assist her, offering cover and opportunities to distract them. She had absolutely no intention of going with them.

"That is wise, lass," the leader said. His chin and neck were thick and muscled, but he was clean-shaven.

As she approached, she gave Huette a reassuring gesture. "I thank thee for thy hospitality," she said in port speech. Then she looked at the man holding Jouvent and said simply, "It is a wonder, Captain, that you only brought five."

"Why even bring five when only one will do?" he replied tauntingly. His eyes suddenly glowed silver, and that was when she noticed the whorl of tattoos crawling up his neck.

His will reached out and clamped around her mind, sending a gush of fear and panic inside her heart. It swelled her anxiety a hundredfold, and even though she knew her emotions were being manipulated, the feelings were real—like a night terror that will not fade after waking.

Lia stomped on the nearest man's foot, so hard and so sudden she felt his bone snap, and he howled with pain and dropped to the floor. Whirling as fast as she could, she dropped low into a crouch and bashed another knight's manhood with her fist. As he crumpled, she reversed the blow, bringing her knuckles up as he bent over, smashing his nose. Already two were incapacitated, but the other three had managed to draw their blades and fan out around her.

"Do not kill her!" the leader said, his eyes glowing. His will crushed against hers, trying to force her to cower before him. It may have worked on a weaker person. It may have worked on every other person he had used his kystrel against. Though she experienced the surge of fear, it did not overcome her.

She drew her gladius and dagger in a fluid motion. "Do not expect the same terms from me," she said threateningly, hoping he would not hear the tremor in her voice.

The leading knight shoved Jouvent roughly away and came at her hard and fast. Lia deflected his blade with the gladius and stepped around him, keeping the others from getting behind her. She kicked a chair over and moved again, forcing them to adjust to her actions.

"You are quick witted, lass," he said. "But I will wear you down. We have all night to play this game. They say you bested a kishion at Muirwood with nothing but a dagger."

Another knight lunged at her, grabbing her arm. In a moment, his strength would overmatch her, but she had been trained by the Evnissyen and knew what to do. While twisting her arm hard and down, she struck his hand with the sword pommel and broke his grip. She cut his cheek as he backed away and nearly took his eye with it. He snarled with pain and jabbed his weapon at her. Lia caught it between her gladius and dagger, slid her longer blade up its edge, and sliced his hand open. He dropped his sword.

Lia whirled fast and hard, for the other two were charging in as well. She ducked a blow aimed at her shoulder and thrust her dagger at his stomach, but the hauberk deflected it. Lia brought her knee up into his gut, making him cough. The leader was reaching for her when he slackened and stumbled, and she realized Jouvent had wrapped himself around the man's leg.

The door of the inn shuddered open, sending wind through the gap with a howling sound. Lia gritted her teeth, expecting more enemies, and then she saw Malcolm enter, his face furrowed with anger. He turned and called behind him, "She is here! Hasten!"

The leader of Dieyre's knights hammered his fist at Jouvent's head and hair, but the boy did not shriek or cry; he only squeezed harder and ducked away from the blows. When at last the boy was thrown off, the knight stood and saw he was surrounded by twelve iron-hard sailors from the *Holk*.

Malcolm had a cudgel in his hand and tapped it menacingly against his palm. "Why threaten the lass?" he said roughly. "What beggars are you to do that? Drop your swords or we kill you here and now."

"Captain?" one of the knights moaned fearfully as the crew quickly surrounded them.

Malcolm glanced at the frightened man. "You should fear us. We are the crew of the *Holk*."

The leader of the knights cast his weapon to the floor with humiliation in his eyes. The other man cast his down as if it burned him. The three wounded men were writhing still.

Malcolm looked at Lia respectfully. "Shall we escort these hostages to our hold? They be Dieyre's men. He may not miss them for a while yet. That will give us some sport and you a chance to leave Vezins."

"Thank you," she replied. "If they ever disturb this place again, I want them to know they will be killed." She approached the captain of the knights, his eyes full of hate and fear. She reached up and gripped the edge of his sturdy chin, meeting his hateful gaze with her own. "You tell Dieyre that she will not come by boat or by sea. She is out of his grasp forever. He is nothing but a coward and a fool, and so are you for serving him. May the Blight take you all."

Reaching down, she glimpsed the chain, pulled the kystrel out of his shirt, and snapped the links with a swift jerk. Then she smacked him with her open palm, so hard her skin stung. His lips quivered with rage and desperation.

"You give that message to your master for me," she warned. "He would not heed my words in Muirwood. I do not think he will listen now."

Turning back to Malcolm, she nodded for the sailors to take them away. She listened to the kicking and punching as the crew overwhelmed the knights. Staring at the kystrel cupped in her hand, she remembered Almaguer and Scarseth. She walked to the ovens and tossed the medallion into the pit. She stared at it, amidst the ashes, as if it were a great contorted eye. She summoned the Medium, and it was difficult, like drawing a breath through water. The flames obeyed her, though, and lit her skin with golden hues as the fire consumed the kystrel and melted it.

Hearing a scuffle of a boot near her, she looked over, seeing Jouvent staring up at her, a trickle of blood coming from his nose and forehead. He stood bravely, gazing at her with admiration.

"I will take thee now," he whispered. "It is not safe in Vezins for thee."

Lia tousled his dark straight hair and nodded. "Fetch me some woad, Jouvent. Let me heal you first."

I tremble as I write this. I should not tremble. I must never surrender to my fears. As the Aldermaston of Billerbeck taught me, the soul attracts that which it secretly harbors, that which it loves, and also that which it fears. The Aldermaston of Muirwood taught this. So has the Aldermaston of Dochte. It must be true. If so, then I must proceed with caution. The young king desires to marry me. He said it will end the rift in our kingdom. He wants me to be queen at his side. He has promised me lands, servants, and riches if I accept him. I resist the idea. I do not love him, and I do not desire those things. I do not believe that he loves me. He will sacrifice himself for the good of the country, but he will never love me. Therefore, I make this oath to myself. If it is true that we will always bring to us that which we most secretly love, and if it is true that our thoughts will be set within our reach, then I have but one chance at true happiness. I will marry no other save Colvin Price, the Earl of Forshee. I will marry him at Billerbeck Abbey under the hand of his aldermaston and by irrevocare sigil. We will marry by Twelfth Night. It is written now. I feel strangely calm. Calmness is power. When I go to the dance tonight, I will be calm. Colvin will dance with me tonight—even if I must ask him.

—Ellowyn Demont of Dochte Abbey

CHAPTER SIXTEEN

The Water Rite

Dahomey was a strange land with many strange sights. The woods were thick with beeches and oaks that reminded Lia of Muirwood. At dawn, they reached the edge of the Huelgoat Forest without seeing any sign of Dieyre's men in pursuit. Lia had used all of the tricks Martin had trained her on to disguise their path and trail and to be wary for any sign of pursuers. Worry throbbed in her heart, and she constantly glanced backward, trying to discern the sound of anything amiss. The forest was crowded with moss-covered boulders, jumbled together for leagues, as if some mighty mountain had been smashed. Some of the rocks were amazingly balanced, huge, round heads topping smaller stones that gave them the appearance of mushrooms. It gave them plenty of places to hide, but it also shielded sounds from reaching them. Without the orb or Jouvent, she would have become hopelessly lost amidst the treacherous path, but he knew the way and guided her through the forest by noontime.

"Thou art not from Dahomey," he said astutely. "I know not where, but not here. Why seekest thou the Abbey? 'Tis not safe for mastons there."

Lia glanced down at him. "Why do you say that?" she pressed.

His nose pinched. "The Dochte Mandar. They be the ones who offer coin for a maston's telling. Silver eyes and painted faces. They see into your heart. I shudder when I cross one."

"Who are these Dochte Mandar?" Lia said. "Did they come from the Abbey?"

"Aye, they did. They say that all 'un should go inside the Abbey—that the secrets should be known by all. In Dahomey, all the abbeys are opened. And the Dochte Mandar taunt and prod and snare any lad or lass who wander by. Their faces were painted black, and they were strange to be seen. Nowadays every person is staining their faces and arms like the Dochte Mandar. There are needles and black ink. Folk get poked and stung. It hurts, so they say. But thou are not painted with ink or shadows." He looked at her shrewdly. "They at the Abbey are painted. They will see thou art a foreigner."

Lia nodded, thinking about the predicament. In her mind, the Dochte Mandar were the minions of the hetaera. They painted themselves and others with tattoos to hide the kystrel's curse. Instead of it being a mark to separate themselves from others, they forced others to embrace the branding to mold them after their image. The notion repulsed her, but she realized that not having a tattoo would make her stand out among them. With offers of reward for turning in mastons, she would need to be very cautious as to whom she could trust. She believed that with the Cruciger orb's help, she could find her way to Colvin, Ellowyn, and Martin. However, it was only a matter of time before Dieyre went looking for his men and discovered that she was heading there. As they walked, she looked backward constantly toward the forest, hoping to catch a sign of riders with enough time to hide themselves.

"That way," Jouvent said, pointing toward the shore. "The tide is gone now. Thou wilt get wet as we pass to the Abbey."

They changed direction and followed into the wetlands, which were spongy and soft, and little bubbles appeared all along the sandy shore. Tall boulders loomed in the distance, offering a jagged edge to the horizon. The air smelled of salt, and dozens of gulls glided overhead. The walk was slow going because of the shifting sand, and they left a trail of pockmarks that slowly filled in and vanished. It would be difficult tracking someone in the sandy muck. At times the water was up to the cuffs of their boots, but it was always low enough to keep trudging and would disappear entirely as they reached little cusps of land. The walk was long and tedious, and Lia's heart vexed her with anticipation. Each step brought her closer to him. Her stomach fluttered with nervousness.

"There," Jouvent said, pointing. "Dochte Abbey."

At first it looked like a boulder, but then she noticed the slender silver spike rising from the center of it. As they walked, the boulder became more distinct, and she realized something she had not when seeing it from the *Holk* near dusk. Her initial thought was an abbey built on top of a hill in the midst of the ocean. The ocean had receded all around it, exposing the land and sea grass. The side facing them showed not just an enormous abbey jutting from the hilltop but row after row of houses, walls, battlements, and turrets farther down. From the rear she had seen forested slopes and cliffs. As they approached, she could see an entire village had grown up around the lower walls of the Abbey, and it was thick and crowded and teeming with chimney smoke and people. There were darker blotches showing some small parks or woods, but the majority of the face was built up and defended. The Abbey was taller than a castle, grander than any structure she had ever beheld. How had something so large and beautiful been crafted by men?

"She is a beauty," Jouvent said with a proud smile. "That is *our* Abbey. The finest mountain in the world."

His words summoned a memory. Long ago, she and Colvin had followed Maderos up the Tor, which overlooked Muirwood far below. The climb had been strenuous, though the older man had hardly struggled for breath. She remembered him telling her, quite cryptically, that there would be other mountains she would climb. To find Tintern Abbey, she and Colvin had climbed a mountain in Pry-Ree. To reach Colvin, she would climb another one. A wave of emotions smothered her suddenly, and she choked for a moment.

"Other travelers," Jouvent said, his face going from grin to grim. As Lia looked around, she saw others crossing the wetlands toward the great Abbey. "It is still safe to cross now. Best be there before supper, or the sea will trap thee inside. The inns will cheat thee. I must get back to Mother soon. It is a long walk, but thou walkest well."

Three dark dots appeared in the shimmering sand ahead, and she realized it was three travelers leaving the Abbey for the mainland. Her heart began to pound when she recognized the black cloaks and cassocks riding dark steeds.

Jouvent hissed through his teeth. "Dochte Mandar."

There was no place to hide. The broad expanse of sand and sea grass left nothing for shelter. Lia gritted her teeth as they approached her at a calm walk, in no rush to leave the Abbey. She tugged her cloak tightly about her, trying to conceal her gladius the best she could.

The Dochte Mandar wore black with white ruffs about their necks. The cassocks were black velvet and designed with silver trim, reminding her instantly of the Queen Dowager's henchmen. Their boots were lined with white pelts, and each had gems studding their belts and saddle harnesses. Swords were fastened to their belts, each with a large ruby set into a silver hilt. Their faces were mazes of tattoos, which disguised their features and drew in her eyes.

"Thou art never to meet their gaze," Jouvent warned, staring down at the sheen on the water. "'Tis disrespectful."

"Thank you," Lia answered and followed his example. The horses snorted as they approached, and Jouvent stopped, his head bowed meekly.

"Another set of pilgrims," said one in strong Dahomeyjan. It was the formal speech she was used to, not the port speech. "They throng like locusts."

Lia was not sure if she was supposed to respond or not, so she said nothing. Another answered instead. "Each soul must be saved, regardless of how petty."

The first stopped his horse in front of them imperiously. "Well met, travelers. What village do you hail from?"

Jouvent took his cap and wrung it in his hands. "Vezins, masters."

"Ah, a lad from the port. Can you tell me, child, if the Earl of Dieyre arrived? The foreign lord?"

Jouvent nodded vigorously. "Aye, he be there."

"Excellent, excellent. Thank you, child. The Medium's blessing be on you."

"He does not have the mark," one of them murmured softly, but Lia heard it.

"Indeed, he does not. Boy, have you received the water rite?"

"No, masters," Jouvent said, his face twisting with discomfort. "Not yet."

There was a snort of dissatisfaction. "Why not? Why do you delay it?"

Jouvent wrung his cap more fiercely. "Mother. I am her only child. Her only help. She cannot spare me yet. But soon."

"Look at me."

Jouvent shook his head, his body quaking with fear.

"Look at me," repeated the command. Lia could sense the churn of the Medium in the air. She could feel it swallow her whole, as if some great glass jar had clamped down on them both. She risked a glance and saw the one speaking, his eyes glowing silver.

Jouvent looked up at him, his face pale.

"You must understand it is important. Believe me when I tell you that you must disobey your mother if necessary to receive the water rite. You have until Twelfth Night, child. Remember that. If you do not receive it by then…" He paused, his voice so somber it chilled Lia's heart. "Your mother will regret it with great pain. Twelfth Night, child. Do not delay."

Jouvent was trembling. "Yes, masters," he whispered hoarsely.

"Have you seen any mastons?" he asked next, his voice supple and inviting.

The coils of the Medium wrapped around Jouvent. She could see him struggling against it, fighting against it, but it was too powerful.

Lia pushed against their thoughts with her own. *Do not fear them,* she thought to the boy. *Do not fear them, Jouvent. They cannot hurt you with me here. I will protect you.*

The Dochte Mandar who had asked the question suddenly turned on her, as if he had heard the thought. "What village do you hail from, lass?"

The full weight of the Medium slammed into her, nearly making her mind go black. There were three of them pushing against her, using their kystrels to swarm her feelings with the sensations of worthlessness, shame, humiliation, and foreboding. It struck her so forcefully that for a moment she lost thought of who she was and could only stand there blinking, trying to remember her own name.

She almost said Muirwood. The compulsion to say it was so strong that the word nearly slipped out of her mouth. They would know of her Abbey, she realized. Yet she also realized she had to speak truthfully.

"I hail from Pry-Ree. I seek work as a cook at Dochte Abbey," she said, fighting against the surging feelings.

"You hail from Pry-Ree?" came a startled response.

"It is true," answered another. "She speaks the truth. She is from Pry-Ree."

Lia swallowed, struggling against the feelings of unworthiness.

"We have enough scum from Pry-Ree as it is," said the third. "Go your way then. You are a foreigner, child. I can hear it in your accent. But if you would stay in Dahomey, you must also accept the water rite. Do it while you are here. It will protect you from the Blight."

"Thank you, masters," Lia said respectfully.

"Have you encountered any mastons in your journeys?" he asked her.

Lia nodded. "Several. There are a few left in Pry-Ree. Most are in hiding."

"The mastons are the source of the Blight that comes," he responded. "They must be sought after and found. If you find a maston, you must tell one of us. Do you understand, child?"

The Medium crushed against her will. She resisted it, but the weight of it was so strong she nearly revealed that she was one. "Yes, masters."

The three horsemen rode on, muttering among themselves as they passed.

Lia breathed deeply. It took several moments for her feelings to subside. She understood better what had happened to Marciana. A Dochte Mandar had manipulated her feelings. Even knowing it was not real, she could not deny that the feelings she experienced were quite real. They were so powerful that she wondered if she could have resisted if more had been there. Their power increased with numbers, she realized. A lone maston would not be able to stand against many.

"Jouvent, you must tell me this. What is the water rite? I have not heard of it."

The boy looked terrified. "It is one of the maston rites. When the Dochte Mandar opened the abbeys to all, they said that all must join in the rites. The water rite is one. They have a holy bowl and cup their hands and pour water on your head. For babes, they dip their fingers in the bowl and swipe it across their foreheads, here…" He demonstrated. "I did not know there were babies to be mastons."

"There are not," Lia replied, sick inside at what was happening. "This is wrong. This is very wrong."

"I must get back to Mother," Jouvent said. "Thy way is clear to the Abbey. I must be past the forest by dark."

"Jouvent," Lia said, stopping him. Her feelings still trembled from the power of the Dochte Mandar. "The mastons are not causing the Blight. That was a lie."

"I know."

"But he was not lying about one part. Something *will* happen at Twelfth Night. If I do not return to Vezins soon—if I am delayed—you must seek the captain of the *Holk*, the ship that I sailed on. His name is Tomas Aldermaston. You and your mother must be on board by Twelfth Night." She gripped his shoulder and forced him to look at her. "Do you understand me, Jouvent? The Blight is coming, and it will come by Twelfth Night. There is not much time left."

"Aye." He smashed the cap back on his head and started back the way they had come.

"Good boy," Lia said. She turned and faced the giant mountain, the Abbey where Colvin and Ellowyn had come earlier and could not leave because of the Queen Dowager. She was in custody in Muirwood. Colvin and Ellowyn were in custody in Dochte.

She had the suspicion that it was not by chance that it had worked out that way.

Squaring her shoulders and striding forward, she approached the outer walls of Dochte Abbey and walked toward the nearest gate. After reaching into the pouch at her waist, she withdrew the orb. Whom should she find first—Colvin or Martin?

As she stared up at the sculpted stone walls, the endless rows of shingles and chimneys and trees, she was awed by the Abbey's presence. The sight of Muirwood had always made her experience the Medium. It felt like home. Dochte Abbey was ancient and splendid. It dwarfed any structure she had ever seen, including the castles at Comoros. But there was no feeling of light and warmth coming from it. The feeling it exuded was one of utter blackness.

CHAPTER SEVENTEEN

Hetaera

The entire hillside of Dochte Abbey was a maze of walls and an endless parade of stone steps that ascended higher and higher. Every time she passed through another arch, it would curl upward again, another laborious ascent bringing her higher and higher within the grounds. Her legs burned from the effort, and still she had not reached even the lower portion of the outer walls of the Abbey. There were fellow pilgrims everywhere, thronging the grounds and visiting shops and bakeries for food. There was cider in abundance. As Lia finished mounting one particular set of steps, she looked back the way she had come and over the outer walls saw far below the rippling waves of the sea that now smothered the lowlands beyond, trapping her inside. There were several tall, sturdy trees spreading their foliage over the lip of the walls and offering patches of shade. The walls were cut of square stone blocks, forming guardrails and even steps, so meticulously laid that it seemed as though every portion of the grounds had been sculpted. Lia rounded the corner and started up again, trying to keep her breath. The pilgrims around her were marked with tattoos, and she shielded her face with her cowl. Hawkers tried to sell pies or cider, but she waved them away.

The Cruciger orb was her guide, helping her maneuver the twists and bends as she ascended the heights to the Abbey proper. What she needed and desired was a secret way into the Abbey, one that would bring her past the eyes of the sentinels—the Dochte Mandar. She did not want to meet any more and hoped the orb would guide her to a safe entrance. It did.

Near the fifth level of the city as she walked down a long corridor full of inns and shops, the orb guided her to a secluded park set off by a wrought-iron gate that was not locked. It was rusty and squeaked as it opened, but she walked down a narrow aisle between two crammed buildings that opened to the park full of mature pine trees and stone benches. The inner walls were thick with rose trees as well, which were interspersed and offered a splash of color and wonderful scents. There was no one in the garden. It seemed tucked away and hidden from the main ways she had passed. Lia rested a moment, trying to summon her strength, and then studied the orb again. The pointers directed her to the wall.

As she approached a dark hollow, hidden by the shade, an ominous feeling confronted her. It sent a rushing tingle down to her stomach and caused a swarm of conflicting emotions, which she recognized immediately as those caused by a Leering. She ground her teeth as she pushed forward and the sense of dread heightened so much that her teeth chattered and the urge to run nearly overwhelmed her. She reached out to the Leering with her mind and silenced it, but the feeling persisted, growing worse with each step. In the shade, she saw a symbol carved into the stone wall—two intertwined serpents. It was the symbol she had seen in her visions.

Seeing it caused a sense of dread and fear deep inside her. It was the mark of the hetaera, she realized. It was one of their Leerings. How would she be able to get past it? There was a password, she realized. Just as existed within the tunnels beneath Muirwood, there were Leerings that guarded this Abbey as well. Without the password, she would not be able to enter.

But what was the password?

Lia breathed deeply, staring at the twisting snakes defiantly. She had come too far to be thwarted now. When she had passed the maston test at Muirwood, there was a password she did not know. The Medium had whispered it to her. Confidently, patiently, she waited, pushing down the awful feelings of dread; instead she thought of Muirwood and how calm and peaceful it was. Closing her eyes, she thought of its beautiful grounds, the brilliant tendrils of fern, flowers planted in sculpted stone boxes, the laundry and fragrant sprays of purple mint. She fell inside herself, drawing deeper into the memories. There was the Aldermaston, Pasqua, Prestwich. From the core within herself, she sensed the Medium hiding, aware of her—unafraid of the surroundings but seeing if her fear would get the better of her. She would not let it. Gently, she bid it to assist her with the password, to teach her the command that would silence the Leering and open the hidden passageway beyond.

The orb glowed in her hand, and she thrust her eyes open as a single word appeared on the surface. The Leering was tamed, and the stone moved silently open, allowing her a way inside. Thanking the Medium silently in her mind, Lia ventured inside.

It opened to a narrow walkway between stone walls. One of the walls stretched up so high that she realized she was staring at the base of the Abbey itself. In her mind, she repeated the command. She wanted to find Colvin but in a place where she could meet him privately. If she could not go where he was, then she wanted to go where he would be. She judged that the orb could do this, as it had done it before when she sought him after Almaguer's men had captured him. It would guide her on the safest course, not just the most direct course.

The spindles spun and pointed, and she followed the base of the wall for a good distance before it stopped at another section of wall that contained another Leering. She repeated the request with the Medium, and again the orb flashed and the Leering obeyed. Once more she stepped beneath a short archway and found herself inside another garden. This one was enormous and sculpted, full of shade and fountains and trimmed hedges. There were stone paths winding in lazy circles and rows of flowers and terraced stone boxes. Some plants hung from iron chains in dishes. The cloying smell of star jasmine filled the air. There were small benches and cushioned seats arrayed for guests, though the park was empty. She was grateful to find a stand of plum trees that still were full of ripe fruit. She ate several and savored their sweetness and then stowed some in her rucksack for later. As she looked past the screen of branches and leaves, she saw the citadel-like walls of Dochte Abbey loom above her and noticed windows set into the towers and small balconies. The view must have been breathtaking.

Lia consulted with the orb again, and it led her to the outer wall of the Abbey. She crossed the grass and hedges swiftly, anxious not to be caught wandering there, and she listened carefully for the sound of any intruders. There was a shallow alcove and a door. She reached for the handle, and it opened without resistance. Within was a corridor completely engulfed in stone, as black as a tomb. She swallowed, staring at the orb once again, and it blazed with light as she entered and the door shut behind her.

Lia found herself in a maze of interconnected, narrow tunnels deep within the Abbey walls. The passage was not straight but went up and down, forking this way and that as it followed between the walls of the lower portion of the Abbey. It was designed for stealth and moving unseen. Without the orb, she would have been completely lost. With it, she managed to find her way to a section that led to a winding stairwell. Sweat beaded on her forehead as she climbed the steps, the path so narrow that she nearly felt the walls rubbing against her arms. Higher she went until the orb directed her to a massive stone block set on hinges. There were metal braces set into it, and she saw the place where a loose stone could be pushed from the other side to unlatch it. She put her hand on the wall, her breath nearly bursting.

Was Colvin there?

She waited, stilling her breathing until she was calm again. She tripped the latch and pulled on the stone wall, which slid soundlessly back and opened to the full view of a small, square bedchamber. The only light came from the orb and from a thin curtain covering the sole window. It was not a spacious room. It seemed more fit for a scullion than an earl. There was a small bed, a single leather-bound chest, and a chair. There was no changing screen and no garderobe, only a chamber pot. Lia stared at the room, wondering if the orb would lead her farther, but as soon as she entered, the spindles stopped moving.

The walls were made of stone and very cold. There was a small brazier by the window, but it was full of white ash. Was this Colvin's room? Her heart sank with the realization. The small, confined place was where he was being held prisoner? She walked to the bed and touched the thin blanket covering it and then leaned down and smelled it.

The scent was unmistakable. It smelled like Colvin, and it brought tears to her eyes. There was a pillow and dusty velvet hangings from the square frame. It reminded her a little of Pasqua's bed—narrow enough for only one person and high off the ground.

There was a small cup near the window with sprigs of desiccated purple mint. Lia parted the curtain and saw the windows were dirty, but there was a latch that allowed them to be opened, so she did and stared out at the vista. Iron shutters were recessed but open to the view. She could see the gardens below. The balcony was a decoration; there was no room for a person to stand on it. From her vantage, she could see the ocean stretching before her as well as the cusp of land known as the Spike. The air had a salty smell.

Lia went to the door and tested it, but it was locked. That gave her a measure of comfort that she would be able to hide if anyone came, for the key jangling in the lock would be her warning. She set about studying the room, looking at it with her hunter's eye. There was no food, for example. It meant Colvin did not eat there. The leather-bound chest opened to her touch, and there were several folded garments within. The leather tunic she recognized instantly. There were still blood spots on it from the battle outside Muirwood. She clutched it instinctively and smelled it, squeezing the leather as if it were him. There were linen shirts beneath, and she had memories of washing them. A sturdy pair of boots and a belt with star-stud designs were seen beneath. That was all.

Lia went to the window and pulled down the cup with the shriveled sprigs and smelled them. There was a hint of fragrance clinging to the brittle stems. She imagined Colvin holding the cup and smelling it, trying to remember what it was like to be free.

Was it only a place where he slept? Where did he spend his days? What did he do to prevent the oppression from stealing his spirit?

The Cruciger orb had brought her to the place where she would find him. She knew she would have to wait for him to return.

A chilly sea wind came from the open window, and she shut it, realizing that her long walk during the day had exhausted her and that she was very tired. The sun was beginning to sink toward the sea, and she realized that other than the plums, she had not eaten much during the day. Opening her travel sack, she pulled out the apple she had saved from Muirwood and slowly pulled it free. It was firm and hard in her hand, and she held it near her nose, breathing in its deep smell. She set the apple down near the cup.

Lia waited. The sun set, and the room became thick with shadows. She waited until the moon cast squares of light on the stone floor. She waited, and still he did not come. She was anxious, tired, and worried. Still she waited. There was no sound except her breathing and stony silence. It was cold in the room, and she pulled the cloak more tightly around her, wondering what she would say to him. What would he think when he saw her again?

She waited.

There was no end to the waiting. Drowsiness finally won over, and she found herself huddled on the floor near the bed, dozing. She was not sure how much time passed, but the moon shifted on the squares until even they were gone and nothing but shadows remained. Dozing—waking. Listening—was that a footfall somewhere? A distant laugh? Nothing—nothing but stillness. Deep stillness and smothering darkness. In the dark she began to hear whispers in her mind. The Abbey lulled her to sleep. *Dream of me*, it said to her. *Learn of my ways. We are ancient. You are our sister.*

The rattle of a key in a lock jolted her awake. Lia blinked quickly and was through the stone portal in a moment, pushing it shut but leaving it ajar so she could see and hear into the room.

Torch fire illuminated the doorframe, and she winced, shielding her eyes from the fierceness of the flames.

There were voices, a mocking tone, but she could not make out the words. Then the door was shut and locked again, the keys jangling as the door was bolted. Inside the room, framed only by a single taper, stood Colvin, looking exhausted, stern, and dressed in a rich outfit of Dahomeyjan style. He leaned back against the door a moment, sighing deeply, and then shuffled forward toward the bed.

The gleam of the taper was enough to illuminate his face. There was the scar at his eyebrow, the pucker of concentration, of barely controlled anger rumbling under the surface of his expression. He set the candlestick on the ledge by the window, next to the cup and the apple.

She watched his eyes glance away, and then slowly, his face turned back to the ledge and he stared at the apple. He blinked quickly, seeing it, his expression turning more intense, more focused. Reaching slowly, hesitantly, he extended his hand until it closed around the fruit, his expression all astonishment and shock, as if he expected it to be nothing more than smoke.

He took the apple and brought it to his nose, smelling it deeply. His eyes were shut in intense concentration.

"Lia?" he whispered in the blackness.

Marciana once told me of something that Ovidius wrote: "Happy is the one who has broken the chains that hurt the mind and has given up worrying once and for all." It is true. I feel free at last to act as I desire to act—to be bolder with my feelings than I have been before. When the king taunts and teases me, instead of blushing, I confront him. Today he stammered with surprise and looked genuinely pleased at my rebuke. There was something in his eyes that was not there yesterday—a genuine interest instead of a duty. Even Colvin began to change his attitude toward me today. I am acting more like Lia did, with more courage and determination. We spoke for a long time, and I told him how much I longed to dance. He said he did not wish to dance the way that is acceptable in Dahomey. Here every man gives his partner a kiss when the dance is done. I think that is what troubles him. I said I did not expect him to change his customs or beliefs. That seemed to satisfy him. We did not dance tonight, but I am satisfied that he will change his mind. The king dances with me often. It is but a small kiss on the cheek. There is no harm in that.

—Ellowyn Demont of Dochte Abbey

CHAPTER EIGHTEEN

A Cemetery Ring

Lia answered Colvin's whisper by pulling open the wall and revealing herself to the light of his taper. He stood there staring at her, his eyes growing wider and wider. He seemed not to breathe, as if one more word would make her vanish.

"Is this is a dream?" he said. "You are truly here, Lia? This is no conjuring from my mind? Say something. Let me hear your voice."

A smile spread across her mouth, one she could not have withheld if she had wanted to. "What would you have me say then?" she answered, stepping into the room and leaving the stone doorway ajar.

"How is it you are even walking?" he demanded incredulously. "Show me your hand."

She offered the hand where an arrow had transfixed her palm. There was a puckered scar there, but it was healing and rarely pained her.

"Not that hand—the one with the maston scar," he said.

She offered the other, which was but a pink little blemish against her skin. "Now are you satisfied?"

He stared at her with a mixture of emotions on his face. They were conflicted. She could see part of him was overjoyed at seeing her, yet there was also the look of blatant panic that she was in such a place as Dochte Abbey. He took her hand tentatively. His hand was warm. It had not succumbed to the chill of the room yet. His eyes continued to stare at her face, a battle of emotions going through his expressions, two warring sides that collided and struck and raged inside him of how he should react to her presence.

"You are here," he whispered again, struck with amazement.

"I am here. I am hale. And your sister is safe."

Her words were like crumbs to a starving man. He reacted to them instantly, pulling her into an embrace so tight she nearly squealed with surprise and shock from its violence. His body shuddered as he clutched her, and she held him just as tightly, burying her tears against the velvet jerkin at his throat. His chin rested against her hair at first, and then she felt his mouth pressed against her hair, as if reverently blessing her head. The room had been so cold, and now he was there, all warmth and softness. The velvet jerkin smelled of incense smoke. So did his skin, but she could still make out his own scent, the one she remembered so well.

His voice was just a whisper. "Several days ago there was a storm, a brutal storm that raged in the sea. The storm ended abruptly, and then there was a ship. I saw it from my window. It was a massive ship that sailed toward this accursed place. I could see it from that window, and when I saw it, the Medium whispered to me that you were coming." He pulled back slightly and took her face in his hands. "I have worried for you in recent days. I have been desperate with worry. Something was happening to you. There was danger. It brooded over me like the storm clouds had. I have held vigil for you for several nights now, focusing my thoughts on your safety and protection." His eyes drooped wearily. "I am so tired, Lia. I have never been this weary before. Was that your ship? Was that you...coming?"

She beamed and smiled. "Garen Demont brought word that you were held prisoner here. We were told that they would not release you until Pareigis was set free."

Colvin's eyes widened with panic. "Is she free?"

"No, she is still prisoner. Deliberately, I think. I used the orb to help me find you. I set sail from Doviur several days ago and was caught in the storm."

His eyes crinkled with worry. "How are you even here, Lia? How are you standing? When I left you...how fragile and weak you were. You could not walk. Yet I see you standing before me, and I marvel at your recovery." He pulled back from her to stare at her in amazement, but his hand strayed and grasped at hers. The warmth from his fingers sent shivers down her.

"The Abbey healed me," Lia answered, trying to keep her voice from shaking. She had never felt so flustered being near him before. She savored the way he was looking at her, the attention. "Muirwood has always mended things. The Leerings there are powerful."

His eyes suddenly narrowed, as if she had said something that pained him. "They are, I am sure." A dark look came across his face. "But they are not as powerful as this place." His hand squeezed hers hard. "Lia, you cannot stay here. Of all places, this is the most dangerous for you. If they caught you here, if anyone learned that you are a maston...Lia, you do not understand the danger."

"I understand a great deal of the danger," she replied. "Which is why I came to free you. There are no mastons left in Dahomey,

I fear. If they would destroy me, they would kill you as well. I am grateful you have been preserved."

His smile was bitter. "I am preserved because of Marciana. I had heard she was bound on a ship for Dahomey. I have been in misery because of it." He gripped her shoulders and lowered his voice more softly. "This is the place where the hetaera make their oaths. This is the place where they are trained in the Medium. The whispers at night…they are unbearable. This place is awful beyond imagining. It is a nest of serpents. Lia, the things I have heard…the rituals that exist here. You remember the Whitsunday fair? How the Aldermaston said not to watch the dancing? It happens every night here. I am forced to watch it, Lia.

"I am a prisoner, but this is not my cell. This is my only refuge. And even this refuge is not safe. There is a lavender who is assigned to me. She is a hetaera, Lia. Every day she wheedles me, trying to tempt me. The Gifting you gave me before I left, I cannot tell you how much I value it. I see Dochte Abbey for what it truly is. The encounters here are no coincidence. Every person who speaks to me is trying to wear me down, to make me violate my maston oaths. Every oath. Every one of them. They do not want me dead, Lia. That would be a mercy. They want me to join them. They want me to forsake my oaths as they have. That is what they want from me. But what they would want from you is different." His fingers pressed hard into her shoulders. "They would turn you, Lia. They would turn you into one of them. You must not stay."

The look in his eyes terrified her, but she strengthened her heart. "Why is it that you have not succumbed, Colvin?"

He seemed surprised by the question. Realizing he was probably hurting her with his grip, he looked abashed and drew his hands away from her shoulders while he unclasped his shirt collar from the velvet jerkin. She noticed in the dim firelight the pattern on the fabric, the ribbed shoulders, and golden threads and intricate buttons going down the front. He unfastened several buttons and then withdrew a twine necklace with a ring. The firelight flashed on its surface, and she thrilled to see him wearing it.

"This little ring," he answered her, pinching it between his fingers. "This is what saved me." He stared into her eyes. "I have worn it since I left you. Every day I could feel it against my skin. It reminded me of you and Muirwood and the feelings of the Medium. It has helped me to focus my thoughts when everything about threatened to confuse me. The Dochte Mandar are powerful, but they cannot subvert your thoughts unless you let them. I was not sure how long I could survive in such a place as this. Your ring is the only way I have escaped succumbing."

A surge of gratitude and warmth filled her. She took a tentative breath. "We must get you out of here. Do you know where… do you know where they are keeping Ellowyn?"

He shook his head. "They restrict my contact with her. The Aldermaston here—he is corrupted. I have not revealed to him that I know that. The Dochte Mandar rule. They are making everyone submit to the water ritual. There are whispers that something will happen to those who do not after Twelfth Night. It is fitting, though. Twelfth Night is the celebration of the advent of winter, of the twelve days before the darkest day of the year. Every day the sun is getting shorter and shorter. I dread the Blight will come soon after."

Lia nodded. "It will come that very night. Did Ellowyn deliver her message? What happened?"

Colvin folded his arms and shook his head. "It was treated with great interest and respect at first. The Aldermaston was grave and listened patiently. Then he started to ask questions over the days that followed. He is a cunning man, Lia. He is dangerous. His questions seemed honest at first, and he would listen to our persuasions calmly. But everything he asked caused doubts as to whether he believed it. For example, why was the warning given in our country and not in Dahomey? Of course, he never denied that the Blight was coming. But he challenged and questioned and poked at the circumstances. I realized through the Gifting that he was trying to learn from which abbey we had learned of it. Ellowyn mentioned an abbey in Pry-Ree but could not remember the name. I refused to tell him, claiming I cannot speak Pry-rian. He continues to seek the name of the abbey in Pry-Ree. Would there was a way we could warn them."

"The Medium will do that," Lia said, touching his arm confidently. "Just as the Medium sent me here. The warning has been given. Now we must find a way to get you both out of here. There are secret tunnels within these walls. I am sure one will lead to Ellowyn's room as well. I will get Martin to help us, and we will leave on the ship you saw."

"Martin is here?" Colvin asked, perplexed.

"There is so much to tell you. Here, enjoy the apple while I tell you what happened and where I left your sister."

He gratefully accepted her idea but offered her the first bite of the apple, which she accepted. Never had an apple tasted so sweet to her. She enjoyed watching him devour the fruit, eating it slowly and savoring each bite, while she related her adventures. There was Kieran Ven and the Evnissyen of Pry-Ree and how she had learned that the Apse Veil would not take them to Dochte Abbey. She related finding Marciana in Dieyre's castle in the Stews and watched his face turn pale with anger at what the Dochte Mandar had done to her and what Dieyre had done to Reome. She described Augustin Abbey and its treacherous aldermaston. He coughed with surprise when she described how she had humbled him in front of his steward and thrashed his guardians. She mentioned the cave outside of Doviur where she had slept, protected by a Leering, and confessed how she had thought of him and wondered where he was. As they discussed it, he said he had been wakened that night by whispers that had tortured him with thoughts of her. He had not slept since then, anxious about her and her safety. Finally she mentioned Tomas Aldermaston and the crew of the *Holk,* which had brought her to Vezins, where she had met Dieyre's men the night before and how a lad name Jouvent had brought her the rest of the way.

"I am amazed," he concluded at the end of her tale. "Truly the Medium guided your steps. I will be able to sleep now, knowing that you are nearby. But I must warn you again, Lia. If you are caught, and if they learn you are a maston, they will turn you. There are Leerings in this Abbey that are ancient. There is one that I have come across. It bears the mark of the serpent—two serpents woven together like a strand. There is a Leering down in the gardens that bears this mark. When I touched it, it burned me. Only a woman can touch it, I was told. But in that brief touch, Lia, I saw that it guarded a doorway leading deep into the earth. It led to a chamber full of serpents. Lia, that is where they send girls who will become hetaera. The image I saw in my mind, just in that brief, scalding touch, was enough to frighten me to death. If you do not have a kystrel, they will bite. It is full of bones and death. It is a place of pure fear. There is something unnatural about serpents that make us fear them instinctually. It is such a place." His face was white. "You know that I fear enclosed places. To be buried alive in a pit of snakes that will kill you unless you accept the hetaera oaths. Lia...please...I beg of you. You must not be captured. They would put you in that place. I have feared they would put my sister there when she arrived. I could not bear it if either of you became one of them. Please, Lia. You must be careful."

The image of the serpent's lair sent a shiver of disgust and loathing through her. Yet it also sparked a memory. She had seen the symbol of the entwined serpents. She had seen it burning. An awful anticipation welled inside her as she realized that she would need to find that place. That it was the reason she had come to Dochte Abbey. The Medium throbbed in her heart, calming her. But it also told her not to tell Colvin.

"I will be cautious," she answered, smiling at him. "I want you to sleep, Colvin. I will watch over you."

He shook his head. "Not yet. I hunger to talk to you. There is so much I have learned in this place. So much the Medium has taught me. There is no one here that I can talk to. There is no one here who knows my heart as you do." He leaned forward. "Lia, there is something that has weighed heavily on me. It has been growing heavier and heavier. This is a dark place, but I know that I will be free from it. I long to leave these shores, to leave the shores of Comoros and find a place where such evil cannot exist. There will be a scourging. I can see it. Those who accept the ways of the Dochte Mandar will fall to the Blight. Those who support the hetaera will be killed. I know this is a place of pure darkness where the Myriad Ones roam free. Yet despite this knowledge, I still feel the Medium with me. I have remained true to my oaths. I have not surrendered to their ways." He looked down, his face turning anguished. "I hardly know how to say this to you."

"Tell me, Colvin," she answered, leaning forward. "You can always tell me."

He looked haunted. His eyes were full of emotion. "The Medium bids me do something." He breathed heavily, his jaw trembling. "It is not what I wish. But I cannot mistake the intent of it. Every day the urgency grows stronger. The Medium bids me…it whispers to me with great urgency…that I must marry Ellowyn Demont by irrevocare sigil." He licked his lips. "That I must do this before Twelfth Night at Billerbeck Abbey."

CHAPTER NINETEEN

Martin Evnissyen

For a moment, Lia was breathless. The force of the Medium rushing inside her heart nearly made her gasp, confirming what Colvin said to be true. It was her heart's deepest desire to be his, and only his, and to hear it spoken from his lips caused a surge of pain and excitement she had never experienced before. The problem was that he did not realize that Ellowyn Demont was in front of him.

She tried to say it out loud, but her jaw clenched shut, swollen by the Medium before she could say anything. She swallowed, nearly choking on the words and looked down, struggling with her feelings.

"I am sorry," he whispered in anguish. "I wish I could express to you my feelings—that I could make you see how it made me suffer, knowing…"

Lia put her hand on his and squeezed hard, silencing him. She felt tears in her eyes, tears born of frustration and hope. Blinking the tears away, she stared into his eyes, using every scrap of strength to push the thought at him.

I am Ellowyn. It is I, before you now. I am Ellowyn Demont!

He stared at her in confusion. "Say something," he pled with her. "I have disappointed you so often. I cannot bear your silence. I deserve your rebuke. I deserve your scorn." His eyes burned with emotion. "I love you still. But my heart bids me on another path. It grieves me to cause you so much pain."

Lia shook her head violently, trying to master herself, to find safe words that she could speak. Instantly, she thought of the orb. What if she used it to prove to him who she was? As soon as the thought entered her mind, she felt a wedge of blackness divide her. Shuddering, she understood what it meant. That any attempt to thwart the Medium's will would rob her of its use. The orb was the Medium's tool to help her discover her own identity. But it would not help another to that knowledge.

Lia was desperate. If there was a way to find her father's tome and undo the binding, she would be able to tell him then. If they could find it before reaching Billerbeck Abbey, then she would be free to admit the truth. Hillel would suffer, but Lia knew that Colvin did not love her.

"Tell me what you are feeling," Colvin said, his expression one of tortured confusion. Yet she was not free to speak her true feelings. Her words had to be guarded and permissible.

With a quavering voice, she answered, "I am struggling with my words and my feelings. My heart bids me tell you that..." she swallowed, yearning to speak words that she could not, "...that you should. It is the Medium's will."

He looked at her in astonishment. "You encourage me? You are not hurt by this? It threatens to rip me in half. I do not love her. Yet still the insistence."

Lia closed her hand on top of his again and patted it. "It is not for us to understand why the Medium wills something. We cannot see all things now. But I have learned to trust it, as you taught me to in the Bearden Muir. When you were abandoned at the Abbey, we did not perceive this moment. Yet we were supposed to meet. I believe that. I will trust that all will happen for the best."

His eyes looked doubtful. "You are stronger than I am, then. I will do what it commands me to do. It means that we can only be friends, Lia." He stared at the ground, mastering himself. "You are stronger than I."

No, just wiser, she thought. She reached out and touched his cheek. He looked up at her. "Trust the Medium, Colvin. Trust it. I know you are tired. I will watch over you while you sleep."

He looked at the window. "It is nearly dawn now. You should go while there is darkness to conceal you. You must find where they are keeping Ellowyn. The sooner we leave this awful place, the better. She sleeps late and then studies the tomes with the king and the Aldermaston. Then the dancing again. I will wait for you tomorrow night, and you can tell me what you have learned."

Lia nodded and squeezed his hand. He squeezed hers in return, and the swollen expression on his face made her heart ache. Even though she had given him leave to marry Ellowyn, the thought of it clearly tortured him.

His voice was husky. "You must be careful, Lia. Take very great care. Do not let them find you."

She smoothed some of the hair from his temple, gave him a nod, and then silently slipped through the stone portal into the hidden passageway.

***

The pale blush of dawn crept over the island city of Dochte Abbey. As Lia quietly roamed the street, she was the only being up that early. In many other villages and towns, there were those who started working before daylight. But Dochte was as quiet as ossuaries, row after row of stone houses and shingled roofs. Near the rear of the Abbey grounds on the fifth level still, the Cruciger orb led her to the Abbey stables. There was a sound heard at last, the sound of a rake dragging across muck. The pointers directed her toward it. The paddock was open, though it was dark inside. There was only the sound of raking and the slop of mud and manure. The smell announced it well in advance.

Lia stuffed the orb away and quietly entered the paddock. The inside was full of shadows. Snorts from horses interrupted the stillness as she entered. A heaving noise sounded, and she saw a man hefting a bale of hay and carrying it toward the trough. She recognized his size and features. He wore leathers and a hood but no weapons.

"Martin Evnissyen," she said in a firm voice, announcing herself.

He did not break his stride and slumped the bale down in the trough, where a few hungry horses began to feed on it. He briskly brushed muck from his hands and strode toward her.

"By Cheshu, lass, it took you long enough to arrive." As he entered the shaft of light coming from the dimly lit dawn, she saw his fingers black and filthy and his tunic stained from his work. He smelled horrible.

"Look at you," she said, shaking her head. "If Pasqua could…"

Her voice froze in her throat as the light fell on his face and she saw the black tattoos zigzagging around his eyes. There was a frightening aspect in his expression, a darkness and emotion that came from his look.

He grinned at her, a fierce grin. "Look at you, lass. So tall. Aye, but what you are thinking the way you look at me? Do you fear I took the water ritual? How can I smell thus and have taken the water ritual, I ask you? These lines and marks on my face are an illusion, my girl. Ink and a steady hand. But it keeps the Dochte Mandar from looking at me twice. A rag and some soap and they are gone. It is you who do not look the part being here. Any lad with even one eye would take you for a foreigner here." He glanced around her. "Where is Kieran Ven?"

Lia was relieved and shocked at his banter. He spoke as if nothing had happened between them—as if their separation had only been earlier the previous evening.

"I know who I am," Lia said, looking him deep in the eye. "I suspect that you are not ignorant of it yourself."

He gave her a pleased look. "Come, lass. I must finish mucking the stalls. We will talk as I work." He started back, grabbed the rake again, and headed toward another stall.

She followed close behind him. "Why are you doing this?"

He looked at her and laughed. "To be close to the Abbey walls. I need to work, girl, to pay for my bread. To learn the comings and goings of the Abbey. Waiting for you." He bent forward and started raking the sludge into a pile. "Where is Kieran Ven?"

"At Muirwood, healing," Lia answered.

"Careless, was he? Poor lad. I thought he knew better."

"*I* was careless," Lia said, feeling roused to anger. "And he suffered for it. Many have suffered needlessly, I am afraid. You know the Blight is coming by Twelfth Night?"

"The...Prince said as much. It comes soon. Three days? I was never that Gifted with numbering." The rake made a horrible scraping sound.

"That is true," Lia answered. "Martin—look at me."

"I hear you well enough while I rake."

"Please, Martin."

He stopped, resting his chin on the butt of the pole. He glanced at her, as if the look of her pained him.

"Why did you betray the Aldermaston?" she asked.

His eyebrow quirked. "Is that how you see it? How little you know the ways of the world. The ways of men and kings. Very well, I betrayed him. But you must recognize that I had an allegiance prior to *his*, lass. I had my *own* oaths to fulfill." He started raking again, more vigorously. "An Aldermaston cannot lie. He must speak the exact truth. The Queen Dowager knew this. So did the Earl of Dieyre. I did promise the Aldermaston to take them to a safe haven. There was not an abbey safer in any kingdom than the one I took her to." He paused a moment, using the edge of his boot to control an edge of the sludge. "You had the orb, child. You hunted us, as I knew you would. You surprised me crossing the Myniths and the lair of the Fear Liath. Only mastons can cross that way unharmed."

"I thought you were killed," she whispered sorrowfully.

He snorted. "It would take a greater brute than that to kill me, child. By Cheshu, am I your first visit in Dochte? Or have you found your way inside the lair of serpents yet?"

She looked at him in shock. "How did you...?"

He struck the rake hard against the ground, dislodging cakes of dung. The look he gave her was full of inner meanings. "I know where you are bound. My duty is to help you accomplish yours. That is why I am here. And to clean the stables. They are filthy, as you can see. Do you know where the garden lair is?"

Lia walked to his other side. "I have been to Colvin, that is all."

"Pah! That is *not* why you are here. Forget the lad. Put him out of your mind."

She glowered at him. "How can I put him out of my mind, Martin?"

His expression was full of angst and smoldering anger. "The same way that I must. There is a duty to be done here. The Medium has brought you to see it done."

"To warn the city?"

"Yes!" he answered fiercely. "To warn them even though they will not listen. The Medium is just. There must be a warning before the scourging begins. Who better to give it than a wretched?"

Lia licked her lips. "Whom must I warn?"

He snorted again. "Whom do you think, lass? How can you ask such a question? Is your mind muddled? Who, you ask?"

"The Aldermaston of Dochte Abbey."

"By Cheshu, I almost took you for a simpleton. Well done. Do you know where the garden lair is?"

"Yes, I believe so. It is behind the Abbey, hidden in the trees. There was a plum orchard there."

Martin nodded and jabbed his finger at her. "The very one. I have seen it myself. I work in the morning, very hard, so that I might snoop and sneak while everyone gets drunk on the cider. How did you get through the wall?"

"There are Leerings guarding the portals. The orb opened them."

Martin nodded again, looking triumphant. "Well done. I must climb the walls. There had to be an easier way. The Prince…he told me of the Queen Dowager and her ilk." He looked around surreptitiously and then nudged closer to her. "We must speak cautiously. These walls can hear even whispers. I dare not forget that. There is more I must tell you. Judging by your haggard eyes, you have not slept all night. Do you see the ladder and the loft over there? That is where I sleep. There are some scraps of food, and I will fetch you a meat pie from the market." He started raking again. "I told the stable master that my granddaughter was coming to live with me. I will bark and rave at you. That is my disguise. When my chores are finished and you have slept, we will visit the Abbey again through the secret ways. Go rest, child. Clear your head. There is much to do before you face the Aldermaston."

Lia swallowed and was about to turn away. She was so grateful to have him nearby. His presence filled her with determination to face the horrors ahead of her. The thought of descending into a pit of snakes made her soul cower with dread. But the look of iron in Martin's eyes offered a bit of courage.

Lia gave him a fierce hug, ignoring the dirt and the smell that came from him. He trembled slightly, not soiling her with his hands. As she pulled away, she caught the glimpse of a tear in his hard blue eyes. He fought against his feelings, his bearded face jutting and scowling.

"Well met, lass. By Cheshu, well met." His eyes turned deadly serious. "I will not forsake you. You know that, lass. Not for all the coin or all the glory in all the world. I am faithful to you. I am yours to command."

"Then we understand one another, Martin Evnissyen. I would have you advise me how to free Colvin and…and…Ellowyn. I want them free from their prison before I face the Aldermaston."

There was a half-smirk on Martin's face. "A prison of velvet and gold. A prison of cider and dancing. But a prison, indeed. The Myriad Ones rule this place. The people are all under their thrall. They are blinded to the death that awaits them."

Lia nodded. "It blinds them slowly."

A wooden door banged somewhere nearby, and Martin nodded for her to flee up the ladder while he began mucking another stall.

I do not know what to think. The entire Abbey is fluttering with the news. The Earl of Dieyre arrived. He was set free from Pent Tower under my uncle's orders. He brought parchment stamped with the privy seal giving him wardship custody over me. This means my uncle took the wardship away from Colvin and gave it to Dieyre. I do not understand how that could happen. I am dismayed. Dieyre said that my uncle has given his consent for me to marry the king, that it will heal the rift between our warring factions, and has ordered it to be performed here at Dochte Abbey. If it is done, Demont promises to release the Queen Dowager, and we all can return home in peace.

I have never seen Colvin so angry. He challenged the seal and said it was a forgery. The whole Abbey is in an uproar. Dieyre promised that my uncle was coming in person and would vouchsafe for his instructions. There was a truce agreed upon after we left the kingdom. I do not want to marry the king. I do not wish it. Colvin took me aside and asked if I desired the marriage. I could not stop trembling, for he was touching my hands. I do not wish it. I wish Colvin to take me from this place. I would go anywhere with him. This is not my country. I belong in Pry-Ree. That is where we will hide until the ships take us away if the Blight comes.

—Ellowyn Demont of Dochte Abbey

CHAPTER TWENTY

Leigh Abbey

In Malvern Hundred near the border of Pry-Ree stood Leigh Abbey. It was fashioned in the same image as Muirwood, though it was smaller and not surrounded on all sides by a rotten mass of swamps. The village of Leigh was full of rich and fertile farms, with fat sheep grazing in the lowlands. Those sheep were tempting targets of Pry-rian bandits who were known to cross the border and steal them. What very few realized, however, was that the sheep were Pry-rian by origin and generations before had been stolen from Pry-Ree to feed the hungry during a period of famine. What those from Comoros labeled as theft was true—from a certain perspective.

Prince Alluwyn stood by the windows, where he could observe the approach of the riders and the covered litter. The Aldermaston of Leigh stood nearby and tried to engage him in conversation, but the Prince seemed lost in his thoughts as he stared down the road with uncanny patience. The outriders appeared first, and that was sufficient for the Aldermaston to beg his excuses.

"I see they have arrived. I must greet the king, my lord. You will excuse me while I attend them. I will bring your…betrothed when she has disembarked from the litter."

The Prince did not reply and stared as the Aldermaston scowled at him and then hefted toward the doorway, for he was a very portly man.

As the door shut, the Prince's bodyguard, Kieran Evnissyen, spoke disdainfully in Pry-rian. "The rake. He calls your marriage to Lady Demont a sham. Insufferable."

"Patience," the Prince muttered. He glanced at the young man pointedly. "A man can see contempt in your eyes. Remember that when treating with him."

"This whole affair is contemptible, my lord," he said acidly. "For three years she has been kept under guard since she was captured by that pirate off the coast of Bridgestow. For three years!"

The Prince smirked. "I know the length of time better than any man, Kieran." He turned back to the window. He parted the curtain. "There she is, taking the king's hand."

Kieran rushed to the frame, but the crowd was thronging them, making a view of her impossible. The rotund Aldermaston shuffled back toward the Abbey manor, leading them.

"Look at the gold collar the king wears," Kieran said disdainfully. "He is flaunting his great wealth. But at least he looks like a ruler. Your dress is too plain, my lord."

"It will suit her, I hope. She was raised at a small abbey after all, far from the wealth and splendor that is so ripe within Dahomey."

"But she has been held at Pent Tower where even the butler's costume is finer than yours. It is beneath your dignity."

The Prince smiled tolerantly and waited as the muffled sound of feet quickly approached the door. Kieran retreated into the shadows again, becoming as inconspicuous as a page. He was young, even for an Evnissyen.

The door opened, and the Aldermaston entered again, bringing the guests with him. The king showed his years well, and Alluwyn nodded to him deferentially. His blond hair was well silvered, but it belied a ruthless jut to the chin and penetrating green eyes. His presence reeked of hetaera. The Prince could see their influence on his countenance as marked as any blemish. Rather than exuding light, he seemed to swallow it; every aspect of him was like a vortex, dragging all cheer and brightness and joy from the room. His presence caused a ripple of doom to spread across the opening. The Prince saw the necklace chained around the king's throat and knew it was a kystrel.

"We meet again, great king of Comoros," the Prince said with a bow.

"Well met, Alluwyn Lleu-Iselin," the king answered in a throaty, raspy voice. "King of Pry-Ree for now. May I introduce my fair cousin, Lady Elle Demont?"

As the king stepped away, the Prince was unprepared for the reaction the sight of her would bring. His emotions welled like a flood. She had her daughter's face—the face that had haunted him in dreams and visions for years, the ghost that walked through life near him, whispering of what was to come. The mother and the daughter were distinctive, beautiful, and for a moment he could only see his visions until tears swam and he lost his composure. Summoning his strength, he subdued his feelings, but there was no hiding his wet lashes from the king.

"The Aldermaston will perform the ceremony straightaway in the Abbey itself. You are both mastons and I am not, so I cannot accompany you inside the sanctuary. You may not believe it, but I do not seek your death, Lord Iselin. I seek peace between our kingdoms. In that vein, I suggest a truce to be consummated with this marriage. There will be no incursions into Pry-Ree for five years. In exchange, you will agree that henceforth there will no longer be three kings in your domain. There shall be one ruler. With my cousin at your side, you will do well. Do we have an agreement?"

The Prince stared at the king's audacity, at his interference with Pry-rian custom. It was not for the king of Comoros to decide the balance of political power within Pry-Ree. But the Prince was wise enough to realize that if he refused the request, his wife would be returned to her prison at Pent Tower.

"The nobles of Pry-Ree will balk at this arrangement," the Prince said, doing his best to keep the emotion from his voice.

"But surely you can manage it?" the king replied smugly, his eyes probing and earnest. "What other choice do you have?"

"Indeed," the Prince replied flatly. He saw the situation as it really was. With only one king to rule the entire kingdom, it would undermine the ambitions of the realm. Rather than co-ruling, others would expect greater favors and privileges. It would also mean jealousy, as those who craved the right to rule would be tempted to do away with the Prince. It is so much easier to over-throw a smaller kingdom when it is squabbling internally.

"Shall we ready the ceremony?" the Aldermaston suggested. "To acknowledge, of course, the secret marriage you conducted earlier. Shall we go down, my Lord Iselin?"

"May I speak with my wife before giving you our answer?" the Prince asked.

The king looked startled and then shrugged. "We will await you without then. Come, Aldermaston. Let us retire to another chamber."

The door shut softly behind them.

There was a pause, a moment when they looked at each other, unspoken words passing between them in a rush. Before the Prince knew it, the girl was on her knees in front of him, head bowed submissively. "Forgive me, my lord. I have been a burden to you. I did not know my cousin would place those demands on you. I knew none of it. I am ill to think what harm this will bring to you and your kingdom. If we must delay, I will bear it. If we must part…"

The Prince knelt in front of her and took her hands, smiling through his tears. "No. Hush your fears…I will not be parted from you so soon." He squeezed her hands and stared deep into her eyes. "You will not spend another day in a Comoros prison. You are the lady of Pry-Ree. You are our rightful queen. I will pay whatever ransom to secure you."

She seemed not to comprehend his words. Tears fell from her lashes, but her look was confusion. "How can this be? I know who I am. My father was murdered on the field of battle by my cousin, the king. My mother and I have been outcasts in Dahomey since that time. I was raised in a poor abbey in a poor province. I bring you no wealth, no lands, no position. And because I am a Demont, you incur the king's enmity. All of this is due to a promise you made long ago to my father. I am a burden to you in every possible way. If it would help your kingdom to send me back to Pent Tower, I will face it. Think of your people, my lord. Think of the burdens they must bear if the king gets his will concerning Pry-Ree."

Very slowly, deliberately, the Prince kissed her hand. He stood and pulled her up with him. "You are mistaken. As I look at you now, I see a prize worth having. A prize worth any wait. It is not because of lands or coins or promises that I desired to marry you. It was not even because of your lord father, though he was my ally and my friend."

He escorted her to the window and parted the curtain. "Do you see the mountains? Those are the Myniths of Pry-Ree. They are treacherous to cross. Wedged deep inside is another Abbey—a small Abbey known as Tintern. That is where I passed the maston test, just as you passed yours at Montargis. It is not the size of the abbey that matters. It is the strength of conviction. When I spoke to your father of marrying, you were but thirteen. I knew that you were not ready then, for you were too young. Since the troubles of your Family, I have watched and observed you from afar. I have observed you through the Gift of Seering, which I possess."

He pressed her hands in between his own. "It was not by chance that you traveled by ship to Pry-Ree and were captured. You are a maston, Elle. If I had communicated to the Abbey where to meet me, you could have crossed the Apse Veil immediately. Your years in prison were a proving ground—do you understand? The Medium must prove us before it trusts us. It must prove us that we will be faithful, no matter the temptation. Only through the greatest sacrifices are the greatest powers of the Medium unleashed."

He paused and carefully brushed a strand of hair from her temple. "I was willing to wait to have someone like you. Someone who has passed every test, who has remained constant and true. Being trapped in the tower would have broken the spirit of others, but it did not break yours. You were firm and resolute. I see it burning in your eyes. Your desire was never for yourself. Sweet lady, you are my equal in every way that matters most. That is who I wanted to marry. That is who I swore I would cherish. By irrevocare sigil, it is done. You have sacrificed enough for now. Of this I am certain: you will not leave this place with anyone other than myself. We will cross the Myniths, you and I. There are trees taller than any you can imagine. Giant husks of trees that are fallen and burned out by fire. There are waterfalls beyond imagining. There are fords and coves where the waves obey any who hold the rank of maston. We will see them all together. There is much I have to share with you."

The girl's eyes were wet, and she hugged the Prince fiercely, protectively, and sobbed against his shoulder. He held her, pressing her close, smelling the scent of purple mint in her hair. He was grateful she could not see his face and the storm of emotions that raged across his features as he clutched her. He had loved her since she was a child, loved her in abstraction for who she would become and his knowledge of what her character would be as a result of all her suffering. But squeezing this woman, this woman of flesh and blood, was deeper than an abstraction. He could already feel his heart throbbing with joy as well as looming sadness. *What a contrast,* he mused silently, *loving the woman so strongly who will break your heart with her impending death.* The pain of the thought was exquisite, a deep, poignant shard that penetrated to his soul. The tighter she clung to him, the deeper the burr stabbed him.

When she had recovered from her tears, she pulled away and looked up at him, relief shining in her wet eyes.

"You were worried I would abandon you," he said hoarsely, collecting a tear from her chin.

She shook her head. "No. I was more worried that I had heard the whisperings of the Medium incorrectly. I am relieved that I hearkened to them—that I trusted them."

He smiled. "Well…I will offer you what relief that I can. You have suffered the ill will and opinion of the world long enough. When you leave Leigh Abbey, you will not return to Comoros again. You will spend the rest of your days in Pry-Ree, a queen-maston. It has been several generations since our people had one." He cocked his head to the side, drinking in her face, her expression, the light he saw emanating from her face. The insidious whispers that she and her mother were hetaera were almost amusing if they had not been so insulting. He would not see any marks of tattoos on her skin or a brand on her shoulder to know the truth. Her very countenance radiated warmth and light and liveliness.

He was thoughtful as he asked her, "Do you know how they pronounce this Abbey in Pry-rian?"

She nodded confidently. "I do—for I have studied your mother tongue since I was thirteen. It sounds similar, but there is a different inflection. They would call it *Lia*."

The Prince smiled as he felt the barb stab even deeper. "A beautiful name."

CHAPTER
TWENTY-ONE

Hillel

Lia was asleep almost before her head rested against the cushion of the pallet in the loft, and she slept deeply. The weariness had seeped into her bones, and with little more than a flittering thought at Colvin, just lingering on the memory of his smile and the forcefulness of his arms wrapped around her, she slept and did not stir until Martin crept up the ladder and shook her shoulder. For a moment, everything was a blur, her mind still lost in the fog of sleep, his face foreign with the criss-cross of tattoos, almost menacing. She blinked rapidly, hungering for more rest, but she noticed the slant of the light coming into the paddock and realized the day was ebbing fast.

"You should have woken me sooner," she said, rubbing her eyes.

He shook his head sternly. "Best that you were not seen today. A retinue arrived from Vezins, bearing the tunic and badge of Dieyre. I did not see the man, but I understand that he and For-shee are enemies."

Lia's heart strained with worry. "Colvin," she whispered.

Martin gazed at her sternly. "Focus on your task, lass. Not on his. Dieyre was looking for you. His men were asking if a flax-haired lass had been seen—one without tattoos and who carried a blade. It was wise when you arrived as you did, before the other stable hands were here. I have waited until they all left to drink their cups of cider. Now we can go, but keep your hood up. Here—some food. You must be hungry."

She was, and she took the meat pie gratefully and devoured it. The spices were different from what she was used to, but it was still tasty and satisfied her hunger. He also produced some nuts, a wedge of cheese, and a half-eaten piece of bread.

After she finished the meal, she followed him down the paddock ladder, and they left together through the rear, heading back to the hidden garden she had emerged from at dawn. The weariness was replaced by strength. They walked stiffly together, listening keenly for the rowdy sounds of onlookers and passersby.

"You know more about what will happen than you can say," Lia said, seeing how deliberately quiet he was.

"Aye, lass." His face was stern, his blue eyes narrowed.

"Is it because of the binding? Is that what keeps you from telling me?"

He glanced backward to see if they were being followed. "It is and it is not. I do not know everything that will happen. Or what order it will happen in. What I was told was very sharp at times and very curious at other times. It has been a great many years, which have faded my memory. I know the most important points. But some of it I expected to happen at Muirwood Abbey, and it did not. Maybe it will happen here."

That was not the answer she hoped for. What clues had her father left with Martin to act on? How much had been revealed in his tome? She was anxious to find it—to use the Cruciger orb and find where it was hidden. If she could overturn the binding sigil, she would be free to tell Colvin the truth and end his torment. But as Martin had warned her, it was best to focus on the task at hand. It was probably one of the reasons her father had given her the orb, knowing that she would one day see to find her father's tome with it.

"There," Lia said, directing him toward the shallow alcove that led to the garden. They advanced cautiously, listening to the din and laughter that came over the rooftops from another street, which was more crowded and blustering. She pushed the gate inward and walked to the hidden spot in the wall where the Leering waited. This time, instead of warning her away, it greeted her with an intoxicating smell. There was no feeling of danger at all, only a thrilling sense of excitement.

She paused, staring at it, confused. She touched the Leering and felt at its powers, trying to understand why it had changed. In a moment, the Medium supplied the answer. Once it had admitted her presence with the proper password, she would be allowed to pass it without barrier. In a word, it thought she was a hetaera because only a hetaera would have known the password. Within the stone, she could sense its formidable defenses. Much like the portals at the Abbey, which prevented intruders from entering, the Leerings at Dochte were equally powerful. She questioned the stone with her thoughts, probing to see if another hetaera had passed it since she had left that morning. She had the strong impression that none had.

"What is it?" Martin asked, studying the expression on her thoughtful face.

"The prey is careless," she answered. "It is safe to pass."

They crossed the maze and emerged into the garden beyond. In this case, they were not as lucky as before. There was one person in the garden, which forced them to halt and remain hidden. They observed her from behind the hedgerows and trees, meandering down the walkway, lost in thought. The sunlight was fading still, but there was enough light to see her face when she turned and came toward where they were hiding. Her long dark hair and supple walk were mesmerizing—until her face lifted, and Lia nearly gasped with shock. It was a beautiful girl, probably her own age, with dark eyes and raven black hair. She looked so similar to Pareigis that Lia almost darted from her hiding place and ran as fast as she could. That moment of panic soon passed when she realized that though the features were similar, she was staring at the Queen Dowager's sister. She followed the path and then started when a voice reached them from the far end. Lia recognized the voice immediately.

"There you are," Dieyre said. "I was told I would find you here."

"This is a private garden," the girl said, her voice sly and sultry. "Which of the girls let you in?"

"I hardly remember her name. You are all alike to me."

"Is that so? Even my sister?"

"She is…unique. There is no woman like her in the world."

"Is she still in bondage at Muirwood?" the girl asked with a grin in her voice.

"You know as well as I that no abbey can hold her. She will seduce them all before Twelfth Night. I am certain of it. How fares the little lark from Sempringfall? When do I get to see her? I hear she is much changed."

"You will see her tonight at the fete, of course. You have not forgotten our quaint ways, have you?"

He took her hand and kissed her open palm. "I have nearly died of boredom in my kingdom. Dahomey suits me better. I understand your brother the king arrives on the morrow. I will get the princedom he promised me?"

"You will get everything you were promised," she replied with emphasis. "Including the Earl's sister as your wife. Our spies have seen her. She is being followed."

"Where?" Dieyre demanded, his voice betraying a hint of anxiety.

"In due time. All in due time. Come—I must change before the fete. I have a new gown I have had tailored. You will like it."

Still holding her hand, he escorted her back toward the Abbey walls. "I look forward to seeing Forshee's face when you arrive wearing it. Dahomeyjan customs suit me quite well. I enjoy watching a maston squirm."

Their voices trailed off, leaving Lia smoldering with anger. Martin appeared at her elbow. "Use the orb," he whispered. "You must find the girl and the serpent's mark. It is somewhere here in the garden."

"The mark is everywhere," Lia said, untying the pouch strings and pulling out the orb.

In her mind, she pictured the image she had seen in her visions: the coiling double snakes—the image that burned with fire. The orb swung sluggishly, as if the very air around them was too thick for it to move freely. A dread filled her heart, a deep, poignant dread. They followed the trail through the garden, listening for even the smallest scuff of a boot, a sigh, or a whisper that did not belong to the wind or the leaves. The garden was sprawling, weaving itself around the entire rear of the Abbey proper. Nestled within a maze of hedges, a maze that would have made her hopelessly lost, she found it. The hedge opened and revealed a sunken pit of stone, with a single stone lid as a shield to the opening. Night had fallen fully, and she summoned just a hint of light to observe the area. The feeling was utter blackness. The strength of the Medium in the place startled her—but it was not the familiar essence of Muirwood. It was raw, raging power—a force that made her feel insignificant and loathsome. The power was chained there, like a mighty beast sulking with fury at its captivity. She sensed it brooding beneath the stone.

"This is a fell place," Martin whispered hoarsely. She looked back at him and saw his teeth clenched, his face twitching with concern as the tide of emotion surged around them. "Great evil lurks here. Do what you must, girl."

Lia reached out and touched the surface of the Leering, closing her eyes and preparing herself for the battle of wills that would follow. The impression struck her like a pillar of pure stone, nearly crushing her with its weight. She lost all sense of herself for a moment, all sense of who she was. The blackness solidified around her, and she recognized she had no power to speak, to move, or even to blink. It was nothing but blackness, so thick she could see nothing, nothing at all. Her heartbeat's frantic wail was the only sound that she heard. Not even a breath escaped her.

Then the smothering sense was gone, and she could move again. The Leering had accepted her. She could almost feel a smug smile emanating from it. *Tame me, child?* it seemed to be saying. *I am without beginning of days or end of years. Open my chasm and be acquainted with our ways. We are older than the stars. You will join us or you will die. We welcome you here, child of fallen Pry-Ree.*

Lia's skin crawled at the sniffing, mewling hissing of the Myriad Ones that dashed around her gleefully. They swarmed her, nudging and writhing around her as she knelt next to the stone. It made the small hairs on her skin pucker. What was she to do?

The pull and tug of the Myriad Ones shrouded her, wrapping her in their folds so tightly she almost did not hear the Medium when it spoke. It was more of a gasp—a faint hint in deepest part of her soul.

Seek Hillel Lavender.

She heard it. She understood it. Rising, she shrugged away from the twisted beings lurking within the hedge maze. She walked quickly, following the orb through the maze until they emerged. Martin was chalk-white, his face haunted as he walked.

"What did you see?" Lia asked him.

He shook his head.

"Tell me," she pressed.

"It was not what I saw but what I felt," he answered. "The vilest thoughts came into my head. I dare not utter them. By Cheshu, a wicked place this is." He looked at her fiercely. "You must end this, child. You must end this taint."

She nodded. "That is why I came, I think." Looking down at the orb, she asked it to find Hillel.

***

Without the Cruciger orb, she never would have found the way. It was not a door hidden within the stone past a maze of secret tunnels that led her to Hillel's room. The way was from the garden itself. A series of stone steps, hidden by the trees and the shrubbery, snaked their way up a single tower that rose like a great white torch into the star-spattered sky. The steps were narrow, the width more for the gait and size of a girl than a man. The stair coiled around the tower, ascending steeply round after round. Lia motioned for Martin to wait below, and with the orb in hand, she ascended. There was no railing to prevent a fall, only the wall itself to flatten herself against as she climbed higher and higher. The wind chilled her and made her shiver. Her legs burned as she continued to climb, coming around the tower again and again as she went up the neck of it toward a balcony she spotted high above her. Her heart thundered with the exertion. She knew she would find Hillel's room at the top. There was no doubt of it.

Each step weighed against her, causing her to rest and gasp as she continued up and around, over and over. From the vantage of the tower, she could see the whole of the garden and realized some had lamps lit, which revealed little domes of light. She coughed against her arm to muffle the sound and pressed upward, grateful her leg had healed so well. Another mountain to climb. One wrong step and she would plunge to her death. Best to keep focus on each step as she went. Another and another sweep around the tower wall. The breeze tugged at her cloak, giving her a sense of nausea. She licked her lips, trying to focus her courage. She was almost there.

The steps intersected with the foot of the rail of the balcony. The balcony was not spacious but large enough to stand on and overlook the entire gardens below. Without knowing the stairs were there, one might never notice them at the corner of the railing wall, on the other side of the balcony, without a thorough search. Lia grasped the lip of the stone rail, with stubby pillars creating narrow gaps in it, and pulled herself over it, grateful to be in an enclosed area again and away from the risk of falling. There was a doorway beyond, well-lit with lamps and a cushioned seat. From the edge of the railing, Lia could barely discern the hetaera gardens below. Had Hillel seen the gardens and wondered what they were? Had she attempted to find them and been thwarted? Or had she discovered the steps leading down and found the courage to brave the descent?

Lia heard voices and pressed herself against the wall. She stuffed the orb into the pouch at her belt and waited, listening intently. What would she say to the girl? How could she impress on her the danger they faced and the need to flee?

Very cautiously, Lia waited and then peered around the edge of the doorway into the room. The door was wooden, but there were enough gaps for the light to exit and sound to carry. Lia stared through the crack in the door first and saw movement in the room. There were three girls in the room, but two of them seemed like servants. One of the girls disappeared through a door on the other side. The other lingered, waiting for the third, who Lia hoped was Hillel. She pressed her ear against the crack.

"Yes, you go down ahead," said Hillel's voice, which she recognized. "I am going to write again in my tome and then will join you at the fete. No, do not wait for me. I am slow in my engraving. I know you are excited to see that young knight who danced with you last night."

She spoke in strong Dahomeyjan, but Lia still recognized her voice clearly.

The other girl did not need to be encouraged to find her beau and soon followed the first out the door, leaving Hillel alone. Lia held her breath a moment, waiting just a moment longer to be sure no one returned for a shawl.

Carefully and slowly, Lia pulled on the door handle, and it bucked and resisted, causing her to worry that it was locked. But after the initial resistance, it opened quietly to her touch, the hinges oiled. Lia slipped into the torchlit room, amazed at the gauzy veils covering the enormous velvet bed, the ornate chests, hidebound and trimmed with gold, the fresh rushes, and the smell of purple mint that was almost staggering in its intensity. The fragrance clung to the entire room. There were dishes, shelves, and polished marble tiles beneath the rushes. It was the palace of a princess and contrasted sharply to Colvin's small booth deeper below in the fortress.

There was a waxed wood changing screen, with several gowns hanging haphazardly across the top. It was from the changing screen that the sounds emerged, the rustle of fabric, and then Hillel Lavender appeared immediately around the edge, facing Lia as she struggled to fit an earring into her lobe on her own. The two stared at each other, startled by the suddenness of their abrupt meeting.

Lia took the image in with a rush, her hunter's eye clinging to every detail in a blink. The low-cut gown revealed ropes of gold and pearl necklaces to fill the open bodice. The gown was elegant, worthy of the tailor's praise, but it was just the sort of gown Pareigis would have worn. Lia saw the rings flashing on Hillel's fingers, the rouge on her lips, and smears of kohl at her eyes. But what startled Lia the most was her hair. It was lighter than she remembered seeing before. It was almost a pale blond, and the tresses had been crimped from excessive braiding. She realized immediately why. Hillel was slowly transforming herself to look like Lia in the hopes of winning Colvin's heart.

For a moment, neither could speak. Lia had the queer sensation that she was staring into the eyes of an enemy.

CHAPTER
TWENTY-TWO

Secrets of Dochte

Neither spoke; it was too much of a shock for both of them. But Hillel recovered and her demeanor changed to a look of ardent relief. "Lia!" she gasped exultingly. "I should not have doubted my senses seeing you here. The orb led you?"

Lia could not shake off the feeling that the other girl's first reaction was not friendly. It was an oily feeling lodged in the quick of her bones. "Look at you," she said, staring openly at the transformation. Hillel had always been so meek and timid—but now there was a fire in her eyes that was not there before. "You have changed."

"I have!" she said, nodding quickly. "I am desperate to leave this place. Thank the Medium you have come. It is a boon, Lia, truly." She rushed forward and embraced Lia, squeezing her with affectionate warmth and the tremulous waver of a suppressed sob. Lia smelled her, inhaling the rich fragrance of purple mint. It swarmed them both.

Hillel pulled away, still clutching Lia's hands. "When are we to leave? Tonight?"

Lia was dazed at the response, confused by her initial reaction. She was wary, though, her experience with betrayal reminding her of how uncertain their friendship appeared to be. "I do not know. We must be cautious, for the tide prevents any rash departures. Look at you, though. How changed you are."

The other girl nodded in agreement. "They took all of my clothes, Lia. They promised to launder them but said they were ruined by the salt air and brought me these instead. I feel ashamed to be wearing it, but I have nothing else. More than anything, I long to be away from this place. We must go immediately. Do you have a way out? A way to escape?"

Lia nodded mutely.

"Will you tell me?"

There was that feeling of uneasiness again. Lia shook her head. "The plan is still being formed. I needed to find you and see that I could reach you. It would be best if we could leave in the early morning. The city sleeps late, and there would not be many witnesses."

She nodded enthusiastically. "Yes! Yes, we must go. Have you told Colvin yet? Why am I asking that? Of course you have told him. He was so different today, and I could not reason why. There was a look in his eye—a hope that I had not seen earlier. Do you know what has happened, Lia? The Earl of Dieyre is here!"

"I know—it is impossible how quickly he travels. He came on my heels."

She nodded, her face flushing with emotion. "He brought word from my uncle. I am to marry the king and heal the rift between our factions. The deal was struck, and my uncle said he was coming."

"It is a lie," Lia said. "I left your uncle a few days ago. Dieyre was a prisoner in Pent Tower and managed to escape. It is all a web of lies." Lia gripped her shoulders. "The Blight is coming. It is coming by Twelfth Night. There are only a few more days to leave before it strikes, and it strikes here first. We must be gone."

"I know," Hillel said, nodding. "Colvin and I must go. I do not want to marry the king. I have delivered the message, but they do not believe it. They think the Aldermaston of Muirwood has invented the tale of the Blight to frighten us all. They say so much about him here. The Aldermaston of Dochte—he said that he will wait until the High Seer of Avinion rules on the matter. He says that Muirwood will be stripped of its aldermaston and a new aldermaston will come to power. Did you know this?"

Lia bit her lip, trying to force down her anger. "I met him. I know who they will put in his place. The kingdoms are unraveling like seams when the threads are pulled out. We must get to the ships, Ellowyn. We must leave these shores."

There was a firm nod of agreement. "Yes, we must. But first we must go to Billerbeck Abbey. Colvin wishes to see his aldermaston one last time and warn him to flee. We will try and persuade him to come with us. The Aldermaston of Muirwood too, if he is not ailing."

"Very well," Lia said, still uncertain how to interpret Hillel's actions and words. "There is a secret way out of this tower."

"The steps, yes…I have seen them. They lead to the gardens below."

There was something in her eyes—something that made Lia wary. "Have you…been to the garden?"

"Goodness, no! The steps are so narrow, and there is no railing. It terrifies me to think of it. But the Medium has whispered to me that my escape lies that way. That I must brave the steps if

I am to escape. There are woods beyond the gardens, down the slopes of the hill. I have heard that there are snakes in the woods. Poisonous snakes. With a hunter, I will not be afraid to face them. And with Colvin there." She said it with a blushing smile.

Lia had a thought. An idea struck a chord within her. "Can you get a message to Colvin?"

Hillel smiled demurely. "I will see him shortly."

"Tell him we will leave tomorrow night. I will come for him first, and then we will get you. During the fete, I want you to feign illness and come back to your room before midnight. That will give us more time to get away before the dawn. Dismiss your ladies in waiting. Can you arrange that for tomorrow night?"

"Yes, but where will we go? Do you have a ship waiting for us? They would hunt us, I am sure. We must be able to get away quickly."

"Leave that to me."

The girl nodded with enthusiasm. Her hand touched Lia's shoulder. "I am so grateful you came, Lia. More grateful than I can say. I will be waiting for you tomorrow night. Let me go and warn Colvin. I know he is anxious to depart."

"Thank you," Lia said and slipped back to the balcony. She started down the tower railing, going as quickly as she dared. It would be another long climb to reach the top, and she knew she had to conserve her strength—for she had no intention of waiting another night. They would flee after the fete, ready or not.

***

The garden was wreathed in shadows when she arrived, panting, at the base of the tower. Her breath was ragged in her ears, and her throat was scorched for a drink. She waited a moment, catching her breath, when a dark shape emerged from the trees.

Martin's voice was thick with reproof. "I heard your steps quite plainly," he said savagely. "That was careless."

Lia looked at him and shook her head. "There is not much time. We must go tonight."

"Too hasty," Martin warned.

"That may be true, but I do not trust the girl anymore. She has changed."

"Tell me," Martin said in a flat voice, but she heard the slight growl in his throat.

Lia paced the footpath, motioning for him to follow. "She looks like Pareigis. The same cut of the gown. The same ornamentation."

"Does she wear a kystrel?"

Lia shook her head. "Not that I could see, but the Queen Dowager concealed hers in a necklace, and she had several she was wearing. She has changed the color of her hair. The style of it too. She dresses in the fashion of Dahomey. I fear that the time she has lingered here has corrupted her. Best if we get away tonight. She seemed anxious to go."

"Why is that?" Martin asked. Again, his voice was sullen, deliberate.

"Because Dieyre arrived and said she was supposed to marry the king."

"By Cheshu," Martin said softly.

She looked at him. "Do you already know about this? Is this part of the knowledge you cannot reveal?"

He looked at her pointedly, his features sharp in the darkness. "Speak on. Why must we leave tonight?"

"I told her to warn Colvin we would leave tomorrow night. If she cannot be trusted, she will plan a trap for tomorrow night to catch me before I can free Colvin. I did not tell her about you. If you can get Colvin out, then I will get her out. Then they can escape."

"And?"

"And what?"

"What of you, child. What will you do?" His voice seemed to throb with emotion.

"If they are safely hidden, then I can do what I must do. I will warn the Aldermaston of Dochte Abbey about the Blight. I have already told Colvin about the ship waiting at Vezins. I will meet you there."

Martin was silent for a long while. "It is a sound plan, being brief. There is much that can go wrong. Much that likely will. But you are wise to plot against her before she plots against you. That is thinking like an Evnissyen."

Lia experienced a warm surge of pride at his praise. "Why do you think Dieyre is doing this? Surely he cannot defend his lies? Demont will not come as he said he would."

Martin watched her as they approached the hidden entrance at the wall. It opened for her, and she guided Martin inside. Once the stone door sealed shut, she withdrew the Cruciger orb, and it flared with light.

"When you get Colvin, you will not have much light. He had one candle last night. You must remember the path back to this door."

"It was I who taught you the mazes beneath Muirwood, child. I think I can manage it. Lead on."

She used the orb to point the way and quickly moved through the tunnel. "Why is Dieyre acting this way?"

"He is acting because he knows something we do not," Martin replied. "The Queen Dowager is very subtle. Perhaps he is counting on her subverting the Earl of Demont. If he subverts, then the alliance can be solemnized."

"But he is a maston," Lia said, alarmed at Martin's thinking.

"Even mastons succumb. Even mastons can be plagued with doubts. Turn here. I see the broken segment midway. A good marker. But a wise hunter is prepared." He withdrew from a pouch at his waist a chunk of white stone. He marked the wall with it. "Chalk, from the cliffs," he explained.

They continued through the passageway, winding through the hidden tunnel quickly. Lia remembered the tortuous passage, but the orb was her source of light and comfort. She could not imagine how difficult it would have been to find the way in the dark without it. Martin was wise to leave streaks of chalk to mark the way.

"Yes," he continued sagely. "Dieyre is a crafty man who serves a crafty mistress. Be wary of his lies. The world is full of fools eagerly waiting to hear what they long to be told. A devious man will use that."

"You seem as if you knew him," Lia said. "You described him perfectly."

"I have never met the man. But I am acquainted with his kind. He is driven by his anger. When he does not get what he wants, he calls it injustice. The anger feeds itself and destroys him from the inside. A wise man once taught me this saying from his tome. 'For as the wood of the forest is, so the fire burns. And as a man's strength is, so shall his anger be, and according to his riches he will increase his anger.' Is it not strange that the more someone has, the less he feels he has? Envy can never be sated."

"This way," Lia directed, thinking on his words. It reminded her of the Aldermaston of Augustin. He had a wealthy Abbey and more fine things than she had ever seen before. Yet it was not enough. He coveted Muirwood and its supposed riches. She sighed, longing to be back home and hoping things were not as desperate yet.

They reached the small conclusion to the tunnel, and Lia demonstrated the latch to open it. As expected, the room was empty. She knew Colvin would be with Hillel and she would be telling him of her plan. He would suspect that Lia would be waiting for him in his room, as she had the previous night. The memory of it still burned. It was still too new. Billerbeck Abbey was their destination. That was where they would marry.

She noticed Martin's expression as he studied the room, glancing over the furnishings, the simplicity and sparseness of it. He nodded with approval.

"Thank you," Lia told him, reaching out and touching his sleeve.

The fierce grin answered her. "I am proud of you, lass. Whatever happens, know that I am." He struggled to speak as his eyes brimmed with tears. "*He* would be proud of you as well." His jaw clenched shut, and she could see him fighting against his tongue—unable to say more.

Lia clasped him tightly, kissing his bearded cheek, and then stole back into the tunnel, anxious to return to the tower and wait for Hillel's return. She would do everything within her power to persuade the girl to leave. But if she chose not to go, Lia would leave her trussed up in the room and unconscious.

Suspicious and wary, Lia made her way back to the hetaera's garden.

Lia is here. I am astonished that she found us so easily. Somehow, I knew that I would have to face her again. The Aldermaston said it would happen. Not directly, but he said that before I could gain my deepest desire, I would face an obstacle to that desire that would seem insurmountable. She is the one person who threatens my happiness with Colvin. I imagined her far away, safely away, and that it would be too late when we next met. But here she is, come all this journey to save us. I know she will resent me for taking Colvin away from her. But she does not deserve him. It is a mockery to think that a wretched deserves an earl. If I were but a wretched at Sempringfall, I would not aspire to someone like him.

When I think of her, I remember that terrible dawn when Colvin abandoned me in the ossuaries to rescue her. It was not until that moment when I realized how much I cared for him, and how much he would not return my love because of her. I hate to admit it to myself, but I was glad when she was injured. I even secretly hoped she would die. She did not. There is an image that keeps coming to my mind, again and again. I am putting rocks on her grave. I am burying her beneath a mound of stones. Colvin is with me. I know it is the Medium. I do not know what it means. I think the stones are symbols. They are concealment. They are walls. I must help Colvin bury his affection for this girl so he can then in turn care for me as he ought. There is a noise.

—Ellowyn Demont of Dochte Abbey

CHAPTER
TWENTY-THREE

Dieyre's Chamber

L
ia finished ascending the spiraling stairs outside the tower, and her legs throbbed with the exertion. The night was cold and windy and threatened to yank her from the steps. She focused on the final blocks and reached the balcony ledge, as she had before. It was nearly midnight. Sweat trickled down her ribs as she raised her arms and pulled herself over the lip of the balcony. Her breath was harsh in her ears, and she waited a moment to rest and calm the wild shuddering of her heart. Soon, if her plan worked, Colvin and Hillel and Martin would be gone and slipping away with the tide. She still had a duty to perform—to confront the Aldermaston of Dochte and give her warning. The orb would guide her on the safest route to him and away again. She longed to be back at Vezins, aboard the *Holk* with the others and casting off. The feeling of Dochte Abbey filled her with dark thoughts. Something ancient and terrible lingered in the stones.

The door was shut from the balcony, and she peered through the gap. There was little light—only a few candles burning, filling the room with shadows. It meant the residents were still cavorting at the dance. Lia pushed on the doors, and they opened soundlessly. There was no one inside. Her heart filled with courage, as she knew she would have time to search the room and learn of Hillel's existence at Dochte. First, she needed to find a place to hide.

As she entered, she caught sight of a large desk nearby and on it, an open tome. There were scriving tools around it and small shavings of aurichalcum. It drew her there, or was it the flame of the candle next to it that shimmered off the gleaming surface? She approached, and a feeling of envy struck her next, seeing the words etched on the tome but not able to understand them. It was her place to be studying; it had always been her wish to read. Lia stared at the tome, feeling a surge of resentment threaten to overwhelm her. It was a violent feeling, one that bubbled up inside her with great force and power. She was envious of Hillel and the time she had been granted to spend with Colvin. The wood of the desk was highly polished, the work of a master artisan. The tiles on the floor were shiny and clean. All her life she had lived in an Abbey kitchen instead of the palace she deserved. The envy twisted darkly into resentment.

Why were these feelings so strong? She had not given her upbringing much thought recently. She had never regretted being raised at Muirwood. It was leaving the Abbey that had made her miss it most. Why the envy now? Why the dark thoughts to brood on?

Almost to answer the impression, she felt the Medium warn her—because the thoughts were *not* coming from inside her. The feelings came from outside herself.

Lia turned and saw a set of glowing eyes approaching. Then another. Then yet another. There were six in the room, dressed in black cloaks and wearing the black cassocks she had encountered previously. Her heart shrank. The Dochte Mandar had found her.

Fear engulfed her, a sick tide of fear that swamped her senses, black as night and terrible as the creature in the mountains of Pry-Ree she had faced. They had been waiting for her to return.

Lia fled. She rushed to the window balcony, knowing she had precious moments to get outside. They would have soldiers waiting for her below, she knew that now. But better to face soldiers with steel and fist than struggle against the compelling emotions the Dochte Mandar attacked her with. The night breeze was caressing, but her heart was too frantic to care. She planted her hands on the edge and nearly vaulted it when she realized to her horror that the stones of the stairwell were gone. There was nothing but the naked face of the tower wall below.

In a wild moment of pure panic, Lia wondered if she should jump over the ledge and fall. Where were the steps? The question made her notice the Leering—the shallow indentation in the stone floor in the sculpted shape of two entwining serpents. It was the hetaera's tower. She realized that her previous trips had not gone undetected at all. The trap was left open invitingly.

Martin! He would be trapped inside the Abbey too. They were all trapped.

The glowing eyes formed a wall by the balcony. The man in the middle spoke, his voice thick with the Dahomeyjan accent.

"Welcome, child. Have you received the water rite?" She recognized his voice from the day before as she and Jouvent had been met.

She struggled against the flood of feelings, but she was no match for six of them.

***

They escorted Lia down the inner well of the tower, three in front and three behind her. The only other way down was a plunge down the center of the shaft. Torches burned in brackets on the walls. The wrought ironwork of the torches was shaped into coiling serpents, whose mouths breathed out the flames. Lia shuddered. The air was cloying with the smell of incense. She remembered it from Augustin Abbey. The smell lingered in the air, thick and heavy with its aromatic spice.

When they reached the base of the tower, it ended at an enormous wooden door, which they opened. They proceeded to march her down the corridor.

"Cover your hair," one of them ordered her, adding a flex of the Medium to the command that made it horribly compelling. She complied and raised her hood.

She was terrified. Her mind refused to work, as if the Dochte Mandar were shrouding her thoughts with such terrors that she could not focus on anything, not the path they walked, the number of doors they had passed. She did not know how deep she was in the Abbey. It was elegantly crafted, with beautiful velvet draperies and ancient tapestries. There were pedestals and gold etching everywhere, filling her eyes with the extravagance of the expense.

They ended the journey at a door, and the leading man knocked on it.

Lia prepared to meet the Aldermaston of Dochte. She tried to steel herself, but she could not stop trembling. Her heart ached with despair. Would Martin be able to escape? Would he come for her? Or were the Dochte Mandar truly waiting for him as well?

The door opened, but Lia could not see inside yet, for the wall of black cloaks covered it.

"We have her."

It was Dieyre's voice. "Leave her with me."

"The Aldermaston wishes to speak with her."

"He will. But I paid you to allow me the first chance to speak with her. Give us a moment before the Aldermaston comes. Go."

"As you wish," came an arrogant reply. The curtain of men parted, and Lia saw Dieyre in the doorway, a goblet in his hand, his shirt collar unbuttoned and open, exposing his chest, damp with sweat. His unruly hair was just as she remembered it, and she felt a spasm of dread. The last time they had faced each other, she had tried to kill him, and he had succeeded in killing her.

He seemed amused by the expression on her face. "Come in, Lia."

The Dochte Mandar allowed her to pass them, and she did, entering the room. Dieyre shut the door behind her, letting her pass near him. He seemed to smell her scent as she passed by. It made her feel terrible.

"Are you thirsty?" he asked. He brought the goblet to his mouth and took a sip from it. She could smell the cider on his breath.

It was a bedchamber with no windows. It reminded her a little of the one in the Aldermaston's manor, the one where Marciana and Hillel had slept. There was a fireplace and an enormous canopied bed with huge velvet curtains sprawled open, revealing a disheveled mattress and blankets. There was his sword, propped against a cushioned seat.

"I will not drink the cider," Lia said, turning slightly to glance at him.

He sauntered into the room and set his goblet down on a table after taking another swallow from it. "How about a bath then? I was about to bathe when the knock sounded. You are filthy, Lia.

Such a girl as you should be in a gown instead of that hunter's garb. Would you like me to fetch a gown for you?"

She turned and faced him, angered by his impertinence. "You want Marciana. I know where she is."

Dieyre smiled hungrily, his eyes narrowing with pleasure. "Of course you do. I am sure she was headed to Muirwood when you burned down my castle in Comoros. Really, Lia, that was unfair. I liked that castle." He sighed dramatically. "The question is not where Marciana is now. The question is where she will be going. There is an Abbey in Pry-Ree where she and the others will be sent. Which Abbey is it?"

Lia licked her lips. "You think I will tell you?"

"I know that you will, sooner or later." He lifted the goblet again and took a sip. His eyes smoldered with anger. "For your sake…I mean for Forshee's sake, I hope you relent sooner than later. But relent you will. Tell us everything, you will. You will even join us before this is over, my dear. So why not skip the unpleasantness? You have been running a good long while. But I am a hunter too, and I have chased you down. Have the grace to admit you are caught, you are defenseless, and that nothing you do or say will deliver you from this place until you agree to join our cause. I granted you the chance to join me at Muirwood, and you spurned the offer. I extend it now on the most agreeable terms. Join us, Lia. One way or the other, you will."

"Join you?" Lia asked, nearly chuckling with amusement.

"I am serious. Look at you, girl. Mud-spattered and filthy. Weary from marching across this land. Look at the bath. Does it not look inviting? We can talk while you bathe. I promise you that I will not look. At least we can discuss the terms of your surrender. There are privileges you can barter for. Come, Lia. Take off your cloak."

She stared him in the face. Her voice was low and full of hatred. "Is this how you wooed Reome?"

There was dark fire in Dieyre's eyes. She had no idea how much he had been drinking the cider. "Smell like a pig if you wish," he replied blandly. "I do not have much time with you, so I best dash all your hopes quickly. This is all part of the Queen Dowager's plan. Muirwood will fall by Twelfth Night. She is still there, Lia. She is plotting its overthrow. All the pieces were in place when I was sent to Comoros in chains. Do you think I was under guard for long?"

He stepped closer to her, his eyes having lost all their acidic humor. "There is a traitor at the Abbey, Lia. The Aldermaston will be betrayed, and he will be killed. Demont is already dead. Poisoned, actually. Yes, I know it for a fact. The Aldermaston will take the blame for the Earl's murder as well as the king's murder. Another aldermaston stands ready to fill the void. It all happens by Twelfth Night. The Abbeys have fallen, Lia. All the mastons will be killed—except one. Forshee lives. But *only* if I get Marciana. If she vanishes into the woods of Pry-Ree, then Forshee will die. A terrible death, Lia, I assure you. It will make the death of the Demont Family seem like a blessing. What is coming to those who do not accept the water rite is really cruel. I submitted myself already. So will you. But we do not just want the water rite for you, Lia. No, you have a special destiny. Do you understand me? Muirwood will fall. The stupid warnings you have been sending so urgently are a sham. The Blight is coming at Twelfth Night, just as you predicted. But it is the destruction of the mastons. Their power has failed. No one is left who believes that you must be good, honorable, and self-sacrificing and all that rubbish. I choke on it, Lia." His face quivered with rage. "I have choked on it since Billerbeck Abbey. That will be the last abbey to burn."

"Is that what this is all about?" Lia demanded, stepping closer to him, jutting her chin at him. "You are angry because of what you learned at Billerbeck? That in order to harness the power of the Medium, you had to give up part of yourself? Look at what you have become, Dieyre." She felt the stirring of the Medium inside her, welling up with words. "You are angry because you cannot be as selfish as you want without feeling guilty. You are angry that Colvin's sister does not love you willingly because she will not love you for who you really are. All this rage against the unfairness of the world. You...who were born to privileges and wealth. You...who are gifted with the sword and clever with your words. You...who have everything a man could have and yet still are not satisfied. Do you think that gaining Marciana will make you happy? Do you think it will make the anger go away?"

He stared at her, his eyes narrowing coldly.

"Listen to me, Dieyre. The Blight *is* coming by Twelfth Night. It is not because of the water rite. It is not what Pareigis is planning. It is in *consequence* of what she is planning. It is a terrible sickness that will destroy everyone in these lands—every man, woman, and child. It is truly a Blight, and it will come. This is the last chance to escape it. This is the final hour to flee before it is too late." Lia looked at him desperately, trying to make him see the urgency in her eyes.

His expression was flat, full of skepticism. "How can you say that the Medium will do that? What right does it have to judge and destroy everyone? Who gave it that right? No, Lia. It is you who are wrong. The Medium is real—I have no doubt of that. But it can be controlled by whichever side forces it to obey."

He stepped closer to her, his expression welling up with hatred. "Up until now, it has been controlled by aging old men who strain to pass their airs! For too long they have scolded and nagged and manipulated everyone into accepting their version of controlling the Medium. You are a wretched, so you do not truly understand. Read the words of ancient aldermastons who have handed down the secrets and meticulously copied them in tome after tome. But it is a lie, Lia. Anyone can control the Medium. Even a wretched. Even you. The future belongs to the young. It belongs to those with vision and feelings, not to doddering men who lust after children. It ends at Twelfth Night, Lia. Their rule of shame ends. You will see it before you leave Dochte Abbey. I promise you that. You will see the fulfillment of what I have said. You will see that no Medium comes to save you. No Medium will scourge the land. No—what you will see is us *using* the Medium to scourge the land—to purify gold by fire, as it were. You will live to see it, Lia. And when you have, you will join us, for you will not leave this place until you have joined us. And if you will not join us, then you will be killed. You will not faint like you did last time."

Lia felt the shell of doubt and anger encrusting Dieyre. Nothing she could say would change his mind. He was well past hearing her words.

The Medium forced her to speak anyway. She saw it bloom in her mind, the image as vivid as the noonday sun.

"It is you who are wrong, Dieyre," Lia said, shaking her head. "You will realize it one day when you are the last man alive in all the kingdoms. You will be alone, Dieyre. You will be left all alone. Remember my warning. You are the last man."

Dieyre snorted contemptuously. "You are raving mad," he whispered with a chuckle.

Another knock sounded on the door.

He smirked. "That will be the Aldermaston of Dochte to introduce himself." He reached for the goblet again and took a long, ponderous sip. "When you have finished suffering needlessly, say the word and you will be brought back here. Then maybe you will accept my offer of a bath and a drink."

CHAPTER
TWENTY-FOUR

Almaguer's Revenge

L ia did not expect the Aldermaston of Dochte Abbey to seem so young. She had expected someone as old as the Aldermaston of Muirwood—someone with silver hair and a thick, full beard. Instead, she found a handsome man with thick walnut hair and only slivers of gray at the edges. He had penetrating hazel eyes and an almost pleasant-looking smile. The ceremonial cassock and robes were black and fringed with gold and fur pelts.

He looked at her, gazing at her with his penetrating eyes, studying her for a moment as if nothing else mattered. The look filled her with ice. She had never met someone whose presence was so powerful with the Medium; it seemed to radiate from him. However, she noticed that it sucked the Medium out of her. It was a strong force, a tidal force that leeched life out of everyone near him. Even the Dochte Mandar were made to seem insignificant in his presence. Lia cowered, struck by his presence as if he were on fire.

"Take her to the dungeon," he said in a simple, calm voice.

She glanced at Dieyre, who smiled at her knowingly and inclined his head, as if providing the offer one last time. She was tempted to stamp on his foot. She would have except for the overwhelming compulsion that tugged at her when the Dochte Mandar entered and seized her arms.

Lia was escorted into the bowels of the fortress, plunging into a lair of darkness lit occasionally by the stain of fire from the serpent-torches. She was weak with hunger and fatigue. Fear gnawed at her incessantly, each step bringing her deeper and deeper into the lair. Her heart struck like a hammer on an anvil. There she could not even feel the dregs of the Medium now, except for the Aldermaston's presence. He radiated it so blindingly, yet it was false. It was an aura that seemed to mask his true nature. She blinked, staring at the trim of his hair, the polish of his rings. His clothes were easily the most expensive she had seen.

Ahead a huge iron-bound door was opened, and that is when she heard the scream. It came from a man in agony. The sound made her shiver and shudder. It was pain—a total abandonment to pain. As the scream ended, she heard the voice sobbing and shouting out in Pry-rian, "By Cheshu, I will kill you all! You will all..." The threat was interrupted with another scream.

It was Martin.

The interior was hazy and wreathed with smoke. She smelled something burning. It was a sharp smell, an unfamiliar smell. Her heart lurched with despair.

The room had three men, two of whom were Dochte Mandar. In the center of the room was a Leering. She could not see its face, but she saw its pocked surface glowing red hot. Kneeling before the Leering was Martin, in chains, his hands smoking as they were held and pressed against the burning stone. The Leering was blackened, diseased, and constantly burning, as the one in the grove she had seen before. The torturers were pressing Martin's hands against it, and he howled with pain.

Lia shook with rage, and she felt the hands tighten around her arms. She tried to quell the Leering with her thoughts, but it would not obey her. She ground her teeth, breathless with agony at seeing him suffer. Her mind went black with fury.

With a quick pull on her arms, she slammed her heel on the foot of the Dochte Mandar holding her. He yelped with pain as she tugged her arm free. With her free hand, she struck the other Dochte Mandar in the throat, and he let go as well, gagging at the blow. Lia rushed the two holding Martin, and that was when she saw the other man, the third who had been there all along. He clipped her from behind, grabbing her arm, and then she found herself face first on the floor, arm yanked back so hard she wailed in pain.

"Thank you, kishion," said the Aldermaston. Her cheek scraped against the floor. She could only see the Aldermaston's fur-lined boots. "Chain her hands and ankles. She is as dangerous as this one, just as Dieyre warned. Strip her weapons."

Lia wanted to struggle, but she could not think beyond the excruciating agony happening in her shoulder. The kishion controlled her as the chains were brought. Her boots were removed and her ankles shackled. Her leather bracers were stripped away and replaced by iron locks as well. Lia struggled as they took away her rucksack, her dagger, her gladius, but she could not resist. Someone untied the pouch at her waist and opened it.

"Ah, a Cruciger orb!" the Aldermaston crooned. "How delightful. You are gifted, as we were told. Wonderful. Take the other wretch to his cell. I would speak with her a moment."

Lia was dumped unceremoniously to the floor, her shoulders still throbbing in agony. She panted, blinking the tears away as Martin was dragged to a door made of iron bars and thrust inside.

"Leave us," the Aldermaston said pleasantly.

"Be wary," the others warned. "Be on your guard."

"The kishion will keep me safe. He is trained to kill mastons and hunters—even Pry-rian hunters." The others of the Dochte Mandar abandoned the chamber, and the door was shut and locked from without.

Lia scooted away from the Aldermaston as he approached her. The feeling of everything light and good was sucked from her as he approached. The kishion loitered in the shadows, his eyes on her constantly. She glanced about the room, seeing five doors made of bars on five of the six walls and the other one they had entered from made of solid iron. She could see Martin slumped on the floor, trembling and moaning.

"The only reason you would have this," the Aldermaston said, hefting the orb in his hand, "is if you could use it. You are strong in the Medium, child. That will serve you well here."

Lia clenched her jaw, staring at him with fear and loathing.

He crouched down, squatting close to her so his eyes could focus on hers. The feeling of blackness made her dizzy, forced her to tremble and cower. Her arms were heavy with the chains. "I know who you are," he said. "Who you truly are."

She swallowed, amazed but wary. "You do?" she asked, wondering if the binding would prevent him from speaking it.

"What did the Aldermaston of Muirwood tell you? Or did he ever tell you?"

Lia was silent, waiting for the other man to speak. She slowly slid away from him, until she felt the cold iron of the door press against her back.

He rose, looming over her. Every feeling of warmth and goodness disappeared from her heart and soul in his presence. Every spark of kindness or love sapped away. She shivered with the feeling, even though the Leering in the room made the dungeon stifling.

"Almaguer recognized you," he said softly, almost in a kindly tone. There was nothing kindly in the way it made her feel. "I see it before me as well. You are a Demont. Rub away the dirt and grime and you have your grandmother's features. The slope of your chin. The clever expression when you smile. You are a Demont, child. It is plain for anyone to see." He stepped closer, squinting at her thoughtfully. "It is a wonder Garen Demont did not recognize you. But then the man has always been self-righteous and blind. Yes, child—you are a Demont. How old did they tell you that you were? When was your name day?"

"I am nearly sixteen," Lia said, confused and wary.

"No, you are eighteen. At least eighteen. You likely had your first year before you were abandoned at Muirwood. Too little to remember anything of where you came from. Or who your mother was. Your father was a Demont—a warrior of great ability. He was Sevrin Demont's oldest son, and he died with his father at Maseve. When they sought an alliance with the kings of Pry-Ree, he fell in love with a woman of the court, a lady-in-waiting to the nobles of Pry-Ree. A lady-in-waiting who was a hetaera."

Lia flinched.

"You know the word, for you are a maston yourself. You have studied the maston lore. She betrayed her lover, as all hetaera betray those they love. She betrayed him to his death at Maseve. But she was carrying his child. You. It was in secret, of course. No one was to know that you had been born or when you had been born. You were sent to Muirwood deliberately, child. You were sent there to destroy it."

His smile was cold and cruel. "You are gifted with the Medium. I can sense it in you. You have only begun to learn its full potential. So you see, child—Dochte Abbey welcomed you. The gargouelle let you pass because it recognized the kinship in your blood. You have betrayed the Evnissyen. You have betrayed the Aldermaston of Muirwood. And very soon, you will betray Colvin Price, the man who loves you so fiercely. When you do, you will pass the hetaera test and realize your full power as a daughter of Ereshkigal. You will learn all of our poisons and their many potencies. There are a variety of serpents, after all, each one with venom that can control the thoughts and minds and bodies of those bitten. Your mother killed the Prince of Pry-Ree's young wife after she birthed her first and only child—Ellowyn. Betrayal is your heritage, child. It is the heritage of all wretcheds and the reason they are not allowed to study." He laughed softly. "Poor fool, Gideon Penman. By trusting you, he destroys himself."

Lia's stomach swirled with odd, conflicting feelings. He had unleashed a hurricane of doubts against her mind. But she held firm in what she knew to be true. There was some element of truth in his words. She sensed it but could not discern the specks of gold with all the mud of lies. Instead of trying to, she clamped her mind shut to his ideas. He was trying to poison her thoughts, seed her with doubts so that the Medium would abandon her. When she doubted who she really was, he would then manipulate her feelings.

She remembered her charge.

"I came here with a message for you," Lia said, looking up at the void that threatened to swallow her.

He smiled, seeming impressed with her boldness. "Another warning of the Blight, child? Truly, how tiresome."

"It may be tiresome, but it is still true," she said. "It will strike here first. It will strike the heart of Dochte Abbey. Then it will spread and consume all lands. This is your final warning."

The Aldermaston looked at her, amused. "And who told you of this Blight coming? Hmmm?"

"An aldermaston," she replied.

"From which Abbey? There are many, as you know. I must judge the reliability of your claim, after all. From which Abbey does this warning come?"

Lia felt a pulse of warning. "I cannot speak it. I will not say it."

"Of course not. It is probably a trifling little Abbey hidden in the mountains of Pry-Ree. The warning did not come from Muirwood, the ancient Abbey of your country. It did not come to Dochte of Dahomey. It did not come to Bruge Abbey in Paix. Neither did it come to any of the other chief abbeys. Yes, young Ellowyn gave us the warning when she first arrived. But when pressed as to the facts, she said the warning was given in a language she did not comprehend the nuances of. She was learning a bit of Pry-rian, of course, in her deep studies at Billerbeck. But the Aldermaston spoke the warning to you, and you translated it for her. You, who serve the machinations of Muirwood. You may understand why I am loath to take your word for it, child. It is a warning so obviously self-serving. If it is true, then why have not all the other aldermastons been made aware of it themselves?"

Lia knew the answer. "Because they are drinking your cider, my lord—the poisoned cider that has been so expensive to buy. Only the wealthiest can afford it."

He smiled tautly. "The cider comes from Muirwood, child," he reminded her.

"I know what I speak to be the truth. The Medium has confirmed it to me."

"Yes," the Aldermaston said, nodding sympathetically. He paced slowly within the small confines, his brow gleaming with sweat. "You will find, child, that everything you were taught at Muirwood is a lie. The Medium can make anyone feel anything. Even I can make you believe that what I tell you is true." The force of feelings slammed against her, causing her emotions to well up so quickly and strongly that tears pricked her eyes, and she found herself sobbing uncontrollably. Then she was laughing, hysterically and violently, and she fell against the floor, twitching as the mirth and giddiness swarmed against her. Then sadness—a sadness so deep and terrible she drowned in it. She could hardly breathe through the pain, the pain of a thousand deaths, the pain of a million deaths. Of mothers clasping their dead babes, of girls jilted by love, of widows for husbands. The depth and immensity exploded inside her, blinding her mind to everything but the suffering. Then it was gone, and she found herself huddled on the floor, choking on her tears, clawing at the stone. Her entire body was drenched with sweat.

Sniffling and still feeling the dregs of the emotions, she did not have strength to raise her head as the kishion hefted her body and dragged her into an open cell. From the slits in her eyes, she saw the Aldermaston leaving, mopping his brow with a silk kerchief.

As the kishion dumped her on the floor, she proceeded to retch violently, expelling everything within her stomach. The stink was vile and made her thirsty for water. The heat from the Leering had drained her, and the millstone of emotions had left little else inside her. As she turned to look for something to drink, the kishion returned with a goblet of cider.

"Water," she begged him.

His eyes were flat and cold, and he set the goblet down near her.

She knew that they would never give her any water. The only thing to drink would be the poisoned cider. She remembered seeing Marciana in the tower, frantic with emotions. She also understood what Dieyre meant about her suffering.

It was only just beginning.

All is well and safe. They caught Lia in my chamber in the tower. I knew she would return. I could sense her distrust. They will test her. She will fail. The Aldermaston has told me that she will. She will fail because a maston cannot pass the hetaera test without succumbing to a kystrel. We will leave soon for home. Colvin will take me to Billerbeck Abbey. The thought is already sprouted in his mind. Soon—so very soon.

—Ellowyn Demont of Dochte Abbey

CHAPTER
TWENTY-FIVE

Ordeal

There was no way to tell if it was night or day. There was no way to distinguish sun or shadow. The only light came from the pitch-soaked torches and the incense braziers. The smoke made her mind cloudy and her skin stink. The goblet lay before her, tempting her. Her tongue was dry, her lips aching. Her throat was on fire with the desire for a drink. She was still weak from retching, and they had not brought any food. The kishion stood guard within the shadows, occasionally changing position, pacing like a caged animal. He kept glancing at their cells, and then he would smile, as if relishing the opportunity to torture them.

"Martin?" Lia whispered.

"Aye, child," he said, groaning. She heard him shuffle along the floor of his cell.

"I am sorry," she said.

There was no reply.

The kishion appeared outside her cell. His gaze was full of eagerness. He said nothing, only stared at her. Actually, he leered at her. Prowling the small room, he kept looking over at her, his eyes hungry.

She met his gaze, refusing to be ashamed by his look. She was angry and struggled to control her fury. At long last, there was a jingle in the lock, and then it was opened. The Aldermaston of Dochte entered, but there were guests with him. In his wake came a young man, richly dressed with Dahomeyjan finery. He was tall, well-built, and quite handsome. The young woman holding his arm was Hillel, but he would not have known her true name. Then Dieyre entered, followed by Colvin.

Lia tried to move quickly, but the weight of the iron chains slowed her considerably. She came to the bars and gripped them, hungry to see his face yet tormented by the prospect. Dieyre glanced at her, failing to hide an amused smile, and sauntered around the room, gazing at the torches, nodding to the kishion, and looking rather pleased with himself. She could have strangled him.

The young man in the finery squinted in the gloom. "Where is he? Where is the man who murdered my father?"

The Aldermaston motioned with his long arm. "In chains in that cell, my lord of Comoros."

"Bring him to me," the young man said icily. Lia's heart started to churn with worry.

The kishion nodded and unlocked the cell door. There was a grunting noise, the sound of a blow, and then Martin was thrown in front of the young king.

His face was puffy and bruised, dark with clotted blood. He trembled, his burned hands pressing against his chest. Martin raised his head to look at the young king, his eyes burning with hate.

The young king stared back at him, meeting his baleful look with one of his own. "At long last," he said stiffly. "My father's murderer." His face knotted with fury. His hands clenched Hillel's arm. "Is he the one, my love? Is he the one who abducted you and brought you to Pry-Ree?"

Hillel looked at Martin shyly, demurely. "Yes." She turned her face away, as if she could not bear to look at him.

"Colvin," the young king said next, looking back at the Earl. "You can vouch for his identity? Do you recognize him? Is he the Aldermaston's hunter? He is the one who led you into the trap?"

Colvin was also wearing Dahomeyjan finery. She did not recognize his costume, but she would never have mistaken his dark, brooding look. He gazed down at Martin pityingly. "His name is Martin. I do know that he served the Aldermaston of Muirwood, but I do not know if he serves him still."

The young king released Hillel's arm and crouched before the prostrate hunter. He seized a thick handful of Martin's hair and jerked his head up, to meet his own. There was fury in his voice, pure hatred in his eyes. "You murdered my father. It was your arrow by which he was slain. I have seen the arrow, you filthy wretched. You served Prince Alluwyn of Pry-Ree. Then Muirwood. It is all part of the plot to dethrone my father and to prevent me from achieving my inheritance. You will die, dog." His mouth curled into a grimace of hate. "You will suffer the death of traitors. I avenge him at long last." He cast away Martin and turned to the Aldermaston. "These grounds are under your authority, my lord. May I beg the use of your gallows for this man? I want him hanged. Now."

Lia's heart lurched with dread. *No!*

The Aldermaston of Dochte had a look of sympathy on his face, as if he understood the deep pain that the young king had felt losing his father early to a murderer's arrow. Lia clenched the bars tightly, watching with growing horror.

"Hanging is not the punishment of death within Dahomey," he said. "In our kingdom, the guilty are burned."

The young king's expression was cruel. "Even better," he said. "Dieyre, see it done. Fetch me to watch the execution. Thus will all traitors in my realm be punished."

"As you command," Dieyre said with a flourish.

It was that moment when the Medium whispered to Lia. It was in that moment of terror that she knew what to say.

"My lord king," she said, speaking boldly, pressing her face against the bars.

Their eyes turned to hers, even Colvin's. She saw his expression of shock and then immediate torment. His focus had been on Martin. He had not seen her in the shadows of her cell until she had spoken. The look of anguish on his face tortured her.

The young king turned curiously at being addressed by a prisoner.

"Who is that?" he whispered to the Aldermaston.

Before he could reply, Lia spoke out boldly. "I am Lia of Muirwood. My lord king, you cannot punish this man for murder." Her heart was wild with emotions. She kept speaking, looking into his eyes. She licked her dry lips. "You cannot punish him for that crime, because he did not commit it. My lord king, it was I who killed your father. It was with a hunter's bow and a Pryrian arrow. I was at the battle of Winterrowd, my lord king. I was there, near the hillock where he fell. I confess it, my lord king. The truth of my words can be established by Lord Price, the Earl of Forshee. He knew I was there. And I told him what I had done.

He is a maston, my lord king. He cannot speak a falsehood. Ask him, if you doubt my word. Ask him."

She could not bear to look at Colvin's face. She held the king's gaze, stared at him with intensity.

The young king was astonished. He looked at her in the dim torchlight. He walked closer, examining her face, her hair. "Colvin?" he asked over his shoulder. "This cannot be true."

Lia stared down at the floor, unable to meet Colvin's eyes. She did not want to see the look on his face. The only sound was the sharp hissing of the torches.

"Colvin?" the young king repeated.

"It is true," came the hoarse whisper, full of pain.

"My lord king," Lia said, forcefully and clearly. "I did not act under the orders of the Aldermaston of Muirwood. When I helped Lord Price reach Winterrowd, I did not know myself what would happen. My lord king, the Medium commanded me to kill your father. If I speak truly, then the Medium will not allow the fire to harm me. It commanded me, my lord king. It was the Medium's will because of the many murders your father committed and allowed to be committed in his name. The mastons have been persecuted and murdered throughout your realm…" Lia's voice cracked, and she began to choke. She needed a drink desperately. Squeezing the bars harder, she swallowed and continued. "I submit myself to your judgment. If the Medium spares my life, you will know that I have spoken the truth. This man who has been tortured did nothing. He was not even at Muirwood when Winterrowd happened. He arrived a fortnight after."

The young king stared at her. Hillel stared at her. Lia lifted herself up and dipped her head deferentially to him.

"You serve the Aldermaston of Muirwood?" the young king said, his voice thick with scorn. "I should have known. She has

226

confessed her crime in the presence of two earls of the realm. There is no other need for witnesses."

"Indeed," the Aldermaston said. "May I propose, Your Grace, that we accept her confession as fact? All that remains is whether the Medium sanctioned the act. There is in the gardens on the grounds a Leering that tests the truthfulness of someone falsely accused. In Dahomey, it is called a trial by ordeal. Beneath the Leering there is a cave full of poisonous snakes. If the Medium is truly with her, the snakes will not harm her, as she said. If she is guilty, the venom will kill her."

In Lia's mind, she saw the stone with the serpent image burning. She had visited it with Martin earlier. As she struggled with her fear, she realized that she was going to that Leering. She also realized that it had nothing to do with establishing her innocence.

"A pit of snakes," the young king said, his voice sounding almost amused.

"I submit myself to the ordeal," Lia whispered, shuddering with dread.

"Very well," the Aldermaston said, sounding pleased. "You will face the ordeal at sunset. If you survive at dawn, your innocence will be established. Let us depart and make the preparations. It will be nightfall soon."

Those in the room were compelled to leave, and the kishion dragged Martin back to his cell and locked the door behind him. The Aldermaston let everyone else leave the room first and then motioned for the kishion to approach. He whispered something in his ear and then left the dungeon as well.

Lia's skin crawled as the kishion appeared at the bars, his eyes gleaming with delight. He looked down at the goblet, untouched, on the floor near her. The amber liquid made her thirsty, but she kept her eyes on the kishion.

He took the ring of keys and unlocked her door.

"You look thirsty," he said, bending low and lifting the goblet. "The Aldermaston said you looked very thirsty."

Lia scooted away from him. "I will not drink it," she warned him, tensing her body to fight.

"I think you will," he replied with equal tenacity.

With reflexes faster than she expected, his hand was tangled in her hair and he jerked her head backward. The goblet lip smashed against her mouth.

She knew at once it was a fight she could not win.

CHAPTER
TWENTY-SIX

The Ring

The cider sloshed against Lia's sealed mouth, entering her nose, and she started to choke. By yanking her hair, the kishion would try and make her cry out in pain and allow him to force the liquid into her mouth. There would be no victory if she was wearing chains on her wrists and ankles. Yet she had other gifts that might aid her. Be quick and unpredictable. Force the enemy to react to her.

Knowing he would anticipate her shoving the cup away, she used the chains at her wrists to her advantage. She grabbed the base of the cup and tilted it too fast, splashing her face and front with the amber drink. It drenched her, but now the cup was empty.

The kishion hissed out a curse. She anticipated the boot strike at her ribs and managed to tuck her arms just in time as it landed, but it hurt ferociously. She jerked with pain but did not cry out. Her arm throbbed, but it brought her a moment to collect herself as the kishion skulked out of the cell to refill the cup.

She stank like the cider; it was in her hair, her face, her clothes. She pushed backward until she felt the wall and then climbed to her feet. The cell was small and humid, the Leering in the outer room blazing still. Again she tried to tame it, but it would not obey her. Sweat mingled with the sticky drops of cider. She breathed deeply, fully, preparing for the next confrontation.

The kishion returned with another cup, so full it sloshed on his wrist. His face was twisted with anger and purpose.

"You will drink this," he said savagely. "If I must, I will dunk your head in the barrel and drown you in it." His teeth were crooked. The look on his mouth was horrifying.

"Why must I drink it?" Lia challenged, meeting his gaze with her own.

"Because the Aldermaston commands it," he replied, walking closer. "Before you face the ordeal, you must drink the cider."

He was closer now, and Lia's mind whirled furiously. Even without chains, she was still no match for a kishion. He closed the distance.

"I will do it!" Lia said, shoving at him with her mind. She willed all the force she could muster to keep him away from her. He seemed to stagger a moment, blinded by the intensity of the thoughts she hurled at him. "Do not force me! Give me the cup, and I will drink it."

The kishion looked at her warily, confused.

"Give me the cup," she said, holding out her hands.

He looked skittish for a moment, unnerved by her change of heart. She focused on his eyes, pushing her thoughts at him savagely. "Give it to me," she ordered.

He scowled, still looking confused. "If you splash it at me, I swear you will suffer. If you dump it on the ground, I will dunk your head in the barrel."

"I understand. Give me the cup." She shook her hands at him impatiently.

The kishion reached out and extended it, watching her carefully.

Lia grasped the cup between her palms and stared at the sweet cider. She stared at it hard, smelling it. The idea came to her in a whisper. Ideas always did.

Closing her eyes, she focused on the thought. The Medium began to swell inside her. She did not look at the cider; she ignored the smell of it. In her mind, she pictured the Leering at the laundry in Muirwood. She remembered its face, the curve of the profile, the mouth that spewed water. When the trough was empty, it was used to summon water to wash the clothes. Water was what she needed—clean, cool, refreshing water. The Medium throbbed in her heart, which hungered for the safety and shelter of Muirwood. She experienced it again, the longing for the peace of her home. There were birds chirping in the branches of the sprawling oaks. The grass and flowers tended throughout the grounds gave the air the scent of autumn. The kitchen, with Pasqua and Sowe. In her mind, she could almost see them, hear the cackle of voices, smell the baking bread. She thought of the Aldermaston, his flowing beard and dark eyes, the brooding look on his face. In that moment, her heart panged with regret at all the naughty things she had done as a child in his service. He had been so patient with her. Truly, he had been a father to her. Her belief in the Medium came from him. Even as a small child, she had experienced its power first from her exposure to him, emanating from him as he performed his duties. She longed to see him again, to thank him for all he had done for her.

With the chains on her wrists, she could not make the maston sign. But she did it in her mind as she held the cup. *Make this water.*

She did not open her eyes. She did not want to risk doubt or the fear of failing. She experienced the confidence of the Medium, could tell it was engulfing her like a flood. Lia raised the cup to her mouth and drank deeply, not holding back.

It was water, precious water. She gulped down the entire cup, slaking her thirst. When it was gone, she opened her eyes and saw the kishion squinting at her, as if she were too bright to look at. She set the cup down and then knelt on the hard, warm stones, thanking the Medium silently for intervening. Without another word, the kishion locked the cell door and vanished into the other room.

***

Lia had dozed on her knees and awakened with the sound of keys in the lock. Her knees were cramped and sore from her posture, and she found herself leaning against the wall, her chin touching her chest. Her toes had lost all feeling, and tiny pinpricks of pain flooded her feet and legs as she struggled to stand.

"Lia," Colvin said huskily.

She blinked and rushed to the bars separating them, her heart surging with fire to see him again. Glancing over his shoulder, she saw Dieyre, hand on his hilt. He had a smirk on his face that was infuriating.

Colvin clasped his hands around the bars. "Why did you tell them?" he said sharply, his face flushed with emotions. "Why?"

"Because she is a fool," Dieyre answered, pacing the room languidly. "We already knew it was her at Winterrowd. The cloak and hood were a disguise, but the hair is remarkable. Many saw it. Old villagers saw her roaming the battlefield afterward. Even some children. It was a girl they had seen."

Colvin's hands clenched tightly around the bars, his head bowing slightly. "Why, Lia?" he begged her. His hands slid down the bars until they rested on hers.

I cannot tell you why, she answered with her eyes. She longed to stroke his hair and whisper that it would be all right. To trust her. She was following the Medium's will. She knew her path had destined her to the serpent Leering.

Her voice was firm and purposeful. "You cannot stay," she said. "The Blight is coming by Twelfth Night. You must go from here. You must all leave Dochte Abbey before Twelfth Night."

Colvin raised his head. "I cannot leave you here," he said in a strangled voice. "Do not ask that of me."

"Oh please," Dieyre said plaintively. "Just kiss the girl and be done with it, Forshee!"

Something was pressed into her hand just an instant before Colvin shoved away from the bars and whirled to face Dieyre. Lia nearly dropped it, but she saw the glint of metal and snatched it before Dieyre could see.

Dieyre gazed at Colvin with contempt. "Ah, the fury awakens! You are so easy to goad, Forshee. I have the weapon here, not you. What do you intend to do, glower me to death?"

"You will be silent," Colvin said tightly.

"For the love of beauty, man, act like one! I despise you for your timidity." Dieyre chuckled mercilessly. "What good is your vaunted self-control? When there is something I fancy, I take it. No harm has ever come to me. No black cloud or rain shadow. You are a fool. You crave this girl. Why not take her? I will not stop you."

"If you utter another word," Colvin said with raw fury, "you will regret it. Do you understand me, Dieyre? By the Medium's power, say nothing more or you will be cursed." Colvin's hand lifted to the maston sign. "Another word while in this cell, and you will never speak again. Do you doubt the Medium's power? Then test it. Utter a word and you will see that you cannot." There was a blinding intensity that seemed to shake Dieyre to the core of his soul. He stared at Colvin sharply, his eyes mocking. But would he speak? Would he test Colvin's power?

The two men stared at each other balefully. Colvin waited for the other to speak, to challenge his claim. But Dieyre said nothing. He looked at Colvin and then at Lia. A little curl came to his lip, part sneer, part snarl.

Colvin turned around and then came back to Lia's cell door. He gripped her hands through the bars. "I will hold vigil for you tonight." His hands were trembling. "I will hold vigil, and I will be there when the ordeal is over. I will not leave while you are down there. You can do it, Lia. I know you can." He reached through the bars and cupped the side of her face, his fingers meeting strands of her hair. His face blanched.

"You smell of cider," he whispered, his eyes widening in alarm. He seemed to notice the splotches on her skin, the stiffness in her hair as the cider dried. His expression turned to horror.

Lia looked into his eyes. "I will be all right," she whispered. "Trust the Medium. Trust what it tells you to do."

"Lia…" he gasped, his face twisting with conflict.

A new voice entered the dungeon. "It is time for the ordeal," the Aldermaston said. "I would have the two of you leave. I must speak with the accused and make her ready."

Lia looked over Colvin's shoulder and saw the Aldermaston wearing ceremonial robes. She clutched the piece of metal in her hand, hidden. Colvin stared at her, his eyes piercing her with his worry.

"I will not fail," she promised him.

Colvin and Dieyre left the sweltering room. Lia faced the Aldermaston as he approached, watching as the Dochte Mandar filled the room behind him. There were so many that her heart throbbed with despair.

The eyes of the Dochte Mandar began to glow. Instantly Lia was seized by doubts and fears, whispers of worry, and shudderings deep within her soul. The Aldermaston stared at her cunningly, appraising her appearance.

"When did the Aldermaston of Muirwood first corrupt you with the Medium?" he asked.

"He did not corrupt me," Lia answered steadily, trying to keep the tremble from her voice.

"How old were you? Eight or so? The roots are deep inside of you. It will be difficult to pluck the weeds out. He should not have permitted you to learn. I can sense your strength, child. You are powerful. You will become an even stronger hetaera."

Lia clenched her teeth. "I will not."

He smiled smugly, approaching the bars. His finger grazed one, stroking the iron tenderly. "No man can enter the lair and survive. The gargouelle will destroy any man with madness. Only a girl can enter. It is the hetaera's test. Like the maston test, there are oaths. If you do not make the oaths, you will die. You will die to be reborn. When we next speak, child, you will be one of us."

The feelings in her heart made her tremble with dread. She had never felt so terrified, so alone, so abandoned. They were feelings, but they were not real. Yet they were real. They slithered through her defenses.

Lia stared at him. "I am already reborn. I died at Muirwood. You cannot kill me."

There was delight in his smile. "Remember, child. To survive the ordeal, you must forge a kystrel. It is the only thing that will save you when the light of the torch burns out. The light is the only thing that will keep the serpents from biting you. If they bite you, you will die. Take her to the garden."

As the Aldermaston turned away from her to walk away, Lia glanced down at the thing Colvin had pressed into her hand. It was the cemetery ring she had given him to wear—the ring she had worn as a child since the storm. Even amidst the despair, fear, and doubt, she clung to the thread of knowledge that the ring represented.

They brought Lia to the Leering stone at dusk tonight. We could see it from the balcony as they marched her through the hedge maze. I remember how it felt. The anticipation and dread. Colvin was upset, but I soothed him. He watched as the Aldermaston handed her a torch and she was lowered into the pit. The stone was pushed to cover the opening. She will be there all night. Colvin says he will hold vigil instead of dancing. I will keep him company and soothe his fears. I will stay in his room all night. He does not understand where we are or what is happening. I whispered in his ear that I wanted to leave Dochte Abbey. I whispered that we needed to find a way to escape. He believes me. He believes everything I tell him. It will all be worth it, when he is mine.

—Ellowyn Demont of Dochte Abbey

CHAPTER
TWENTY-SEVEN

The Fear Oaths

As the stone lid of the Leering scraped into place, Lia experienced the sense of utter abandonment. She was in a grave, a narrow slit of a tunnel that stank of rot and decay. Long, wriggling centipedes twisted in the exposed earth. There were mushrooms everywhere, spongy brown with black splotches. The air was stale and fetid. Lia wanted to cover her mouth, but the shackles on her wrists and ankles prevented her. She wore the ring beneath her bodice and felt its firm edge against her skin. The walls were pocked with holes, and as Lia began to walk, she could sense the eyes staring at her from within the holes. There were hundreds of holes, and she could hear the sound of slithering coming from all sides, even above her. She clenched the torch tightly, swinging it as she walked to illuminate the path ahead. The narrow, crooked shaft opened to a small, round room. A power from that room summoned her. She felt the pull of ancient Leerings, vast in power and centuries old.

Leaving the narrow shaft, she entered the room. Immediately the feeling of blackness intensified. The room was full of Leerings, carved into the pillars. It was like the Apse Veil at Muirwood, except the images were different. There were six Leerings, all human-like, women's faces. The expressions were all savage, tortured. There were no doors or archways, only the six pillars on the walls. But there was something beyond the room, beyond the walls—a Leering she could not see with her eyes, but she could see it in her mind. It was a stone Leering with the symbol of two entwined serpents burning with fire. It was awake, eager for her presence. A deep longing filled her and made her shudder. She heard slithering noises and swung around, scattering light down the shaft. The ground was thick with snakes, sliding toward her, tongues testing the air. When she turned with the light, the black, coiling serpents hesitated. Some hissed at her, and it was as if she could understand them.

Learn of us, sister.

Join us, daughter of Ereshkigal.

Know us, mother of abominations.

The mewling sound of the Myriad Ones filled her senses, and she shuddered with the nuzzling of them, as black as soot. Lia turned and faced the Leerings again, walking around the small circle to get a better look at them. Six faces, each with a different expression—and none of the expressions were good. She realized that they were the guardians of the last. She would not be able to visit the final Leering until she had mastered these. The Medium throbbed within each of the six. They were Leerings carved by an aldermaston, so long ago—anciently. They had been assembled to this place by the hetaera, but they were not crafted for evil. They were each unique, different. It reminded her of the maston training.

Lia wiped her forehead on her arm and saw a serpent gliding by her foot. She swung the torch at it, and the creature darted back with the hiss and swish of the flame. How long would the pitch burn? She knew there would not be much time. The room was shaped like the Apse Veil. It was a mimicry of the maston order. At Muirwood, the Leerings had all spoken at once, and she had taken the oaths to silence them. None of them was speaking to her. What was she to do?

Lia approached one of them, its face twisted into a grimace of torment. She licked her lips, wondering if she should touch it. The Medium throbbed in the room, slamming against her mind as she hesitated. She was here for a reason. There was a part of the hetaera ritual she needed to understand. But she should not succumb to it. She knew she had to resist its lure. With trembling hand, she reached forward gingerly to touch it. The torch wavered in her other hand.

As she touched the stone, her mind opened up, and she gasped with amazement at the strong feelings emanating from the rock. The Leering was carved into an expression of hunger, a woman starving to death. She felt her own stomach as it had been for days, fed on meager crumbs instead of the wonderful variety of Pasqua's fare. In her mind, she saw a desperate mother with starving children, pleading and begging for stale bread. The mother had nothing to give the children. The many children. Her husband was missing or dead. There was no wood for a fire, and it was winter—the middle of winter. There was nothing left to eat. Her children were starving. Lia could see the woman in her mind, could see her clutching at Lia's skirts in desperation and realized that the woman was she, in the future. She saw the strands of curly gold hair, the worn lines on her face, the terror of death by hunger. *Please give me something to feed my children! Please do not let them die! Have pity on us! Please! I will give anything—any-thing! Please, a little morsel for my children. Please! There are so many to feed!*

Lia would have done anything herself to shut the screams from her ears. Then she felt it—the answer throbbing beneath the panic. She must give up something. She must give part of herself. She recognized the feelings contained in the Leering. It contained the fear of want. She needed to overcome it.

Lia was a wretched, not a noble, but she had never known hunger until she had left Muirwood Abbey. There was always enough to eat at the Abbey. Pasqua had never let her or Sowe go hungry, not even as a punishment. Hunger had afflicted her on her travels, but with her skills as a hunter, she knew where to find thimbleberry bushes or catch game. Food was scarce, but she had never experienced the fear of want before.

Please save us! Please! A morsel only. Just a morsel! For my children! Only for them!

She tried to take her hand off the Leering, but she could not. It was fastened tight, the feelings growing more desperate. The children were sobbing and tugging at her clothes. What could she do? Then the Leering spoke in her mind. She had to offer something—a part of herself. Something she did not need. That would feed the suffering woman and her children.

Lia thought a moment, and then then insight came. She would give the chains off her wrists.

Instantly they disappeared. The Leering was tamed.

As Lia looked down, she saw snakes weaving around her ankles. The serpents filled the chamber, sliding and weaving through the tangled fray. She swung the torch down, her hands fully free now that the chains were gone. The serpents retreated again, hissing savagely at her. Her heart shuddered with dread and fear, but she did her best to control it. Just seeing the snakes made her want to scream. Carefully, she moved to the next Leering. It was an expression of remorse, of guilt. Lia stared at it, preparing her feelings to be overwhelmed again.

Then she began to understand.

There was nothing to be feared from them except what they represented. There were six fears that troubled the world. Every imaginable fear could be linked to one of these. The Leerings were important because a hetaera faced the training to overcome her fears. By overcoming fears, they could make the final oath that would bind them to the Myriad Ones forever. Overcoming their fear would help them make the final covenant.

Lia reached out and touched the second Leering. Immediately she was swarmed by the sound of jeering laughter. It was mocking, cutting, humiliating. In her mind, she saw a wealthy palace full of beautiful girls wearing expensive clothes and dazzling jewelry. They were all mocking one girl. She was not dressed like the others; she was in hunter rags, filthy, her hair spattered with dirt and sticky with…cider? Lia saw herself, cowering before the onslaught of the humiliation. There was Pareigis among them—and Reome—and even Marciana. There was Sowe, a disdainful look on her mouth, a condescending look that made Lia feel as if she were the ugliest girl in the world. They laughed and scoffed at her. They snubbed her. They pointed at the shackles at her feet and tittered with wicked delight at how uncomfortable she was. The fear of shame.

She would have given anything to stop the sound of laughter. Lia knew what to do. She surrendered the shackles at her ankles. As she thought it, they disappeared.

Lia opened her eyes. Part of the room was glowing now. In the center of the room behind her came the aura and heat of fire.

She had not noticed before, but there was a hollow in the center of the floor, an indentation in the rock in a whorl pattern. It was full of shimmering metal, the liquid metal of the chains now reduced and purged by great heat. The metal bubbled and smelled acrid. It was a kystrel being forged.

She gasped with shock as she realized another purpose of the Leerings. The kystrel was being forged out of her own fears. The Leerings took her feelings away from her and implanted them within the amulet.

Confusion struck her. Was she doing the right thing? She hesitated, but she felt the throb of the Medium again, guiding her to the next Leering. The torchlight was fading, the pitch being consumed.

The next face was full of pockmarks. Lia bit her lip and reached out to it. Again she was plunged into a swarm of emotions. The fear of sickness and disease. The fear of plague. She smelled rotting flesh. She heard the hum and buzz of flies swarming all over her body. Lia recoiled, disgusted by the feeling. The air had a putrid stink to it. Fever raged through her body; Lia could never remember ever feeling so terrible. Every bone and muscle ached. Her stomach and insides clenched and twisted. Her throat burned with fire. She had to surrender something—to give a part of herself. Her outer garments—her cloak and girdle. With the thought, she realized that each surrender stripped her of something more and more important and made it easier to lose something else. It was like the story she had heard as a child, one that Pasqua told that came from the Aldermaston, about the lark who gave up her feathers for treats until she could no longer fly. After losing her cloak, what would she lose next? She had no possessions—no knives or gladius. Not even the bracers—but she had her leather girdle and cloak. She gave that, and the festering feelings vanished.

Lia's breath came in shuddering gasps. Each time she had quelled the Leerings, she felt a giddy sense of excitement swelling inside her. It was billowing, growing stronger with each one. Her thoughts warned her of the danger. Being free of those fears brought with it a sense of triumph and glee. With the kystrel around her neck, she would never go hungry. She would never get sick. She would never be taunted again. It gave her power over all those things. It had the power to banish any fear—any at all. She blinked with the magnitude of the thought. What a temptation. The snakes were still coming in, slithering through the stones, hissing at her. Part of her no longer feared them.

Lia touched the next Leering, one with a face so worn away by time that she could hardly tell it was a woman. As her fingers grazed the stone, she saw herself as a shriveled old hag, stooped with age. She was sitting in a cushioned chair, speaking to someone…but she could not remember his name. She was desperately trying to recall the name, but she could not. It was an old man, a man she should know. A man with a brooding face and silver hair. She should know his name. She had spent a lifetime with him. What was his name? Why could she not remember it? Her heart spasmed with fear. There were faces of little ones surrounding her, patting her hands—her wrinkled, fragile hands. She stared at the splotches on her skin, the tangled veins. The fear of losing her beauty and body. The fear of losing her memory. The fear of age.

What did she have to quell the Leering? What could she give? Her clothes? Lia wrestled with the decision. What would be required of her next? Her chaen? The ring at her neck? Yet she was trapped, unable to release the stone unless she gave something up. She would be trapped in that vision, those thoughts, until the fire sputtered out and the snakes bit her. She had to do something. She had to act.

She could see why a girl would be tempted to follow the trail. The fear of growing old and decrepit. Could the kystrel keep her forever young? She felt the surge of the Medium and the horrible truth it showed her. The kystrel could create the illusion of youth. It could make someone feel young, even if he or she was not. It was a deception of the cruelest kind. By being a maston, by learning the full depths of the Medium, she could forge a new body that would be forever young. A kystrel could not offer her that—only the illusion of it.

Ugly. Hideous. Revolting. Lia was stuck in her mind, trapped by the doubts of what she should surrender. Hetaera would find it easy to surrender. For them, the fear of ugliness was worse than the fear of hunger or the fear of shame, or even the fear of sickness. They would give up what was asked, and if they did, they would find the next surrender even easier.

Lia understood. The hetaera test was robbing her of all her outward things. It was taking away everything external so it could mold her into a new creature. It would take away her rags and replace them with silks and velvets. It would take away her chains and replace them with bracelets and necklaces and ropes of jewels. And it would eventually take away her chaen, the only thing left that would protect her.

But the Leerings were not evil. Why then was she being tempted to give up her possessions? Why was the hetaera's path the only path? The mewling sound coiled around her. She felt the snakes weaving around her legs.

It was the Myriad Ones influencing her thoughts, she realized. Surrounded by them, deep within their lair, she was hearing them more clearly. They were luring her down the path, but it was not the only path. It was not the only way to be free of the Leer-ings. She must surrender something. She must surrender a part of herself.

If everything she had learned at Muirwood was true—if the maston oaths she had taken would one day entitle her to receive a new body that never aged or died and that would allow her to cross the Apse Veil and return to Idumea—why should she fear old age? If joining with another maston, bound by irrevocare sigil, would eventually produce children so strong in the Medium that they could raise her dusty bones and give her back her life—was there any reason to fear growing old or losing her youth?

No.

She remembered what she had seen when she had died, how the Apse Veil had drawn her toward it, summoning her back home to Idumea. It was real. The Medium was real. That fate…that future—was real. What she needed to surrender were her fears.

It came as a blaze of light to her mind. She had gone hungry, but she had never starved. The Medium had always provided her with food—thimbleberries in the woods or the flesh of a quail. It would never let her starve to death, even it required food to appear with the dew of the grass in the morning. Why should she ever fear it? And what of shame? What did it matter that Pareigis wore gowns and jewels? She had never sought or cared about hav-ing Reome's good opinion while so many others did. What for? She was a silly girl who had been seduced by a powerful man. What did her scorn mean? Nothing! What power did disease have against the power of the Medium? It could heal any wound, recover any illness. Why be afraid of sickness when the Medium could overcome it?

That was what she needed to do. She realized that the Leer-ings could be crossed if she surrendered her fears. The Leerings were not trying to subvert her. It was the Myriad Ones who were trying to subvert her, to tempt her to put on the kystrel in the promise that it would banish her fears. She did not need a kystrel to accomplish that.

In her mind, she made promises to herself: *I will never fear hunger. I will never fear shame. I will never fear sickness. I will never fear age.*

The grip of the Leering ended. A small gleam of light came from the flickering torch. She stared at it, knowing it was almost out. The serpents coiled around her body. Carefully, she lowered the torch until its light touched their black scales. The serpents hissed and withdrew from her. Lia lowered herself down and crawled to the next Leering, using the torch to clear the path. The kystrel burned hideously, the metal bubbling with anger and frustration. The keening in her ears warned her of the anger of the Myriad Ones. Reaching out, Lia touched the next Leering. It was in the shape of a corpse, eyes closed. She knew it already. The fear of death.

As Lia touched it, she saw in her mind the vision she had seen before. She was dead and being buried beneath a mound of stones. Colvin and Hillel were there, placing the rocks that became her bier. It was a vision of the future. She had seen it before. Dread swelled inside her.

Learn of us, sister.

Join us, daughter of Ereshkigal.

Or you will die.

She knew that if she did not join the hetaera, she would not leave the ordeal alive. Those who did not pass the test were killed. Was she prepared for that? Was she prepared to fail in her charge? Twelfth Night was in two days. It was early still. Was there a final warning to give? Was there something else she must do?

Was her life required by the Medium? She had given the message. She had warned the people of the coming of the Blight. Would her death trigger the Blight? Was that what the Medium wanted of her?

In her mind, she saw Hillel sidling up to Colvin, comforting him, stroking his arm as they stared at the mound of stones. Colvin's face was ravaged with grief. Lia saw the look in Hillel's eyes—the gleam of triumph. Her blood boiled with fury.

Take the kystrel. You are stronger than her. Your feelings are stronger than hers.

Take the kystrel. He will be yours. If you join us, he will be yours.

If you scorn us, he will be hers. Give yourself to us. Know our ways.

The light of the torch was nearly gone. Lia hesitated, her soul wrenching with pain. But she would not surrender to it, even if it cost her life. The Medium had whispered to Colvin that he needed to marry Ellowyn Demont by irrevocare sigil. If he took Hillel to Billerbeck, he would marry the wrong girl—but perhaps the Medium would bind him to Lia regardless because of who she really was. Could she give up having Colvin in this life in the hope of having him forever?

The pain of the decision was excruciating. Jealousy, greed, hatred—and worst of all, fear—all of the negative feelings swarmed her. She crushed them beneath the heel of her mind. No, she would not give in. With her hand still on the Leering, she set the torch down on the ground and stretched to reach to the final Leering. Its crushing weight slammed upon her.

The fear of betrayal.

Oh yes, she was expecting it. She saw Hillel for who she was. She saw that she had visited the hetaera garden already. During each visit, she had slowly given away her fears, one at a time. Her last act was to betray someone. She had chosen to betray Lia.

Caught in the crushing grip of two ancient Leerings, Lia experienced the salty sweat streaking down her body. The agony was unbearable. Fear of betrayal was worse than the fear of death. Colvin would succumb to Hillel. After all, he was only a man. The Aldermaston had taught her that women were more powerful. It would take time to wear him down. But if Lia died in the pit, would he keep faith to her memory?

The choice is yours. Join us, and you can avert this fate. Join us, and live forever!

You are a daughter of Ereshkigal.

When the mastons are dead, the hetaera will rule the kingdoms.

Lia bowed her head, knowing what would happen.

I will not fear death. I will not fear betrayal. I will do the Medium's will.

The two Leerings released her. The serpents surrounded her, eyes and forked tongues probing her. There was only one more Leering, the one she could not see—the one beyond the wall. Lia stood, heart heavy but feelings firm.

She left the small cone of light and wandered into the dark, no longer caring what the serpents did. The Leering pulled her forward, beckoning her with its power.

The stone wall blocked the way. She reached out and touched it. Immediately she was overwhelmed by a force so powerful it dropped her to her knees. There was a rush of pain and pleasure, a jolt so violent and heavy that she was overwhelmed by its power.

A voice thundered in the stillness of her mind. She recognized the voice from the night before the battle of Winterrowd.

Speak your true name and enter. Give me power over you. Speak your true name!

Lia stared, dumbfounded, paralyzed by the weight and ferocity of the voice. She tried to open her mouth, but the binding sigil prevented her. She could not say it. She would have. Her will was so small and frail next to the strength she faced. It was Ereshkigal's voice. She had never experienced something so powerful before, something that was ancient beyond anything. A presence stirred in the room.

Speak your true name!

But Lia could not. Of course it would be this way. The hetaera would never risk their lair to any maston. They would not risk it without the assurance that any who entered would fail.

Lia's mind burned. She could not let go of the stone. She saw the burning image of the twin serpents just beyond the wall, mocking her.

You thought to tame me? I, the mother of hetaera? You are nothing compared to my power. You will give your body to my minions. You will surrender who you are to me. You will surrender your will to mine. Speak your true name!

Lia could not.

The fire from the torch guttered out.

The first fangs bit the flesh of her legs as she knelt near the stone. Then another bite. Then another. The poison rushed through her, burning from her legs up to her waist. It was quick and painful. Then there was blackness.

CHAPTER TWENTY-EIGHT

Birth

The horse was lathered in sweat and foam as Prince Allu-wyn crossed the threshold of his ridge-top palace. He had not slept since learning that Elle was laboring with the child, too early. They were not expecting the babe to be full term for another cycle of the moon, and the news had shocked him. As someone with the Gift of Seering, he knew that he would die shortly after the babe's birth. He had hoped for another fortnight or more. Clutching the leather reins, he swiveled off the saddle as his steward, Davtian, approached.

"Where is your escort?" Davtian said, his eyes wide with out-rage. "Did you leave the Evnissyen behind?"

"They are not far behind," the Prince said, tossing the reins to a stable boy. "How fares my lady?"

"My lord, there are traitors to Pry-Ree lurking everywhere, some even in your own household. You should not have risked riding alone, even a short distance. Your enemies seek to ambush you."

"How fares my lady?" the Prince repeated, striding toward the keep.

"My lord, a moment first." There was a firm tug at his sleeve.

"What is it?"

"My lord," the voice was full of pain. "The birthing was early, but she did well. She was healthy yesterday. Her cheeks full of color. She was anxious to greet you with your daughter. But my lord, during the night, she fell sick. A raving fever has taken her—the milk fever. The Aldermaston has laid hand on her, but she will not recover. There is no Gift of Healing to be given. She is so weak, my lord. Every moment we fear is her last, but she strains to stay alive. To see you." The steward's lip quivered. "My lord, I am so sorry. She awaits you in your bedchamber."

The Prince had prepared his heart for this. But even then, when the hour was come, he shrank from it. The pain of losing her sent shards of agony piercing him like arrows. His vision blurred with the rush of tears, but he shook his head and stumbled forward, dizzy with the news. His temples throbbed with thunder. A cleft had opened up inside him, gaping and savage. Nothing could have prepared him for that moment. The weight of it amazed him.

He took the tower stairs, rushing past servants until he shoved his way into the bedchamber, dark with shutters and curtains, only sputtering torchlight to see. The smell of the room was death and blood. The midwife was there, her face ashen when the Prince entered. She fell to her knees, sobbing.

The Prince walked past her, touching the crown of her head tenderly, patting her hair. Then he knelt by the bedside and gazed at the colorless face of his wife, her skin glistening with sweat. Her fevered lips were panting.

The urge to heal her was so strong that he almost could not control himself. She was alive, barely. She clung to the threads. Beneath the coverlets, she only wore her chaen—her sweat-soaked chaen. It was torture seeing her ravaged by the fever. A word of rebuke and the fever would depart. By raising his hand to the maston sign, he could preserve her life.

But the Medium forbade it. He knew what he wanted to do, yet he also knew what he was meant to do. He leaned down and kissed her forehead.

Elle's eyes fluttered open. "You…came."

His throat was too tight to speak. Her hair was listless, the color draining from it. He took her frail hand in his and kissed it. "I will not leave you," he whispered huskily.

"She is…so beautiful. Our child."

"From her mother," the Prince said. He smoothed the clumps of hair from her forehead.

Her eyelids were shutting. "It is time. I waited…for you… long as I could."

"Thank you. I love you, dearest. I love you, my heart."

"I see it," she whispered, her eyes shutting. "I see…the Veil…I see…"

His throat constricted, and he stifled the moan before it escaped his lips. He kissed her hands, her eyelids. Like water seeping through his fingers, she left him. Her body remained, enshrined in the coverlets and blankets, sheathed in a blood-flecked chaen. But with his other eyes, he saw her, radiant and beautiful, rising from the bed. Tears coursed down his cheeks, and he shuddered as she laid a ghost-like hand on his head. With her other hand raised in the maston sign, he heard her ethereal words.

I Gift you, Alluwyn Lleu-Iselin, with the Gift of Death. That you will not suffer fear. That you will not suffer pain. That you will feel nothing but the joy of having served the Medium faithfully. I will wait for you, my love, in the kingdoms of Idumea. Join me there, with my father and mother. With all our ancestors who have gone before. While the abbeys still stand.

There was a tug as the Medium drew her away. In his mind's eye, he could see her go, a shaft of light that winked and was gone, passing the Apse Veil into a better world.

"My lord," Davtian said, his voice choking. "Do you wish to be alone with her? Shall we depart?"

The Prince rose shakily to his feet, using the bedstead to brace himself. "Where is my daughter? Where is Ellowyn?"

The midwife stared at him, her face ravaged with grief. "My lord, I beg your forgiveness. I did my best. There was no one sick in the chamber. I swear it!"

He looked at her with sympathy. "I do not blame you. Thank you for bringing my child safely into this second life. Where is she?"

"With the wet nurse, Myrrha."

"Thank you." His heart shuddered with dread. Myrrha was a hetaera.

"Davtian, I would see my child. Take me to her."

They walked through the chamber and went into an adjoining one where the servants slept. His worry intensified, but he held it in check, trying to calm the rage that bloomed inside. Davtian went ahead and opened the door. Then he warned the Prince back a moment because Myrrha was suckling the child. The girl covered herself and stood, cradling the little bundle. There was another babe playing by the stool, another girl, but she was a year old and toddling, though she was tiny.

"My lord," Myrrha said, surprised at the arrival. She gave him a sultry smile. "You have a fine daughter. Your lady said she was to be named Ellowyn. She is Ellowyn Demont, by our customs. She is healthy, my lord. No sign of the milk sickness."

"Let me hold her," the Prince murmured softly, approaching the girl as he would a poisonous serpent.

She sidled up next to him, brushing her shoulder against his arm. He gritted his teeth, keeping his expression guarded. She wore a perfume that was cloying and sweet. Her mistress lay dead in the other room, but she showed no indication of grief.

"Such a delicate child," the girl said soothingly. "Each is a gift. She has a special destiny." With a long finger, she ran it down the babe's nose. Little Ellowyn tried to nuzzle it.

"Thank you," the Prince said, carefully taking the babe into his arms. She seemed reluctant to let her go. Though her eyes were smiling cheerfully, the look did not match her smile.

The Prince stared down at the flawless little face, the pink skin so warm and soft. He stroked her cheek with his nose, savoring the smell, the wisps of hair, the tiny fingers that curled and reached. As he stared at his daughter, her eyes parted, chalk-gray as most newborns were. There was a serious look in her expression, a contemplative look. His heart broke again with pain.

"You will want to be near her, while you can," Myrrha said. "The invaders have entered Pry-Ree's borders. The king of Comoros hunts you. I will be near so that you can see the child often before you return. I will keep her safe, my lord." Her eyes gleamed like a cobra's.

The Prince looked from her to Davtian and noticed the Evnissyen had finally caught up to him. They were standing outside, staring at him with smoldering anger and budding concern.

"Leave us," the Prince said to Davtian.

"My lord?" the steward asked. The Prince never allowed himself to be alone with women other than his wife, no matter the circumstance.

"Leave us," he repeated.

Davtian obeyed, his face betraying his alarm. The door shut softly, but it caused the baby to startle.

The Prince turned and looked at Myrrha coldly.

Her expression turned from anticipation to alarm. She stroked the ridge of the chair with her finger. "It is normal, my lord, to feel the loss keenly. She was a great lady. A noble lady in every way. If I may be any comfort to you...?"

A spasm of lust went through his body. With ice-like control, he turned his thoughts to Tintern Abbey. He remembered the oaths he had made, one by one, when passing the maston test. One by one, he recommitted himself to them. She stared at him, curiously, her face ranging through complex emotions.

"Where is your kystrel?" he asked her. "Who wears it?"

It was as if he had thrust a goblet of chilled water on her face.

"My lord?" she asked, pretending to be confused.

"Your thoughts betray you, daughter of Ereshkigal," he said, taking a step closer to her. "So do your fears."

"I fear nothing," she replied, her eyes darting one way and then another.

"Who wears your kystrel?" he asked again, tauntingly.

He could feel the Myriad Ones now, mewling and hissing throughout the chamber. They skulked and glared at him, at the child out of their grasp. He clutched the baby close. "Who wears it? Speak—I command you by the Medium."

Her voice came out unnaturally. It was full of loathing and was more of a snake's hiss than a voice. "Your brother." Her fingers, which a moment before had gently stroked the baby's nose and the smooth wood of the chair, were hooked like claws, as if she were preparing to strike him.

"Which of my Envissyen will betray me?" he asked. "Speak!"

"Tethys," came the hissing voice.

He stared at her coldly. "I speak your true name. You are Chione, the Unborn. You will depart."

The hissing sound turned into a rush of wind and a screech. The Prince made the maston sign. "You are Chione, the Unborn. Depart."

The girl's face was stricken with fury and rage. The Myriad Ones howled with torment as the wind blasted against them.

"You are Chione, the Unborn. Depart!"

On the third command, the wind stopped. The Myriad Ones were gone, and Myrrha slumped to the floor. Her body convulsed, and then she slowly, shakily, lifted herself up on her arms. She looked confused, bewildered by her location. She looked up at the Prince, her face a mixture of dread and sickness. She looked around quickly, scanning the floor.

"Was I…dreaming?" she whispered. "Where is the babe? Oh, you hold her. Was I asleep?"

The Prince stared at her. "Yes…in a way. What do you remember?"

"A room was full of serpents. One of them bit me. Where am I? My lord? Is this Dahomey?" She glanced around the room. "These are Pry-rian curtains. The rushes are from our moors." She looked up at him, and then her face quivered with horror. "What have I done?" she whispered, gasping.

"You are a hetaera," the Prince answered sadly. "How can you use your power without your kystrel?"

Her hand went to her shoulder, as if it burned her. She nodded, her eyes filling with tears. "What have I done?"

"I will tell you, Myrrha. You will not wish to hear it. You killed your mistress, my wife, the Princess of Pry-Ree." His voice was thick with emotion. "You killed her with your hands. Days before, you murdered a man with a dagger. His body was found, but no one knew who had done it. It created suspicion. It caused distrust amidst my servants. After this child was born, you went to the corpse and handled it. The bodies of the dead bring diseases. You carried those diseases on your hands and touched my wife as you washed her. She is dead from the milk fever because of your hands and what you touched. Why do the Myriad Ones want my daughter?"

Myrrha's eyes blazed with terror at the Prince's words. As he spoke, it was as if she had witnessed everything she had done but from another's perspective. The horror of it made her face twist with pain and dread.

"Answer me," the Prince said forcefully.

The girl doubled over and vomited on the rushes. She trembled and quivered, her face turning as white as milk. "I am undone," she moaned. "They will kill me if I betray their secrets. I will die if I do not, for I am a vessel of the Myriad Ones." She looked up at him fiercely. "Save me, my Prince! I beg of you, save me!"

We buried Lia this morning. We covered her body with stones, just as the vision showed me. There were serpent bites all over her body, and she was black and bloated. Colvin wept silently, crouching before the makeshift ossuary. He kissed her forehead, despite the threat of venom there. I thought he was going to take the kystrel from her bodice, but he did not. The knowledge that she had succumbed to the hetaera test crushed his spirits. It is dusk now, and the fete is about to begin. Tonight we will depart Dahomey, arm in arm. We are lovers now, in secret. He will defy them. He will betray the young king and forswear his oath of fealty. Together, we will sail for home, where we can marry at Billerbeck Abbey, bound together for all the ages to come. My work here is complete.

—Ellowyn Demont of Dochte Abbey

CHAPTER
TWENTY-NINE

Ereshkigal

The struggle for Lia's soul began with the serpent's bite. When the venom from the fangs entered her blood, she collapsed in agony. The snakes engulfed her, slithering around her, biting, striking, and piercing her skin with their poison. Her body convulsed, and she became rigid, paralyzed by the venom but still awake. She could sense the Myriad Ones snuffling around her; she could hear the eager whine in their voices. Lia could not move, but she could hear everything. Another bite, another sting in her flesh. The venom overwhelmed her physical senses.

Darkness engulfed the room as the torch finally failed. Strangely, she could see. There was something in the dark, a form shifting, coalescing from the blackness and rising up until it formed the image of a woman. She had felt the presence before the venom had made her fall. The Leerings in the room shuddered with power as the woman appeared, their carved faces distorting, the stones glowing white hot. She wore a violet robe,

decked with gold and jewels and precious stones. She was dev-
astatingly beautiful. The sheer essence of her drew Lia in with
admiration. A child of Idumea, a presence and a force that went
beyond anything Lia had felt. She felt ashamed looking at her, for
the woman was staring at her, eyes silver-white. In her hand she
clasped a golden cup. Mist wreathed the rim.

Daughter.

Lia shuddered at the greeting, for it was full of warmth and
empathy, not the anger of before.

"I am not your daughter," Lia whispered, staring at the
woman. The gold gleamed about her wrists and throat. The violet
shape of the robe clung to her tightly, swaying as she approached.
She paused to stroke the side of a Leering, and it burned even
hotter.

*You are my daughter. I am your mistress. I am Ereshkigal,
mother of the Unborn. Serve me.*

"I will not," Lia said, trembling with dread.

The white-silver eyes flashed with anger. Gracefully, she lifted
the cup and swallowed some of its misty contents. The drink
smelled inviting, like cider and sugar, and sent pangs of cravings
inside Lia.

*You will serve me, daughter. All who enter this sanctuary serve
me or perish.*

"Then I perish," Lia said.

The woman's will lashed against Lia's, so strong and vicious it
seemed to pluck her by the head and strike her against the walls
of her own mind. She remembered the feeling, the night before
Winterrowd, when she had stumbled against the king's thoughts.
She was insignificant next to this power. It could crush her mind
with a simple flex of thought. It could reduce her to a gibbering
mass of flesh.

Behold!

The scene changed, and Lia was suddenly back at Muirwood, within the cloisters. It was nighttime, and the two of them were alone. Row after row of shelves, mound after mound of tomes. The wisdom of the ages, compiled in a single Abbey. They were written in different languages, from hundreds of aldermastons. Each one contained specks of wisdom and the knowledge of how to interact with the Medium.

All these are yours, if you join me. My daughters speak every language. They read and engrave. It would take a lifetime to master all of the knowledge amassed here. But as my daughter, you would be able to read them all. My gift to you, child. I give you this. Serve me.

Lia hungered when she saw the stacks of tomes. All her life she had wanted to study at Muirwood. She had wished to learn its many secrets. All were laid before her. The entire collection would be hers.

"It is a lie," Lia said, shaking her head. "You offer what is not yours to give. What use would the tomes be without the abbeys?"

Again, she saw the woman's eyes flash with anger.

The power of life and death is in my hands, child. Would you have your precious Abbey survive?

Immediately she was drawn back, swept away in another vision. This time, they stood together on the Tor, overlooking Muirwood Abbey in the valley below. The Abbey was burning. Lia gasped as she saw the flames searing the sky. The stones were burning. Burning! She could hear screams coming from the Abbey, even that far away. Lia's heart wrenched with pain and sorrow. No! Not her Abbey. Not Muirwood!

Everyone you have ever loved in your childhood is trapped inside. We have barred the doors. Will you listen to them burn, child? Know that you can save them. You alone have the power to save them. Join with me, or they die. Surrender your true name. Your earthly tongue cannot speak it, but your mind can. Think the name and you give it to me. Give it to me, and I give the Abbey to you. The only one that will not be destroyed by fire. I will give you the lives of your friends in return for your allegiance. Serve me!

Lia heard the shrieks and hugged herself in agony. She could not bear it. Was Pasqua down there? Sowe? Brynn? Was Edmon there? The Aldermaston? They were her Family. What about Reome and her unborn child? Had she sent them both to their deaths? Lia struggled with despair. A thought. It begins with a thought. If she only thought the name, surrendered it to Ereshkigal, she would have power to save her friends and those she loved.

Lia trembled with purpose. "I will not," she answered. "Though you kill everyone dearest to me, I will not serve you." Lia glared at the woman, seeing the anger flare even brighter in her eyes.

The scene changed again.

She had seen this vision before. Colvin and Hillel were placing rocks on her body in the hetaera gardens at Dochte Abbey. The look of grief on Colvin's face made her long to reach out to him. He knelt by the column of stones, his eyes wet with tears, and he gently lay his hand on her head. No prayer came from his mouth. There was nothing there—only deadness. Slowly, he stood. Hillel leaned against him, her face pinched with sadness and a concealed smile.

Lia watched as Hillel received the Cruciger orb from the Aldermaston. She used to it direct Colvin to the dungeons. There was a short fight between Colvin and the kishion, who drove the man backward into the bars, and then Martin strangled him mercilessly. The cage was opened, and Martin nodded in sadness as

JEFF WHEELER

he was told of Lia's death. The image flashed to a ship, the *Holk*, crashing through the waves as it struggled to reach Comoros before Twelfth Night. The wind lashed at it, heaving on the water. The storm threatened them, but it was Hillel controlling the skies with Ereshkigal's power. The wind blew them home. Another change, and there were horses riding hard for Billerbeck Abbey. It was dusk, the eve of Twelfth Night.

You cannot stop them, the woman whispered. *He is under my thrall. All men succumb to me, child. No one can resist the power of desire. I can stop the ceremony. I can prevent the binding of their union. Or he will be hers forever. He will be banished here, as I was. Forever. When he dies, he will become a Myriad One. Is that what you wish, child? When the abbeys are all burned, there will be no gates back to Idumea. The dead will be trapped here forever. Join me, and one abbey remains. One gateway will be left open for the dead to return. This is your gift to the world, child. Join me, and you save him and yourself. He will be yours and not hers.*

It was the hardest choice of the three.

Lia bowed her head, pained to the deepest clefts in her soul at the thought of losing Colvin to Hillel. But even more painful was the thought that if all the abbeys were burned, it was true—no one would be able to return to Idumea after death. The abbeys were the links. Without them, it would take years and years to construct another. Even the survivors of Pry-Ree, even those who escaped by ship, would have to start building them anew, stone upon stone.

Lia could see Colvin's face in her mind as he knelt across an altar from Hillel. He looked determined—fiercely determined. Their hands clasped.

You are so young, the woman said soothingly. *Why lose your life when you are but the bud of a flower and have not yet tasted the*

264

first kiss of sunlight? Do you desire children? Do you desire posterity? You will die here, child. Join with me. Save the tomes you crave, the abbey you adore, and the man you love. A thought is all it will take. A single thought. Give me your true name. Think it.

The feelings were so intense that Lia thought she would die from them. But how could she die if she were already dead? Drawing back into herself, she realized that everything Ereshkigal had promised her was a lie. She had no such power. Her only intent was to make Lia surrender to her will by promising anything she could imagine that would tempt her. It was a deception. All of it. Had she not promised Hillel that she could have Colvin? If that promise was broken, then why not any other promise made? Why did she want Lia to surrender her true name?

Then she understood. It came as it always did when the Medium spoke to her. It was a little whisper of insight, a bit of wisdom broken free from the chaff. The Myriad Ones were the Unborn. They did not have bodies of their own. When they were banished from Idumea, they hungered to take by force what they could not enjoy naturally: a body. Her body. If she surrendered her true name, a Myriad One would enter inside her body and control her. She would do Ereshkigal's will in all things, enjoying the body, using it, and then fling it aside when it was past its usefulness. Then she would inhabit another and then another. Lia was not needed. It was only the shell they craved, not the pearl within.

Lia looked up at the woman, her flowing robes and dazzling jewels. Illusions. She had nothing, wore nothing. Despite her strength of will, she was powerless against Lia. She could not force her to relinquish her right to her own body.

Lia stared at her. "Be gone."

The look in Ereshkigal's eyes hardened with fury. *You will give me your true name!*

"Be gone."

The feeling in the room swelled with hatred and fury. It was so shockingly strong that it stunned Lia for a moment. The woman shrieked, and the sound scalded Lia's ears and made her flinch.

"I speak your true name. You are Ereshkigal, the Unborn. Be gone!"

Lia felt the Medium churning inside her, growing stronger and stronger.

I will destroy them all!

The woman's form began to hiss and dissolve.

They will all die, one by one! You have no boat. No orb. You have nothing! You are nothing but a pitiful little wretched. I killed your father and mother. I will kill all you love or who love you. I will kill them all, and they will be banished here as I am!

Lia stared at the fading form. "I am coming for you, Pareigis. I know your true name."

It was at that moment that she awoke, eyes blinking against the glare of lamp lights. She smelled cider and incense and heard the crackle of a hearth fire. She also heard a voice—the Aldermaston of Dochte's voice.

"She is waking at last. The transition took longer than I expected. Come closer. They are very strong when they awaken. Do not be alarmed; the skin blotches are fading now that the poison has finished its work. Bring the lamp and some cider. She will be thirsty."

Another voice was next to her, Dieyre's. "Can you hear me? Do you remember your true name? Waken, hetaera."

CHAPTER THIRTY

Awakening

Lia was surrounded by men. As her eyes opened, she saw them hovering at the bedside. There was the Aldermaston of Dochte, the Earl of Dieyre, and three Dochte Mandar, one holding a blazing torch.

"The bite marks are fading," the one with the torch observed in a low tone.

"She must have struggled fiercely," murmured another.

The Aldermaston stared at her, his face betraying a certain eagerness. His hand strayed toward her hair. "Are you awake now? What is your name?"

Lia's mouth was parched and thick. Her body was weary, for she had not eaten in a long while. She tried to lick her lips, and the Aldermaston gestured for a chalice of cider.

"Drink it," he offered. "It will soothe your thirst and strengthen your hold on her mind. Does she fight you still?"

Dieyre's arms were folded and he looked at her curiously, his face crinkling with thoughts. "Are you certain it worked?"

The Aldermaston gave him a waspish look. "Of course it did. No one has ever returned from the lair themselves. No one." He turned back to Lia. "What is your name?"

Lia parted her lips to speak, to whisper, and the Aldermaston bent lower to hear it.

She hit him as hard as she could in the face. The blow crushed his nose, and there was blood everywhere, spurting as he roared with pain and flailed backward. Lia swung her leg around and kicked one of the Dochte Mandar in the chest, shoving him back. Her strength ebbed like sand gushing from a ripped bag, but she managed to find the floor and continued the attack.

The two Dochte Mandar in front of her snarled with fury, and their eyes blazed silver-white. She was assailed by terror, their own terror, but she brushed the emotions aside. She dropped low and clubbed one in the groin with her fist and then back-turned her knuckles as he crumpled in agony and struck his temple. The blast of emotions intensified like a storm, but she fought against it. The fear rolled over her like oil and slipped away, unable to sink inside her. The Aldermaston cupped his face in his hands, cowering from her, but the other Dochte Mandar barraged her with emotions, trying to smother her with them as if they were heavy blankets. But the feelings would not stick. They slid off her harmlessly.

Her knees buckled with weariness, but she was determined to fight to the last.

"I am Lia!" she said savagely. "I am myself and no other. I passed the ordeal. I spoke the truth."

The Dochte Mandar's white eyes blazed with determination. They thrust feeling after feeling against her as they backed away, amazed at the strength of her will. Lia rushed forward and tripped one of them, yanking on his sleeve to topple him to the ground. She was about to tear after the other when she remembered Dieyre.

Too late—his arm clamped around her throat, and he hoisted her backward so that her feet left the ground. She struggled and thrashed, trying to claw him with her nails, but his leverage and stance were perfect. Her air vanished. She could not breathe. The bulging muscle in his arm flexed, and there were dots spattering in front of her eyes. She pulled against his arm, trying to clear her throat for a gasp. Dizziness washed over her, and then she was face down on the bed, coughing and spluttering.

"You are pathetic," Dieyre snarled. "The lot of you. Stanch the blood, Aldermaston. Your nose is broken, but you will not die of it. And you—do something useful instead of clutching your manhood and moaning, you craven sot. Send for the kishion. Move, man, before I get even angrier."

Lia heard sounds, but she was gasping for air. It took several moments before she could see again, and she whirled on the bed. Dieyre stood over her, arms folded, his eyes intense.

"They are gone," he said, nodding toward the room. She recognized it as his bedchamber. "I will grant you that when you last left this place, I truly believed you would return a different person. I am in shock but not…surprised. You have always had a habit of thwarting my plans. Yet I can see that it is you still. I recognize the defiance that should have been purged by now. How did you manage it, Lia? You are as stubborn as an ass in the mud."

Lia trembled with rage. She wanted to flail at him with her fists, but she knew she was too weak and tired.

"What day is it?" she asked him in a low tone.

"Twelfth Night," he replied. "The sun is about to set." His face twisted with irony. "So I would assume it means that the Blight is truly coming?"

Lia nodded.

"How?"

"I do not know," she answered, her shoulders slumping. "Where is Colvin?"

The smirk that came in answer was infuriating. "He left the night before last. We gave you a proper burial, of course. You looked disgusting with all those purple bite marks when you were lifted from the lair. But the bruising is fading." He gave her a scrutinizing look. "The venom of the snakes is not fatal, as you have no doubt realized. It feigns death. But it does not kill. It makes it easier for the Myriad Ones to take over. To settle."

She was relieved that Colvin was gone. He thought she was dead, however. That was a problem.

"So you do not know how the Blight will come?" Dieyre pressed intently.

She shook her head. "It comes tonight. It will strike here first."

"Do you remember the promise you made to me?" he asked. "More like a prophecy than a promise."

"I do."

Dieyre leaned closer, his arms still folded. "Is it too late for me to switch sides again?"

It made her stomach twist with rage and anger. "I despise you, Dieyre."

He glanced at the door and then at her. "I can live with your scorn, Lia. Truth be told, I have a fleet of mercenaries ready to sail to Comoros and invade in the king's name. I was intending to bring you with me. This is not your kingdom. This is not your land. I could use a hunter in my service—especially one as talented as you. I need your help to find Ciana because I know she will not submit to the water rite, and I wish to be on the ships when they leave. Whoever will not submit will be executed. It begins tonight. They will kill even you if you do not submit. Comoros is the last kingdom to fall. We have mercenaries and Dochte Mandar in the ships. Demont is already murdered. There is only Forshee and the mastons left to defend, and we outnumber them. They will not stand against the fear. The king wants Forshee's head on a pike, for he took his betrothed and ran away with her. It has all happened according to Pareigis's plan. Yet despite all these advantages, I have a nagging feeling inside me that you may just win. I have never met anyone as persistent as you. As determined as you. I can get you on my boat and bring you to Comoros. If you help me find Ciana, I will help you save Forshee."

There was the sound of footsteps coming down the hall. Dieyre glanced toward the open door and then back at her. "What say you? Will we help each other?"

Lia pushed herself up and glared at him defiantly. "I can never trust you, Dieyre. I will get free without your help."

"I highly doubt it, Lia," Dieyre said, glancing again at the door. "I know what they will do to those who will not take the water rite. They will kill you tonight. Right now, in fact. Let me help you."

Lia shook her head. "If my work is finished, then it does not matter if I die."

His face twisted with frustration. "You are too stubborn, girl."

"I know who you serve," Lia said tautly. "I know who she really is. You are a puppet."

Dieyre's eyes blazed with anger, and his face flushed with emotion. He grabbed her arm and hoisted her off the bed. His gaze was like fire. "But you resisted her!" he hissed in a whisper. "Show me how! I did not believe it could be done, not after you have first surrendered. You broke her spell on that mute slave. Break her chains on me!"

Lia saw the panic in his eyes. It was the look of a drowning man who had long abandoned flailing in the water. "I cannot break the chains you forged against yourself," she answered. "She snared you long ago in the form of a girl you desired. She lulled you with false promises. But in the end, she betrays us all. As she will betray you. I cannot stop that, Dieyre. And I cannot break your chains any more than I can make you an honorable man. I cannot undo all of the choices you have made."

His jaw clenched with frustration as the Aldermaston returned, his nose purple and his face still sticky with blood. His eyes were murderous as he pointed to Lia.

"Take her above, and let her join the others doomed to die."

Dieyre's expression hardened. "What if she submits to the water rite?" he asked.

The Aldermaston's expression was mottled with hatred. "She had her chance already. Take her."

***

Lia's wrists were chained again in irons, and she was dragged up the steps, exhausted. When she reached the outer doors, she felt the cool breeze, but the air was sharp with a burning smell. Even though the sun had set, the sky was illuminated by fire. As Lia struggled to see, she saw a crowd of fifty or more, forced to kneel in the turf. They were surrounded by Dochte Mandar who wore the kystrels openly on top of their cassocks. Their faces were striped with the twists and insignias of tattoos. Some of the prisoners were children.

Lia was forced to kneel amidst the other prisoners. The faces around her were drawn and pinched with fear and dread. Many were whimpering. Some were crazed with the anticipation of death. The firelight was coming from the wall of the Abbey. It was not a bonfire but a furnace-like opening that gushed with violent flames—like a giant hearth large and wide enough to fit twelve people. She sensed the Leering in the back of it, summoning fire from some nether world in a roar and rush that made it seem like a living thing.

The Aldermaston's voice rose over the noise. "You are condemned to die this night because you have refused to submit to the water rite. You have been warned that this would happen. Some of you cling to the mistaken belief that the Medium will save you. It will not. There is a new order for worshipping the Medium now. The order of the mastons has ended. In every realm, in every kingdom, across every land, the abbeys will burn this night."

Lia stared at the flames, mesmerized by their ferocity. She breathed deeply, knowing that she would not be harmed. But those around her did not share her Gift. She glanced from face to face, her heart panging with sadness. As she looked at each one, she saw that they had been warned, at one time or another, to flee. They were stubborn, refusing to heed the warning that had been given to them. In her mind's eye, she saw them clinging to that stubbornness, not to their belief in the Medium. Now it was too late. She saw a boy and craned her neck, but it was not the boy Jouvent. The mother near him was not Huette from Vezins. She had warned them both to go to the *Holk*. She hoped they had listened to her. One by one, face by face, she looked at them, feeling dread and sadness at what would happen to them. The warning had been given. Now it was too late.

Lia sighed deeply, preparing to be ushered into the flames. Deep inside, she knew her work was not finished. There was something remaining for her to do.

273

Lia felt someone's eyes on her. She looked up and noticed the man near her. His face was familiar; she had seen him on the *Holk*, one of the crew. His gray eyes were staring intently at her face. Her mind rushed furiously for a moment, and then she remembered his name. Malcolm. His hands were bound behind his back as well.

Slowly, deliberately, he nodded to her.

The Aldermaston's voice rose in a shriek. "The moment has come! The stars are in alignment to our cause. The silver moon smiles upon us. The sun has set in the ebony sky, hiding his face in shame. Throw them into the gargouelle! May all who defy us be burned with fire."

We were married this evening at dusk, bound to each other by irrevocare sigil by the Aldermaston. Bound to each other forever. He is mine. At long last, he is mine. Colvin says the last loyal men to my uncle and myself will gather and fight in the Demont name. We ride on the morrow for Bosworth town to rally them. The orb will guide us there, as it has guided us here. The guest quarters are beautifully furnished, though not as richly as Dochte. I must douse the lamps before he returns. He cannot see my shoulder. I have commanded the Leerings to burn when we leave.

—Ellowyn Demont at Billerbeck Abbey

CHAPTER THIRTY-ONE

The Blight Leering

Screams filled the night sky in a terrible melody. It was an unearthly sound, of fear and terror and pleading all mixing together into an agonizing chorus as, by twos and threes, the prisoners were clutched, dragged, and then shoved into the flaming maw of the Leering furnace. Lia stared at the bright flames, made even brighter somehow as the night deepened. She watched children, mothers, fathers, the aged—all corralled by the Dochte Mandar and thrust to their deaths. Some tried to recant, swearing they would accept the water rite, but there was no compassion. One after another were sent to the flames, the crowd of prisoners thinning moment after moment. The silver eyes of the Dochte Mandar gleamed, their power driving away any feeling of resistance or anger. Lia's heart panged seeing the destruction and realized that on many nights to come such a scene would be repeated.

The Aldermaston of Dochte strode toward her, his face flushed and gleaming with sweat. His look was exultant. "Behold your Blight," he sneered at her. "Where is your power now, child?

Where is your faith? It is nothing but ashes." The look he gave her was savage and full of delight. "Send her next."

Lia rose without being yanked to her feet as the others. She noticed, from the corner of her eye, that Malcolm rose, just a shadow behind her. She gritted her teeth, trying to summon the power of the Medium. She remembered the fire that had consumed Almaguer's men in the Bearden Muir. More than anything, she wanted to unleash it on the Aldermaston and those who served him. But it did not heed her plea. It was a selfish desire, she realized. Forcing down her hatred, she marched toward the Leering.

"Make sure she goes in," the Aldermaston warned.

Malcolm strode next to her, his wrists in chains as well. The grass crumpled under her feet. Strange that her thoughts strayed to the feel of the grass. She felt no fear. The air was acrid, the smell sending a revolting lurch into her stomach. Soon the roar of the fires began to drown the shrieks of fear coming from those few remaining. Glancing down and to the side, she saw Malcolm walking step in step with her, shuffling forward toward the doom of the furnace.

"Stay with me," she whispered to him. "I will try and save you."

"Aye," he replied gruffly, closing the gap.

The light from the furnace was blindingly bright. Lia strode forward, ignoring the wave of heat and tongues of whipping flames that sought her. She clenched her teeth, sinking inside herself, dropping into the calm memories of Muirwood. Even in death's maw, she felt it—the peace and reassurance that she had grown up experiencing. Her love and admiration for the Aldermaston throbbed in her heart. She wondered where he was at that moment and if he was aware of her somehow. She had the deep impression that he knew much that he had not told her.

Malcolm sidled up next to her as they stepped into the jaws of flame together. There was heat and wind and jets of molten stone—and behind them all, an enormous Leering, blackened and ravaged by the forces compelling it to destroy the innocent. The chains that clutched her wrists and ankles melted in the heat. But no part of her was burned or even blackened with soot. She willed the protection to envelop Malcolm as well. She walked deeper into the throat, seeking the face carved in the rock. It was corrupted, of course. It would not obey her willingly. She prepared for the fight and walked closer, reaching out with her hand to touch it, to tame it, to crush its will with hers.

A hand closed on top of hers and brought her arm down. Lia turned, surprised. She did not know if Malcolm would survive the blaze. She had not dared to look at him, fearing any sliver of doubt. As she turned, she saw that he was no longer next to her. In his place, there was another man. She had not seen his face since she had sworn the maston oaths at Muirwood.

Maderos.

He shook his head slightly. "This way, sister," he beckoned, drawing her toward the side of the vaulted furnace. Her heart thrilled to see him. As they stood near the side, he waved his hand over the rock, and the stone beneath them began to sink and shudder, descending gradually down a well shaft that brought them lower and lower beneath the ground. The shaft opened below into a stone chamber, black and carved of sculpted rock. They were deep beneath the Abbey. After the stone settled, they stepped off it and it quickly ascended back up the shaft, floating alone until it plugged the hole and muted the furnace's roar.

Maderos nodded to her to follow, and several Leerings erupted with a soft, tranquil light along the walls. The tunnel had been abandoned long ago, but it was not like Muirwood's, carved out of dirt and earth and braced with timbers and stones. The whole tunnel was carved from stone, and the sound of their boots clipped as they walked. It was musty and stale but firm.

The light preceded them and opened to a large circular chamber. A stone railing blocked the way forward, which prevented a fall into a deep pit. The lights continued to wink as they circled the chamber from both sides, revealing other corridors leading out of the circular room. As Lia looked down past the rail, she saw an enormous basin, perched on the backs of Leerings in the shape of oxen. A small stone bridge led to the lip of the basin, which was empty.

"What is this place?" Lia asked, marveling.

"We are in the depths," he answered, his voice heavily accented. "It was shut away long ago when the grounds were enlarged. Hmph," he snorted. "Always getting bigger. But bigger does not mean worth. Bigger does not mean useful. It does not even mean respect. It is a sign of corruption."

Lia stared at the vast chamber, feeling the Medium coming strongly from one of the tunnels.

He saw her gaze and nodded. "That is where you go, but not yet, sister. You are not ready."

"It was you on the *Holk*," she said.

He nodded somberly. "I have always been nearby, child. A servant. A sailor. A gardener. But my calling is to write your story. The story of your Family. A story that has spanned a thousand years and will span another thousand years. I engrave it, tome by tome."

Lia's eyes filled with tears. She was so relieved, so grateful to see him, that she grabbed his neck and sobbed against his chest. The horrors she had faced overwhelmed her. Trembling, she clutched him and felt a comforting pat on her back, a gentle sigh in her ear that all would be well.

"You have done well, child. A little further. Your work is not done. Courage."

Mopping her eyes, she nodded and backed away, looking at him piercingly. "What must I do, Maderos?"

"You must bring the Blight," he answered. "You must fulfill the warning. But before you enter that passageway, you must be an aldermaston, and you must know the irrevocare sigil. I am here for that purpose. Kneel."

Lia slowly dropped to her knees as Maderos reached inside his gardener's robes and withdrew an ancient jeweled vial. The vial had a gold stopper and had several gemstones encrusted on the ridge. Its craftsmanship was beyond description, with tiny, elegant symbols etched into the surface. Maderos removed the stopper and gently tipped the vial over her head.

"Patience," he said.

"What is it?" she asked.

"It is oil pressed from fruit in a certain garden in Idumea. The garden is called Semani. The Garden of Semani. It does not sound as grand in your language, but it has deep meanings. It is the anointing oil."

Lia felt wetness on her head as the oil seeped into her wild hair. Maderos stoppered the vial and set it back within his robes. Then he placed a hand on her head and made the maston sign.

"I Gift you by your true name, Eprayim. I Gift you with courage and strength and power in the Medium. I bestow on you the rank of aldermaston, the servant of all. May you speak no falsehood and honor your oaths. I grant you the demesne and grounds of Muirwood Abbey, rightfully and properly to defend them as Aldermaston. To guide those who come there seeking escape. To guide them to Pry-Ree where the ships await. You will do this until you are released from your service or until death takes you. Be it thus so."

As he spoke, Lia felt a flood of warmth descend from the skin of her scalp all the way down to her soles. With the warmth came a weight—intangible, but very real. It was a burden of responsibility, a shifting of responsibility from the Aldermaston of Muirwood to her.

Lia's eyes fluttered open in shock. "Is he dead, Maderos? Why did you Gift me with Muirwood? Is he truly dead...?"

"Hush, child. Too many questions. You must be an aldermaston to learn the irrevocare sigil. That is all you need know right now. Do not pester me with questions. All will be revealed in time. Stand—you must learn the sigil."

Lia rose, her legs trembling. She worried about Muirwood—about what was happening there. The feeling of uneasiness was as palpable as a shroud. There was danger and fear. The Abbey was in terrible danger.

"Look at me," Maderos said, cupping her chin. "You feel the burden already. I can see it. But you have another duty here to perform. Do you hear me?"

Lia swallowed, nodding.

"This is the irrevocare sigil. Watch my hand. You trace this shape in the air with your palm. Think of a block of stone. Down, over, up, and across. A square. There is another square. It starts in the middle and goes this way. It is an eight-pointed star. It is the seal of Zedakah of the first Family. It is the sign he taught his posterity. It is the sign of the aldermastons, the irrevocare sigil.

Whatever you bind with this sign is bound forever, child. You will be commanded by the Medium when to make the sign. If you Gift someone and then make the sign, that Gift will remain with him forever. If you curse someone, the curse will last forever. You can never use it for yourself. You cannot bind someone to yourself or bind yourself to someone. Remember this, child. It is an important responsibility. Never use it against the Medium's will. Great calamities have happened when that occurs. Do you understand?"

Lia nodded. "I understand."

"You are an Aldermaston now. You have the authority of the irrevocare sigil. Go where the Medium bids you. I will wait for you here."

Lia walked carefully around the rim of the circular chamber, staring at the cool light coming from a passageway on the other side. The stones were ancient and carved with masterful details—little patterns of leaves and symbols cut into the stone and interspersed with glowing blue stones. There was a solemn feeling in the air, a whisper of centuries past. She did not know how long it had been since mastons had walked it, but she felt a peculiar reverence for the place. The pathway led to another tunnel, and from that tunnel, she experienced a Leering calling to her.

As she stepped into the tunnel, her heart spasmed with fear and terror. It struck her with such force that she nearly screamed and ran. Behind the terror beckoned the Leering, commanding her to come forward. She recognized that the fear was caused by stone faces carved into the archway ahead, their eyes white with power. She silenced them with her mind, and they obeyed. The fear departed.

Walking hesitantly forward, Lia entered a small cupola. It was small enough to admit only a few people, but the space was consumed by a massive boulder. She did not know how the boulder managed to be there in such a confined space but then realized immediately that the stones had been laid around it, shielding it from the eyes of the world. The boulder was crumbling in places and seemed as ancient as the world. The face was so worn by time that it was unrecognizable. It could have been a man's or a woman's face. The stone was smooth, as if touched by the sea for a thousand years. The power emanating from it was fearsome and immense—a huge presence that made her feel like the child she really was. This Leering had stood there for thousands of years. Who had carved it and when?

Instantly she knew. The whispers told her it had been carved by King Zedakah himself. It was nearly as old as the world itself. It had been protected by the elements and safeguarded at Dochte for generations. Lia stared at it in awe. What kind of Leering was it? What powers did it hold?

Lia hesitated, staring at the face—imagining the man who had carved it. The first Aldermaston. The story of her Family. A story that had been written and scrived for thousands of years. She swallowed with nervousness, feeling the weight of the responsibility. With a trembling hand, she reached out to touch the stone. Her heart pounded in her chest. Her fingers trembled as they brushed the stone.

Knowledge flooded her as she pressed her palm against the Leering.

It was the Blight Leering—a carving that would summon devastation. In her mind, she saw images from the past whirl by, instances where aldermastons had been summoned by the Medium to Dochte Abbey to unleash a Blight on the world. Some of the figures she saw in her mind were old men. Some were young. Some were women of various ages. Always the Medium warned before the destruction came. Always it offered a chance to flee or escape. But throughout the centuries, there would come times when the people were so hardened by the machinations of the hetaera that they would not listen to the whispers of the Medium. They drowned the whispers in drink, in music, in dance, in smoke. They were lured by the wiles of the daughters of Ereshkigal until nothing could save them. In her mind she saw the horrors of what happened when the hetaera ruled. There was murder and lust and actions so terrible they made Lia shrink to even consider what occurred. The only way to reverse it—the only way to bring humanity back to its senses again—was the coming of a Blight.

Lia's hand began to burn.

She had never experienced the pain of fire before. She tried to take her hand away, but she could not. Her hand burned, but it was not just the sharp, scalding pain of fire. She felt it passing through the Leering to her. The Leerings were just conduits. They connected two points, bringing together two separate forces, combining them.

Knowledge of the Blight filled her mind. In the past, the Blight had manifested itself in many forms. Some it had killed by drowning. Some it had killed with famine. This Blight was different.

The Leering released her.

Lia nearly stumbled back, staring at her glowing hand. She could not see the Blight, but it was there, cupped in her glowing palm. The Medium whispered for her to return to the hetaera garden. Instantly, she knew what she had to do.

CHAPTER THIRTY-TWO

The Secret Veil

The hetaera gardens were empty, of course. The populace of the Abbey still thronged around the furnace—leering as the last remaining prisoners were thrown to their deaths. The night was calm, and the air smelled of jasmine. Lia entered the hedge maze, walking quickly until she reached the round stone lid that covered the lair. Staring at the stone, she knew in her mind the password that opened it and spoke the word aloud. The stone began to slide downward, sinking into the pit. Lia stepped on it quickly and descended into the black chasm. When she had entered it previously, she had been terrified. There was no fear this time. Lia walked forward quickly, past the black gaps where the serpents waited for their victims. Her hand glowed more brightly now, the light keeping the snakes at bay.

Lia entered the chamber with the oath Leerings. They did not speak to her, for she had already made her oaths. In the center of the room, still in the floor, was the half-made kystrel. It was shallow in the grooves. The Medium commanded her to pick it up with her other hand, which she did after stooping. The kystrel was cold, lifeless. It was not a threat to her.

Walking forward, she met the barrier that had thwarted her before. Behind it, she sensed the Leering she had seen so often in her mind—the Leering with the twin snakes twisting into a circle. She felt its power throbbing, but it was pale compared to the Blight Leering she had just traveled from. She stared at the stone barrier. There was a dirge that would open the door—a command spoken by a Myriad One. But she was not controlled by a Myriad One.

"Open," she commanded, drawing on the full power of the Medium.

The stone groaned in rebellion, but it could not defy an aldermaston. It swiveled open silently, opening to the sound of rushing water and mist. The room beyond contained a giant pool crafted from stones and tile and filled with overflowing water. There were three Leerings carved into pillars high on the wall, and the rushing waterfalls came from them. The center of the pool contained a whirlpool. The waters swirled and churned in a spiral around the whorl. A single Leering rose from the edge of the water in front of her, the stone with the burning snake insignia.

The tiles and stone leading up to the Leering were beneath a shallow layer of water. Lia looked at the water and felt the thundering mewling of Myriad Ones within the pool. There were millions of them.

Lia raised her glowing hand into the maston sign. The waters parted away from her, leaving a path of dry stone to the Leering. She approached the serpent Leering, listening to the churn and foam of the waterfall, feeling the mist on her face as she approached. The room was dark, except for the light coming from her hand and the burning snakes carved into the Leering. This was the final place. This was where a girl became a hetaera after making the oaths and forging her kystrel. She stared at the Leering and experienced a rush of blackness inside her soul just looking at it. The water bubbled and hissed as if flames from beneath the pool were beginning to ravage the waters. The mist turned into steam. It burned hotter and hotter as she approached. The entire stone shuddered with power, trying to blast her away from it. But Lia pressed on, approaching the stone, her hand in the maston sign as she walked.

The Leering began to crack with power, the stone vibrating and humming as it tried to force her away.

Lia reached the Leering, barely able to see it through the haze of steam. The waters bubbled like a livid cauldron. Reaching out, Lia touched the image of the serpent with her glowing hand.

As Lia closed her eyes, she saw in her mind every girl and every woman who had ever stood before the awful Leering. In her mind's eye, she watched them press their naked shoulders against the burning image and watched it sear their flesh with a brand they would wear the rest of their days. The kystrel was a token of their power, but their power came from the binding they received by touching the stone—a binding of a Myriad One inside their body. The Myriad Ones were given complete control over the hetaera, to use them as they wished until they were finally persuaded to kill themselves, thus releasing the Myriad Ones and making them available to join with another hetaera. The cycle had been repeated over and over for centuries. Young girls, inexperienced in the ways of power and manipulation, were suddenly wiser than their limited years, able to seduce and influence even the strongest minds. She saw Pareigis, a shivering little girl who was barely thirteen at the time of her binding. She saw countless others. The last girl, the one who had made the final oaths and promises, was Hillel.

Lia felt the power of the Medium thrust through her hand as it touched the stone. The Blight began its work. Every hetaera had a brand on her shoulder, the brand of the twin serpents. The Blight infected the Leering and every woman who had the brand in her skin. Lia shuddered, realizing what she was doing. The Blight would take the form of a disease, a sickness, a plague that would ravage the land. The disease would be transmitted to its victims through a kiss. Lia's mind opened up, and she saw the devastation that was coming. It would come slowly, creeping stealthily. Every kiss from a hetaera would transmit the plague. Every victim would die an agonizing and slow death. It would take time—weeks and months, even years—before the survivors began to understand who was causing the plague. Then every hetaera would be hunted and killed. Women would be forbidden to read or study from tomes. The deaths would still continue, plague after plague, secret after secret, until everyone in every kingdom had been destroyed. The last man alive would be the Earl of Dieyre. She saw him in her mind, alone in the world. The glow disappeared from her hand. The curse had been invoked.

The Medium whispered to her. *Bind it with the irrevocare sigil.*

Lia wept at what she had seen. She sobbed as she realized that she was causing the death of untold thousands. Hundreds of thousands. Her hand had brought the plague that would destroy the world, save those who escaped on the ships. She remembered the Aldermaston of Tintern, how he said that the name of Ellowyn Demont would be spoken for good and evil by many. She remembered Maderos at Muirwood Abbey after she had passed the maston trial.

This hand—will impact the lives of millions of souls. Your name will be had for good as well as for evil. But to those who know the truth, they will always hold you in reverence for what this hand will yet do.

With tears streaming down her cheeks, she raised her hand and made the sign of the eight-pointed star. The irrevocare sigil bound the curse to the Leering forever.

It was done.

Lia knelt at the foot of the Leering and sobbed, wracked with emotions too vast to control or even understand. A single thought burned through the storm of feelings. Colvin was with Hillel. Somewhere, the man she loved was with a woman she hated. A woman who Colvin believed was Ellowyn Demont. And one kiss from her would kill him.

***

Maderos had taught her the password to open the slit in the outer wall of the Abbey. Her feelings oppressed her with crushing weight. Colvin was in danger—immediate danger. Muirwood was also facing a threat. She could feel both looming in front of her eyes, a shadow that blinded her to all other thoughts. Thrusting through the dark shaft of stone, she entered the room with the strange basin and oxen and found Maderos standing by the shaft leading to the Blight Leering. The shaft was covered by a length of silk cloth, a narrow sheet that rustled as she disturbed the air with her presence. The shimmering sheet looked like an Apse Veil.

"Maderos!" she cried, joining him around the walkway. "Maderos, where is Colvin?"

The look he gave her was stern. He turned away and smoothed the fabric, letting it settle once again. "Billerbeck Abbey." He stared up at the length of sheet and stepped back from it. "Yes, your *pethet* is there."

"Maderos, please tell me. Has he…has he fallen? I know he is with her…"

Maderos waved his hand impatiently. "Do not ask me, little sister. Do not ask me about the pethet. What if he has fallen, eh? What if he has kissed the hetaera? Does that alter what you must do now?"

"Maderos, please!"

His expression was as solemn as stone. "I will not influence you, child. I will not give you the answer you seek. It is your choice." He gestured toward the shroud. "This is a Veil. An Apse Veil. There are only two abbeys standing still. You must choose where to go. Both choices have consequences. But I cannot choose for you. It is yours to make."

Lia stared at the Apse Veil in agony. She knew that Muirwood was threatened. She could feel it deep in her bones. She longed to go back there, even knowing that the Queen Dowager was there. Yet there was also the Abbey at Billerbeck. There was Colvin and Hillel. If she went there first, could she warn Colvin in time and then travel to Muirwood? Was there time to do both?

Maderos's eyes were fixed on hers.

Colvin thought she was dead. Hillel believed she was dead. Was it already too late to save him? Had he, by error, bound himself to Hillel by irrevocare sigil? Even if he had unwittingly bound himself to the wrong person, would it matter? Was it the name that mattered or the person he had clasped hands with? Would he kiss her, believing her to be his wife, and receive the curse of the Blight as a result?

It was pure agony. Was she already too late?

She could not know the answer to that. In the end, it did not matter. As much as she wanted to save Colvin, it was her duty to save Muirwood. Even though the thought of losing Colvin forever tortured her, she knew she had to do her duty. She could not force the Medium to do her will. She could only submit herself to the Medium's will.

Tears had pooled again in her eyes, but she brushed them away harshly. "I will obey," she whispered. She gripped Maderos by the arm. "If I understood the Aldermaston of Tintern properly, once I go to Muirwood, I will not be allowed to leave. I must remain there and help direct others to the safe haven. The Blight will afflict slowly at first. Then it will increase, faster and faster, as more fall to the curse."

In her mind, she remembered the stories about the maypole dance in Dahomey, how Pareigis had taught the youth to be bound to the pole and then steal kisses when the boys were free. She shuddered, realizing how quickly the traditions would cause the fall.

Maderos eyed her somberly. His cheek muscle twitched.

Lia swallowed and nodded, firming her resolve and her courage. Then, with a glint of determination in her eye, she approached the Apse Veil and passed through it to Muirwood.

CHAPTER
THIRTY-THREE

The Prince's Death

Prince Alluwyn Lleu-Iselin stroked the baby's cheek with his finger. Tears welled in his eyes and blurred the image of the child, his daughter. She was asleep, her little mouth puckered and at rest. Little tufts of golden hair crowned her fragile head. Bending low over the basket, he kissed those curls.

"Hold it steady," he asked. The Evnissyen's name was Nuric. He was young, but he had proven himself trustworthy. He was fluent in three languages and looked like someone from Comoros with his straight, dark hair. He would blend in better than the fair-haired Pry-rians. Nuric clenched the basket to his chest and held it still as the Prince placed two fingers on the babe's head. "Close your eyes, Nuric."

He obeyed, and the Prince made the maston sign.

"I cannot speak your name, child. My tome is sealed. I cannot claim you as kin in words, but my heart is full. From this moment, you are a wretched. I Gift you that you may accomplish the work the Medium plans for you. This little hand, this tiny little hand will change the world. It will destroy. It will also build. You are dear to me, little one. I face my fate with courage that you may face yours. I Gift you with courage. I Gift you with faith. You will be strong in the Medium, child. Stronger than I. Until we rejoin on that day to come in Idumea, I give you all that I have and all that I am. My life for yours, dearest one. I die that you may live. Be it thus so."

As the Prince lowered his hand, he saw wetness in Nuric's eyes. The Medium was strong in the room. The Prince had not felt it very much of late. His heart was heavy with sorrow at the death of Elle and the devastation throughout Pry-Ree. Reaching out, he clasped Nuric's shoulder. "Guard her, Nuric. Bear her safely to Muirwood."

"I do not know the way," he whispered hoarsely. "But I will find it."

The Prince opened the pouch dangling from his belt and withdrew the Cruciger orb. "The Abbey is surrounded by marshland. It is desolate country, but it has its own beauty. When you are lost, and you *will* be, put the babe's hand on the orb, and the spindles will point the way for you."

Nuric nodded and watched as the Prince tucked the orb within the blankets in the basket. Afterward, he clenched the rim of the basket.

"It is crucial that she has the orb when she is older," the Prince said, looking deep into his eyes. "She must have the orb. Only an aldermaston can command it or one of my blood. She will need it to find her way to safety. Without it, she will fail in her mission. I trust you, Nuric. I trust you to deliver her and the orb safely to Muirwood."

"I will, my lord," he promised. "I will do as you have commanded me."

The Prince's hand was still clenched around the basket. "Be faithful to me, Nuric. You must do all that I commanded you. If you fail, then we have no hope."

"I will not fail you, my Prince," he promised soberly.

"Go then. Take the secret tunnel so that no one sees you. The household is moving to Dungeurth castle for protection. The king's army is nearing the river crossing. There is little time remaining. The orb will guide you past the army safely."

With a nod, Nuric hugged the basket tightly against his chest. The Prince reached down and hoisted the trapdoor, exposing the ladder below. With a cautious step, Nuric managed his way down into the darkness. He looked up once, his eyes meeting the Prince's. He nodded firmly. The Prince closed it and kicked the rushes back into place.

The ache in his heart deepened. A wretched; his daughter, the princess of Pry-Ree, soon to be the only heir of the kingdom—she was only a wretched now.

***

Prince Alluwyn reined in his stallion as they approached the turn that would lead to the river shallows. The path was obscured by enormous trees, towering redwoods that were wreathed in mist. The ferns swayed in the gentle breeze, and the cackle of birds and buzzing of insects filled the air with chatter. Four Evnissyen flanked him, also mounted, each peering keenly into the mist.

"Do you hear the river?" said Braide. "We should hear it by now."

"Too far," muttered Tethys. He glanced back into the woods the way they had come. He seemed to be looking for something.

The Prince noticed the tightness of his jaw. The brooding expression. He had the sullen look of a guilty man. He would not meet the Prince's eyes.

"After they cross the river," the Prince asked, "how long can we hold them in these woods?"

Braide sniffed the air. "Two days at most, my lord."

"Two days!" argued Kent. "We could hold them here a fortnight if we had a mind to do so. You speak rubbish, Braide."

Braide shrugged but did not change his answer.

"A fortnight," Kent continued. "This is unfamiliar ground. They will move warily, expecting us to strike their flanks, which we shall. If we harass them, striking and fleeing, striking and fleeing, we can twist and pull their army in several directions. A smaller force, striking hard and fast, can convince an enemy it is larger than it is."

"But you forget," said the Prince, "that our enemies have joined forces. They have Pry-rian hunters among them. They know our tricks. They know our tactics. In a matter of force, we cannot prevail. We can only forestall them."

Kent angrily scowled, not willing to concede the point. "Where is Campion? It is nearly dusk. The river is not far."

"Coming," Braide said, tightening his grip on the reins and nudging his stallion forward.

The sound of galloping was heard a moment later, piercing the cluck of birds and sending several keening into the wind as they flew away. Around the bend came an Evnissyen, hunched low over the saddle. His face was streaked with sweat, his eyes wide with terror.

"Ambush!" he shouted when he saw them.

The Prince saw the arrow protruding from the meat of his massive arm as he reined in next to them.

"Ride, my lord!" Campion gasped. "They have already crossed the river. They were waiting for me in the woods, silent and still. Two hundred knights, if not more. They tried to shake me from the saddle, but I fought my way through."

His hands were bloody. Campion looked backward at the road. "They ride hard behind me. We will be hard pressed to make it back to the castle. Ride, my lord!"

"Crossed the river!" Kent seethed. "No one knows of the shallows here. No one save one of us. How could they have found it?"

"Ride to the castle," the Prince ordered, his heart beginning to shudder with anticipation. His breath came in little gulps. "Ride hard while you can. They will be without the walls by morning. The women and children, make sure they are—"

The arrow struck him in the center of his back. The pain was excruciating, a hot fire that stole his breath and made him gasp. Already his fingers and legs were useless, seized up in a fit of agony. They would not respond.

"By Cheshu!" Kent roared. The Prince was facing the river. The arrow had come from behind.

"In the trees!" Tethys shouted, pointing. "I saw a man! Over there!"

The Prince fell from the saddle and struck the ground with a jolt that smashed his arm and stunned him. The pain in his back burned hotter and hotter. Spots danced in front of his eyes. He could not move. He could not scratch an itch on his nose.

"My lord!" Braide was off his saddle in an instant, gladius in hand.

"Ride," the Prince wheezed. "They...come..."

The sound of hooves, a chorus of hooves, an avalanche of hooves sounded from the trail ahead.

"Carry him!" Kent ordered. "Toss him on my saddle. We can ride with him."

Braide looked at the Prince's eyes. His face turned as hard as stone. "I had hoped you were wrong, my lord," he whispered.

"Go…" the Prince moaned, shutting his eyes as the pain overwhelmed him.

He heard the sound of stirrups, the creaking of leather. "Ride hard," Braide ordered.

"But we cannot leave him!" Kent shouted.

Braide whistled crisply, and his stallion plunged into the forest.

"There he is!" Tethys warned. "I will draw his fire. He must be a kishion!"

The others rode hard, their hooves thundering in the loam. It was not long before the knights of Comoros arrived. It was not long before they were assembled to stare at their fallen foe, jostling and jeering with each other, trying to get a better look at him. The Prince listened to the mocking laughter and felt the boot jabs that nudged his body this way and that.

"Roll him over," said a voice. It was a voice he recognized and knew—a voice he had not heard in person since the day of his wedding to Elle. It was the king's own voice.

"The arrow," someone said. "In his back."

"Well, you had best pull it out first," came a chuckled reply.

The prince readied himself for the pain, but he was not prepared for it when the arrow was yanked from his back. He nearly choked on the vomit the pain caused. Someone twisted him roughly on his back, facing the sky. He blinked, teeth clenched, and tried to see or even breathe. There was the king of Comoros, on his war horse, in full armor. The Prince could sense the power of the kystrel around his neck. He could sense the despair and hopelessness that were showered on him, thrust on him, swirling around him. The king wanted him to feel every awful emotion before he died.

"Where is the traitor?" the king asked.

Tethys approached, flanked by several knights. The king looked at him disdainfully. "Give him his pay," he said. "I keep my promises. Of that you can be sure."

Someone thrust a bag of jangling coins into Tethys's hand. He looked at the king in confusion, at the distaste and distrust on his face. There was a subtle nod, and then Tethys slumped to the ground without a sound.

Each breath was a torture. The Prince's mouth would not work. He tried to turn his neck, but the pain in his muscles prevented anything but blinking. Someone scooped up the bag from Tethys's dead hand.

The king turned back to Prince Alluwyn. He had a similar expression on his face—a look of utter contempt. "Die, maston," the king said with a look of satisfaction. He nodded to a knight with a huge battle axe gripped in his hands.

The Prince stared at the king, heard the mash of the earth as the boots approached him. He did not have much air for words. Already part of him was slipping away from his body. He felt the pull of the Apse Veil drawing him. He spoke in a clear voice, in the king's own language. "Fitting that an arrow...brought me down. You will die the same way. A Pry-rian arrow...in your back."

He remembered an oak tree struck by lightning on a hillside near a village called Winterrowd. He died just before the axe came down and severed his head from his body.

CHAPTER THIRTY-FOUR

Muirwood Burning

A sickening lurch plunged into Lia's stomach as the Apse Veil drew her inside, hurtling her to Muirwood in an instant. She stumbled from the Apse Veil on the other side, falling to the ground with a rough jolt. Tremors shook her, and clenching her fists, she squeezed her eyes shut to stop the sensation of spinning long enough to brace herself. She opened her eyes again as she realized by the heat, haze, and smell that the Abbey was burning.

No!

Lia struggled to her feet, but the clues were unmistakable. The dread and warning that had oppressed her in Dahomey was revealed fully—the Leerings throughout the Abbey were all burning, consuming the stone with raging fire. She marched past the Rood Screen, the intricate woodwork separating the inner sanctum from the large interior corridors. As she passed through the portal, she saw in horror that the vaulted ceiling was thick with swirling smoke and green tongues of fire.

The stones were blackening quickly, charred and pocked by the intense heat coursing through the rock like blood. Smoke masked everything, and it wasn't until she took several halting steps that she saw the bodies.

Her heart panged with terror.

"Lia!"

As she approached, she saw a circle of individuals, kneeling and clasping each other's hands, binding themselves together in a ring as they awaited their fate—death by fire or when the walls came down and crushed them.

"It *is* Lia!"

She came from the smoke fog and beheld faces that she had longed to see. Faces she had treasured and loved. Faces she would never forget. There were Sowe and Edmon, hand in hand, fingers tight and clenching, knuckles white. Marciana and Kieran Ven clutching each other, as well as Pasqua and Prestwich. She knew the faces—Brynn, Siler, the children, all clustered together, holding each other's hands—waiting for their fate. She recognized others, but her heart was too full and tears stung her eyes along with the acrid smoke. She did not see the Aldermaston among them.

"Where is the Aldermaston?" she begged as she approached, embracing Sowe after she surged to her feet and hugged her so tight it made both sob.

Sowe's eyes were wet. "They bound him in ropes. They said… they said they would take him to the Tor to watch Muirwood burn. The Queen Dowager will kill him there."

Lia nodded, her heart aching with pain. She was ferociously angry and knew she had to move quickly.

"Lia!" Marciana said, grasping her in another tight hug. Her face was joyous but alarmed. "Where is he? Where is Colvin?"

A chunk of burning stone whistled and crashed against the tiles, exploding with a shower of sparks and hissing flame. Everyone flinched.

"Everyone, come with me!" Lia shouted. "Bring nothing with you."

"They have barricaded all the doors, child," Prestwich said. "There is no way out."

"There is," Lia said. "Everyone, follow me!"

Another hissing rock landed nearby, another shower of sparks. Lia realized the flames would consume the Abbey in moments. Drawing deep within herself, she willed the fires to stop.

I am the Aldermaston of Muirwood Abbey; obey me! she ordered, shoving the thoughts with all her might. The flames resisted her authority, roaring in defiance as they licked up the stones and consumed them. She shoved the thought again, commanding the fires to be tamed. Again they resisted. She pressed harder with her mind as she ran to the corridor heading down to the lower chamber where she had received the first maston rites. She waved at the others to follow her. Down the steps they herded.

Obey me!

The fires began to give way, not losing their strength, but she felt the Abbey resisting the spread of the flames, holding it back from consuming everything.

"Scream," she said. "Make them believe you are dying. Make them believe we perish in the flames."

It did not take persuasion. Everyone was terrified already. A piercing chorus of fright rose from the throat of the Abbey. In her mind she had seen the future when she had taken the hetaera test. She had seen Muirwood burning and heard the screams.

"Scream!" she said, adding hers to the noise. Down the stairwell she marched until it opened to the long room full of polished wooden benches. At the head of the room was the main altar. She remembered going there with the Cruciger orb, seeking Colvin at the Pilgrim Inn. The thought of Colvin succumbing to Hillel nearly overwhelmed her concentration with sickening feelings that would have made her go mad. She blasted the thoughts aside, focusing on the matter at hand. If she hurried and saved them, she could go to the Tor and rescue the Aldermaston. She had no weapons, but she experienced the rush and thrill of the Medium, strengthening her. As she crossed the center aisle, she reached the small antechamber at the side and hefted on the stone slab on the floor. It raised with ease, showing the hidden entrance to the tunnels beneath.

"Kieran Ven!" she said, turning suddenly and realizing that the last time she had seen him, he had been unable to walk. There he was, striding boldly with Marciana still clutching his hand. "You lead them. There are lamps and flint to light them at the bottom of the shaft. They should be trim with oil. Take the tunnel on the right; it will lead you to the woods beyond the Abbey grounds. Go down, all of you!"

Marciana was very close to Kieran Ven. Her hand did not leave his, as if he were a possession. Lia's hunter eyes had noticed it, but she could not remark on it yet. There was not time.

"How far to the woods?" he asked, his eyes wide with concern. "How deep the passage?"

"It is not far. A maston word will open the portal. You may have to dig your way out if the Dowager's folk buried it." Lia grabbed his shoulder. "Take them to Tintern if I do not come for you," she whispered.

He looked at her in shock. "Tintern has already fallen, Lia. I tried to return there days ago, but the portal was closed."

She looked him hard in the eyes. "The Abbey may have fallen, but there is an aldermaston there. I know he is there. He will direct you to the ships."

Marciana grabbed Lia's arm. "What will you do?"

"What I must. Go now, while you can."

Kieran plunged into the tunnel shaft and helped Marciana come down after him. Lia felt the weight of the Abbey pressing on her. The fire pushed against her will, but she refused to let it win. *Not yet,* she ordered.

There was Sowe next, followed by Edmon. They both turned and helped Pasqua down, and it took time for her to manage the ladder steps.

"I am hurrying, quit fussing down there," Pasqua snapped. "I was once as skinny as you two and could handle ladders quite with ease." Her eyes gleamed with gratitude and relief when she looked at Lia. "I knew you would save us, child. I never doubted it."

One by one, Lia helped them down, holding back the flames with sheer will. Siler and the children clambered past, one after another. The flames burned even hotter, and she realized that another presence was commanding them to burn faster. She knew it was Pareigis.

"Hurry!" Lia warned. Reome was next, her eyes wide with wonder, and she gave Lia a grateful smile. One after another they went, Prestwich lingering in the back, insisting that others go first. He coughed violently against his arm, for the smoke had seeped into the lower chambers. Another family from the village went down. So few, Lia realized. So few had believed.

At last it was just her and Prestwich. The weight of the Abbey strained against her. She could not bear it any longer.

"Go," she said with a moan, beckoning for Prestwich.

He shook his head. "I will die here, Lia. This is where I want my bones to sleep. With my Aldermaston."

Lia stared at him hard, exhausted by the strain of holding back the Leerings.

"Prestwich," she said.

He shook his head. "I am done, child. This Abbey was my life. The ships are too far. I would never make it."

Lia clenched her teeth, shuddering under the weight. "I cannot hold it back. Go down. You are needed, Prestwich. Your wisdom. Your experience. The little children need you. Someone to tell them stories. Of what it was like before the Blight." She groaned. "Please, Prestwich!"

His face wrinkled with livid emotions. "They are killing my Aldermaston," he said with grief. "I cannot...abandon him."

She looked at him, a strangling feeling in her throat. "I know, Prestwich. I know. But *I* am your Aldermaston now," she said. "Please, Prestwich. There is nothing you can do to serve him more. Help these children escape. Do it for me."

The look he gave her was raw with suffering. He nodded and then ambled down the passageway. He paused on the rungs, looking up at her. "Come down with me, Lia."

Her hold on the Leerings failed. She felt the blast of fire already sucking through the shafts as she slammed the stone lid down and whirled. The torrent of flames came jetting at her from all sides.

Lia walked through the shroud of flames as if they were a gentle breeze. She went back up the stairs as huge chunks of burning rock hurtled from the weakened beams. They exploded around her, sparks and whorls of flame. She walked without thinking, without wondering whether a stone would strike her. She had no fear. Somehow, it was lost during the hetaera test. Remembering the kystrel she had taken from the lair, she removed it from her tunic and tossed it into the flames, watching the metal turn bright orange before becoming a puddle of sizzling dross. In her mind, she saw the Abbey consumed, the Apse Veil vanishing in the conflagration. The Rood Screen turned to ash. The floor tiles were all cracked and black with soot, the pewter and silver vases and stands warped. Her soul grieved seeing the ravaged insides of her precious Abbey. For moments, she stared at the devastation, tears streaming down her cheeks, only to hiss and vanish when they struck the floor. It was midnight, she realized. The darkest hour. And somehow, deep inside, she realized with shock and sadness that there were no abbeys left in all the world.

She felt a presence and turned, startled, seeing the Aldermaston walking toward her.

He walked through the flames in his golden robes, approaching down the long aisle. She knew it was him, even through the billows of smoke and flame. Yet she felt his presence more strongly than what her eyes beheld. She squinted, not sure what she saw in the smoke.

"Aldermaston?" she breathed in surprise.

There he was, a wraith, a shadow that was visible one moment and vanished the next. A glimmer of his former self. But she recognized who it was; she recognized his presence. She felt him looking at her.

She reached out, but her hand passed through the haze and smoke, touching nothing. He was there, right beside her.

Aldermaston? She thought the word.

Redeem the Abbey. You are the Aldermaston of Muirwood now.

It was as if he had spoken the thought aloud.

Her throat clenched shut with horror. *You are dead? I am too late?*

Redeem the Abbey. Your posterity will build it anew.

She wondered how he was in front of her. When she had died, the part of her existence that remained had drifted toward the Apse Veil. But there were no Apse Veils left! With sickening realization, she understood what she had not even conceived of before. The abbeys were the gateways back to Idumea. They were the gateways for the living and the dead. With no abbeys left standing, the dead souls would be stranded, unable to return back to the city gardens.

She saw his eyes, his angry, brooding eyes. He had known all along. Her father had told him, before she was even born, what would happen to him when the Blight came. He had known that his Abbey would be the last to fall and that he would be tortured to death after its fall, unable to return back to Idumea.

Redeem the Abbey and build it again. Build them so the dead can be set free. You are our hope, child. You are our last hope.

He had always known, but the binding sigil prevented him from ever speaking it. He had known that his death would be followed by other deaths. Millions of deaths as the Blight swept across the land. Millions who would not be able to return to Idumea.

Lia's eyes were wet with tears of sorrow and hatred. This was the work of the hetaera, and they had succeeded in destroying all the abbeys. Their dominion would be short-lived, Lia vowed. Raising her head, she walked toward the burning walls and summoned the power of the Medium to aid her.

It is midnight on Twelfth Night. The world is ours.

—Ellowyn Demont at Billerbeck Abbey

CHAPTER THIRTY-FIVE

Rage of the Myriad Ones

L ia passed through the burning rubble of Muirwood, immune to the heat and tongues of flame. The fire consumed the stones, leaving stumps and stubble. The Abbey would burn until dawn, and there would be nothing left—unless she stopped it at the source.

She left near the pond, the waters befouled with chunks of ash and floating debris. As she crossed, she saw a huge ring of Dahomeyjan knights inside the cloister. The cloister walls and gates were down and tossed aside. The Leering in the middle of the fountain was in flames, shooting blasts of fire into the night sky. The knights carried tomes to the Leering and heaved them into the fountain, which was now full of molten aurichalcum. Lia gazed in shock as she saw the Leering consuming tome after tome, each one someone had spent a lifetime engraving. Crouched nearby were goldsmiths, dozens of them, scooping up the molten stream and fashioning them into rings and bracelets and tiaras. The smell of cider was strong in the air. Knights staggered and laughed, clapping each other on the back as they continued the work of destruction.

Lia saw a speck in the distance—in the night sky in the direction of the Tor. There was something burning on the crest of the hill. With a sickening dread, she already knew what it meant.

Closing her eyes, she fell deep inside herself. She journeyed through her memories to a night long ago. It was after her ninth name day, the night of the great storm. She remembered the smells from the kitchen. The plop of the water seeping in from the roof. The Aldermaston and Pasqua were there. Sowe was asleep in the loft. The storm—the flooding of the cemetery. She remembered the lightning, the sound of thunder, the torrent of rain that had lasted for days. The mud and grass she had tromped in earlier that day. The ring she still wore around her neck, its hard edge still a reminder of that night. A storm. A great storm. A storm greater than any Muirwood had endured for hundreds of years. That was what she desired. Water to put out the flames, to quench them once and for all.

Come to me! she commanded. *I invoke a storm to purge the Abbey, to cleanse it from this defilement.* Lifting her head, she opened her eyes, her hand up in the maston sign. "Be it thus so. May storms always come to defend this ground should any seek to ruin it again." She made the sign of the irrevocare sigil.

Someone had seen her. She heard the cautious footsteps approaching.

"Lia? Is it…is it you?"

She turned and saw Duerden, clutching a cider cup. He gaped at her, his eyes wild with astonishment. He looked older. Worse, he looked a stranger to her. There was something more serious in his eyes, an expression of a much older man and not a boy her own age. As she looked at his face, she saw it clearly through the Gift of Seering. He was infected with the plague.

"Oh, Duerden," she murmured with a throb in her voice. "What have you done?"

"It is you!" he said, his voice plaintive yet his expression was wracked with guilt and confusion. "But look at you. Where is… Lia…the baby? Where is the baby?"

She saw it on his face with her hunter's gaze. There was a dab of rouge on the corner of his mouth where a woman had kissed him.

"You wanted to become a maston," Lia said, her heart breaking. "Instead, you helped destroy them. What are you talking about, Duerden? What baby?"

His face twitched with spasms, his voice choking with emotion. "You were sent away to another abbey. To keep it secret! You were with child. The Aldermaston's child—the baby. The child. You…you were with child. What…but…were you not with child, Lia? Like Reome?" His eyes were desperate and helpless. The cup dropped from his hand.

"No, Duerden," she said, shaking her head violently. "That is a lie! You were deceived by the Queen Dowager. Duerden, do you not understand? The Aldermaston was murdered. He was not a traitor. It was not an execution. He was murdered. Demont was murdered!"

Duerden shook his head in a daze. "No, he fell sick. He was poisoned by Pasqua."

"No, Duerden! He was murdered. All of the mastons have been murdered. The abbeys are no more. When, Duerden?" She gave him a fierce look. "When did you begin listening to the Queen Dowager? You are hers. I can smell her on your clothes. Her stain is in your blood as well. When, Duerden? When did it happen to you?"

His expression was haunted, his voice quavering. "Before… Whitsunday. She spoke to me while I was walking in the gardens. She…oh, Lia, what have I done? She was so friendly to me. She did not tease me. She…Lia…she…what have I done?"

"You are infected," Lia said, shaking her head. "The Blight. You are infected with it. She kissed you. She kissed you again tonight." Lia's heart broke with pain. "You cannot leave these shores. You will die, like everyone else. I am so sorry, Duerden. You will be sick. You will be very sick, very soon. Leave Muirwood while you can. A storm is coming. If you stay here, you will die tonight. Go as far away as you can, but you can never return. Go!"

Duerden began to sob like a child, overwhelmed by his despair. He was devastated. She grabbed his shoulders and shook him. "Go!"

Lia felt the Myriad Ones surround her. Their mewling sounds and hisses filled her senses with loathing and animosity and pure hatred. They were drawn to her, wheedling at her mind with their thoughts. She turned around slowly, and there was Pareigis, the Queen Dowager, in a gown as dark at the night, the silver fringe glittering. Her eyes glowed silver, and the wind rustled her hair. Her fingers were curled like talons.

"He is not yours to command," Pareigis said with an imperious voice. "You spurned him, girl. Remember? A broken heart is easily seduced."

Lia gritted her teeth but did not back away. "I broke your hold over Seth. I will break your hold over him. I do not fear you. I know who you really are."

A gust of wind swept across the grass, bringing the scent of fire mixed with flowers. Pareigis's hair whipped across her face. Pressure began to build in the air. Lia felt it inside her ears.

"It is your pity that you do not fear me," Pareigis said. "You have been troublesome to me. That trouble will end tonight. You are the last maston. I have saved you for last."

The wind began to whip more violently.

"You summon a storm?" Pareigis said with delight. "I am the Queen of Storms. Water is my dominion."

"You have no dominion," Lia said. "You only steal. Nothing is truly yours. I know your power. I do not fear it. You cannot harm me."

Pareigis's eyes flashed with murder. "Harm you? I will kill you, little one. You also will be trapped on this pitiful earth. The mastons who fell before you were fortunate because they could return to Idumea. But not you. This is your reward, foolish child. This is what the Medium bestows on you for your faithfulness." She spat the word. "Misery. That is your reward. I give you misery for bread and suffering for cider."

In the distance, there was thunder.

Lia stared at Pareigis, unconcerned. "You will go. Depart from Muirwood and never return." She took a step toward her.

"You cannot command *me*!" Pareigis shrieked in fury. "I command the oceans and the waves, and they obey *me*. The winds come at *my* calling. Fire burns at *my* will. You cannot command *me*!"

"By the Medium, I command you to leave," Lia said, holding up her hand in the maston sign.

Lightning lashed the sky. The wind began to keen and howl like a wolf. Lia's hair was whipped about her face. Her clothes thrashed with the fury of the gale. She took another step closer.

Pareigis's raven hair spun wildly around her. She was hunched, as if under a huge weight. "This is my world. You are my daughter. I have destroyed all of the mastons, and I will destroy you! Do you think you can defy an army led by the Dochte Mandar? I allowed this Abbey's defenses to destroy my army. It was part of my plan to ruin you. This is my dominion!"

Lia took another step. The air felt as if it would burn. "You have taken everything from me. My true Family. My real home. The one I love. There is nothing else you can take from me. I surrender all that I am and all that I have to the Medium's will. I speak your true name. You are Ereshkigal, the Unborn. You will depart."

"No! You cannot command me! You are a child! Nothing but a child!"

The sky lit up with jagged shards of lightning. The trees swayed wildly. Plump drops of rain began to splatter against the walls and against Lia's face.

"You are Ereshkigal, the Unborn. You will depart."

The look in Pareigis's eyes was wild with frustration and fury. She screamed then, a sound so loud and startling and unearthly that it made Lia shrink inside. The scream grew louder and louder, drowning out the booms of thunder. Pareigis's fingers, hooked into claws, swept forward as she rushed to rake Lia with them.

Lia grabbed her wrists, holding her back with all her strength as the storm cracked open and torrents of rain began to dash from the skies. Lia clenched Pareigis's wrists tightly, digging her heels into the ground to help her balance.

"You are Ereshkigal, the Unborn!" Lia shouted. "You will depart!"

It was as if all the strength gushed out of Pareigis's body. Lia found herself holding the frail girl up by her wrists as she sagged and collapsed. Lightning seared the air, revealing on-looking Dahomeyjan knights who stared at Lia and the Queen Dowager with awe and terror.

On her knees in front of Lia, the Queen Dowager's eyes fluttered open.

"Where am I?" she whispered, her voice a tiny, frail wheeze. She spoke in Dahomeyjan. "What abbey is this that burns?" she said, gazing at the fires raging within Muirwood. The rain began to quench the flames.

The Queen Dowager's hair was soon drenched with rain, and she stared up at Lia in confusion and terror. "What land is this?"

Lia helped her to stand. "This is a foreign land. You must return to your country. You are sick, my lady. You will make others sick if you kiss them." She stared into her eyes. "Please, do not make others sick."

Pareigis blinked with the rain, confused.

"Duerden," Lia said, turning around. He was on the ground, huddled against the downpour. "Help her to get away. Take her far away. The storm will get worse until she is gone. Go or it will kill you both."

He nodded mutely and came forward, helping Pareigis to stand. He supported her and guided her in the rain toward the broken outer gates.

Chunks of ice began to thud against the grass and trees. Lia knew the storm was still building its strength. It was far from spent. It would be the greatest storm that Muirwood had ever known. And somehow, in her heart, she knew that it would last for three days and three nights.

Hugging herself and her dripping clothes, Lia walked slowly to the Aldermaston's kitchen, seeking shelter.

CHAPTER THIRTY-SIX

The Battle of Forshee

The ultimate force of the storm did not strike Muirwood until just before dawn. The noise came as the sound of a rushing wind so mighty it was as if ten thousand wagons were hurtling by at the same moment. Lia watched from the windows of the loft but could see nothing but raindrops and ice lashing against the panes. The wind made a ghostly sound, shrieking and roaring. Hunkering within the kitchen, Lia felt no fear. She knew the Medium would protect her. But even still, she clutched her childhood blanket and listened to the chaos and havoc whipping and whirling outside.

When dawn arrived, the storm had abated somewhat, but the light revealed the damage. Lia stared in shock.

All that remained of Muirwood Abbey were trusses and struts, tall, lonely chunks of stone that had once formed the mighty walls.

"It is gone," she said to herself, amazed at the devastation. What sort of wind had come that would hurl away stone?

After pulling on a cloak, Lia wandered out in the rain and stared in astonishment at the skeletal remains of the Abbey. A few segments of wall still stood, but they were like broken clay fragments, giving only a shade of resemblance to the original.

In the midst of the Abbey, a gaping hole exposed the dungeon room where the maston rights were instructed. Oddly, the benches and altar were still there. It was now open to be seen, and even the stairwell leading there was still intact. It was while Lia wandered the wet grounds around it that she saw the floor stone raise up and curious heads began to poke out. Kieran Ven and the others emerged from the tunnels below ground. Lia watched their faces as they emerged into open air where once an abbey had stood.

***

The traveling supplies had been gathered. Sacks and blankets, sturdy boots, and thick cloaks adorned everyone, even the little children. Pasqua had tears in her eyes as she tried to determine which of the five ladles she would bring to Pry-Ree and then beyond. Lia bit her lip and hugged Pasqua tenderly, helping her to choose her favorite.

The door of the kitchen opened, and Kieran strode in, spraying beads of water. He reminded her of Jon Hunter with his unshaven face and unruly hair. He wore a gladius at his side.

"It is the third day. The storm has broken, just as you said it would." He gazed at Lia and then reached for Marciana's hand. Their fingers entangled. That news had been a surprise to Lia. The two had been married by irrevocare sigil by the Aldermaston days before the fall of Muirwood. Marciana had passed the maston test. Sowe clung to Edmon's arm and stared at Lia with worried eyes.

Kieran glanced at those assembled. "We must go."

Marciana looked hard at Lia. "I wish you could come with us." Her voice caught. "But since you must stay, as Maderos bade you, you may hear what became of my brother. I still hold him in my thoughts. I have not given up hope."

Lia experienced the deep ache of pain that happened whenever she thought of Colvin. "It was not my choice to stay behind. But it is certainly my duty. There may be others seeking to escape the Blight when they realize what form it has taken. I will send them to Tintern, after you. Unless they are infected—I will not send on any who may bring the sickness among you."

Sowe came and gave Lia a hug. "Will you be safe here? All alone?"

Lia smiled and wiped her eyes. "If that wind did not kill me, I doubt loneliness will. This kitchen has always been my home. It brings me comfort knowing that it still stands. Please take good care of my sister," she said to Edmon, giving him a hug farewell. "Make her laugh. Every day."

A crooked smile contorted his mouth. "I will. If we by chance have any daughters, we will name the first after you. That way, we can be assured of a mischievous child!"

Lia laughed through her tears, hugging them both again. It was painful, saying good-bye. But the roles had changed, for it was her Family that was leaving her behind. Pasqua was next and then Prestwich, who was holding one of Siler's children by the hand. She gave a kiss to each and a firm hug.

Reome lingered in the back, uncertain about what to do. She had transformed since they had last seen each other. The haughtiness was gone. The swell of the babe was visible, but still just barely. Lia approached her and took her hands.

"I was always a little afraid of you," Lia said softly.

"Were you?" Reome asked, looking baffled. "I am sorry, Lia. I am sorry for all of the dreadful things I said and did to you. Teasing you and mocking you." Her eyes squinted thoughtfully. "I suffered greatly from my guilt and shame until I spoke with the Aldermaston. We really spoke, Lia, as I am sure you often did with him. He was so gentle and kind to me. He helped me see that punishing myself accomplished nothing. He taught me to be grateful for what I have instead of what I lost or never had." There were tears in her eyes, and she blinked rapidly. "If I have a boy, I will name him Gideon." She bit her lip. "I will never forget what you did for me, Lia Hunter. May the Medium comfort you and keep you. I believe in it now as I have never believed anything in my life. You gave me the first spark of it." She squeezed Lia's hands and then gave her a kiss on her cheek. "Bless you, sister."

Lia's heart shuddered with emotion and she clenched Reome tightly, amazed at her surging feelings. The two had never shared a hug in their entire lives together at Muirwood. It truly was the end of all things.

As they left the kitchen into the chilled morning air, Marciana and Kieran halted while the rest gathered outside.

"Do you think Pen-Ilyn will still be by the shore?" Marciana asked. "With his boat to ferry us across to Pry-Ree?"

Lia pursed her lips. "I believe…someone will be waiting for you. The Medium responds to our needs. I cannot see who, but I sense it. Someone will take you to the ships."

Marciana swallowed. "Do you think…that Colvin…? Do you have any sense, Lia?"

She frowned. "I cannot see his future, any more than I can see mine or yours. There is nothing but fog, like the mists that often settle over these grounds. My Gift only works when I benefit others, not myself."

"But in your heart," she pressed in a low voice, her eyes desperate for assurance. "You said Hillel…that she was a hetaera. Do you think he resisted her?"

Lia's heart twisted with pain. "I do not know. I cannot think on it without getting ill. They were to be married at Billerbeck. He believes I am dead. I had hoped to find him here at Muirwood." She clenched her jaw and stifled her feelings. "We can hope, Ciana. That is all that we can do for him now."

Tears trickled down Marciana's cheeks. She nodded, and Kieran put his arm around her shoulder, hugging her. She leaned against him, trying to master her feelings.

"Good-bye, Lia," she whispered. "Would we were sisters. Thank you for saving me from Dieyre. Thank you for saving me from what you suffered at Dochte Abbey." She put her hand on Lia's arm. "I would not have been as strong as you."

They hugged each other one last time, and then Lia watched the group begin the slow walk toward the ring of oaks surrounding the grounds and then toward the Bearden Muir. The lake that had surrounded the Abbey had long since receded. The Abbey's defenses were broken.

As she watched them go, she turned her gaze to the Tor and the dark duty that awaited her there.

***

As Lia climbed the Tor, her heart grew more and more heavy as she neared the charred stumps of the twin maypoles at the peak. Her stomach clenched with agony at seeing the blackened shells, the stick-like figures still chained there. The last time she had climbed the Tor, she was with Colvin on a stormy day hunting

Seth's footprints with the Cruciger orb. The wind whipped about her, moaning softly against her ears.

The evidence of death lay ahead of her, but the memories of hearing what had happened tortured her soul.

She had woven together the threads of story in strands from everyone in the kitchen while the storm had raged over the Hundred. Marciana and Kieran had been escorted from Comoros but ambushed. Since Lia had Gifted him, his recovery had been startlingly dramatic. As Dieyre's men attacked and began killing the knights who escorted them, he had fended the attackers off, killing them all and stealing their tunics and horses to disguise their movements as they rode back to Muirwood. Upon reaching the Abbey, they had hidden as wretcheds, wearing simple clothes and helping with simple tasks to aid in their disguise. Edmon had finally summoned the courage to face the maston test, and when he learned it was more about oaths and promises than knowledge learned from tomes, he had encouraged Sowe to face it as well. It was Marciana's wish that Sowe be adopted into her Family when she learned of Colvin's promise. The Aldermaston had permitted it, knowing they were approaching the end of his authority at the Abbey.

The day after they had passed the maston test, the Aldermaston of Augustin arrived, claiming to be the new aldermaston. He presented his charge and then summarily dismissed Demont and his mastons from the Abbey under his new authority. With the new aldermaston against him, Demont had left, and they had heard he was murdered by poison as he journeyed to Comoros to take control of the city and prepare for an invasion.

With a new aldermaston, the Queen Dowager was finally released from her captivity, and she summoned her vassals to Muirwood to bring her safely away. But the entourage did not leave immediately as they had promised. Each day brought another delay. Her power and influence continued to grow, much to the surprise of the new aldermaston, who found her to be intractable and unwilling to simply walk away. He also began to discover that the wealth he had suspected to exist at Muirwood was as elusive as the wind. There was no treasury, no hoarded funds supporting Demont's army. He realized at the end that he had given up a wealthier abbey for a lesser one.

On Twelfth Night, both aldermastons were executed on the Tor. They were bound to maypoles and forced to watch the Abbey below begin to burn. From what Lia had heard, the Aldermaston of Augustin had howled and wept and begged for his life. The true Aldermaston had silently faced his death without a word after Seth, his hunter, had been stabbed by soldiers while trying to defend his master. His body had been left on the lawn, but it had vanished with the storm.

Lia looked up at the charred remains of the Aldermaston. She knelt before the post—knelt in the soaked ashes—and she sobbed. She had lost two fathers in her life, and she was not sure which hurt most—the one she had never met or known or the one who had been prepared for her by her true father. In anguish, she had let the others leave for Pry-Ree, never able to tell them who she really was. Somewhere in the world was a tome, written by her father, sealed with a binding sigil. Until it was found, she would be forever silenced. Her true story would never be known. It was the same for the Aldermaston. He had died in disgrace, accused of horrid crimes he had never committed.

She spoke out loud, to herself but also to him. "If only I had come sooner, I could have saved you from your fate. Or you could have died and the Apse Veil would still be open. I am sorry for that. I did not know what was happening to you. I was mostly only aware of my own pain. I am sorry."

The wind tugged at her hair. She cried softly.

"There were so many lies told about you. People always believe the worst, even when rumors might later be proved false. I know the truth, and so do a handful of others. It seemed sometimes that you never cared what others thought about you. But so many will never know who you truly were. They will never know you as I knew you."

She squeezed her eyes shut. "I miss you, Aldermaston. I miss your counsel and your advice. You believed in me. I always felt that from you. I remember when you sent Jon Hunter to rescue me from the Bearden Muir. He told me that I was welcome back—that you said I could come back home. Do you know how much that meant to me? How much your trust meant to me?" She hugged herself, shivering with her emotions. "I wish I had told you how much I depended on you. How much I learned from you. How sorry I was for all the rude things I said. My disobedience and childishness. You were so patient with me. I see now that I was not just a wretched to you. Thank you, Aldermaston. I am grateful I was sent to your care. You helped to mold my faith. I could not have done what I did at Dochte Abbey without you."

She knelt there until her knees cramped and ached and her tears were finally exhausted. She breathed deeply and swallowed the hiccups that threatened her.

"I will carry a mark on my heart for the rest of my life. I will never forget your words and teachings. And I will never forget what you suffered because of me."

In the stillness that followed the storm, she felt something light graze the back of her head. It was feather-light. She opened her eyes and turned around, but there was nothing behind her. It had felt like a…hand?

She blinked in the stillness and closed her eyes again.

"Are you with me, Aldermaston?" she whispered.

The faint pressure came on her head again. Instead of looking backward again, she closed her eyes and opened her mind to her thoughts. The Gift of Seeing opened up to her again, and she saw the Aldermaston in her mind. He was crossing the Cider Orchard painfully, each step an agony to him. The branches lashed at him, but he walked firmly ahead, his arm cradling something that glinted gold. Then he was moving through the forbidden part of the grounds, his expression writhing in pain. She watched as he made it to the floating stone beyond Maderos's lair. He clambered down upon the rock, almost losing his balance and plunging to his death. He knelt, exhausted, on the stone, his body trembling with the exertion. He bowed his head, and then the floating rock began to move, easing downward to the base of the hill that was still submerged beneath the waters of the lake. With a mighty heave, he shoved a tome of aurichalcum off the boulder and watched it splash in the waters. It sank instantly, coming to rest amidst the stone ossuaries that she used to play in as a child.

The vision faded.

Lia opened her eyes. "Thank you, Aldermaston. Thank you for showing me where your tome lies."

***

She buried the Aldermaston's bones in an ossuary near Maderos's lair. The tome was where she had seen it and had not been difficult to see hidden within the crevices. As she knelt before the sealed box, she raised her arm in the maston sign.

Her voice was thick with emotion but grew stronger as she spoke. "By Idumea's hand, I do not know all the words. I am a young maston still. But I kneel and through the Medium dedicate this ground as the final resting place of Gideon Penman, the Aldermaston of Muirwood Abbey. By the Medium I invoke this, that when the time of his reviving has come, at some future dawn, he may be restored, every whit. May all who love truth always remember this final spot that others may remember what he did for us. That we may remember him through our words. Make it thus so."

As she crossed the Cider Orchard to return to the kitchen, she heard the snort and whicker of a horse. The trees were skeletal, but there were enough to shield the source of the sound. She stopped, listening carefully and trying to discern the location of the sound. It was coming from ahead—some distance ahead. She could hear the distant mumble of a voice, and her heart began to hammer in her chest with longing. Carefully, she set down the Aldermaston's tome and began to stalk forward, weaving through the trees carefully but quickly. Her blood throbbed in her ears. It was approaching noontide, but the day was overcast, veiling the sun.

Colvin?

She emerged from the grove and approached the oaks shielding the kitchen. The sound grew louder, an impatient grunt from an animal followed by a soothing whisper. A man's voice. Lia's heart beat wildly.

She had no weapons, but she did not feel they would be appropriate for her now, as an aldermaston. She had the Medium to warn and guide and protect her. But still, she craved a blade dangling from her side.

The sound came from the kitchen, the clang of a pan falling. There was a muttered oath and then the shuffling sound of boots.

Only one person and one horse. She had not heard anything to make her think otherwise.

Lia peered around the side of the kitchen and saw the brown mare, lathered with foam and sniffing and nibbling at the brush and plants outside the kitchen. The beast was saddled and there was a scabbard dangling from the horn, but it was empty. The horse raised its head when it saw her and nickered softly.

"What is it?" murmured a man's voice as he emerged from the kitchen holding a maston sword.

She saw the hilt first, the gleaming hilt with the symbol she had recognized as a child. The tunic was of a knight of Winter-rowd. Disappointment crushed her as she saw his face, the curly, dark hair and slim, sallow cheeks. She had never seen him before in her life. Or if she had, she did not recognize him. He was not as tall as Colvin. He was a stranger.

The sword was leveled at her immediately. "Who are you?" he demanded hotly, his face full of suspicion.

"I am the Aldermaston of Muirwood," Lia replied. "Please, put away your weapon."

"You are the Aldermaston?" he said, his face scrunching with irritation. "Is that a jest?" He waved his free arm toward the rub-ble of the Abbey.

"I am the Aldermaston still," Lia replied. "You are a knight of Winterrowd. I recognize your clothing, but I do not know your name. Were you looking for food?"

The word made his eyes widen with hunger. "Yes! I am half-starved. I have ridden for two days without rest." His horse val-idated his words. The mare looked exhausted and worn out. "I have eaten little, not trusting myself into the hands of strangers. I had hopes that Muirwood had not fallen, despite the stories. But

I see that I arrived too late. It has already fallen to the Blight." He ran his hand through his tangled hair.

"You are a maston?" Lia asked, staring at him.

"Yes."

"Let me see your palm."

Only another maston would know to look there for the scar. He lowered his sword and shifted it to his other hand. After tugging off his glove, he showed her his dirty palm, and she could see the mark of the stone where it had burned him.

"You wear a necklace?" he asked her, his eyes squinting warily. "A charm of some sort?"

"Not a kystrel," Lia answered with a nod and showed him the ring she wore on the string. He looked relieved.

"I am grateful it is not," he murmured somberly. His eyes glowed with inner fire. "They are powerful. Even the strongest mastons succumb to them. The strongest of us all."

Lia looked at him, her stomach lurching. "Where did you ride from, sir knight?"

"The Battle of Forshee—though it was not much of a battle." His teeth gritted together. "We abandoned the Earl and each rode our own way." He rubbed his mouth on his arm, his face livid with memories. "I should have left for Pry-Ree when Demont was murdered. I thought Forshee would redeem the mastons, but he could not. Not with *her* as his wife." He looked at her blackly. "The Earl's wife is hetaera. I know she is. You could see it just looking at her. I could not serve him. And now he is ill, and…"

Lia did not mean to, but she started. "Ill? What do you mean? The Earl of Forshee?"

"Who other?" he replied with a growl. "He came back from Dahomey with Demont's niece and said he was bidden to marry her, even though the king had sworn peace if she became his queen. Instead of ending this business, he began it anew. They were married at Billerbeck Abbey on Twelfth Night, and then the Blight struck him. He fell sick two days ago. He was coughing and retching. The Dowager's forces were closing in when I took flight. They were closing the ring around us, but I made it through. Forshee was too sick to ride. Pareigis hunts every maston now. I heard in Wells town that the king's army of mercenaries will land now that the storm has passed over, but the Queen Dowager already has the kingdom under her grip. They will kill Forshee for treason, they will. If the sickness does not end him first."

CHAPTER
THIRTY-SEVEN

Fallen Blossoms

Winter ended with an abruptness that surprised Lia. It seemed as if snow crusted the forlorn Abbey grounds one day and then the next, a warm, humid breeze floated in and the ice melted away all at once. For a fortnight at least, she had experienced the stirrings of the Medium preparing her that when spring came, it was time to leave Muirwood. Something would happen—she did not know what. Perhaps the Queen Dowager would send her army. Perhaps the Dochte Mandar would arrive. Something was coming, and she felt uneasiness, a warning to prepare. Perhaps Maderos would come and relieve her of the burden he had placed on her. She thought that the ships would not leave during the winter, not when brutal storms lashed the seas with their utmost ferocity. They would have gathered to a safe haven, to a secret place. Spring would bring calm waters, and she would need time to track them in Pry-Ree quickly. Without the Cruciger orb, the search would be more difficult.

The winter had been sad and lonely for Lia. Every so often, a traveler would appear at the Abbey looking for shelter and safety. Some had heard a warning from a family member to flee to Muirwood. Occasionally it was an entire family, mostly poor and desperate. They brought news she did not want to hear, but she listened to the stories of the world beyond. She listened, and her heart died a little bit each time.

Colvin was no longer called the Earl of Forshee. His titles and lands had been stripped by the young king and given to his sister, Marciana, who was still missing. Marciana was placed under the wardship of the Earl of Dieyre, who would control the lands in her absence. He was by far the wealthiest noble of the realm. His influence with the young king and the Queen Dowager was unmatched by any. It was clear by the reward offered that he would pay handsomely for any information regarding Marciana's whereabouts. But Dieyre had never come to Muirwood himself.

The Traitor Forshee, it was said, was languishing in a dungeon at one of Dieyre's many estates in the north country. Abandoned by the knights of Winterrowd before the invasion, he had been captured by the Queen Dowager's men and taken. It was said he was so sick that no one wished to be near him or tend him for fear of catching his illness. The very thought of him alone and ill in a dank, lightless place made her heart clench with dread and misery. She would have tended him to the last, bathing his forehead with cool rags, if she only knew where he could be found. She did not try, though, because it was her duty to remain at Muirwood. She was the Aldermaston of a grave.

With the spring came a revival of the Cider Orchard. The skeletal branches that had lain dormant during the winter frosts and snows were budding with blossoms. The entire orchard was wreathed in snowy white petals, and Lia walked amidst the trees every day, feeling the soft kiss of the petals as they began to trickle down like snow. The air was alive with smells as the grasses and flowers began to bloom amidst the toppled garden boxes. She roamed the grounds, trying to remember where the laundry was. The small shelter had vanished with the winds that night so long ago. The cloisters were gone as well. The only tome that had survived was the Aldermaston's tome—a tome she could not even read.

She lingered by an apple tree, pausing to stare up at the trunk and the flurry of blossoms that shook with the breeze. It was a tree she remembered, and she gazed at it longingly, rubbing her hands along the smooth bark. Memories were things. Dwelling on them could summon feelings as powerful as anything a kystrel could create. It was the tree where she had first revealed to Colvin that she loved him. It was the place where he had spurned her. So much had happened to her since then, but as she stood, conjuring the memory and the emotions, she thought for a moment she could make it real if she just wished hard enough. To hear his voice again, one last time. To see the scar at his eyebrow. To touch his hand. To smell him, close and tight in a hug.

It was the distraction of her thoughts and emotions that made her fail to hear the approach, until a boot cracked on a branch and alerted her with a startle. Lia turned her head, seeing the man approach. The wind rustled the trees, sending a blizzard of apple blossoms, veiling him. Her heart wrenched with longing. Was she dreaming? The gait of the man walking, the height and size of him, was as familiar as her own shadow. She began to tremble and clutched the apple tree, afraid her senses were tricking her.

The petal flurry slowed, and she saw him—Colvin.

Her heart thudded in her chest, her eyes widening with shock. He looked hale, not sickly. He was staring at her, walking purposefully closer. Was he a shade? Had he died in the dungeon and now came to her from the dead as the Aldermaston had done? Tears stung her eyes, but she saw something else.

She noticed the orb in his hand—the Cruciger orb. The spindles were pointing at her.

Colvin stuffed the orb in a pouch at his waist and cinched the strings closed with a tug. He ducked past a looming apple branch and came near her, his face lighting with an expressive smile of pure delight at finding her there, in the Cider Orchard.

Lia bit her lip, feeling tears blur her gaze. Was it real? Was she only dreaming? The bark felt real against her hands as she scraped them, squeezing the wood so hard her knuckles blanched.

"Colvin?" she whispered breathlessly, her legs trembling. Her whole body trembled.

He stood in front of her, looking deep into her eyes, and grabbed her hands so she could feel the flesh and warmth. He was real, and his eyes were shining with warmth and love.

"You are truly Ellowyn Demont," he said softly and then squeezed her hands fiercely. "But to me, you will always be Lia."

She gasped when he spoke her name. "Is the binding broken then? You can speak my name?"

A languid smile stretched over his mouth. "The binding sigil is broken. It has been broken since Twelfth Night. I know who you are, Lia. I know everything about you now. Your father's tome is in my rucksack with mine. I know everything, Lia." His hand strayed and brushed aside a lock of her hair. "You did it. You did what he meant you to do." Tears filled his eyes. "I am so proud of you, Lia. Your courage did not fail." He gazed at her pointedly. "Neither did mine. If I could have sent you word,

I would have. Believe that. But I only just escaped, and I rode hard and fast."

Lia was so startled and shocked, and she clutched him, seizing his tunic front and hugging him so tightly, breathing in his smell, the texture of his tunic and shirt. She squeezed him so hard she was afraid she was hurting him.

"What of Hillel?" she asked fearfully.

Colvin stroked her hair. "She weds the young king in a fortnight. After all, I am dead now."

She looked at him, seeing the humor in his eyes. "You seem very sturdy for a ghost. What are you saying? Please do not jest! My heart is still near breaking. I fear that this is a dream and I will awaken."

"I will tell you all," he answered. "But first, may I kiss you? My darling. My wife."

She stiffened.

He looked at her, gazing at her face, feeling through her wild hair with his fingertips. He brushed the back of his hand across her cheek. "Do not fear my touch, Lia," he whispered. "Your father foresaw it perfectly. I knew who Hillel was truly. Your father's tome told me what I had to do to bind myself to you forever. When I was at Billerbeck, I shared the knowledge with the Aldermaston since I had broken the binding. I showed him the tome. He saw what was written, and he agreed to perform the ceremony, binding me forever to Ellowyn Demont. We are bound, you and I, by irrevocare sigil, the same way your mother and father were bound together while they were apart, she in Dahomey and he in Pry-Ree. The orb works for me now, you noticed, because of you. Because of that binding. I share many of your Gifts. Hillel took the hetaera oaths, but she did not deceive me. I let her believe she swayed me. But I never let her lips touch mine. I am saved from the Blight." His fingers clenched in her hair and his forehead brushed hers. "You are mine. Forever."

With his hands tangled in her hair, he brought his mouth down on her cheek and kissed her. Then he kissed her chin. And then finally, as her heart nearly melted with fire, he kissed her mouth. It was not a soft kiss or a tender one. It was a kiss that stole her breath with its urgent claiming of her mouth. She wrapped her arms around his neck, pulling him closer until their bodies touched, and she leaned into him, grabbing his hair, kissing him back with every pent-up longing and feeling she had experienced. He kissed her again and again, breathing her in, clutching her as if she would float away and leave him. She trembled inside, awakened to feelings she had never experienced except in dreams. The world blurred around them for that moment, gasping and breathless. She could not believe how it made her feel. The worry and torment since he had buried her in Dahomey melted into nothingness. The agony and loneliness of winter were gone like the frost. He was there. He was hers. And they would go together to a new land and build new abbeys together.

She thought she would faint with joy and was grateful his hands had managed to loose themselves from the tangled weave of her hair and clutched her shoulders to keep her up.

Glancing up at him, she blinked as if in a dream. "Are you saying, Colvin Price, that we are married?"

"I am," he whispered huskily, greedily.

"But do not I get a say in this?" she asked with a teasing voice. "Am I bound forever to you, then, with no choice of my own?"

His eyebrows raised in mock solemnity. "You must accept the binding for it to be sacred. I suppose I was presuming…?"

Lia ran her finger down his mouth. "Yes."

"Yes?" he asked.

JEFF WHEELER

"Yes, I accept it," she answered. "I give you all that I have and all that I am."

"Then kiss me again," he demanded.

She was only too willing to oblige.

***

Lia awoke first before the blush of dawn lit the windows of the kitchen. After rising from the pallet, she summoned fires from the oven Leerings to warm the tiles and quickly set about making something for them to eat. She was starving and knew Colvin would be too when he awoke. For a moment, she remembered the day she had made him porridge and he had tried to guess her age without asking and how they had argued. She warmed the kettle and added some spice to the dish before tossing the seeds into the boiling water.

As she fretted by the trestle table, she heard him shift and come away and slowly pad over to her. His chin nuzzled her neck, and she smiled and trembled, enjoying the bristled feel of his cheeks and chin, the tickling feeling it caused down to her feet.

"I thought you would sleep longer," she said, glancing over her shoulder at him.

"I was cold after you left. I want you near me…always."

"The ships will be cramped; I imagine you will get your wish," she said playfully. "Now, you said the *Holk* will meet us on the coast?"

He nodded, kissing her earlobe and making her gasp. "Please, Colvin. I do not want to burn your food. You must let me concentrate. The *Holk* will take us to Pry-Ree and then…?"

"We cross the mountains to Tintern and bring the Aldermaston back with us. He is the last to be saved. We will be on the boats for some time. The land we sail to is very far. Across the great ocean."

"You said that the orb was meant to direct us there," she continued, stirring the porridge and nodding with satisfaction at how it thickened. "The *Holk* will be the lead ship." She frowned. "What about Martin? We did not speak of his part to this story yet."

Colvin nodded sternly. "He has chosen to remain and protect his granddaughter. Hillel will become queen of Comoros, and he will be her advisor and protector. There is still some time before the Blight consumes everyone. At least she knows now what she truly is and what she must never do."

Lia sighed. "It must have been difficult for you—ruining her sense of who she really was. You were the one who discovered her at Sempringfall. You were also the one to tell her the truth."

Colvin looked askance and shrugged slightly. "I suppose I do not judge or consider her pains and loss equal to what you have suffered, Lia. She will be queen. It is hardly confinement in a dungeon. Her marriage will not be a happy one. But she will have more comforts than she would have enjoyed as a wretched. And more power."

"You learned her true name from my father's tome?" she asked.

Colvin nodded.

Lia served up two bowls of porridge, flavoring both with treacle and raisins. They ate it ravenously, washing it down with pure water that Lia summoned from another Leering.

"You told me to wait until today to tell me how you escaped Dieyre's dungeon," Lia said when they were finished. "I had thought perhaps Martin rescued you. But now I think not."

Colvin shook his head. "No, but he did mix the herbs that feigned my illness. He is an astute poisoner. I was truly sick for many days, and he used juice from some berries to add little poxes on my face and arms. The important thing to create was the rumor of my illness. Rumors get exaggerated with each telling. I knew that I would be spending the winter below ground in a dungeon. Considering what you endured in the hetaera's lair, I faced my task as bravely as I could. There were no serpents to torment me—only rats. Dieyre visited me often, trying to get me to reveal where my sister was being held. He kept me alive for that purpose, using his influence to forestall the queen's plan to execute me. As long as I revealed nothing, they had no choice but to spare me."

"Yes, but how did you escape?" Lia pressed.

He paced the kitchen as he had before, back when he was healing from his wound. She wondered if he would reach for a broom and start swinging it like a sword. The thought almost made her laugh.

"Dieyre let me go," he said simply.

"What?"

"You must understand that we spent much time talking together. He did not come to that decision all at once, but he slowly turned his thinking. He saw people around him begin to die of the plague. He saw that your warning would eventually be fulfilled. He asked me about you. He said he believed you did not die in the furnace, that you were alive somewhere. He wondered where you were and if you could be convinced to remove the curse you had put on him. I think he kept me so long because he believed you would eventually come looking for me to save me. But how could I explain to him that you were an aldermaston and were bound to Muirwood's fate? You will be bound to Muirwood forever, you know. We both will."

"Yes, but as you explained last night, it means I am bound to rebuild her. Not myself, but one of my posterity must do it. I did not know I could freely leave, but now I do. Imagine it, Colvin. A child or grandchild of ours, returning to this land to rebuild the abbeys. It will take centuries to rebuild them all."

Colvin nodded. "Until we do, the dead will multiply and roam the land. They will be in chains like the Myriad Ones. We must free them, Lia. We must free them all."

She nodded, remembering the Aldermaston. "So you convinced Dieyre to let you go?"

He shook his head. "No. None of my persuasions ever convinced him. In the end, he arrived one night after one of his servants had perished by the plague. He stripped the man's clothes and gave them to me and replaced mine with his. He said he would announce to the world that I was dead and that I could leave that night."

Lia wrinkled her forehead. "Surely he was letting you go to follow you to Marciana," she said, suddenly concerned.

Colvin nodded. "Naturally. Which is why I went to Forshee first instead of here. I went there for two reasons: to find my tome and to get something for you. There is something I wanted you to have."

"What is it?" she asked, leaning forward curiously.

He retrieved the pouch with the Cruciger orb and pulled it out. Then, fishing at the bottom of the pouch, he withdrew a wedding band.

"This was my mother's," he said. "You remember I told you that she was buried in an ossuary at my manor house? That I had feared she was buried alive?"

Lia nodded, her eyes widening in wonder.

"I opened the ossuary, and there was nothing left but grave clothes and this ring. As you pointed out to me in the past, if the dead do not wish to wear rings in Idumea, then we may as well use them here." He walked up to her and took her hand. "Will you wear this, as a symbol of our binding?"

Trembling with happiness, Lia nodded, and Colvin slipped the ring on her finger. It fit well. It was beautifully crafted by an expert goldsmith, with little designs made of maston symbols along the band.

"In return then," she said, reaching into her bodice and removing the ring she had found as a child, "would you wear this ring? When you gave it back to me in the cell below Dochte Abbey, I fashioned a little necklace from some threads and wore it beneath my chaen." She snapped the threads and put the ring on his matching finger. It fit perfectly, as if it had always belonged on his hand.

"I have carried that ring since I was a child," she murmured. "To think, all along it was meant for you."

Colvin leaned down and kissed her warmly. She enjoyed it immensely.

"You still have not finished your tale. How did you escape your manor?" she reminded him, tugging at his shirt front. "Dieyre is not known for being generous or a fool. I am certain he had his men follow you."

"Yes. But neither he nor I was expecting Nuric. That is his Pry-rian name. I knew him as Theobald, my father's steward. He was an Evnissyen who served your father. His mission was to deliver you to Muirwood Abbey as a baby. Because of the binding sigil, he could not speak of it, but he hinted as best he could. As I child, I had heard his stories about the Prince of Pry-Ree's miss-

338

ing daughter. I assumed he had family in Pry-Ree, not that he was of Pry-rian descent. Do you see, Lia? Your father sent Nuric to Forshee to serve my father. He was my advisor and a friend. He knew about you and where you were, but he could not say until the binding was broken. Remember, when I told you last night that Hillel and I went to the *Holk*, I was given the room of a shipmate, the one belonging to the crewman Malcolm. That was when Maderos told me who he really was and gave me your father's tome. He was the one who kept it safely all these years."

Lia smiled at the thought, grateful to her father and his Gift of Seering. "And the password?"

"The tome had passages for me, written in my language, by your father. He explained that to get the password, I needed to take the orb from Hillel and bring it to Maderos. He would be able to read it and make it work. The password was, as I told you last night, the name you were given in the maston ceremony."

"And you read the tome during the journey home, at least the parts you could read. Then Twelfth Night came. That was when you betrayed Hillel and banished the Myriad One who was with her. You cannot banish it permanently, because of the mark on her shoulder, but you drove it away for a while and could explain to Hillel who she really was and what she had done."

Colvin nodded, rubbing his chin. "Nuric helped me escape Forshee undetected. He is a skillful man and helped me cross to you undetected. He knew I should visit you alone and has gone ahead of us to the *Holk* and will leave with the ships for the new land. He is so anxious to meet you, Lia. He served your father faithfully for so many years."

Lia looked out the window again. It was dawn. "I suppose it is time to leave for Pry-Ree." She smoothed her hand across the trestle table. "I will always remember this kitchen. My earliest memories are here. It will be sad to leave Muirwood, knowing we will never see it again."

He took her hand and kissed it. "We will build it in the new land. It will look the same. Someday our Family will return and claim it once more. We will rebuild it, Lia. We will rebuild them all."

She squeezed his hand. "Make it thus so," she whispered.

EPILOGUE

My dearest daughter, this tome is my only opportunity to speak to you with my own voice. If all has happened as I have foreseen, you are on a ship bound to a new land. I provided instructions that this portion should not be read to you but that you must learn to read it yourself as you have always longed to be able to do. I have watched you from afar, from the very shores of Idumea. It is there that your mother and I await your return. You have been tasked to open the gates that bind the worlds together, and you have set in motion the destruction of the hetaera. You have been faithful, obedient, and courageous. I am so proud of you.

In this tome, you will learn about your future and the future of our Family. Your work is not yet done. You and your husband and your children and their wives and husbands will be kings and queens in the new land. I have left you my tome to aid you that you may rule in wisdom and humility. When I sent you to Muirwood, I trusted you would learn the pains and feelings of common people. Their tears and pains and sorrows weigh more on the Medium than the whims and greed and beauty of the rich and the powerful.

I have seen deeply into the future, my darling girl. Our Family will play a great role in events to come. Your writings and wisdom will be added to this tome, helping save generations yet unborn. In the future I have seen that your posterity will chain and shackle Ereshkigal for all time and bind her in prison under irrevocare sigil. She knows this is her destiny, which is why she has persecuted our Family. Teach your children to be strong, for she will always seek to subvert them. Some will fall under her sway.

Cold aurichalcum and shavings is a poor medium in which to express a father's love. Clasp this tome in your hands, my child, and think of me. Through the true Medium, you will feel my love for you, stronger than death and deeper than the depths of Sheol. We await you, beloved daughter. We offered up our lives that you might live and fulfill and begin the destiny of our Family.

Your servant,

Alluwyn Lleu-Iselin

Father

AUTHOR'S NOTE

I dedicated this novel to Sharon Kay Penman because she is the inspiration for this story. I first read her novel *Here Be Dragons* while I was in college and fell in love with medieval English history. My friend Jeremy told me of the book, which he found in a used bookstore in Switzerland. After *Dragons*, we discovered *Falls the Shadow* at a used bookstore in downtown San Jose. It tells the tragic story of Simon de Montfort and his death at Evesham Abbey. The trilogy concluded with *The Reckoning*, which describes the subjugation of Wales to Edward I. It was while reading this book that I first learned of the lost princess of Wales, Gwenllian ferch Llewellyn, who was banished to the Gilbertine Priory at Sempringham, where she died fifty-four years later. Her story is a sad one, and it inspired me to create Lia in her memory and give her a much happier ending. Many of the political details in the Muirwood series come directly from this era—yes, even the bit about Tomas Aldermaston abducting her mother by sea (history named him Thomas the Archdeacon).

Writing novels is an endeavor full of surprises. When I first began plotting Muirwood, it was a more comical series than it ended up becoming. The characters began developing their own personalities and would often buck against the paths where I tried to coax them. For example, Sowe was supposed to go along with Lia and Colvin when they first left Muirwood, but she ran off and told the Aldermaston what was going on and whimpered in a corner instead. Another example was that the confrontation between Lia and Almaguer, in book one, was supposed to happen at a tavern in the village of Winterrowd. Sometimes my best intentions were deliberately waylaid by the characters. And some scenes ended up writing themselves just by throwing Dieyre into the mix. I enjoyed each of the characters in a different way, but Lia is clearly my favorite.

Last, I wanted to thank many of the early readers of Muirwood for their extreme patience in waiting for the story to be finished, and especially for those who read it in little gulps, five chapters at a time. Thanks to Muirwood's biggest fan, my sister, Emily Bradshaw, for her persistent enthusiasm and sharing. My niece, Jenna Wheeler, who could pass for Lia in a pinch if you saw her. For Melanie Hoem and her late-night IMs with Emily about the series (which they forwarded to me!). I would also like to thank Kate, Colleen, Rachelle, Cousin Melanie, and Steve for their feedback on the series. Your feedback and enthusiasm helped keep me motivated to keep writing, one chapter at a time.

For readers who want to know if this is the end—an author rarely shuts the door and locks it when creating new worlds. I wrote a novella years ago called *Maia*, which is set in this world in the future, after the ships return and the kingdoms begin anew. The main character is part of Lia and Colvin's posterity. There is more to be written still, as that novella was just a foreshadowing of the plot and characters. You can find this story on my website: www.jeff-wheeler.com.

Thank you for reading!

ABOUT THE AUTHOR

Jeff Wheeler is a writer from 7 p.m. to 10 p.m. on Wednesday nights. The rest of the time, he works for Intel Corporation, is a husband and the father of five kids, and a leader in his local church. He lives in Rocklin, California. When he isn't listening to books during his commute, he is dreaming up new stories to write. His website is: www.jeff-wheeler.com